LET'S GO TO CHURCH: NAKED!

HUMMINGBIRDMAN

This is a work of fiction.

Ordering Information:

Prime Seven Media
518 Landmann St.
Tomah City, WI 54660

Printed in the United States of America

Table of Contents

About the Author

I was born in 1959 25th of march in Utrecht Netherlands; and I am a dual citizen by facts of birth and parentage; Father: Richard Leroy-USA & Mother: Greta-Dutch; and the first seven years of my life I was in an orphanage without my parents and I observed life without the codification of parental behavior imprints; and following I was adopted at seven years of age by my adoptive parents Peter and Tinus with my adoptive sister Anne Claire; and my adoptive father died in 1975; I felt lost and went to India to find Enlightenment with the Gurus before my physical death; and I came back to being "Normal" in this world and studied Physical Therapy and Progressive Medicine; and in 1990 moved back to the States to practice physical therapy and went on a Native American journey and participated in the Lakota Sundance for five years; and on 9/11/2001 I left the States returning to the Netherlands to continue physical therapy; and, also in the States I was studying with the Erwin Rommel School of Law and became a legal analyst; and so I created an international treaty: Peace Treaty trust for the living man and woman in anticipation of the singularity split; and, filed an UN-ICC document: "Pacta Sunt Servanda" to stop the Pact of the Future, which in essence wanted to hijack our Bio-Mimetric-DNA title ownership; and, the Covid-19 was a definite motivator to stop this piracy by the privatized Elite Billionaires; I am a single father with three children, who are the love of my life; and, so there is much more to my story.

Explanatory Memorandum; of

Controversial cover drawing: Jesus on the cross embraced by Mary Magdalene; and,

In order to <u>transcend-transform-transmute</u> peoples dogmatic points of view, religious perspectives, sexual polarities there has to take place a paradigm shift, which will usher people towards unconditional LOVE; and,

As a Christian, is it a sin to look at the naked body of a woman?

Of course not.. There is nothing that we can do that is a part of human nature, that can be thought as "sin". There is only following the path of love, for God is love and following the path of fear which is the illusion of being separate from our divine truth. No amount of self inflicted guilt, shame or punishment will change what is in the heart, because the heart precedes the mind so healing, resolution and change can only take place in the heart.

The behaviour that is attempting to be averted here is the identifying ones self with their "animal body" or as the many parables say the beast.

So long as we believe the self to be the body, to be the mind and so our "knowledge" of what is right and wrong…we judge, condemn and vilify. And so in choosing to do this, we are choosing to live in the illusion that separates us from our divine nature, as children of God, that why these too are attributes to be averted.

Animals cannot stop themselves from their instinctual natures of feeding, procreating and competing for dominance.

The difference…IS that we having the freewill of discernment to choose our path of abiding in the higher OR fulfillment of temporary bodily desires that simply keeps us in darkness to the higher aspects of our human evolution. Thats it.. No lake of fire, no eternal damnation, just stagnation, in our lifes experience.

Once we have transcended the lusty sensations of bodily things through meditation, right practice and proper wisdom, we will find are then free to enjoy more things more consistently. So we indulge again and again until the sensations can no longer quell the infinite discontent with distorsion from paradise . And so even into addiction we can go in the pursuit of happiness but this is the self imposed hell and so we suffer until we opt (through freewill) for more fulfilling things like love and creative expression rooted in expansion.

160v: **Mary Magdalene Washing Christ's Feet** (Luke 7: 38) "This is the story: How Saint Mary Magdalene washed the feet of Our Lord Jesus Christ with her tears and wiped them with her hair.

Luke 7:36-50; **A Woman Washes Jesus' Feet**; and, Mary Magdalene? She seems to me the only true follower of Jesus. Her authenticity, her daring, is immense. Jesus had come to her house and she poured precious perfume on his feet, washed the feet with the perfume, then wiped the feet with her hair. She was sitting there crying tears and tears, and naturally the virtuous were offended.

And somebody said to Jesus, "This is not right. She is a sinner, and she should not be allowed to touch you!"

The prostitute had no mind. She had lived a very simple existence of selling her body. She knew nothing of the scriptures, she had no time to read them. She could not have the ego of a virtuous person. How could she have? She was simply humble, crying. She couldn't have any ego, and that is the door to the divine.

Simon said, "Teacher, tell me."

Jesus said to Simon, "You are right." 44 Then Jesus turned toward the woman and said to Simon, "Do you see this woman? When I came into your house, you gave me no water for my feet, but she washed my feet with her tears and dried them with her hair. 45 You gave me no kiss of greeting, but she has been kissing my feet since I came in. 46 You did not put oil on my head, but she poured perfume on my feet. 47 I tell you that her many sins are forgiven, so she showed great love. But the person who is forgiven only a little will love only a little."

48 Then Jesus said to her, "Your sins are forgiven."

49 The people sitting at the table began to say among themselves, "Who is this who even forgives sins?"

50 Jesus said to the woman, "Because you believed, you are saved from your sins. Go in peace."

God said in Jeremiah 1:5, "Before you were formed in your mother's womb I knew you. Before you were born I consecrated you and set you apart." God was saying, "Before you showed up on this earth, I already knew everything about you. I knew every weakness you would have, every shortcoming.

Job 1:21; And he said, "Naked I came from my mother's womb, and naked shall I return.

Hosea 2:3; Lest I strip her naked and make her as in the day she was born, and make her like a wilderness, and make her like a parched land, and kill her with thirst.

Hebrews 4:13; And no creature is hidden from his sight, but all are naked and exposed to the eyes of him to whom we must give account.

Matthew 5:28; But I say to you that everyone who looks at a woman with lustful intent has already committed adultery with her in his heart.

Song of Solomon 4:1-16; Behold, you are beautiful, my love, behold, you are beautiful! Your eyes are doves behind your veil. Your hair is like a flock of goats leaping down the slopes of Gilead. Your teeth are like a flock of shorn ewes that have come up from the washing, all of which bear twins, and not one among them has lost its young. Your lips are like a scarlet thread, and your mouth is lovely. Your cheeks are like halves of a pomegranate behind your veil. Your neck is like the tower of David, built in rows of stone; on it hang a thousand shields, all of them shields of warriors. Your two breasts are like two fawns, twins of a gazelle, that graze among the lilies. ...

The Root of these sins are a desire for more and the human need for access. These

Deadly sins are:

1. Lust 2 Tim 2:22
2. Gluttony 1Cor 10:31
3. Greed Heb 13:5
4. Sloth Prov 6:6
5. Wrath Rom 12:19
6. Envy Prov 14:30
7. Pride Jer 9:23-24

Curing these sins, we find the seven virtues: faith, hope, charity, justice, prudence, temperance and fortitude.

But in actuality these sins are all distractions and distortions from the original sin; and that is everything we do for not allowing the everlasting living light from our heavenly father J.C. to shine through our body vehicle and that is your paradigm shift.

How would Mary Magdalene stand before him naked and with pure heart?

No one can only meet jesus weeping, because the meeting with jesus is not of the head, but of the sacred heart in the image and similitude of God; and, she must have felt not worthy, because of her sinful nature; and, the more you feel you are not worthy, the more worthy you become; and,

Why? Because there is One <u>Iniquity-Sin</u> Only: "Everything we do for not allowing the everlasting living light from our heavenly father J.C. to shine through our body vehicle" when she comes in front of him, what does she do? She disrobes; and, why? "Naked I came from my mother's womb, and naked shall I return" And no creature is hidden from his sight, but all are naked and exposed to the eyes of him to whom we must give account; and, she must have had courage; and, jesus he was there utterly showering compassion on her; and, John 17:23; <u>I in them and you in me—so that they may be brought to complete unity. Then the world will know that you sent me and have loved them even as you have loved me.</u>

<u>Perfection of this moment;</u>

    I praise love for this moment in its perfection

    I thank love for my human experience in its perfection

    Love creates me in my perfection

    Isha Judd: Why walk when you can fly?

Preface

Only Sex is! Everything else is peripheral! God has nothing to do with the morbidity of our Sins! It is man himself, who brought these into being, and man is the only one, who can erase his problem seeds of thought! When one is one with the law of love, then one will no longer produce sins, but to merely refrain from producing sins does not place you within the benediction of God's grace. It is doing truth, not merely refraining from that which is not truth! This book is about rebalancing our sexual poetic justice versus their religious righteousness.

The love I feel in my heart has a longing to be embraced, received and touched by the greatest beloved in existence. I feel so much, and yet I feel so little within this vast Universe. Life, has taught me the painful lesson of rejection, which in its turn has ushered me closer to the discovery of 'agape' or unconditional love. My focus on the primal feelings of pain, anger, fear, sadness is egotistical and I am now learning the lesson to feel the magic of life within my heart.

I have to figure out how to have a love affair with the creative life force running through my veins. The intentions behind my will power have been replaced by hosting the awesome power of this magic called love. Love is for real when I become pregnant of it. It is difficult to define this true love with a sense of purity, because the meaning of language has polluted my perception of reality. Language is abstract and the meaning of abstract is: "withdrawn or disconnected from reality." The existential significance of unconditional love is seeded deeply within the relationship dynamics between a man, a woman and their creator God! Conditional love is challenged by the trial and tribulation of: "Rejection and Denial!" When triggered, these relationship dynamics may cause feelings like: "Pain, Anger, Fear, Sadness!" These are the feelings, which will often confuse the feeling and intention of your love life. My yearning for my beloved has to go deeper, much deeper, until it's meaning can no longer be polluted by the mirror of my external reality. The toroidal turmoil in my emotional life can be compared to a scuba dive gone wrong. Imagine yourself at the abyss of your feelings and suddenly you run out of air. Your whole being will now yearn for one thing only: "Life!" As you swim towards the light and break on through to the blue surface of the ocean, you do one thing only: "Breathe." Finally, when your state of panic has calmed down, a thankful state of clarity and purpose will arise, which then may give a new meaning to your life: "Passion!" There is a force greater than myself in control of my life and this has been a humbling experience to me. This book is about a force called the echo of Divine love, which wants to express itself freely within this sexed Universe. It is a passionate search for the Nlem myore 'one heart only' in which the hope for a better tomorrow is being replaced by the loving relationship with my true self connecting with my beloved and the Creator of this Universe. The experience of "one heart only" is nearly identical to the rave scene's own concept of P.L.U.R., which stands for Peace, Love, Unity, and Respect. The power of love is rooted in and ruled by the Law of One. A man or a woman, who moves with the power of Divine love shall be absolutely clean from any Religious, Social or Political conditioning. The echo of Divine love is not a ritual, but instead it is an intimate relationship with the divine force of creation, the God essence from which we all came from. In all of the time on Earth, no progress has been made to resurrect the Garden of Eden, because of the unseen role of denial into distortion. In Christian terminology: "We are born sinners!" To sin means: anything that prevents the everlasting dancing light of your creator to move through your body vehicle.

We have conditioned ourselves to accept the feelings we like, and we have rejected the feelings we do not like! Are we able to allow ourselves to deeply feel the emotions being triggered here, rather than arguing about what is being said as a way to avoid the feelings, which are being felt?

What if the creator has given us feelings just to know what we are thinking? It is the shadow side within ourselves, which has dimmed, compressed and often blinded the living light within our being with the veils of ignorance and denial. We have turned ourselves away from each other and turned towards a magic Tube called television. Television has become the substitute for our: "Beloved!" Is there anybody out there interested anymore in loving a woman at her core essence? A person may wonder: "What is so special about a woman's essence?" Because my friend: "The world is more alive there, than you would have ever imagined it could be any place else!" Colors burn and flicker, sounds vibrate like plucked strings, and each breath you draw into your existence makes you feel a little giddy and light headed as if you are inhaling a purer element. Female energy is beneficial to the essence of your being. Man and woman have lost the courage to feel this unsettling force of love. Our lack of courage is caused by the very nature of love, which in essence is ferocious, because of its pull into the abyss of acceptance of that, which One truly is in this sexed Universe. The tension between man and woman is like an elastic rubber band stretched apart. It is the same energy that wants to get together to relax and feel the love that wants to flow and be felt. A woman has one desire only and that is to open up the floodgates of her Divine essential being, but she cannot, because she doesn't feel safe. See-men want only to possess her love for their selfish pleasure These two "Man's sex and Woman's love" unbalanced love-sexed conditions creatively desire to return to the oneness of balance from which they were divided into two. Man and woman are recharged into a sexed condition by their heartbeats, by the foods they eat, by the imprints on their senses and by the way, they breathe! Every heartbeat creates a sexual pulsation within the creative essence of our being. Our creative life force wants to express its compressed sexuality freely and it seeks a safe container within which it can be allowed to release itself to the beloved. Our sexual pulsation seeks rest and unification within the intimacy of our opposite sex partner. Sex is the compression of our life force into two opposite pressures, which desire release and expansion from their opposition. The heart of every woman is crying aloud to be touched by a passionate man with feeling. She wants to be touched in places where she has never been touched before: "the Heart!" and only then will she open up to release her finest, fundamental, female energies. In return for a gentle touch with heart, she will then release the free flow of her divine feelings. The quest for every man is to find 'passionately' the way to a woman's heart, where he then in return will experience the best gift she can offer: "a divine merging into one heartbeat with the Divine!" Make love without self-indulgence, without emotional self-satisfaction, self-gratification. Make sexual love the Divine way. Make love and go on and on, and your woman will be available all the time and at any time. Feel your woman in the flesh of her heart. Focus only on the fun of pleasing and delighting her, give and give again. Kiss her gently and lightly on the lips and all over her body. The basic unfulfilled need of every woman is to give up her finest female energies to her lover, to express her intrinsic female beauty, her divine fragrance. Every action of motion in this Universe is a result of sex desire for motion into stillness and the joy of the heart. The fears in our Minds have frozen our bodies frigid and yet at the same time we claim to be at service and devotion to a higher being called God. The time has come to defrost our frozen light body and become alive! It is time to free up this energy, which we have invested in the shame and blame issues of our defensive selves. It is time to go to other places. It is time to visit and browse our inner website called: "Joy!" It is time to reach out and touch each other with fingertips filled with the passion of love. It is time to melt down our emotional resistance to: "Change!" It is time to live the incredible lightness of being! It is time to deeply feel each other within the safe container of laughter. It is time to end the suffering and enter the wisdom of true love. Will the change come while we are waiting? Will we burn in heaven like we do down here? Everyone is waiting for the Sun of God, wishing for a better place in heaven. Is it too late to celebrate our ability to have a little taste of God? Orgasm is like having a little taste from God and this feeling communicates to us of what it is going to be like in heaven. Every now and then, we get this like "Wooff" amazing feeling, which makes us long for heaven. This uplifting feeling brings us to a point, where we are completely elevated to a different level within our being. It is like that is how it is going to feel like in heaven. Heaven is like a place, where you will be totally in the "Orgasmic" state of being. The tangible world of orgasm is movement, not a collection or crescendo of moving bodies, but more or less the movement of orgasm itself. There is no personal human identity to be found in a state of orgasm. Orgasm leads to a blissful expansion of consciousness, which leads to an ecstatic expansion into space, which leads to the house of peace in which God lives. Orgasm is the God identity! Are we able to allow ourselves to **move** and **feel the emotions** being triggered here? If the answer is 'no', then please try to consider the following:

1. Close your eyes.
2. Breathe deeply and connected.
3. Scan your body for tension spots.

4. Zoom into the tension with awareness.
5. Feel deeply.
6. Ask yourself: "What am I holding back?"
7. Discover, observe, look into it.
8. Ask yourself: "What would I like to release?"
9. Identify: "Anger, Pain, Fear, Sadness!"
10. Release!
11. Move your body; dance, Humm, express yourself!
12. Ask yourself: "What would I like to activate?"
13. Move your body; express yourself!
14. Enjoy your healing bubble!

When the answer is 'yes', then you need to allow this expression of emotions without harming yourself or others! When a person absorbs an emotional charge, without releasing it into the free expression of it, then the feeling center inside the body will adapt itself into a sense of numbness. Desensitized we then become saturated with emotional crud, and we lose our ability to receive clearly. Denial and rejection are the first indicators, which will make us aware that we have become therapy resistant to the living light, which seeks its way into the dark side of all God's creatures. *Unravel yourself, until you break on through to the other side of your shadow self, that is what God, is all about.* Wouldn't you like to get to know your true self at your most intimate level of being? "That sounds frightening," one might say! That is correct, because this knowing will be in contact with a feeling of irrevocable Change! This book is about the inert possibility to experience a paradigm shift within and to have the choice for a new reality outside of your preconditioned inhibitions. This book will show you, why, how, and what you can do, and who you can be, or what you already are, together, each of us, and all of us. Our whole society is geared towards living in a collective comfort zone, which overrides the feminine essence and principle of individual creativity. To discover our true identity, we must be willing to leave this comfort zone of our baby blankets behind. Letting go of the familiar and the move forwards into the unfamiliar is a frightening process, because at any given moment one may accidentally find God, and be happy. Therefore, my initial suggestion is to move into the deepest intensity of love that is possible. This magic happens in the magic zone, which is outside the comfort zone. Let it be an opening in yourself to the divine. Allow your feminine energies to flower and allow your heart to pulse your feelings of love. God gave us a nerve system to feel each other, God's reflections, and ourselves. To truly feel connected is like having intimacy with everything alive and divine. This book is for those people, who have the courage to activate their sexuality for a full and complete integration into all of the aspects of your divine being. Overcoming the shame and blame issues of your sexuality will enable you to change your perception and recollect yourself at the highest level of self-acceptance. Spiritual purification begins with the acceptance and expression of your sexuality. The journey of the divine begins in your root chakra and as it matures it will rise above you into deep space nine. The free flow of sexual energy has the inner potential to change a man and a woman into a superconscious omni-dimensional human being. We are born with the powers to tap into a full brain capacity. The juice created by our passion may open us up in sweet surrender to the luminous love light of the One we call our beloved. So, I say onto you: "Welcome your passion with Grace, Love and Awareness!" Engage yourself; reach out to one another with the intimacy of an open heart. Surf the waves of your emotions and ride the ripples of your vibrations to the calm lake of inner peace. Be sexual, sensual, emotional, feel, express, share, touch, love, laugh, dance, and be orgasmic. Dare to share your passion for love and dance your way to God. Love must gush and squirt out of every pore of your being as you evaluate and respond to life's opportunities and challenges. Love is to be saturated by every atom of this entire Universe, and its blissful side effect is to be impressed upon every cell of the human form! When you become one with the Law of One, you will no longer produce sins, but to merely refrain from producing sins does not place you within the benediction of God's grace. It is doing truth, not merely refraining from that which is not truth! Some words written in this book will create a gap of awe inside of your being. A Gap is a mystery and cannot be stigmatized as a mystical learning experience. It takes **courage** to remain balanced in the constant flow of **change**! It is in this Awesome Gap of no return where you may find your beloved Creator! WOW! the visible invisible of inner true being. back on rise to inner space where emptiness become wholeness. I AM the Bride that seeks the Beloved within an infinite ocean of dancing light particles. I AM the image and similitude of a Divine creation of the Father Mind into the similitude of his divine creation of nurturing feminine principle of the Mother Earth. I AM an inner child on starry grounds in the enchanted flower world. I AM the Hummingbirdman. I AM here to serve you with the songs of dancing light so that I may guide you home into the bosom of my Father. He is the only beloved who beckons you to move and come on home on rays of dancing light, forever in Harmony and Lovejoy with the Infinite. This book is for those who still believe that love has any meaning. In a dream the Pleiadean sisters told me that all I had to learn was just to create a space of love for my inner child, because I AM the presence within my Divine breath.

LET'S
GO
TO CHURCH
NAKED!

Chapter One ~
Riders on the Storm

Young people, it's wonderful to be young. Enjoy every minute of it. Do everything you want to do, take it all in. But remember that you must give an account to God.

Ecclesiastes 11: 9

Do not change yourselves to be like the people of this world. But be changed within by a new way of thinking. You must see yourself as you really are.

Romans 12: 2 -3

For since the creation of the world God's invisible qualities - his eternal power and divine nature - have been clearly seen, being understood from what has been made, so that men are without excuse.

Roman: 1 - 20.

Before I formed you in the womb I knew you, before you were born I set you apart. I appointed you as a prophet to the nations.

Jeremiah: 1 – 5.

I give you a new command; love each other. You must love each other as I have loved you. All people will know that you are my followers if you love each other.

John 13: 34 - 35.

"Submit to God, and you will have peace; then things will go well for you. Listen to his instructions, and store them in your heart."

Job 22:21-22

"Love is not two souls finding perfection, but two hearts choosing each other's flaws as their home, and in that imperfection, discovering a beauty the world cannot understand." Dostoyevsky. You can feel it. You can feel it in your own dreams. You can feel it in your own trips. You can feel that we're approaching the cusp of a catastrophe, and that beyond that cusp, we are unrecognizable to ourselves. The wave of novelty that has rolled unbroken since the birth of the universe has now focused and coalesced itself in our species. Freedom the End of the Human condition is the Last Frontier of Agape. Love is God's possibility in and with him. Man does not bring about this love on his own strength and from his own initiative. He cannot actually choose it, but it happens to him and moves him, like the Samaritan in the well-known parable 'is moved with compassion'. He himself is not the original subject of this love, but rather the agape is the subject in him. He will 'walk in love' as on a path that he himself has not opened up or chosen and act in the superiority of the love that has happened to him and animates him.

Humble yourself to the sight of the mother
You got to bend down low and
Humble yourself to the sight of the mother
You got to know what she knows and

We shall lift each other up
Higher and higher
We shall lift each other up

Humble yourself to the force of the sun
You got to bend down low and
Humble yourself to the force of the sun
You got to know what he shows and

We shall lift each other up
Higher and higher
We shall lift each other up
Humble yourself: Rainbow Song.

"The most important kind of freedom is to be who you really are. Be authentic and vibrate higher than love daily. Stop trading in your reality for a borrowed role. Stop trading in the purity of your senses for a dullifying modelling act. Do not give up your ability to feel, and in exchange, put on a mask. *There can't be any large-scale revolution until there's a personal revolution, on an individual level. It's got to happen inside first: Jim Morrisson.*"

The Absolute at rest in infinity is a GOD concept straight out of Hebrew mystical philosophy. Even the Christian concept of the Trinity shines through the description of the Absolute as presented in this paper. The description of energy totally at rest, in Infinity fits the Christian metaphysical concept of the Father while the infinite self-consciousness resident in that energy providing the motive force of will to bring a portion of that energy into motion to create reality corresponds with the Son. This is so because in order to attain self-consciousness, <u>the consciousness of the Absolute must project a hologram of itself and then perceive it</u>. The human consciousness is to establish a coherent pattern of perception in those dimensions where speeds below Planck's distance apply. The horizons of its perceptual personal liberation continuum at beyond light speed cause the Absolute to be infinite at which point your perception stops the holograms of or about itself._That hologram is a mirror image of the Absolute in infinity, still exists outside time and space, but is one step removed from the Absolute and is the actual agent of all creation (all reality). And, the eternal thought or concept of self which results from this self-consciousness serves the Motivational Aspect of a Sea of unconditional Tsunami Love.

<u>History is ending</u>, because the dominator culture has led the human species into a blind alley of robotical zombification of singularity. And as the inevitable catastrophe approaches, people look for metaphors and answers. Every time a culture gets into trouble, it casts itself back into the past *looking for the last sane moment it ever knew.* And the last sane moment we ever knew was on the plains of Africa, 15,000 years ago. The 20th century mind is nostalgic for the paradise that once existed on the mushroom-dotted plains of Africa, where the plant-human symbiosis occurred that pulled us out of the animal body and into the tool-using, culture-making, imagination-exploring creature that we are. What this means is that the womb of the planet has reached its finite limits, and that the human species has now, without choice, begun the descent down the birth canal of collective transformation

toward something right around the corner, and nearly completely unimaginable.

Something is calling us out of nature and sculpting us in its own image. We are flesh, which has been caught in the grip of some kind of an attractor that lies ahead of us in time, and that is sculpting to its ends. Speaking to us, through psychedelics, through visions, through culture and technology. Consciousness, the language-forming capacity in our species is propelling itself forward, as though it were going to shed the monkey body and leap into some extra-surreal space that surrounds, but that we cannot currently see. And the confrontation with this something is now not so far away. This is what the impending apparent end of everything actually means. It means that the denouement (the final part of a play, film, or narrative in which the strands of the plot are drawn together and matters are explained or resolved) of human history is about to occur and is about to be revealed as a universal process of congressing and expressing novelty that is now going to become so intensified that it is going to flow over into another dimension.

I believe that I cannot receive any greater gift from anybody then, to be seen, to be heard, to be understood, and to be touched from the heart while dancing on the sound of music. To be a fully integrated male, a man has to assimilate in his body the divine female energies that woman can only release to him through right emotional lovemaking. But the man has to be man enough. He has to be able to love her enough; that is, love her selflessly during the actual act of lovemaking, and love enough to extract the divine energies from her deepest center. *To be able to love in this way is the authority man has lost - his only true authority over woman. A woman's heart should be so close to God that a man must seek him to find her.*

This requires pure love. Love is nourishment in itself. The more you love, the more you will find untrodden spaces where love goes on and on spreading around you like an aura.

Let this story begin now: *"Can you picture what will be? So limitless and free, desperately in need, of some stranger's hand, in a desperate land, Lost in a Roman wilderness of pain*

And all the children are insane, All the children are insane, Waiting for the summer rain, yeah,

Come back, baby, back into my arm, we're getting' tired of hanging' around

Waiting' around with our heads to the ground, I hear a very gentle sound

Very near yet, very far, very soft, yeah, very clear

Persian night babe

See the light, babe

Save us, Jesus, save us:

Jim Morrisson: The End when the music is over.

The writer's journey is expressed by make it real or else forget about it. The body of Drone was resting in a field of wild Lavender flowers somewhere in the Ardêche, a province in the mid-south section of France. A soft breeze of wind is moving the air around him and Drone realizes that a force-greater than his self must be the creator of all this beauty! With his lips pursed, he exhales and blows his circular breathing of life into a hollow pipe called a Didgeridoo. A full spectrum of sound permeates the air around him. His spirit responds and Drone begins to slip and slide in and out of the Dreamtime. In his head he was singing the song: I am a King bee buzzing around your hive. A world unknown to his worldly self-lays hidden dormant deep within the abyss of his subconscious reality. The fields of flowers around him are reflecting the brilliance of the Sun, and his eyes are receiving their flickering colors! The retinas of his eyes are adjusting to the brilliance of flickering colors all around him, and he is taking in the magic of it all. The moment he realizes this gift of divine mystery; his eyes have become adjusted to what now feels like a nostalgic memory of bliss. The cicadas are singing a cosmic song for him, and the cadence of their high droning sound is mesmerizing. A dominant yet attractive fragrance of lavender permeates the air and her scent is riding a gust of wind to the sensors of his nose. Hummingbirds are doing their cosmic love dance from flower to flower. The mesmerizing sound of their high-speed wings tickle his insides in places where he has not been touched before. Drone is stunned, in awe with the immense beauty of this detailed and vast Universe, and It is within his inner world, where the world around him is really happening.

It felt as if his Soul was not in his body, but instead his body was hovering suspended in the vastness of his soul. Suddenly the sound of a ringing bicycle bell interrupted the magic spell he was captured by! Its disturbance made him aware, that he was not alone in this vast Universe. A bicycle was approaching. His head turned automatically into the direction of the ringing echo. Drone's dreamy eyes glanced at two youthful females waiving their hands at him. His hands waved back and signaled them to stop. To his surprise, the girls responded and hesitantly awaited his approach. The wind was playing with their fluffy hair and it wrapped the cloth of their yellow summer dresses around the curves of their heavenly bodies. One could see that these young girls were naturally biologically blooming and really ready for the ecstatic process of procreation. Only the emotional frustration at not reaching ecstatic union would lead these girls to the consumption of chocolate. The color yellow reminded Drone of a quote made by Albert Einstein, who once calculated the following:

"When a man looks at a woman in a yellow dress, the electrons inside the retina of his eyes, will produce more vibrations in one second, than all the waves that break on all the shores of every continent, over a period of ten million years!"

French girls: "Bon jour, comment tu t'appèle?" (What's your name?)
Drone: "My name is Alex Drone!"

Drone smiled and handed each of them a small bouquet of wild flowers. The girls descended their bicycles, scented the flowers and blew him a kiss on the cheek.

French girls: "Merci Drone, t'es gentil!" (Thank you Drone, you are a nice person)
Drone: "What are your names?"
French girls: "Alice and Cecile!"

His heart was pounding with joy and his hands reached out to touch their hands with feeling. A touch of skins made them feel connected and a rush of shyness made their faces blush. Spontaneously Drone broke the embarrassment with a suggestion:
Drone: "Do you girls want to be my Queen bee and buzz through a field of wild flowers?"

The force of enthusiasm now strengthened the grip of their hands and they stampeded downhill over a field of wild flowers, until they fell down from fun laughter and exhaustion.
Mother Earth felt soft and her breath-taking beauty was now being captured by the natural impressions of her soft surface. Drone's Soul was being uplifted from his physical body and he felt himself being pulled into the light of the Dreamtime. Blasts from the past soon flashed by and Drone silently observed his internal memory screen.

Alice: "What do you see, Drone?"
Drone: "I am a witness to my birth on the 25th of March, 1959 in Utrecht, the Netherlands!"
Cecile: "Tell us more!"

Drone: "My birth mother Greta rejected me for her personal traumatized reasons and she gave me up for adoption to the Salvation Army!"

Alice: "What about your father?"

Drone: "All I know is that he was in the Airforce and from Native American descend."

Alice: "Aho, my brother, May the drums bring you home!"

Cecile: "She must be a horrible person! How can anybody give up their child for adoption?"

Drone: "Maybe my mother was too traumatized by the things that happened to her?"

Cecile: "Yeah right!"

Drone: "Maybe my mother's pain was greater than her feelings of love for me!"

Cecile: "Why are you still trying to defend a mother, who rejected you in the first place?"

Alice: "Maybe you are giving your mother the benefit of the doubt, because the pain you feel Drone, is too hard to bear!"

Drone: "It hurts, when you say that!"

Cecile reached out with the touch of a butterfly and guided Drone's head gently against her voluptuous breasts.

Cecile: "Don't hold back chéri, let it all out!"

Drone cried his eyes out and the pain, which had been entrapped within his body for years, was now being released and set free. It felt good to release and taste the drops of salty tears. The gentle, loving, warm and understanding manner, in which Cecile expressed her nurturing care, assisted him to wrest the iron grip from his emotional mind.

Alice: "What is the Salvation Army?"

Drone: "They are the soldiers of God!"

Cecile: "How did that make you feel?"

Drone: "Make what feel?"

Cecile: "You, being able to release your mother trip!"

Drone: "Oh...(paused), I don't know, eh. Pain, Anger, Fear, Sadness!"

Alice: "What was it like in the Orphanage?"

Drone: "Every Sunday, ignorant parents would pick up their kids for a day trip and give them the lovey Dovey treat. However, many times these parents would not show up or never return at all. I can still remember a strong sense of despair emanating from my fellow orphans!"

Cecile: "What did you learn from your feelings of despair?"

Drone: "A desperate longing for the return of my birthmother, forced me to be a witness to the yearning pain of rejection and grief inside of my body! The world around me began to fade out and it lost her beauty for me. That became the reflection and lesson of my pain!"

Alice: "This I can feel, and I can now feel your pain!"

Cecile: "Thank you for sharing! Do you want to tell us more?"

Drone: "It's hard to open up to strangers and it hurts too much to be rejected again! The pain I feel is too deep, too intense!"

Alice:" Each of us carries their own unique pain, but by sharing it with one another we have an opportunity to set ourselves free from its burden!"

Drone: "I think that life's lessons are unique but the pain we carry is the same!"

Cecile: "True, your pain could easily trigger certain issues, which we are carrying and it in return would then make us feel our pain!"

Alice: "Once we learn to communicate with our primal feelings of pain, then that will enable us to open up to all levels of intimacy!"

Drone looked into the compassionate eyes of the girls and it made him feel safe in the magic zone, so he continued his story.

Drone: "At dinner time we were taught how to pray with our eyes closed. As I opened my eyes, I noticed that my food had disappeared into thin air. The laughter of my fellow orphans explained to me the whereabouts of my meal. From that moment on, I prayed with the appearance of having my eyes closed. I felt determined to catch the thief, which had the audacity to steal my food, and I did! A hand reached out to take my food and I stabbed my fork straight through it!"

Cecile: "Did they punish you?"

Drone: "Yes, the punishment was a three-day confinement to my room!"

Alice: "C'est terrible!" (That's awe full!)

Cecile: "How long did they keep you inside the Orphanage?"

Drone: "When I was seven years old, I was adopted by my adoptive parents and they gave me the name Nirbeeja!"

Cecile: "Your name sounds unusual! What does it mean?"

Drone: "Near-Be-Jah means: A state or condition, where there are no seeds of thought, Mind, or unawareness left!"

Cecile: "So you are what we refer to as a nobody!"

Drone: "Yes, when you are alone, God is and you are not!"

Angelique: "Being ordinary is the greatest miracle in life and if that means that you have to be a nobody, then so be it!"

Drone: "I love the way the French carry themselves with nonchalance and choix the vivre (lust for life)!"

Cecile: "So, why do you call yourself Drone?"

Drone: "Because I am a King bee, the Bees are dying due to the use of pesticides, which creates fungus in the Bee hives. I want this to stop, so I want everyone to remember!"

Angelique: "Remember what?"

Drone: "No Bees, no flowers, no scents, no perfume, no colors, no women, no fun, no sex, no love, no children, no men, no life!"

Cecile: "Have you heard the saying: 'On vit bien en France!"

Drone: "What does it mean?"

Alice: "Would you like to make love to our heavenly bodies and find out?"

Drone: "Ehhh.... definitely Yes!" He responded with a sense of shyness. Who can refuse a magical love offering by two French girls in a field of wildflowers?"

The pulse of life became hard within his erotic zone and Drone thanked the Lord within for the manifestation of an overdue fantasy. The scent of a French woman, wild flowers, flickering colors, droning cicadas, his heart beat, the taste of transpiration, red lips, French kisses, voluptuous breasts, succulent vortices and the burning sun on his back! The alchemical magic of it all made him feel drunk with the divine beauty of France! With each breath his body softened, relaxed and soon the three of them blissed out and for a couple of seconds they experienced an awesome feeling of being one with the Universe.

Alice: "God just gave me a little taste of what it's going to be like in heaven!"

Cecile: "If this is what heaven is going to be like, then I want more of it!"

Drone: "If this is Truth then I am that! I feel as if a Universe just moved through me!

Alice: "Drone, did you feel it?"

Drone: "I am in the flesh baby! True love, or the dawning of real love, longs for love in the flesh of my body. I am feeling your love in the flesh, my flesh.

The reality of the sun burning on their naked flesh brought them back to their senses, and they helped each other getting dressed. The three of them mounted the bicycle and the girls dropped Drone off at the bottom of a dirt road, which led to his parent's summer vacation home. They hugged and French kissed each other goodbye!

The summer vacation home of Drone's parents was built on top of a mountain with a 360-degree view, overlooking St. Pierreville and the adjacent mountains. Each year his family would spend their vacation here in the Ardèche, a province in the southern part of France. Most of his time he spends fly-fishing or hanging out with the girls in town.

Every other day, his parents would send him down the mountain to pick up some French loafs of bread. It took Drone half an hour to run downhill on a small goat trail, which ended in a back alley of the town of St. Pierreville. Running down hill was fun and easy but the rerun going uphill induced a shortness of breath, which humbled him into the realization of being connected to a greater vastness of being. It was not that he was breathing for himself, but more like it was as if a being larger than life itself was breathing through him!

At night his family would sit around the fireplace to reminisce the day. It was during those times that his adoptive mother Tinez Ambhanidhi would have these peculiar psychic insights into Drone's past lives. The name 'Ambhanidhi' means 'Ocean of love' and her name originated from a French Polynesian heritage. She was also gifted in playing the classical piano and skilled in the Art of Past life regression therapy. Tinez is a storyteller and she would always begin a story with: 'My heart belongs to Bora Bora. It is there, where I found my beloved, who gave me the gift to see!' At first Drone would reject her 'juicy' stories, but there were those moments in which he detected a definite sense of emotional recognition. Tinez then would teach him how to get in 'touch' with those feelings, and he learned to embrace his feelings with the art of discovery. The realization of awe and mystification began to grow on Drone Day by day. Little by little, he became a believer of his stepmother's psychic gift, not because of what he felt, but more because of the intense dreams and flashbacks that followed. Drone learned that past life experiences ought to be used for the personal integration of daily obstacles into a higher power of love. Religion should be brought to actual reality. Once it comes to the actual reality you can forget about it and it will continue. It will hover around you.....it will become your aura and you will always be in contact with it.

His family enjoyed their togetherness in front of a cozy fireplace and when the fire got low, it was usually Drone who had to go outside to gather some more firewood. The logs were stacked 500 yards behind their house, next to an old graveyard. Revelations of his past life events were spooky from time to time, but that fear was nothing compared to what he felt during his nightly cat walks to the old graveyard. During those walks, his fear for darkness and death would escalate to a point of terror, obsession and despair.

One day Drone made a commitment to himself to face his inner demons. He raised his arms to the skies and screamed at the top of his lungs:

Drone: "Enough is enough, no more fear, no more demons, only the Light is, and only the Light shall set me free!"

Drone took off his clothes and some unknown force directed him to walk towards to the graveyard: "Naked!"

The moon was full and all the dark silhouettes surrounding him appeared spookier than ever before! At the graveyard, Drone picked out a tombstone and laid his naked body down on top of it. Stunned by the encroaching sense of fear, he became unable to breathe. The spirits of the undead were clearly touching his body. Their presence became so overwhelming, that it triggered him into a state of catharsis. He had to conquer death before it would find him.

Drone: "You can't touch me, I am not my fear, and this too shall pass!"

He screamed and burst out in tears. Facing the intensity of his fear meant, that he had to stay with it, breathe into it, and look at it, until it would disappear. At the abyss of his deepest despair, a pillar of white light appeared, and its stillness had a calming effect on the adrenaline rush, which was pumping through his body. It was this pillar of white peace, which pulled him back into the presence of the here now. The stillness of the light now distinctively moved and a voice spoke to Drone!

The voice: "Give it up to the light my child, give it up!"

Drone raised his arms and he could clearly see a black substance leaving his body. The darkness became the light. Happy feelings arose inside of him and he felt like celebrating a victory won over the demons of fear. Semi-drunk with his victory he began to run down the mountain, stumbling, rolling, and filled with laughter. His spirit felt alive again and he jumped butt naked into a mountain stream. Celebration time! The current took his body downstream for about a mile or so and by that time, the cold water began to sober him up. Butt naked and content, Drone felt like he had just been initiated into a personal breakthrough to the other side of his fear. It took him about two hours to walk back home, where he found his concerned parents waiting for his safe return.

Parents: "Where were you?"
Drone: "I was out facing my fears, but I returned with my victory!"
Parents: "We were so afraid!"
Drone: "So was I!"

That same evening the family members discussed their personal fears extensively and together they came to the conclusion, that there are four basic fears, which control more or less the variable factors of human behavior. Fear itself is deeply rooted within the animalistic triple F reaction: "Fight, Flight, Fright!"

Drone: "What is your most intense fear Dad?"

Father: "For me it is the fear of Death or Non-existence!"

Drone: "What is your most intense fear Mom?"

Mother: "Love is what we were born with, fear is what we learned here! My mother taught me to fear sex and orgasm"

Parents: "What is yours Son?"

Drone: "For me it is Insanity! The fear of losing my sanity!"

Mother: "Now that I think about it, there is one fear which everybody seems to overlook!"

Drone: "What's that mom?"

Mother: "The fear of being alive. The fear of living life, realizing that every moment does contain your very last breath! Life is a process of constant change, but within our Minds we want to secure our level of comfort, hence we sacrifice things like: romance, passion, magic!"

Father: "Do you see any similarity between these fears son?"

Drone: "Hit me, I don't have a clue!"

Father: "As you will mature by the experience of life, you will come to know, that the similarity is a loss of self-identity!"

Drone: "I don't understand!"

Father: "In death, insanity and orgasm, you as you know your 'self' ceases to be. When you feel intensely alive, you are rebirthing moment to moment, which in essence is a constant mode of change!"

Drone: "Are you saying that when I'm having an orgasm, that I'm not really having one?" He asked laughingly.

Father: "No, when you are experiencing an orgasm, you become the energy and you leave your identity behind! But you my son will have to find your identity first before you surrender yourself to the divine!"

Drone: "So I need to find myself first and then commit myself to a Quest for God?"

Father: "Why harass or kill your ego, when one can be free in its play as a needed, useful tool? God bless you my son!"

Drone: "Don't patronize me dad!"

Father: "Just remember son, when there is 'Ego' there is no 'Amigo!'"

The summers in France were divine and Drone felt a deep gratitude towards his parents, who had provided the opportunity for him to have a little taste from heaven. Time flew by and Drone was having fun. The moment he realized that he was actually feeling good, seemed to be the same moment in which it was time to return back to Holland and have a reality check. Back in Holland, Drone continued his high school program, but the blending of life and school just did not seem to match anymore. The testosterone expansion drift of a young man was now yearning for the thrill of participating in the roller coaster of life.

His French lovers had stirred a drift of passion within his heart and Drone began to long for his beloved. The effects of male hormones were kicking in and Drone's emotional behavior began to conflict with the conditioned believe systems of those around him. At first glance they seemed to care for him, but then he realized, that they did not know how to feel the magic of love from the heart. His confrontational efforts to produce more life inside the people who mentored him were being bounced off by the walls of their closed-Minded way of thinking. His heart was not willing to adapt to their restricting Mind set and he continued to seek the thrill of Freedom. Everything became a struggle and a drag for him. School just did not make sense anymore and his heart became increasingly rebellious. Drone remembered specific situations during which he kept asking his teacher:

Drone: "Why is it that I am a mortal being? Why is it that my heart longs and dreams for love and yet at the same time the teachers of this dead Society are trying to kill my passion with dead and abstract knowledge? Tell me oh Great One I want to know!"

Teacher: "Who the Hell do you think that you are!"

Drone: "I'm a child of God and I'm in search for my beloved in Paradise and not in Hell Sir!"

Teacher: "If you do not study and make good grades, you will have no merit in society and that's a sure way to go to Hell!"

Drone: "When there is no love in your Heart, then it doesn't matter if you study or not, because that will be Hell for sure!"

The sincerity of his questions seemed to upset his mentors and Drone was expelled from school. His stepparents were concerned about the continuance of his education and they decided to send him to a private school setting, where he would get all the necessary attention for his personal development and growth. The private school setting was part of the Seventh day Advent Missionary School and it was here, where he learned everything there was to know about God, and they in return were educated on everything there was to know about Drone! Again, he was advised not to ask deep spiritual questions, which were in direct opposition of the foundations of the social order of things, and again he felt cornered into condemnation by a society, which was out to control him. That autumn of 1975 a life-changing event occurred. Drone's step father Pierre, who was an engineer in nuclear science, went horseback riding and he was struck by a fatal accident. The reality of his death triggered Drone into an identity crisis and more questions began to surface from the depth of his being.

"Who am I?"

"Why am I here on this God forsaken planet?"

All Drone could see was a massive void. The world felt empty around him. His girlfriend Renee tried to help him all that she could, but they both realized that their lives were heading off in different directions. Drone was filled with a passion to find his ultimate beloved and that was a thrill too intense for any normal human being to go out on a limb for.

Renee: "You know Drone, you are too intense for me. Do not get me wrong, I love the way you make love to me, but it feels like you are trying to find God in sex, myself, and everything alive. I don't feel like I can combine my sexual intimacy with your driven Quest for the ultimate beloved!"

Drone: "Can't you see that it is the same phenomenon?" Every orgasm feels like God is giving us a little taste of what it is going to be like in heaven. We can create paradise on Earth, when we become able to master our orgasmic bliss from moment to moment!"

Renee: "I want to live a life of laughter and be filled with the incredible lightness of being. I want to Humm like a Humming bird, play like a dolphin, fluff like a butterfly!"

Drone: "Butterfly, that word really triggers me! All butterflies are about Sex, Change and Transformation. You don't think that that is an intense way of living?"

At the time Drone and his girlfriend Renee were having this argument in a bar and the alcohol was dragging them down under into a state of intoxicated unawareness. The intoxication of the brew made them inconsiderate towards each other's feelings, and it is needless to say, that intense and irreconcilable differences of opinion made them end their relationship that same evening. As Drone was about to leave the bar, he ran into Lucy, who was engaged to Willem, the brother of his best friend Frank.

Lucia: "Drone, I need to talk to someone!"

Drone: "What's up Lucia?"

Lucia: "Willem just broke up with me!"

Drone: "I'm sorry Lucia, but I'm kind off in a mess myself right now and this just isn't a good moment for me!"

Lucia: "But I need you now!"

Drone: "Look Lucia, you mean the world to me, but at this moment I don't have the courtesy, time nor energy to listen to your cry for help, because I am drunk!!!"

Lucia: "Drone, feel, see, be the void within me, but can you not fill the emptiness within a woman like me?"

Drone: "Lucia, please do not allow the pressures of emotion or relationship separate you from the void you know so well. As every baby comes out of the void and soon forgets."

Drone turned his back on Lucia and walked away. The next day he heard through the grapevine, that Lucia had committed suicide. Until today Drone still feels guilty for not having been available for her 'feeling void' during a time when she needed him most.

People say, that to commit a suicide is a crime, because one disrupts the divine order of things and people. Sweden is the number one country with the highest suicide rate of the world. Teenage girls commit suicide at the rate of a mass lemming migration. Maybe the cause is to be found within the collective human unconsciousness? One could ask oneself: "What is it that we are doing wrong and what is it that we could do right?"

The burden of every human being is rooted within a hypnotic spell of his/her original sin, which caused him to be expelled from paradise. We feel the pain of rejection by God deep inside of our bodies. It is this pain, which is covered with anger, and it is this anger, which is destroying our environment! All human happiness, health, safety, prosperity, and all things worthwhile depend upon the balance and normalcy of our environment. We are building an environment of death upon the surface of this planet, dolphins are beaching, and Swedish girls are checking out like lemming migrations. God is trying to compress life within us, but our manmade 'Plutonium' produces more heat and radioactivity than we are able to resist. Plutonium sends millions of radioactive particles into our bodies, which accumulate there all of our life, and raise our temperature above 98.6 F, readjusting our entire metabolism, until our body cells explode from their accumulated heat and expand beyond their normalcy. The question is:

"What are we going to do about it and what would it feel like?"

In the back of his head Drone kept hearing the song: "I am the Freedom man, that's how lucky I am. Life to Drone is more so a balance between relaxation and contraction, and hence the song should be: " Relax, soften up, don't do it if you really want to love!"

Drone's best friend Frank Autumn dropped by to show him his brand-new moped. Hitching on the back of Frank's moped was his new girlfriend Rose. Frank and Drone rolled a cigarette and were catching up on old times, while Rose was circling around them on his new bike.

Rose: "Can I cruise around the block?"
Frank Autumn: "Sure, be careful!"

Half an hour had gone by and they began to worry about Rose's well-being. Frank and Drone scouted out the neighborhood, but without any productive result. They waited for two more hours and decided to call around to check if people had seen Rose cruise around on a moped. A large search party was rounded up and it took them three days to find Rose's body. Her body had been submerged in a canal for three days after which it drifted afloat. She must have slipped, snapped her neck and fallen into the water, submerged and disappeared out of sight. When she finally surfaced, the harsh decay of death had gotten a hold of her beautiful body. Frank and Drone were as if in a daze, shocked, stunned and down and out for weeks. Most of their time they would hang out together, smoke pot and discuss the meaning of life and death. Frank had a difficult time accepting the loss of his girlfriend Rose, and he began to suppress his feelings more and more. The death of Rose made their friendship grow apart, because neither of them knew at the time how to handle the pain they were feeling deep down inside. Drone's feelings for Frank as a friend of the heart was never deleted from his memory bank. Even today, he still loves him as another essential part of himself. The death of Rose forced the boys to grow up overnight and Drone did not like the feelings of alienation caused by his inability to deeply feel pain. His person became obsessed with death and feelings of rejection and denial accumulated into a threshold of compressed rage. Pain became a motive towards self-destruction and Drone began to pick fights out in the street and local bars. Many a times Drone got his butt kicked, but he enjoyed the path of self-pity, pain and martyrdom. His defeats motivated him to become a better fighter and he enrolled himself into the world of Martial Arts! His two favorite styles of self-defense were: "Aikido, Wing Chun!" His teachers' 'Sensei' originated from the old-traditional school, which in essence meant: "Learn to love your pain!"

Every winter Drone would run weekly on his bare feet in the snow, which then was followed by an intense routine of Martial Arts practice. The emphasis of his training was to toughen up physically, mentally, emotionally and spiritually. The daily practice of 'Makiwara' or toughening of the hands and feet on a rope padded board, made his callus grow at a rapid rate. It was important to build up a full impact tolerance, because that is the 'character' building aspect of a true warrior.

The repetitive impact of punches and kicks was painful at first, but over time, the nerve-endings would numb themselves out. Drone's hands became deformed by the growth of callus and with his shinbone; he was able to crush a wooden baseball bat. His Sensei taught him how to meditate and how to reinforce his strength with the powers of the Universe. The energy, which was created through continuous breathing exercises, was to be recollected within the Hara! Hara is the Japanese word for 'wheel' or center of life and death. Its location is 10 cm below the navel and inward. His Sensei always stressed out the importance of not showing off in public the supernormal powers he possessed. It is an Eastern belief system, that if one does, and then all the supernormal powers will be taken away. His Japanese master 'Yamaguchi' used to say: "One with the supernormal capabilities developed could also drop to the bottom. If he cannot conduct himself properly, an enlightened person could also drop to the bottom. Even a Buddha could fall down if he cannot conduct himself properly, not to mention a practitioner like you among the ordinary people!"

Over a period of eight years Drone finally graduated to the level of obtaining a fourth-degree black belt for: "Aikido." Finally, he had found a channel for his surging rage attacks. The painful feelings, which he had felt before were now erupting, and releasing themselves through the expressive force of Martial Arts. The practice of Martial Arts motivated Drone to learn more about the physical body and he decided to move to Amsterdam to study the art of Acupuncture. In order to pay for his tuition, he had to find a job on the side. A normal nine to five job would not give him the financial leverage that he needed, and Drone focused in on the odd jobs listing. There was one classified ad, which caught his eye, and it read as follows: "When the going gets tough, the tough get going!" Kick-Ass muscle head wanted! It was a nightclub called 'Zorba the Buddha' and the owner was a Greek by the name of Zorba. The nightclub itself was located in the center of the red-light district where drugs, sex and Rock and Roll were the main center of attraction. The music at Zorba was called the Psychedelic Goa Trance, which in essence is a form of hypnotizing trance dance. The owner 'Zorba' requested from Drone to participate in a skills performance test and he agreed. Drone asked him: "What do I have to do?"

Zorba: "Let me make a phone call!"

Zorba made him wait for about ten minutes or so and to his surprise returned with four humongous Hell's Angel dudes. Their presence made him feel uncomfortable and Drone swallowed a couple of times to clear his throat.

Zorba: "Floor these four and you're hired!"

Inside his brain, somebody switched a knob, which was labeled: "Beware, Rothweiler on LSD!" A dormant warrior became alive and Drone kicked their Asses and broke a few bones.

Drone: "Nothing personal, but Biznez is Biznez!"

Zorba: "You're hired. You'll get paid a $100 flat fee per night and the rest you will earn in tips!"

The Red-light district is a one square mile area of window prostitution in the city of Amsterdam. The neighborhood has a reputation of being safe, because the underworld had an investment in its merchandise. The streets alongside the contaminated canals are crowded with junky's, tourists, and plenty of undercover agents. The working girls are looking out for one another and most of the striptease clubs are protected by the Hells Angels. The Red-light district is run by the Drug Lords, who are always on the lookout for new comers trying to move in on their turf. Therefore, it happened that during one of his shifts a messenger, who claimed to be working for one of the big shots, was approaching Drone.

Messenger: "Do you want to make extra cash on the side?"

Drone: "Who wants to know?"

Messenger: "Dado is the man, who runs the show!"

Drone: "What does he want?"

Messenger: "He rewards those who push his candy and protect his Bunny Clubs!"

Drone: "Can't do candy, but will do protection! What do I do?"

Messenger: "You'll carry a Beeper and be on call as our trouble shooter!"

Drone: "What's the Bottom line?"

Messenger: "When your Beeper goes off, you show up and produce some kick ass results!"

Drone: "What does it pay?"

The Messenger handed Drone a Beeper and said: "It pays a $100. Per show!"

Drone: "I will need a partner to cover my shift at Zorba!"

Messenger: "Call your uncle Danny Steel shoe!"

Drone: "How do you know my uncle?"

Messenger: "Don't ask, we know!" And he walked away.

Drone's uncle Danny Steel shoe is a five-foot raw deal muscular guy, with a no-nonsense attitude to anybody who gets on his nerves. His uncle's fighting reputation had stigmatized him as 'the Pitbull', because of his ferocious nature and persistent choke holds. Danny was always doing shady jobs on the side, but because Drone was family, he knew that he was able to depend on him as his trouble-shooting sidekick. Danny was married to Drone's aunt Willy and that somehow created a 'next of kin' type of relationship between the two of them. They were both impulsive and from time to time even crazy, but throughout it all, they felt next of kin. Drone dialed his number and Willy answered the phone.

Willy: "How may I help you?"

Drone: "Hello Aunty is Pitbull there?"

Willy: "Just a moment!"

Danny: "What the F...do you want?"

Drone: "It's me your nephew and I need your help!"

Danny: "What kind of help?"

Drone: "I want you to be my side kick at Zorba!"

Danny: "When do we start?"

Drone: "Friday at eight o'clock!"

Danny: "I'll be there!" Click beep, beep, beep......!

Drone: "He hung up on me! Can you believe that, he hung up on me?"

The music at Zorba was called 'Salsa Trance' and its mesmerizing beat induces a psychedelic effect of space travel. The customers at Zorba would trip on Acid, Ecstasy or Magic mushrooms and most of them were living in the Dreamtime of an Archaic revival. Zorba became the place for Tribal gatherings, and people would trip from Dusk until Dawn! Zorba was hot and its trendy success stirred a ripple of jealousy in the adjacent nightclubs, which were owned by the drug Lords. The underworld began to lose out on money, and goons were sent in to harass Zorba with the intent to disrupt success!

Zorba was a new kid on the block and it had to be challenged as a way of the survival of the fittest. The drugs Lords send in two of their goons to test Drone's muscle capacity. By their looks and derailed behavior, it seemed obvious that they were feeling over confident within their steroid based muscle outfit. Drone's adrenaline was pumping and the customers, who were lined up and eager to get in, became worried and restless! There was pressure in the air and something was about to go down. The tension became unbearable and Drone could not believe that Danny was still containing himself within the limits of his social tolerance. One of the goons broke the ice and pushed one of the customers out of his way, while the other walked over to Danny to…

It was unbelievable! He unzipped his pants and peed all over Danny's shoes.

The crowd got excited and a girl yelled: "Hey Hot Dog is your wiener made out of real meat or do you sprout one of those Veggie things?" Danny just stood there and Drone had to wait until Danny decided to break his charm. The goon continued to degrade Danny like a big bully, lifted him to eye level, and said: "Where is your bathroom, because I've got to wash my hands!"

Danny: "Would you please be so kind to repeat that to me in Soprano because I love the Opera!"

Danny then kicked the goon in the groin and gave him a head bud. In pain the goon got down on his knees and Danny delivered an upward knee kick to his face and grabbed him by the balls. This move instantly transformed the goon into a choirboy performing at his first ballet session. The death grip pressure on his gonads made him walk on his toes.

Danny smiled and said: "I told you that I love Opera!"

The other goon stepped in to finish off Danny, but the steel lining of Danny's shoes painfully affected his shins. The crowd applauded and Danny took it upon himself to mentor his recruit students and said:

Danny: "Next time around you'd better dress for the occasion sissy!"

Zorba's customers applauded, for they now had a better understanding of why Drone and Danny were there. At the end of the Night shift, one of Zorba's bartenders: 'Jack Hemp', nicknamed 'Hemp Boy', was the designated driver. Hemp Boy is like an Angel, who sheds his Light deep into the shadow side of lost Souls. In the daytime Hemp Boy was running a Coffee/Hemp shop and at night he was a bartender at Zorba. Hemp Boy began to run his own business two years ago. In the beginning, he had a rough start, because during those days he had been diagnosed with a malignant brain tumor. His personal doctor had prescribed him the use of Marihuana for medicinal purposes and since then, it had become his 'Holy Sacrament!' One of Hemp boy's symptoms was that he was speech impaired, which in layman terms is called 'stuttering!"

He did not care when people were joking around about his handicap due to his good nature and great sense of humor. People are not supposed to laugh at each other's handicap, but this one morning, when he gave Danny and Drone a ride home, they did! On their Way Home at five a.m., a street gang of about twenty goons forced the car off the road. When the car came to a halt they then jokingly tried to tip over the vehicle with the three of them sitting in it. Hemp Boy by then had cranked down his window and spoke the following words:

Hemp boy: "Iffy I Wwwwere You, Iiiiiiii Wwwwwouldn't ddddoo that!"

Hemp Boy kept on stuttering while Danny and Drone were out there kicking ass. Eighteen guys were floored in less than a minute and Hemp Boy was finally able to complete his sentence.

Hemp Boy: "Iiii tttttried ttttooo wwwarn you, ddddidn't I!"

Drone's body was pumped up by the adrenaline rushing through his veins and he took a moment to enjoy the thrill of the rush. It felt good to be a winner. Hemp Boy drove them home and Drone slept all day. The next evening it was calm and peaceful at the entrance of Zorba and Danny and Drone had time to joke around with their customers. The groupies were hanging around them as usual and that always boosted up their ego. A groupie is a girl, who offers her body to what she thinks is a VIP. Danny and Drone were the elected VIP's and they were enjoying it thoroughly. The magic that attracted the groupies to these bouncers was rooted within their sense of humor. By joking around, they seemed to have softened up the hard-core macho image, which they represented.

Peace can last only so long, because the intrinsic nature of life on Planet Earth is CHANGE! It is usually during the full moon nights, that the people in the city will go crazy. Just check police records on the effect of the full moon on the crime rate at your local police station or the incidence of violence in psychiatric wards in mental hospitals. In both instances, there is a great increase. It was during one of these full moon nights that Drone's beeper was going off like crazy. The little screen on the beeper was instructing Drone to make his appearance at 'Gi Gi's a Go-Go bar!'

Drone: "Danny, hold the fort for me will you?"

Drone jumped on his motorcycle and drove like a madman alongside the canals to the designated club in distress. The entrance was open and Drone drove his bike into the fighting crowd. No time for questions, but he kept yelling:

Drone: "Who started it?"

Somebody pointed at three men who were roughing up the bouncer of the club. Drone moved in on his target, while delivering low devastating roundhouse kicks to their tender thighs.

When a striking force is applied onto a contracting muscle, its fiber then responds with an excruciating spasmodic cramp, which quickly convinces its recipient into a surrender of the flesh! In a flash of a second Drone then grabbed his opponents by the gonads and escorted them outside the premises to a back alley for the final touchdown. The bartender was happy to tip him a $100 dollar bill for 'service rendered' and Drone was on his way back to Zorba.

It was soon thereafter, that Drone became able to build a reputation for himself as being a 'Bone crusher' who always completes his assignments. Now he had earned himself some leeway for negotiation of his protective skills with the head honchos of the underworld. As a reward for his effective services rendered, the underworld then honored him with the custody of seven gorgeous prostitutes. In return for this favor, the expectation was a 30 - 70 split of revenues on their behalf. Naturally, Drone had to test out his merchandise before he could accept the offer. One by one, Drone asked the ladies to undress themselves and give him the works. They all graduated, because these girls know the Art of sexual pleasure! To his surprise, he found out, that all of them were regular married housewives. The choice for prostitution was not only made out of boredom, but also out of an insatiable thirst for material well-being. 'Freedom' is what a regulated atheistic Democracy is all about? Drone's female employees were housed in the windows opposite Zorba the Buddha, which enabled him to keep an eye on his merchandise. It was Drone's intend to build a business relationship with them, which was based on trust and mutual respect. Every Friday, as a token of appreciation he would buy his girls a box of chocolates and a bouquet of Dutch flowers. On top of that, he would include a box of funny condoms as a tool to increase business. His generosity was always returned with a hug, a kiss and a stead vast source of residual income. His girls were fully aware that if they were to be returned to their former bosses, then that would stigmatize them as being: "a worthless reject!" A return to their old status quo was not an option at this time. The pressure was on them to keep Drone happy and He loved it!

Riders on the Storm; by the Doors

Riders on the storm
Riders on the storm
Into this house we're born
Into this world we're thrown
Like a dog without a bone
An actor out on loan
Riders on the storm

There's a killer on the road
His brain is squirming like a toad
Take a long holiday
Let your children play
If you give this man a ride
Sweet family will die
Killer on the road

Girl you gotta love your man
Girl you gotta love your man
Take him by the hand
Make him understand
The world on you depends
Or life will never end
You gotto love your man

Riders on the storm
Riders on the storm
Into this house we're born
Into this world we're thrown
Like a dog without a bone
An actor out on loan

Riders on the storm
Riders on the storm

Chapter Two ~
Love her Madly

No! Those parts of the body that seem to be weaker are really very important. And the parts of the body that we think are not worth a lot are the parts that we give the most care to. And we give special care to the parts of the body that we want to hide. The more beautiful parts of our body need no special care. But God put the body together and gave more honor to the parts that need it. God did this so that our body would not be divided. God wanted the different parts to care the same for each other. If one part of the body suffers, then all the other parts suffer with it. Or if one part of our body is honored, then all the other parts share its honor.

1: Corinthians 12: 22 - 26.

This man welcomes sinners and eats with them.

Luke: 5: 2.

Frank van Dyk: 'Junior', blue eyed, five foot eight, skinny but muscular, is a good friend of Drone. From time to time, he would pay him a visit in Amsterdam. Together they would get stoned immaculate and take a walk on the wild side of town. Frank's father John van Dyk was the C.E.O. of the southern district of the I.R.S, and somehow that had triggered Frank into doing those things, which would upset his father most. Drone asked him one time why he enjoyed teasing his father so much. His answer was:

Frank; "I must do whatever it takes to wake up and thunder clash my father from his illusions!"

Drone: "What illusions?"

Frank: "The illusion of limitation, inhibition, control, identity, public image.... you name it!"

Drone: "For crying out loud Frank your father is the C.E.O. of the I.R.S!"

Frank: "Yeah, good for him!"

Drone: "Did you ever ask him to free up some time for you?"

Frank: "I did, but he never kept his promises!"

Drone: "What do you have in mind Frankie?"

Frank: "Well, I want to make my dad feel alive again!"

Drone: "That sounds reasonable!"

Frank: "Yeah, and I want you to take my picture, while I'm having sex with the ugliest prostitute in the red-light district! Would you Drone?"

Drone: "Whatever you say man!"

Frank and Drone shopped around the red-light district in search of a prostitute, whom would fit the profile of being ugly. Bingo! Their eyes spiked a match and simultaneously they yelled: "UGLY!" Frank approached 'the lady' and negotiated a price, after which they disappeared behind the curtains of her neon love shag. The lady closed the curtains, but Frank immediately opened them again because he was determined to have his picture taken. Frank had to renegotiate, because 'taking pictures' was an additional charge on top of the regular fee.

Frank coughed up some more cash and she then agreed to have her picture taken by Drone. Drone had to stay on the outside until they were done and ready to have their picture taken. Frank enjoyed his new role of being a puppet master, who was in control of his theatre. From time-to-time Frank would open up the curtains to expose his naked behind. First, he was dancing around naked, not knowing what to do with his energy. Then he would mount his 'lady', who then gestured Drone to take their picture. The sexual positions he created were hilarious and Drone could not stop laughing anymore. Drone shot a roll of film and eternalized Frank's eccentric performance. Finally, when the show was over Frank said:

Frank: "These pictures shall most definitely spike a response out of my dad!"

A couple of windows down the street Drone noticed a fat tourist trying to take his trophy prostitute picture. Moreover, as he was backing up trying to get his lens into focus he stumbled and fell backwards into the city sewer. It took about eight people to pull this guy out of the murky water and he seemed all right, but the water probably did ruin his trophy picture. The guy was lucky, because under the normal circumstances these girls would come running from behind their windows and rip out your film. They do not like to be tracked down by Interpol or the CIA/FBI for 'illegal' overseas prostitution, and every picture taken, has to be paid for! The thing Drone hated most about the red-light district was the excessive amount of Heroin addicts. When he cruised around the Red-Light district, he would often yell at their faces with the expression of disgust written all over his face!

Drone: "Do you know what I hate about you?"
Junky: "What?"

Drone: "That you neglect your personal hygiene!"

Junky: "Screw you man!"

Drone: "Do you know what I hate about you?"

Junky: "What?"

Drone: "That you're begging me to pay for your fix!"

Junky: "Fuck you man!"

Drone: "Do you know what I hate about you?"

Junky: "What?"

Drone: "You smell like a dump truck and I can see little critters move in your hair!"

Junky all upset and paranoid: "Get them out, get them out!"

Filled with anger and disgust Drone then beat the crap out of that person without any sense of remorse. Compassionate bystanders would often try to intercept his ferocious attacks and Drone then turned onto them:

Drone: "I'm cleaning up the streets you M....Fuckers! You want a piece of me? You want some of this too?"

Moreover, before Drone could restrain himself he was fighting off innocent bystanders.

It was until much later that Drone found out that the Dutch Government had legalized Heroin, because the Insurance companies were losing out on 'the big dough' to the small claims Courts, which dealt with issues like: "Car radio thefts etc....!" To Drone it meant: "Let's lower our social standards so we can keep the money in the Bank!"

Money seems to be the conflict of interests in all systems of quality value. Anyway, Frank junior and Drone were cruising alongside the canal, and suddenly this messed up junky girl walked up to Drone and begged him for a fix. As he was about to kick her butt back into the gutter, a voice inside of his head seemed to restrain his surging rage. The voice spoke as follows:

Voice: "Stop, and Look again! She is your beloved?"

In the spur of that moment, Drone was captured by the reflection of her beauty and the grace of her vulnerability was melting down the walls of his macho image. The deepest Emerald Forest green blue eyes embraced his angered being and when their eyes met, a scintillating flame was sparkled inside the walls of his heart. Drone was captured by the fragrance of her being. Her levy jeans were torn and on top, she wore a petite red woolen sweater, which elegantly exposed her pierced belly button. Anyone could see in one glance that this girl was dehydrated, in despair, hungry, and in need of some TLC, tender loving care. Drone stepped backwards and she stepped forwards, stumbled and fell straight into his arms. Drone tried to get her back on her feet but she was unconscious. Frank and Drone carried her over to his apartment and tucked her in bed. Frank Junior left and Drone had to figure out what to do next. The first thing was to get her out of those dirty clothes. As he undressed her heavenly body, she began to whisper to him in an unknown language.

Junky: "Ra tigua ma nouqua a qui the manna desposi na mi lotto."

Drone did not know what she was talking about so he brushed it off. His attention shifted to the expensive lingerie, which she wore underneath her street clothes: 'a red string bikini perfectly matched with a seamless red bra, which had a soft silky feel to it."

The beauty of her complexion astounded him and it left him stunned! Her body resembled the voluptuous succulent perfection of a Venus goddess. She was about six feet tall and well breasted with sensuous stream lined thighs. Her buns felt hard and firm as if she had been working out. Drone stepped back and glanced at this perfected creation of God. All he could say was:

Drone: "Thank you Lord, I praise your name for this blessing!" Unexpectedly, and out of the blue, a voice responded to his prayer and it said:

Voice: "When we can come to this one place inside of our bodily selves, and know that we are all One, and know that we are all members of God's body as much as one member of our body is a part of the whole body, then we are Divine."

Drone thought he was dreaming and he brushed the voice off. He paused and slowly began to gather the clothes of his guest and took them over to a laundromat down the street. Her clothes reeked like they needed a deep cleaning, and 'Toyota!', they got what they had asked for. When Drone returned home he noticed that his guest was about to wake up and he quickly fixed her some hot Coco. Her body was shivering and she stretched out her limbs. Drone coughed as to make her aware of his presence! She then raised her voice and asked in a demonic way:

Junky: "Who the fuck are you? Where the fuck am I? Why the fuck am I here?"

Drone paused, took a deep breath and answered:

Drone: " My name is Drone, you are in my apartment and you are here, because I am aware, I care and I serve!"

He paused again and continued:

Drone: "Here is some hot coco for you!"

She reached out her arms, embraced the cup and pressed her lips softly against the surface of the cup to test its temperature. Her whole being absorbed the invasive scent of chocolate and her body seemed to relax and soften up into the here-now.

Junky: "I felt you looking at my body!"

Drone: "Yes, it's quite amazing!"

Junky: "Man's real body is not a body of material flesh but a body of light. So long as you seek outside of yourself that which is to be found only within yourself, you will not find it!"

Drone: "Thank you for sharing! So, why are you unhappy!"

Junky: "Imagine how long it would take you to become joyous if you had to proceed to concentrate upon each part of your body to awaken it to the state of joy and then proceed with each body center in this way until you finally became happy? This only happens on the other side!"

Drone: "I don't get that! What's your name?"

Junky: "My name is Layla and I am a French Polynesian descendant!"

Drone: "So you are an Island girl!"

Layla: "Yes, my heart belongs to Bora Bora, which is an island surrounded by Blue Lagunes and caressed by warm summer winds. When I close my eyes I dream about Bora Bora and I imagine myself sitting on the bow of a sailboat watching the dolphins swim beneath me. Mumm...........pure bliss!"

Layla then opened her vast blue green eyes and glanced at Drone with a gloom of despair as if saying: "I'm lost, I need a home, please don't send me away!"

Drone: "You can stay with me until you are able to get back on your feet again!"

Layla: "Is there a catch?"

Drone: "No catch Layla, just follow my house rules and we'll get along fine!"

Layla: "What are the house rules?"

Drone: "Thieves and Drugs are not welcome, and please do clean up after yourself!"

Layla: "I have prayed to the Lord to send somebody, who can help me kick my drug habit and I was thinking, that maybe it could be you?"

Drone: "Maybe so! We'll see!"

For the next three days they remained contained within Drone's apartment, and he took care of his guest. Kicking off a drug habit is hard and Layla was shaking like a leaf for hours at a time. Drone kept her warm with blankets and comforted her with gentle body rubdowns. In her vest pocket, he found a cassette tape, which was labeled: "Music of the angels as channeled by Cynthia Rose Young & Friends from Atlanta Georgia."

Drone: "Where did you get this tape?"

Layla: "From one of my customers!"

Drone: "So you exchanged sex for music?"

Layla: "Yeah, Good music for a skin deep quicky!"

Drone: "Unbelievable!"

Layla: "What's it to you?"

Drone: "I would never sell out the privacy of my body!"

Layla: "Sex is music and music is sex and besides music keeps me sane! The sound of angels is soft and soothing and it nurtures me with a feeling of safety. It makes me feel like I'm living in a vast cocoon i.e. a matrix woven by a silken God."

Drone: "Not to change the subject, but I'm going to fire up my sauna and I was wondering if you felt like joining me for a good sweat?"

Layla: "Yeah, I love to sweat!"

Layla jumped up and grabbed his hands and said:

Layla: "I'm all fired up, let's go do it!"

Drone showed Layla where the sauna was and she immediately disrobed and jumped into the steam room butt naked. When Drone entered the sauna, Layla had already made herself at home and she smiled at him without the embarrassment of her naked self. The strong eucalyptus vapors soon brought them in an altered state of consciousness, which in the land of down and under is being referred to as: "the Dreamtime." Layla's pores were opening up and pearls of sweat ran down over her sweaty skin. Layla was doing all the talking, as women seem to have the special need to express at least 30.000 more words or so per day! She took Drone on a guided fantasy tour into the blue Lagune of Bora Bora and he loved every minute of it. From time-to-time Drone would open his eyes and look at the curvature of her naked body. He fantasized about French kissing her private parts but he did not have the courage to ask her for permission. It was better to suggest something less intrusive.

Drone: "Layla would you be interested in a total body massage?"

Layla: "Yes, but no hanky panky!"

They walked back to his bedroom where she laid herself down on his blue satin sheets. With a childish voice she then said:

Layla: "I'm in the bed; I'm in the bed".

It was a definite tease and Drone rubbed his hands with preheated massage oil and pressed them gently onto her naked skin. His hands followed the contour of her heavenly curves and his breathing began to deepen. Watchful he would move around her erroneous zones, because it was not his intent to violate the little trust she had left in humanity. Layla's wounded self-needed a safe container within which she was able to receive and allow her healing to take place. Her inner being responded well to the feeling of safety flowing through the hands impressed upon her skin.

Layla: "You know Drone, when a man touches a woman with tender loving care, it makes her bodily juices flow!"

Drone: "Is that a fact"?"

Layla: "Most definitely! When a woman feels safe she becomes able to relax her body and flow her juices!"

Drone: "Are you saying that the basic unfulfilled need of every woman is to give up her finest female energies to her lover, to express her intrinsic female beauty, her divine fragrance?"

Layla: "Yep, make love with your hands and go on and on, and your woman will be available all the time and at any time."

Drone completed his massage and Layla felt great! They both seemed to enjoy each other's company, but after a three-day seclusion from the outside world, Layla felt a need to get some fresh air. They took the Metro to the Vondel park and it was here, when Layla bluntly asked Drone:

Layla: "What do you want from me Drone?"

Drone: "To be honest with you Layla, I hate junkies and everything that they represent! But when I looked into your eyes, I saw these scintillating sparkles of light, which called on me to take a chance with you! Give me your heart, make it real or else forget about it!"

Layla: "Do you resent that part within yourself, which you have been neglecting?"

Drone: "Don't get smart with me now, will you Layla!" He paused and continued: "But to answer your question, I don't know if I hate myself, why?"

Layla: "Because I just may be the reflection of that other part within yourself, which you are rejecting or which you are seeking!"

Drone: "Does this have anything to do with past lives and karma?"

Layla: "In a way it does!"

Drone: "In what way?"

Layla: "Through the exploration of each other we may just be able to find our beloved!"

Drone: "This Heroin stuff must have done a good job on your brain!"

They both paused and for a moment, there was this gap of silence! The rhythm of their breathing became synchronized and they drifted away in the Dreamtime. Layla was the first to break their magic spell and she said:

Layla: "Whether you like it or not, we were meant to be with each other, because we have issues to clear!"

Drone: "What are you talking about?"

Layla: "At this time the specifics have not yet been revealed to me, but I trust that the details will soon become unfolded!"

Layla's beauty had the spell of infatuation on Drone and he became captured and intrigued by the meaning of her words. Her body responded well to his nurturing care and it almost seemed as if she became more radiant and alive. The hidden beauty within her facial complexion started to protrude more outwardly, as if yearning to explore the world with a more playful curiosity.

Layla: "What's your plan for us Drone?"

The word: 'Us' sounded like music to his ears.

Drone: "Well, first we will have to kick your drug habit and strengthen your mind and body, then we will have to work on your self-esteem and self-love!"

Layla: "Where do we start?"

Drone: "Let's have a medical checkup before we do anything else!"

Drone made an appointment with a local Doctor and a week later Layla received the lab results from her blood work, and it read as follows:

"No VD, C4 cell count within normal limits, AIDS negative, toxic liver with high levels of opiates, recommended 10 intra venous Ozone treatments, detox liver & connective tissue with Homeopathy and boost up stamina."

During Layla's first intra-venous Ozone treatment, the Doctor mentioned a technique, which had effectively been used in Thailand as a way to detox drug addicts. This caught Drone's attention and he asked the Doctor:

Drone: "Explain this procedure to us, will you Doc?"

Doctor D. Hardaway: "The detox procedure is called the 'Salt water meditation', and the recipient has to drink a bucket of sea water daily, for eleven days straight in a row!"

Drone: "That is so bizarre that just thinking about it makes me want to throw up!"

Layla: "I will do whatever it takes to kick my drug habit!"

Drone: "Are you sure?"

Layla: "Yep I am!"

They committed themselves to a mutual goal, right then and there in the Doctor's office. Layla felt delighted and thrilled about her new adventure. The next morning at five o'clock Layla woke up Drone and ushered him to the backyard. There were two buckets of water awaiting them to be gulped down.

Drone: "Man what a wakeup call!" He thought to himself.

It was Layla, who took her first sip of salt water and the intense expression of disgust was written all over her face.

Layla: "How can anybody with a sane mind do this? I won't do it!" Moreover, she threw the bucket down.

Drone: "What does it taste like?"

Layla: "Like a bucket of pussy oysters!"

Drone: "Do you want me to go first?"

Layla: "Be my guest!"

Drone lifted up the bucket and gulped the water down without trying to taste it first. His belly blew up like a balloon and shortly thereafter it felt as if the ocean was trying to give birth throughout the cavity of his mouth. Drone screamed from the top of his lungs:

Drone: "Tsunami, Drone are you there?" and he answered: "Yes, I am here! Drone is here!" Witnessing his strength gave Layla the courage to follow through with her procedure and she drank again from the bucket. She too then gave birth to a 'Tsunami' and barfed her guts out.

Layla: "Layla are you there? Yes, I am here! Layla is here!"

After their oceanic session they hugged, showered and sat down to write up a daily detox schedule, which read as follows:

5.00 - a.m. Saltwater meditation.

6.00 - a.m. Sauna.

7.00 - a.m. Protein shake.

8.00 - a.m. Yoga stretch.

10.00 - a.m. Acupressure.

12.00 - p.m. Lunch.

13.00 - p.m. Salsa dance.

15.00 - p.m. Thai body massage.

17.30 - p.m. Aikido.

19.00 - p.m. Dinner.

After dinner they went for a stroll alongside the city canals and Layla talked about sweet little nothings. It so happened that they passed by Zorba the Buddha, which was closed during the week, but since Drone had the key, it gave them free access to the dance floor. Layla knows how to dance and she takes it all the way, whenever she has the dance floor to herself.

Layla: "Drone play me a song and I'll dance for you!"

Drone always wanted to be a D.J.Nirbeeja "No-Mind" and he mixed the music in a way, which gave her the sensation of a sensual climatic rise. His opening theme was: "My Wild Love." followed by 'Nataraj by Osho', My wild love is crazy

She screams like a bird

She moans like a cat

When she wants to be heard

My wild love went ridin'

She rode for an hour

She rode and she rested

And then she rode on

Ride, c'mon

My Wild Love: Doors

Drone: "Dance sister dance and let it all out!"

Layla swayed to the music and slowly began to open herself up in sweet surrender to the gentle hypnotic beat. The more she danced the more she was able to express her inner self. A moment came in which she totally felt free and uplifted. Layla undressed herself and took full possession of the dance floor, and she danced her divine femininity "womb awakening" away to the stars. This was a time for Layla's healing and they both had agreed upon the therapeutic rule of: "You can't touch this until I feel safe!" Drone longed for a moment of intimacy with Layla, but it was important for her healing process that she would feel safe within the parameters of his touch. Layla and Drone had committed themselves to complete her healing process within an eleven-day time frame. Eleven days had gone by and Layla felt able to embrace life again. In the mean time it was Drone's uncle Danny Steel shoe, who had been covering his bouncer shifts at Zorba and Drone felt that it was his time to go back to work at Zorba. The matter needed to be discussed with Layla.

Drone: "I don't know how to say this Layla, but it's time for me to go back to work!"

Layla: "Can I be with you while you work?"

Drone: "Sure, but remember not to get in my way when the going gets rough!"

Layla: "Meaning what?"

Drone: "Just don't be in the way when I have to kick ass!"

Layla: "Can I be your cheerleader?"

Drone: "Just promise me that you will keep a safe distance!"

Layla: "I promise!"

Drone: "There is something else you need to know!"

Layla: "I am listening?"

Drone: "Ehh...Ughh...Ehh...!"

Layla: "Come on, say it!"

Drone: "Well there are these seven prostitutes working for me as a favor to the drug Lords!"

Layla: "Did you sleep with them?"

Drone: "I had to check out my merchandise Layla!"

Layla: "What else is new Drone?"

Drone: "Well each week I hand deliver my girls flowers and chocolate as a token of appreciation for their services rendered."

Layla: "And....?"

Drone: "And I was wondering if you would mind to come along for an introduction?"

Layla: "You are stretching my level of tolerance, but I'm curious why you want to get me involved?"

Drone: "My girls are like real people, who became my friends!"

Layla: "Yeah right, that is the most ridiculous thing I've ever heard off and you really want me to believe that?"

Drone: "Please take this serious!" Moreover, he gave her the puppy eye look.

Layla: "Okay, I'll do it for now, but I still think it is a poor excuse!"

Together they bought bouquets of flowers and boxes of chocolate. Hand in hand, they then strolled along the windows of his working girls and Drone introduced Layla to each and every one of them.

The Girls: "Is she a new girl on the block?"

Drone: "No, she is your new boss!"

The ice was broken and it was soon thereafter that the girls established a solid friendship with Layla. "That wasn't too bad!" said Layla and they strolled back in the direction of Zorba. Back at Zorba Layla kept herself close to Drone, but from time to time, she would separate herself and mingle with the crowd. In the back of his head, Drone was afraid that somebody might offer Layla some dope and that she would not have the strength to resist the temptation. Layla must have read his mind, because she walked up to him and said:

Layla: "Drone, my body is aching and I need a fix badly!"

Drone hugged her and said: "Take some pot to soothe your pain, but stay away from the hard stuff!"

Inside himself, Drone prayed the following words:

Drone: "Dear Lord, please fill the abyss of Layla's yearning body with the stillness of your light!"

The groupie girls at Zorba had realized by Layla's presence that Drone had chosen a steady girlfriend to hang out with and they kept their distance. Layla in return began to show Drone more of her affection, which soon developed into a mutual romance. From time to time, she would playfully grab his hand, hug and kiss him on the cheek. And at times, she would look deeply into Drone's eyes and sigh. The sound of her sigh and the triggered release of her pheromones would then cause his libido to rise. Not knowing what to do with these feelings, Drone would bang his head hard against the wall as a means to distract himself. Together they danced this push pull thing all night long until his shift was over. Hand in hand, they then walked home like two little lovebirds. At the apartment, it was Layla who always seemed to be the first to crawl into the bed. Seductively she then called Drone by singing:

Layla: "I'm in the bed, I'm in the bed, I'm in the bed!"

Drone translated her cat-tease as: "I feel so cozy, please come cuddle with me!"

So, cuddling they did, but no kissing and nothing sexual! The taboo was still on and all he could do was to nurture and attend to her needs. From within his being Drone knew that 'trust' would soon find a way to her heart and settle down! The heart eventually has to melt down its walls of resistance, because passion can burn like a California bush fire! Layla needed more time to prepare her inner self for the flow of sexual joy and in that sense; he compared her to a crock-pot or ceramic tajine that needed a slow simmering heat to prepare for a delicacy. Every vagina, until loved rightly, is an emotional vagina. The vagina freed of emotion becomes yielding, soft, giving, simple, easy, undemanding and still; then the lovemaking is sweeter and more fulfilling. It is effortless, natural and beautiful. Drone and Layla had issues to clear! On the weekend, they slept until noon, jumped out of bed, dressed themselves and strolled to a coffee shop down the street. The caffeine invigorated their Minds, which then cleared the vision of the looking glass, which framed the windows of their souls. With a smile on their faces, they then welcomed the bright daylight. In the afternoon, it was time for a lovers stroll alongside the canals of the red-light district, where they could not resist the playful urge to window shop for some explicit sexual materials. Layla was feeling better and she used her surplus of energy to joke around with all the sexual toys she saw in the window displays. From time to time, she would then teasingly pull Drone inside one of the many sex shops and show him in a comical way how to use the toys and create sexual pleasure. The truth is that every man dreams of a mature sexual woman with heart. One wonders why there are so many professional women 'prostitutes' with bags of sexual tricks. Is it because 'men' cannot handle a real woman at home with her womb awakening? Or is it that 'men' get bored with women who do not wish to explore their sexual fantasy. The basic unfulfilled need of every woman is to give up her finest female energies to her lover, but men must make love without excitement, expectation or imagination. Simply learning to love for the beauty of loving a woman. The ultimate thrill of any search is to find God, and he can only be found within the ultimate abyss of the heart. Only then, when there is no more search for thrills, will 'He' the Lord dawn in the chambers of your heart. Layla pulled Drone out of his reflective state of being and she asked him:

Layla: "Let's buy a couple of skin flicks Drone, because I enjoy watching other people making out and doing the wild thing!"

Playfully he then responded with: "Layla, you're getting me all excited and I want to kiss you in places you feel very insecure about!" She then replied with: "Ditto Drone, but my kitty is not ready yet to play with your puppy!"

Her push-pull game was then abruptly interrupted by a forceful pull of her arms into the dark corners of the store, where she playfully pushed Drone into one of those private peep-show booths. With one hand she would cover his eyes and say:

Layla: "Pretend you can't see, just feel!"

With her other hand she rubbed over his hardened protruding erotic zone and said: "Can you feel the force?"

Drone pulled Layla close against his chest, but she abruptly distanced herself with a push and said: "Just feel it and enjoy!"

Drone: "But I want to possess your love!"

Layla: "I need more time to heal my inner self and I am asking you to have patience with me!"

Drone: "I will go for a jog around the park and when I return I'll take a cold shower to cool off my passion!"

Layla: "And then we'll talk again, okay?"

Drone: "All right!"

When Drone returned from the park he asked Layla: "What do you want to do tonight?"

Layla: "Do you feel like watching a skin flick together?"

Drone: "I feel like taking a cold shower right now!"

Layla: "This time I'm not teasing!"

Drone: "Now you are singing my whale song and it's surfacing for a breather!"

Layla observed him from head to toe with her oceanic deep blue eyes and changed her mood as swiftly as a strike of lightning. She said: "Let's go dancing and cool off our sex chakras!"

Drone: "What's a sex chakra?"

Layla: "It's your personal procreative energy vortex!"

Drone: "Oh, I get it. You mean my penis!"

Layla: "Yes, Moby Dick!"

Drone: "Your sexual tease makes my head spin like a Roller Coaster ride!"

Layla: "Trust me Drone, you will learn how to love your pain and drop your shame!"

Drone: "What do you mean Layla?"

Layla: "Together we will encounter many painful layers of emotional rejections before we are able to bathe and merge into the eternal bliss of ecstasy!"

Drone: "I don't understand?"

Layla: "It's not meant to be understood! The depth of its meaning lies within the feeling of it! One becomes it by feeling it and once surrendered, one disappears into it!"

Drone: "Your mystical sensuality confuses me!"

Layla: "Don't worry my love! Everything is in Divine Order!"

They changed their clothes, called an Uber cab, which took them down town to Drone's favorite Brazilian Trance dance club: 'Bahia Mia!'

Drone: "This is the place, where it all happens!" He spoke.

The D.J. Misha routinely opened his 'Gig' with a Capoeira dance demonstration, which is a Martial art form that originated from the African tribal dances. Since the colonial days, it has been integrated into being an essential part of the Brazilian culture. Anyone who likes to dance will be attracted to this type of performance, because it shows an energetic flow of dynamic body movements. After the Capoeira demonstration, D.J. Misha would then put on his headphones and work the crowd with his voice operated digitized computers. His music is not from this world, but instead it originates from a homestead, where elevated primal feelings are allowed among the enlightened commoners. It is a hypnotic trance, which will lead you on to a place within yourself, where one can only find a place called Heaven! God's domain is embedded within the musical rhythm matrix of: 'Salsa, Lambada and Kizomba!' Misha's Gig would start with a slow & easy gentle rhythm. The lyrics that followed would soon lead his tribe to unbelievable heights of excitement; and Cazimi climax portals were opening up.

D.J. Misha: "A man should honor a woman, awaken her juices, because her peach is as sweet as Heaven. Rock her spot and make her feel stronger! Come on baby, rock your spot, purse your lips down under, squeeze your juice and let it drip, drip, drip! Open your musky glands, scent your pheromones, feel your endorphins drip, drip, drip! I will suck it for you, squirt, squirt, squirt your little wild thing! Men you better get down on your knees and kiss your woman on her succulent lips. French; and down under, kiss your woman's peach and give her the treat of wild oats and grits. Women you better hold on to your men, because your men want to be uptight, out of sight and in the groove baby. Let it slip and slide until you get dizzy in the knees. Buckle, buckle, buckle up and bob your head. Make her feel alive or you're dead!"

The crowd was getting ecstatic and Drone looked over to Layla, who smiled and said:

Layla: "Taste me Drone, drink me, make me squirt!"

Layla grabbed his arm and directed his hand under her mini skirt, where his fingers slid into her lubricated vortex. The lips of her vortex down under were swollen with excitement and he finger diddled her moist private insides until she began to moan and groan. She then closed her eyes and was fully enjoying her joy ride. From time-to-time Drone would pull Layla gently forwards with a two-finger press on her pleasure zone. Shame kicked in and Drone's hand was pushed away abruptly. Layla giggled and looked around to see if anybody was watching. His hand was now being guided to her mouth and she sucked on his fingers as if wanting to taste her very own juicylicious.

Layla: "I taste sweet!" Aroused and excited by her demonstration Drone replied:

Drone: "Yeah, that's right baby! God wants us to love ourselves first!"

Their bodies began to sway to the rhythm of the Lambada music and they danced into a dark corner, where Layla then repeated her intimate approach. She took his hand, guided him under her skirt into her juicy vortex, and begged him to do her again. The rhythmic movements of his fingers made her breathe deeper until she began to moan again. She begged him for a breather and removed his hand. This time she directed his fingers into his mouth. Drone tasted her love juice and said:

Drone: "Yes baby, your taste is sweet!"

It was an act of trust for Layla, to allow him to explore her most intimate body parts.

Layla: "I want to hear you say it again!"

Drone: "Say what again?"

Layla: "Yes baby, your taste is sweet!"

Drone: "Yes baby, your taste is sweet!"

They both exhaled for a breather. Her sweet musky pheromone flavor triggered an endorphin rush into the nerve endings of his brain cells and for a moment, Drone felt dizzy. His heart was pounding deep within his inner ear and he was imagining her lingerie marinated with her pheromones. From that moment on Drone became drunk with the Divine feminine womb awakening! His taste buds were hooked on Layla's sweet musky flavor like a Buck in the rut of mating season. The Lambada dance brought them back to rhythm of their senses and they began to sway their bodies to the ever-increasing beat. Society has labeled this dance 'the forbidden dance', because of the sensual pelvic tilts that fishtail their way on up towards the forbidden fruit of passion. Energy is like a flow of eternal will power! Eventually it will present itself right back in your face, until one becomes willing to feel and accept the lesson being taught. The technique of the Lambada consists of fishtailing your hips, twice to the left and twice to the right. Yet, at the same time one is to maintain a close centerline rub with the opposite sexual vortex. The juice of the dance flows with the activation of your sexual energy, which then will continue its orbit through the spinal column into the brain. The rising of sexual energy or Kundalini always results into a blissful orbital experience in the outer limits of the brain cortex.

Drone: "How do you feel?"

Layla: "Like Tingle bells all over!"

Layla: "Has your Kundalini risen yet?"

Drone: "My what?"

Layla: "Kundalini is a form of liquid light that rises in the spine as a response to sexual pleasure. Sort of like a barometer responds to the weather!"

Drone: "What do I do with it?"

Layla: "I learned to master the art of recycling my sexual energies and orgasms!"

Drone: "What does it feel like?"

Layla: "It feels like an implosion within a bubble of virgin white light drifting on the matrix of a silken God!"

Drone: "Is that why you call it liquid light?"

Layla: "Yes! All one has to do is to stay in the flow!"

Then they closed their eyes and allowed the rhythm of the Lambada take them all through the night until the break of dawn. At closing time they befriended some Brazilians, who invited them over to their Santo Daime church that following Wednesday. Drone told them that he would keep it in mind, but at this time, he was not sure if he would be able to make it.

A taxi drove them home and Drone felt content about the fact that Layla was showing her affection to him. At home, they took a shower and cuddled with each other until they fell asleep. The next morning, they took a sauna and Layla sat across from him naked! Pearls of perspiration were rolling over her delicate skin. Layla was sitting spread Eagle and Drone watched the pearls of perspiration drip from her exposed vortex. Man, that turned him on in a heartbeat! Drone looked into her eyes for a sign of approval to approach! She blinked and Drone landed his lips on her legs. He followed the trail of pearls until he found her oyster. Layla trembled and shivered! "No tongue, only soft kisses Drone!"

They did not proceed with intercourse, but their lips had a language of their own. Layla engaged with a hellacious lip-lock on his erected vortex and she began to milk him with a gentle sucking traction. From time to time, she would slap his erected shaft against her tongue, which he perceived as a shear punishment of pleasure. Layla then created a surplus of saliva and spit straight on his bobbing head, which then had the invigorating effect of an endorphin rush inside his brain! As soon as Layla felt the pulsing throb in his vortex signaling her that he was about to blow his whistle, she then pushed onto his prostate gland and eliminated his upcoming bubble of sheer joy. With his hands, Drone directed Layla's body posture to stand up and face the wall. She then spread her legs at will and protruded her buns of steel into the direction of his face. Her sweet musky scent drew him right into her hot spot and he sank his tongue deeper in between her legs. With his tongue extended, he opened up her lips and submitted her lips to a cunnilingus treat. Layla began to moan and gasped for air. She begged him for a breather! His tongue stopped for one second, which allowed her to soften up and relax into the sensations rushing through her body. Drone's tongue was driven to touch her again and he slid it right back where it felt most needed. By this time, her bodily juices were really flowing and her rose bud squeaked as he slid his tongue back and forth through her vortex. Layla erupted with the most sensational squirting orgasm right on his chest and she simultaneously released a primal scream, which shivered him to the bone. They glanced into each other's orgasmic bedroom eyes and it felt like they were floating in a pond of blissful silence. Layla was the first to break their pregnant spell of silence and she said:

Layla: "This is the most sensational thrill of personal freedom and only this feeling makes every other feeling bearable, thank you Lord Jesus!"

Layla began to cry and her body trembled as she began to release primal feelings of pains and fears which had been captivated within her inner self, for God knows how long. Drone could feel her pain, but he could not take it away. This time he had to feel everything that she triggered inside his inner self and there was no way out! How good it is too deeply feel one another. Her emotional expressions intensified and her body slid into an uncontrollable state of catharsis. Trembling, muscle spasms, shocks, jerks, quivers, they were all there and Drone was feeling his pain! He felt lost and drifted away into the Dreamtime. It was Layla's voice, which woke him up the next morning.

Layla: "Thank you for being here Drone!"

Drone: "How do you feel?"

Layla: "My female cycle has started!"

Drone: "Then allow me to nurture you for the next seven days!"

Layla: "Are you referring to flowers, chocolate and movies?"

Drone: "Why not, let's hang low and be mellow!"

The next seven days it was a time of low intensity and high quality. Amsterdam is the city for Art, Theater, Museum's, Opera's, Hemp-Coffee shops and Thai massage parlors. It was Layla's wish to experience a Thai massage. Inside the massage parlor, Layla and Drone were positioned next to each other and they waited patiently for the arrival of their massage therapists. Two young Thai females walked in fully dressed in their native sarongs and positioned their bare feet on top of their backs. With their child like little feet, they began to walk over their backs like two featherweights. They knew intuitively where to place their feet and

Layla and Drone were enjoying the gentle intrusive pain. The pleasurable torture lasted for an hour or so and they both relaxed. After their break the girls returned fully disrobed and began to massage them with their heavenly lubricated bodies. This was a massage send from heaven and naturally Drone would have preferred for Layla to do him the honors, but it was her choice to have it done this way. After their massage, they were guided to a sauna, where the instruction was to endure at least four rounds of sweat & heat. Exhausted, but content they completed their rounds and headed on home. On their way home Drone suggested to visit Hemp boy's coffee shop and see how he was doing. Layla's eyes blinked up with a smile, because this little pit stop would give her a chance to smoke pot and readjust her yearning body to a heavenly fix! Hemp boy always talked to his customers in a very angelic way as if he was trying to convey a message straight from God. He hugged them and said:

Hemp boy: "God is light and his light will set you free!"

Layla: "Oh hush preacher boy, just hand me the holy Sacrament and light me up!"

Hemp boy rolled her a joint, prayed over it, lit it up and passed it around. After a couple of hits, they exhaled presidentially and were able to relieve some of their internal stress. Now they became able to digest Hemp boys' words at a more reflective level!

Drone: "You're so cool broh!"

Hemp boy: "God is like the sun it shines for everybody!"

Drone: "I can dig that!"

Hemp boy: "If you only could see through my eyes at this moment, you would be able to know the bliss that I am experiencing!"

Layla: "Life sucks!"

Hemp boy: "Wake up you sleepers! You must make the necessary effort to arouse yourself from your lethargy and look upon each moment as a revelation of perpetual unfolding of magical awe!"

Drone felt as if he was but beginning to realize the deep meaning of the things, he was experiencing.

Hemp boy: "Christ brought forth perfection from within himself. You, of yourself are always Christ, and every child has a right to claim this Sonship, this Divinity. Claim your birthright as the child of the living God!"

Drone: "Yeah right, Drone the Son of God!"

Layla: "Christians will always stigmatize those who claim their 'Christhood' as being an Anti-Christ!"

Hemp boy: "Yeah, but they are incorrect, because the act of expressing is an abundance of reverence for the living God in each and every one of us!"

Layla: *"Jesus never allowed himself to dwell in the external after his illumination. He always kept his thoughts at the central part of his being, where he held himself in conscious communion with God himself!"*

Hemp boy: "Raise your consciousness to His consciousness and behold, you will stand free, above all mortal limitations, abundantly free!"

Drone: "We are but simple commoners!"

Hemp boy: "Don't focus on the Dark Side of the fallible man, but instead always keep your eyes steadfast on the Everlasting living light of the living God!"

Layla: "Let me get this straight, deep inside myself I am an infallible virgin?"

Hemp boy: "If you are satisfied with your present limitations, then remain lethargic, but if you want to engage life fully, you must seek each moment to express life fully. Find your echo, life just wants to celebrate your echo with eternity. Love can be expressed only, when it flows through the one expressing life."

Drone: "Man yearns to fly, and this longing invites him to seek the miraculous that will enable him to rise above the limitation of his senses!"

Layla: "Why walk when you can fly? The thrill of sex ought to be transcended into the benediction of love, but the beginning of love starts with the expression of God from within!"

Hemp boy: "Jesus realized that that for which he was seeking was right within himself. When you behold God and nothing else but God, and know that His Holy Temple is your pure exalted body, a whole and all – including an outpouring vessel for His Eternal living light to flow through!"

Drone: "Thanks broh!"

The three of them hugged and Drone and Layla headed out the door. They tucked in early that evening and experienced a very deep healing sleep. The following morning Layla introduced Drone to her special love potion mixture and he asked her what the ingredients were.

Layla: "You will know it, when you feel it!"

It was very potent stuff and Drone felt an irresistible urge from within to kiss her all over her body.

Drone: "Did you put a spell on me or something?"

Layla smiled and welcomed his affectionate behavior in a playful evasive manner.

Drone: "You behave like the French do when they are courting! First the girl seduces and attracts the male, then she pretends to be indifferent, distracted and finally she distances herself!"

Layla: "Je t'aime Cheri!"

Drone: "Tell me what the secret of your potion is!"

Layla did not give in to his pleadings and she refused to give away her secret recipe.

Finally, on the last day of her menstrual cycle she decided to give in to Drone's pleadings. With an innocent, but sensual tone of voice she said:

Layla: "The secret is that you have been drinking a homeopathic form: 'One drop per 100-CC of Vodka' of my menstrual blood!"

Drone's logical mind was stunned and he began to juggle her words with disgust:

Drone: "Menstrual blood! Are you a witch?"

Layla: "Hey it works and if you could only see the expression on your face!"

Drone: "I feel grossed out!"

Layla: "Most humans eat animal blood 'steak' every day! Don't they?"

Drone: "Yeah, but that doesn't make them long for a quicky with a cow!"

Layla: "To me it feels like I have come to accept you at a deeper level within myself!"

Drone: "I think I need some readjusting and fine tuning to that level of understanding!"

Layla: "Don't you want to surrender your heart and receive all of my loving?"

Drone: "Yes I do, but love needs the innocence of honesty and you took away my right to choose!"

Layla: "That can be painful! Have you accepted all of your past trauma's yet?"

Drone: "When I feel love I tremble, I fear, I feel fragile and everything else becomes so worthless, so transient. Nothing else matters anymore and I can't function!"

Layla: "Love is exciting, but it is also dangerous! One never knows, when it appears or disappears. Love can be ferocious, but in the end it is all about the art of knowing oneself through the intimate experience with another yourself!"

Drone: "Do you feel like I am another part of you?"

Layla: "That I am! Enjoy life with your beloved, whom you love, all the days of this meaningless life that God has given you under the sun!"

Drone: "Let's go out and do something fun!"

Layla: "Why don't we contact those Brazilians, who invited us to their church?"

Drone: "It's hard to believe that you actually want to go to church!"

Layla did not answer, but instead she picked up the phone and called the Brazilian friend 'Gaia' for directions to his church! The fellowship of the church was to start at seven o'clock and neither of them knew what to expect. At the church, there were about 40 people present and Drone and Layla were introduced to every one of them. It was 'Gaia', who explained the Daime ceremony to them as follows:

Gaia: "First we chant songs to mother Mary and her son Jesus Christ, then we consume the holy sacrament 'Daime' and we continue to praise our Lord God with Portuguese hymns until the break of dawn!"

Drone: "What is this sacrament made from?"

Gaia: "It is a bitter form of tea that originates from the Amazon jungle. The tea is brewed from a male vine and a female leaf of the following plants: 'Male is the vine of the soul or Banisteriopsis caapi and it's female counter part is the Chacruna or Psychotria viridis!"

Drone: "What is the effect?"

Gaia: "When consumed it feels like your body is pulsing liquid light and it feels as if God is waking up the innate light potential of your being. It is a great experience for meditation and prayer!"

Layla: "Is it addictive?"

Gaia: "It brings you closer to God and God is contagious!"

Layla: "Is it addictive?"

Her voice was raised and more sternly! Gaia still did not respond!

Layla: "Is it God d…. addictive?"

This time Layla was screaming from the top of her lungs but Gaia remained calm. The church minister walked over to Layla and handed her a joint as a token of mediation. Layla received it in silence and without hesitation.

Gaia: When you ask for God: 'Daime=give me', then God will be in you!

Church minister: "To master an addiction one has to love God, because He is the only Master!"

Layla took a hit and relaxed. The people around her now began to line up towards the altar. The men were dressed in dark blue pants with a white shirt on top and the women were dressed in a dark blue long skirt with a white-green shirt on top. All of the Santo Daime initiates were pinned with a metal Star of David across their hearts, which symbolized their spiritual commitment to God. With his inner eye, Drone scanned Layla's energies to check if she would be up to this challenge. She felt the piercing force of his eyes scanning and said:

Layla: "Let's do this Drone, but be there for me if I fall back into my old habits!"

She grabbed his hand and together they lined up with the rest of the dancers to receive the holy Sacrament. They drank the Daime and it tasted bitter!

Layla: "This tastes worse than the salt water meditation!"

Within no time, there were people around them barfing and this triggered them to do the same.

Drone: "Are you okay?"

Layla: "Stay with yourself!"

Drone: "Let me hold you!"

Layla: "Don't touch me! This one is between me and my God!"

Drone left her be and trusted God to look after her. The Daime's light pulsations by now began to have an effect on Drone and there were these sparkly lights dancing all around him. It felt as if the emptiness inside of him became pregnant with the presence of a million stars. The minister opened the ceremony with a prayer and the band began to jam their nostalgic Portuguese cura hymns. Every body knew the lyrics; **Vossas**

maos curadoras; Mae Natureza; Com Deus. (Reinado do Sol), Drone, and Layla just sang along with it. The Daime juice was enriching him with the experience of feeling liquid light flowing through the silken matrix of his body vehicle. During the dance it was hard for him to be separated from Layla, because his heart longed for her to stay connected while they danced. Layla appeared to be all right because she kept her distance and made the impression as if she was totally submerged within her own reality. At first Drone was watchful, but then he relaxed because deep inside of his being he somehow knew that everything was going to be alright. It was this sense of inner knowing, which soon made him forget his separation anxiety. Every two hours or so the dancers would take a little break and yet again, took another sip of Daime. It was during these little intermezzos that Drone would touch the hands of his beloved Layla. She looked back at him in a very loving way and Drone began to have visions of an Amazon Indian, who kept repeating his name:

Drone: "Isua-Dow, Isua-Dow, Isua-Dow!"

His face was painted with an emerald green-blue paint and he said:

Indian: "I am he who they call: 'Isua-Dow!' I am the shaman of the Hummingbird people. I invite you to enter the Amazone Dreamtime. Spirit animals need to be painted on your skin, which then will guide you back to me! When you find me you will dance the Dreamtime Sundance."

The vision was so real to him that Drone now began to communicate with Isua-Dow.

Drone: "What do you want from me?"

Isua-Dow: "Hello Snow leopard king, your woman who you have come to know as 'Layla' will be divided into the light and it's cast away shadow side. She will then return as a female twin, who will face the challenge to merge as one. As one they shall then be prepared to meet their creator God."

Drone: "Will she die?"

Isua-Dow: "God's light will romance her shadow side to become the light again that she was from the beginning of time!"

Isua-Dow faded out and Drone felt lost! He needed a downer, but the Daime was pushing him further into his cosmic experience. His body kept dancing until the break of dawn. Exhausted he sat down and he felt his body vibrating like a humming bird. Together they hugged everybody goodbye not realizing they were as high as a kite can get! They did not speak a word to each other and it took them about a week to process and integrate their spiritual experience. Inside his heart Drone felt a growing concern for Layla's wellbeing. Layla noticed the concerned expression in his eyes and she said:

Layla: "I am fine for as long as I am able to stay connected to my inner emotions!"

Drone: "What about some nooky?"

Layla: "When a man has sex on his Mind it will disrupt his hormonal pheromone balance. A woman lives her sexuality by being sensual!"

Drone: "I am driven by sex!"

Layla: "Learn how to leave yourself behind and not allow it to enter and spoil our lovemaking. I want a higher form of sex! Sex is the continuous expression of playful intimacy: 'Into-me-See!' I want to be in the perpetual mobile of the great cosmic orgasm!"

Drone: "Now you're talking?"

Layla: "Sex is fun, but there is something amiss! I feel that we are both holding back our true essence behind the walls of our defended selves!"

Drone: "Let's tear down that wall and get straight to it!"

Layla: "It is a more delicate process than the destruction of a wall. Everything is to be done together and discussed and observed together!"

Drone: "Can I share my Daime vision quest?"

Layla: "Sure babe, I'm listening!"

Drone: "During the Santo Daime ceremony, this shaman who called himself Isua-Dow, gave me the name the Snow leopard king and this gave me a vision of spirit animals to be painted on my skin. These animals would then become my spirit guides, which would lead me to his sanctuary in the Amazon jungle!"

Layla: "Did he say anything else?"

Drone: "He gave me a vision that you would be divided into the Light and its cast away Shadow side. Your 'being' would be transformed by Death and return as a twin sister, who in their turn will have to face the challenge of becoming One with their creator God!"

Layla: "Mmm... That sounds interesting! Maybe you should get yourself one of those Tattoos and see what it does for you!"

Drone: "I know of this Tattoo shop on the Oude-zijdse voorburgwal next to that Harley Davidson shop!"

Layla: "Let's go check it out!"

It was a sunny day in the red-light district and they decided to walk their way over to the Tattoo shop. Layla wore her flower-patterned mini skirt with a T-shirt on top, which read: 'God is my Vortex!' As they strolled alongside the canals, they ran into a guy with two vicious looking Pitbulls. Layla felt unsafe and stepped aside. The stranger responded by saying:

Stranger: "They only bite, when I tell them too Missy!"

Layla: "I bet they do!"

Stranger: "You don't believe me?"

Layla: "I do, I do!"

The stranger was driven to give them a demonstration and he kicked against a tire of a car parked alongside the canal. Both Pitbulls reacted immediately and dug their teeth deep into the rubber flesh. The tires flattened instantly and the dogs shredded the rubber into little pieces. Drone looked at the stranger and noticed that his arms were covered with tattoos.

Drone: "Who is your artist?"

Stranger: "You like them?"

Drone: "It's quite impressive!"

Stranger: "Go to the shop next to the Harley Davidson store and ask for Molly!"

It took them about twenty minutes to get to the shop and as they walked in, Drone recognized the stranger from before.

Drone: "We are looking for Molly!"

Stranger: "You found him!"

Layla: "My, my, what a coincidence!"

Molly: "Just look around and see if you can find a picture you like!"

Molly showed us a picture album and it was Layla, who picked a Dolphin pod for Drone. He undressed his upper body and submitted his delicate skin to the spit firing torture of a paint ball needle, which left behind a trail of tears and running blood.

Molly: "If you have to pass out just put your head in between your legs! And uh, how many tattoos do you want buddy?"

Drone: "I want a dolphin, a buffalo, a butterfly, and lots of hummingbirds to symbolize a higher state of sex!"

Molly: "You better pass out buddy, because when I'm done with you, you'll be covered with blood from head to toe!"

The word 'blood' triggered his feeling of well-being and Drone passed out. In his inner ear, he heard a very gentle sound. Very near, yet very far. Very soft, yet very clear. And it sang:

There's blood in the streets it's up to my ankles
Blood in the streets it's up to my knees
Blood in the streets of the town of Chicago
Blood on the rise, it's following me
The Doors.

It was Layla's laughter, which brought him back to his senses. Molly was greasing Drone's bleeding dolphin pod with vaseline and he covered up his wound with a sterile gauze pad.

Molly: "Are you the bouncer at Zorba?"

Drone: "That I am!"

Molly: "Then the tattoos are on the house!"

Layla: "Why is that?"

Molly: "Here in the Red Lights we help each other!"

Drone: "Thanx Molly!"

Layla grabbed Drone's uninjured arm and hand in hand, they walked back home like two little lovebirds. At home, they took a bath and Layla gently washed off his skin from its sticky bloody crusts. Drone felt Layla's love flowing towards him and she welcomed him by opening her legs. She exposed her most intimate private self and invited Drone to French kiss her vortex down under with his lips and he began to tease her succulent lips. As his lips were caressing her electric spot, his vortex became as hard as a python. Her body began to signal to him the arrival of her upcoming squirting orgasm. Her breathing was deepening and the pleasurable tension of his slithering tongue became unbearable. She gasped for air, exhaled, and her vortex exploded into a fountain of pee pleasure. Layla ejaculated her love juices all over Drone's chest and it felt warm and soothing to him!

Layla: "Oh my God, oh my God, I just had a past life vision that we were two gay lovers on a Greek island and you were giving me head!"

Together they laughed so long and so hard that it became painful.

Layla: "That was deep!"

Drone: "All the way baby, all the way!"

Layla: "Let's take a vacation!"

Drone: "Where do you want to go?"

Layla: "Let's leave the country, let's go to Prague!"

Drone: "What's in Prague!"

Layla: "Spontaneity! I've heard that since the collapse of communism people are going through extreme times and changes of social tolerance!"

Drone: "What do you mean?"

Layla: "People are expressing their newly gained 'hardcore' freedom by publicly exposing themselves naked!"

Drone: "And you want to have a little taste of that freedom, Hugh!"

Layla: "Living in truth will set us free!"

In the spur of that moment, they packed their suitcases with prime necessities and Layla called the train station and booked them a trip to Prague! When she finally got off the phone, she said:

Layla: "You are going to love this! I booked us a nice private compartment all the way to Prague and I am looking forward to having great sensual kissing with you!"

Drone: "All the way?"

Layla: "All the way babe!"

Love her Madly: by the Doors

Don't you love her madly?
Don't you love her badly?
Don't you love her ways?
Tell me what you say
Don't you love her madly?
Want to be her daddy
Don't you love her face?
Don't you love her as she's walking out the door
Like she did one thousand times before
Don't you love her ways?
Tell me what you say
Don't you love her as she's walking out the door?

All your love, all your love
All your love, all your love
All your love is gone
So, sing a lonely song
Of a deep blue dream
Seven horses seem
To be on the mark

Yeah, don't you love her?
Don't you love her as she's walking out the door?

All your love, all your love
All your love, all your love
All your love is gone
So, sing a lonely song
Of a deep blue dream
Seven horses seem
To be on the mark

Don't you love her madly?
Don't you love her madly?
Don't you love her madly?

Chapter Three ~
Light my Fire

The man and his wife were naked, but they were not ashamed.

Genesis 2:25

I will show the nations your nakedness.

Nahum 3:5

They were all filled with the Holy Spirit, and they began to speak different languages.

The Holy Spirit was giving them the power to speak these languages.

Acts 2:4

The Spirit speaks to God with deep feelings that words cannot explain.

Romans 8:26

The train ride to Prague would last for two days, and Drone grasped every chance he could get to express his effectuation towards Layla. The mesmerizing effect of their surging pheromones pulled them irresistibly closer to one another. It felt as if they were like two dolphins doing the Lambada in an ocean of love. Pulling close to touch and feel, distancing to take a breather, and again closing in to exchange the heat of their passion. There is something to say about having intimacy in a moving vehicle! The rocking cadence of the train somehow prolonged the blissful experience of their sensual activities. Drone's favorite sexual position during that long and arduous train ride was the doggy mount. Layla was standing naked with her legs apart and her upper body was bent forwards onto the upper bunk bed. She wiggled her rose bud in his direction as to say: "Come on and get me if you can!"

A force greater than his will power to resist brought him down to his knees. Drone placed his hands on her buttocks and with his fingertips, he caressed the curves of her heavenly body downwards. He so dearly loved the curvature of her buttocks! His fingertips touched her inner thighs from behind and he gently separated her labia. Her vortex was now exposed and the pink color of her swollen lips made a vulnerable impression on his intrusive act of passion. Gently he leaned forwards and with his tongue, he slithered back and forth through the crevice of her swollen lips. Layla responded with a deep moan, which triggered Drone to increase the suctional force on her lips profusely. The flow of her sensual pheromonal nectar was really kicking in and it lubricated their passionate drive to get down and into each other. Her juice was flowing lavishly around the sensors of his tongue and he so loved this nectar of his goddess! Their passionate workout induced a strain on their bodies, and Layla's legs felt weakened by the driving force of Drone's sexual drift. The strength in her legs was beginning to give way to the downward pull of gravity and she lowered herself into a squatting position. Layla repositioned herself on her knees and leaned forwards with her upper torso now supported by the lower bunk bed. Drone's vortex by this time was standing hard and with full erected force. Gently he ushered his extended love tool forwards towards the crevice of her vortex. Layla sensing what he wanted now separated her lips with her two fingers and they made an initial contact.

Layla: "My pussy is sitting on your face and I am claiming my squatting rights."

Her vortex squeezed and relaxed, which enabled Drone to slide deeper towards the sensors of her G-spot. From excitement, Layla released a little scream and Drone knew he just hit the jackpot. She wiggled her rosebud a couple of times until they both were calibrated to her sensitive G-spot. They then adapted their position in such a way, that the mechanical cadence of the train would effortlessly rock and rub her G-spot against his extended vortex. Their electrical spots were locked and loaded with the ultimate sensation of pleasure. Their sexual organs were now running on automatic pilot and with his hands freed up Drone became able to caress her breasts. Sometimes he would lean on one arm and hold her head with the other hand, which enabled them to really French kiss each other. Layla's trust in herself and her partner grew slowly, but at a steadfast pace. Her inner self was opening up in sweet surrender like a Blue Lotus flower blossoming in bloom. As a former street prostitute, she had mastered all the tricks and traits of how to work a man's sexual pleasure. The difference with Drone was, that this time Layla allowed herself to feel fragile while her heart was taking baby steps to open up. Sensations do saturate when one gives in to the sensations of the insatiable pleasure zone and from time to time they would distance themselves and break away free from the burning desires of their loving bodies. The brain dopamine levels were running high, and Drone began to experience flashes of liquid light popping inside his head! The pistoning motion of his vortex was making a popping sound and the tickling heat from within his sexual organ became unbearable!

Layla was surging like a volcano and she erupted her nectars and screamed: "Oh my God, oh my God, I'm coming home!"

Her vortex was in a sensual pleasure land and Drone felt her hot lava juice flowing around the base of his shaft. His body kept pumping and his rock-hard shaft pistoned in and out of her warm vortex, until he was about ready to come home in pure bliss. Just before his upcoming orgasm, he quickly turned Layla over and pressed his chest against her voluptuous breasts. He entered her vortex again, but this time their hearts really surrendered, and Drone blasted a full load of Star seed potential into the opening of her womb awakening. They French kissed and down under; and Layla sucked on his tongue hard, as if wanting to pull him out of his body. It was a painful but pleasurable sensation, and as her orgasm subsided, so did her death grip on his tongue.

Drone: "That was sensational!"

Layla: "Do you want us to get dressed and now explore the train?"

Drone: "I'm all for it!"

They slipped naked into a pair of jeans and a T-shirt and as they headed towards the cafeteria, a female passenger accidentally ran into Drone. The lady was very direct and she commented: "You guys are doing it, aren't yah!"

Layla: "Excuse me!"

Passenger: "I can scent your pheromone love juice and I'm loving it!"

Drone: "Do you want me to bottle it up for you?"

Passenger: "For here or to go?"

Drone: "Did you know that sex became a private thing after Adam and Eve were expelled from paradise?"

Passenger: "What do you mean?"

Drone: "Well, look at the overpopulation, everybody is doing it, but nobody wants the other person to know that they're doing it!"

Layla: "Yes, and that makes God an intriguing stalker, because he is watching us doing it all the time!"

They said goodbye to the wild lady and continued their walk to the cafeteria, where they sat down for an hour or so. After their refreshments, they returned to their compartment for a continuance of their lovemaking. Layla was moving swift and Drone was teasingly trying to chase her.

Drone: "I can scent you!"

Layla laughingly responded: "Come on over here and get you some!"

The next morning at seven a.m. they arrived at the train station of Prague, where their Dutch money was exchanged for the local currency. They felt invigorated and their refreshed bodies radiated a love glow. Hand in hand, they searched for a taxi stand and they asked the chauffeur to take them to their designated hotel. The taxi driver was so infatuated with their fresh glow of love, that he only charged them half the price of his normal rate! Layla felt like God above had paved the way for a smooth transition to their destination. Drone's first impression of Prague was, that somebody had sucked the bone marrow out of the city. The buildings were gray, worn down, somber, cold and colorless! His second impression was that the people were very friendly and hospitable. Everybody made some type of connection with them and some individuals were able to express themselves in a broken form of English. Poverty had struck deep into this part of the world and many of the people whom they met, appeared to be homeless. Strangely enough, the poverty did not seem to bother the youth of Prague, because they made an appearance of being filled with a lust for life. Drone and Layla were soon to find out to what extremes they were enjoying with their newly gained freedom. People were dancing all over the place and Layla asked one of the youngsters:

Layla: "What are you celebrating?"

Youngster: "The breakdown of the German wall!"

When they finally arrived at the hotel Layla was all excited to go out and join the party, but Drone wanted to be settled first! The hotel room was a large but cozy place and to their surprise they discovered that the going rate for their royal suite was only ten dollars per night. It felt good to be able to enjoy the best of the best for an yet affordable price!

Layla: "Let us humble ourselves Drone! Let us honor everything that we are allowed to use or partake of in this moment!"

Drone: "For you I get down on my knees again and again Layla!"

Layla: "What I meant to say is; Let us keep a low financial profile, as to not stick a needle of greed into the eyes of those who have not!"

Drone: "Alright!"

Layla: "People are in need of a higher love, and greed will only close their hearts!"

Drone: "The love we feel for each other shall become a public commodity like sunshine does! Layla: "Remember that the sun shines for everybody!"

Drone walked over to their host 'Nagar' and asked him about the tourist attractions in and around the city of Prague. Nagar gave Drone a warm social welcome and spontaneously invited the two of them over to have dinner at his house. That evening Nagar's family welcomed Drone and Layla with unreasonable hospitality, which you can only find at a real family-based home. They intensely enjoyed the friendliness of Nagar's family, and they in return were uplifted by the fact that Layla and Drone were their inner circle guests! Nagar's family was pleasantly distracted from what otherwise was a daily routine of despair and boredom. It was as if they were sent to rekindle their spirits with a light that wants to live and illuminate all the dark corners of despair. After their dinner, they hugged goodbye, and back at the hotel, they decided to take a nightcap at the bar. They met a young Swedish couple: 'Borg and Ingrid' who invited them for a night out on the town.

Drone: "Do you guys know where the action is?"

Borg: "We'll be your guides!"

Drone looked over to Layla for a response and she said: "Why not!"

They swiftly changed their clothes at their hotel room and returned downstairs to meet up with Borg, who already had a cab waiting for them. The taxi took a detour all over town and finally dropped them off at a place called: 'the Catacombs'. The psychedelic sound waves, which originated from the Catacombs, surprised Drone like a Tsunami. Who would have ever thought to find progressive music in this part of the world? They merged with the crowd and became like the waves, which beach on the Anjuna shore of Goa, India! The eyes of these people were in a deep state of Trance as if they were soul searching themselves to find their creator. Some people looked like they were lost and others made the appearance as if they had found God in the bliss of their abyss. There were even couples dancing naked and Drone witnessed some of them having sex, right then and there, on the dance floor. Nobody seemed to pay any attention to the presence of nudity, because a Trance dance is between you and your creator. Only God is allowed to intervene with a payment of homage to his supreme being! Layla asked around what the indecent exposure was all about! She found some young people at the bar, who informed her that everybody was enjoying their newly gained individual expression of freedom! The country had endured a communistic suppression for more than a decade and all of the people's suffering and frustration was now set free. Anything suppressed is given the power to liberate itself! The youth was claiming back their right to live a life style, which before had been suffocated by the systematic indoctrination of communism. There was no money, and all that the young people had left was their self-expression in the form of creative sexuality. The people of

Tsechoslovakia had to accept this excessive naked behaviorism for what it represented: 'A celebration of liberty!' The youngsters informed us that their nakedness was not a preference, but more so a religious conviction!

Ingrid: "Borg and I have been doing it in the streets, and eh! You guys should have a little taste of this experience!"

Drone: "You're kidding me!"

Ingrid: "No serious, you'll see people doing it everywhere; they are doing it in the streets, the movie theaters, restaurants, banks, schools etc...."

Drone: "Doing it?"

Ingrid: "Yeah, you know; the wild thing!"

Drone: "I always thought that the Scandinavian countries were the most sexual liberated nations, as for instance compared to the back drafted U.S.A!"

Ingrid: "Yeah, you're right, America has a long way to go to heal itself from Biblical prudence."

Layla and Drone were enjoying this new expression of sexuality and they considered it as a sign for new beginnings. The hypnotizing beat of the Goa-Trance soon stirred up a spark of sensuality in between them.

Layla: "Drone do you want to go down on me!"

Passionately Layla then guided Drone into a dark corner, where she slowly liberated his droning vortex. She kissed the head of his extended self passionately, and her twirling tongue did not know how to stop. As soon as Layla noticed that Drone began to breathe deeper, she then reached out and tightened her hellacious lip lock around his throbbing vortex. Her saliva was running down and around the base of his shaft. A couple of times she even had the audacity to spit viciously on his erected vortex, and Drone took it like a man. Her hands were rotating and moving up and down, slipping and sliding, trying to get a grip on his lubricated shaft. Sometimes it felt as if an Anaconda was trying to squeeze the juice of life out of his extended self!

Drone: "Be gentle Layla, be gentle!"

Layla: "Like this?"

Drone: "Oeh yeah, do me like that!"

Layla: "Or do you like it like this?"

Drone: "Yes, I like it like that!"

Layla was now giving him a gentle sucking traction, which triggered an intense tickling sensation in his vortex area! Layla was sensing his upcoming orgasm and she pressed her fingers firmly on his pulsing prostate gland. For a couple of seconds Drone felt numbed out and she then retracted her head and said:

Layla: "Darling, contain yourself, let it cool off, because I have a surprise for you later on this evening!"

Drone: "I hate surprises!"

Layla wrestled his Johnny back into his cage and zipped him back up. She then grabbed his hand and pulled him back onto the dance floor, where the rhythm of the music swept them away into the Dreamtime Trance land. They danced back and forth from the darkness into the light and Layla continued to guide Drone's fingertips towards her juicy vortex.

Drone: "You're teasing me!"

Layla: "No, I am romancing your shadow side! You've got to learn to accept every little piece of your fearful self!"

Drone: "My Johnny is not afraid; he feels like Tarzan!"

Layla: "I'm not having sex with a monkey darling, what I meant to say was; explore your areas of shame and blame, while you're publicly exposed!"

Drone: "Are you trying to tell me that you want us to have sex in the spotlights where everybody can see us?"

Layla: "Well we're doing it aren't we? Here feel how wet I am!"

Layla's vortex by this time was voluptuously transpiring her juicy self and her lingerie had absorbed the better part of her inner self!

Drone: "You're soaked, why don't you take it off?"

Layla: "Why don't you earn yourself a trophy?"

Drone: "Are you sure?"

Layla: "Most definitely!"

Drone: "Okay, spread them so I can frisk you!"

Layla made a side step and Drone snapped the strings of her lingerie. With his fingers, he crinkled up her G-string and clenched the palm of his hand around it. He then raised his arm and squeezed the juicy juice from her G-string straight into his opened mouth. Her juice was dripping down on the velvet lining of his tongue and Drone felt like he was drinking nectar from the Gods. This was the holy sacrament, which triggered the Endorphin and Pheromone rush into the discovery zones of his exploring brain. Layla jumped towards him and pulled his arm down and said:

Layla: "You can't do that!"

Drone: "Why not?"

Layla: "It's gross!"

Drone: "No babe. It's love!"

Drone kissed Layla intimately on her neck and down towards her breasts. When his lips touched her nipples, they instantly responded with a hardness, which profiled her T-shirt profusely. His lips were on a journey of love and they kept moving further on down, towards her navel. His tongue could not resist to twirl around and around inside of her belly button. With his hands, he lifted up her mini skirt and Layla now fully exposed her vortex right up and into his face. Drone reached out and stuck his tongue right in between her swollen labia. His tongue began to slip and slide in between the crevice of her vortex and Layla opened her legs even further, which then gave Drone full access to her private area. Seriousness is the worst of sins and it is a shame that people have to feel ashamed for what they truly feel. Drone felt ashamed and he looked around, but nobody seemed to pay any attention to him. Everybody seemed to be too busy with their own little 'wild things'! Layla had her eyes closed and said:

Layla: "I'm sure this is what it feels like when I go to heaven!"

Together they danced their way towards heaven and it lasted until the break of dawn. Drone kept swaying and rocking his Layla like a little baby and finally he said:

Drone: "Keep your eyes closed and let me guide you outside!"

Hand in hand, they walked outside, where the sun was just about to rise and the warmth of its rays made their faces smile. In the middle of the street Drone undressed himself and Layla.

Drone: "Okay, you can open them up!"

Layla smiled and said: "When there is love, there is light! When there is light, there is life! When there is life, there is heaven on Earth!" She looked at Drone and said: "Look at us, we are 'naked' in the middle of the street!"

Drone: "Yeah, isn't it cool?"

The naked exposure of Layla's divine body caused quite a few cabdrivers to hit their brakes and many offered her a free ride back to the hotel. Layla negotiated for Drone to be included and when they returned to the hotel, they crashed on the king size bed and fell asleep! The next morning it was Layla's voice, which woke Drone up.

Layla: "Drone, I love you with all of my heart!"

Tears came to his eyes and Drone took some time to enjoy his moment. The mental fortress, which kept his E~motions safe, was now stirred and he bursted out in tears! Layla noticed his tears and said: "You're crying!"

Drone: "I'm so happy!"

Layla: "Make a wish!"

Drone: "Whatever happened to that sensual promise you made me inside the Catacombs?"

Layla: "You mean the surprise!"

Drone: "Yes!"

Layla: "I'll keep my promise, but first I have to share with you the dream I had last night!"

Drone: "I'm listening!"

Layla: "Last night I dreamt that I was being impregnated by an aspect of your Pleiadian self!"

Drone: "Héh schizzo, are you trying to tell me that you're pregnant?"

Layla: "Yes, that I am! This baby is from an immaculate sex act with your Pleiadian self!"

Drone: "Thanks for sharing! Are you on drugs again?"

Layla: "No, you silly! It was a lucid dream and at this time you may not understand what I'm talking about, but you will come to understand it in the near future!"

Drone: "Let me get this straight; I'm going to have a baby from my extra-terrestrial self?"

Layla: "I'm so glad I can talk with you about the outer limits!"

Drone: "You are out on a limb, and I have got to find a doctor, who specializes in Heroin dissociation traumas!"

Layla: "No darling, why don't we submit ourselves a pregnancy test?"

Drone: "Yeah, let's get the facts straight!"

They bought one of those instant pregnancy test kits and the test turned out to be positive! The results took Drone by surprise and it threw him off balance. Drone was going to need some time to readjust to the news of becoming a father to the child of his alien self?

Drone: "How can you be so sure that my Earthly semen didn't fertilize your egg!"

Layla: "Because I am using the pill!"

Drone: "That's only a 98% safety factor guaranteed!"

Layla: "When a woman feels, she knows!"

The force of love is stronger than its peripheral shadow aspect called reasoning, and a new feeling of commitment and responsibility started to grow on Drone. He felt happy and the idea of becoming a father excited him, but in his Mind, he doubted Layla's sense of reality Layla noticed his inner turmoil and she looked him straight in the eyes and said:

Layla: "Just love and trust me! Our child will need a lot of your great cosmic orgasms, in order for it to evolve with a full brain capacity!"

Drone: "What is a full brain capacity?"

Layla: "The general human population uses only 10% of their full brain capacity. A continuous induced state of orgasm during the pregnancy phase can unlock the Super natural powers inherent to the capacity of our brain."

Drone: "Are you suggesting that we commit ourselves to a nine-month sensual sex marathon?"

Layla: "It will grow on you! It is more like a way of life, a divination!"

Drone: "Let's hope that our batteries and fuse boxes are up to it!"

Layla: "Adaptation is another power we possess!"

Layla's swiftness stunned him and before Drone could figure out what her next move was, she asked him:

Layla: "Would you like to give your new baby a great cosmic orgasm?"

Drone: "Are you sure that it is safe for us to do this?"

Layla: "Absolutely! Are you ready for the promise I made you in the Catacombs?"

Drone: "Most definitely!"

Layla positioned herself in doggy style and wedged herself up with pillows. She prodded her sensitive self with a vibrator and asked Drone to warm up the lubrication oil. Layla lubricated his droning vortex and Drone gently poured the warm oil on her 'cafe au lait' rose bud.

Layla: "I know men like it tight and I want to give you a Mind-bending orgasm! Be gentle baby and do me with ease and grace!"

Drone positioned his shaft and followed Layla's instructions. She felt tight and it took a couple of seconds for her to give way and loosen up her rose bud. The sensation was indescribably fulfilling, but Drone did not want to release it yet. He lowered himself and slid his tongue back and forth through her succulent crevice.

Layla: "Stop, stop, stop, give me a breather I don't want to come just yet!"

She relaxed and her body began to release her mobilized sexual energy with little gentle contractions. Her sweet musky scent was now evaporating all over their royal suite and the endorphin rush inside his brain began to trigger a massive number of pheromones.

Layla: "Do me, do me love?"

With the gentle care of an Obstetrician and the passion of a Don Juan, Drone inserted and positioned a vibrator at her electric C-spot. Layla was moaning and she moved her pelvic region in response to the droning vibes. It was as if she was trying to get away from her pleasure source and she took some time to adapt herself to it! She grabbed the vibrator and repositioned it exactly onto the sensitive neuron receptors of her G-spot. Her body became more in tune with the vibrator and she now made the appearance of having a joy ride of her life. Layla turned her vibrator mode on low and slid it slowly through her well-lubricated crevice.

Layla begged him: "Give me an Aboriginal kiss down under and then French kiss me on my lips, please Drone. I want to taste myself"

Drone kept sucking on her electric spot and her vortex released an abundance of nectar! Within five minutes, Layla gasped for air and she erupted with a vulva tickling squirting orgasm. In fact, her vortex squirted her love juice with such an incredible thrusting force, that it left Drone in awe! Visions came to him in whom Layla's vortex transformed into an erupting volcano. Drone could clearly see himself fire walking on top of hot waves of lava. In the mist of fire, Drone witnessed the angelic body of Layla dancing in the heat of flames. Her dancing silhouette radiated a divine translucent glow. The fire goddess Pele was smiling at them and the sky was releasing the rain of blessings, tiny particles of God light! When they both returned to their senses Layla said:

Layla: "I can feel our child fluttering inside of my womb!" It is sponging up my inner bliss!"

Drone: "Are all Pleiadian babies like this?"

Layla: "Yes these cosmic babies are called; the children of the Blue Ray!"

Layla gently removed the vibrator from her vortex and pulled Drone on top of her. She grabbed his shaft and inserted it in her well-lubricated crevice. Layla pushed him over laughingly and gently rocked her G-spot against his droning vortex. With her pelvic region, she began to move circular and with the cervix of her womb, she massaged and stimulated his vortex glans! It felt like there was an electric surge in between the synapses of their nerve endings. Suddenly she stopped and asked:

Layla: "Are you ready for a tight rerun?"

Drone: "What else can a man wish for, when he has captured the heart of a woman?'

Layla grabbed his extended vortex and completely lubricated it from head to toe.

Layla: "Do you like flower power?"

Drone: "They call me mister butterfly!"

Layla: "Then do me the honors sir and lubricate my rosebud again!"

Layla was trembling with excitement at the thought of feeling his pulsing vortex locked inside her rose bud again.

Drone: "Here I go again!"

Layla tossed back her gorgeous waving black hair, blew him a kiss, and squatted down in front of him. Drone grabbed her hips and Layla sensing what he wanted got on her hands and knees and wiggled her behind. The warm drops of lubrication oil were running playfully over her skin.

Layla: "Mmm, that feels nice and soothing!"

Her well-lubricated rosebud sphincter gently gave way to the forward ushering of his droning stamen. Layla almost lost her breath and Drone began to rock and skewer her back and forth with a rhythmic pistoning. Their level of intimacy reached a depth of perception, which moved them, both beyond the realities of this transient Earth plane. Drone leaned forwards and grabbed her breasts, while his excited vortex continued to piston in and out with the grace of a jackhammer at full throttle. Layla was responding rhythmically to his magnetic thrusts and she put a tight squeeze on her sphincter as if kissing him with a deadly lip lock. She definitely had a sense for rhythm and pleasure! Drone's body started to convulse and he finally blasted a load of warm thick semen deep inside of her body cavity. The world was spinning around him and he felt dizzy. When he returned to his senses, he felt a warm wet cloth covering his vortex and it made him have visions of a Japanese after treat. Layla and Drone looked into each other's eyes and it was through these windows that they began to melt away into the abyss of their bliss. From deep within Drone heard a spontaneous song:

"Layla take me to the depth of your being!"
"Layla take me to the depth of your heart!"
"Layla take me to the depth of your being!"
"Layla take me to the depth of your soul!"

Layla broke their magical spell by saying: "When you came inside of me, it felt as if the warm glow of your life force directly moved towards the embryo in my womb!"

Drone: "That's deep!"

Layla: "Oeh, here feel this, our baby is fluttering again!"

Drone: "I don't feel anything!"

Layla: "Rest assured that it feels you!"

Drone: "Isn't it neat that sex equals life!"

Layla: "Yes, it is beautiful that life equals sex!"

Drone: "You know Layla, you make me feel greater than life itself!"

Layla: "Yeah, isn't it neat?"

Drone: "Let's take a shower together?"

Layla: "Don't you enjoy the love dance of our bodily germs?"

Drone: "All I know is that my body wants to be fed, washed and nurtured!"

Layla: "Mon amour, je t'adore!"

Drone: "Ditto!"

Together they took a bath and gently washed each other's skin with a soft washcloth.

They cuddled in the bathtub for an hour or so and Layla suggested going out for a scenic tour in the city of Prague. Walking through a crowd of people they noticed again that their love vibes had a contagious effect on the people they met! People would spontaneously walk up to them to ask for an autograph or just to talk. When Drone asked: "Why?" the reply would be: "Happiness is God!"

Some locals would even take it as far as asking them for having a picture taken together! Love was definitely in the air and it marked them as 'the LOVE~VIPs of Prague'! On their way back to the hotel, they stopped at a local park for a walk about. Again, they were stunned by the observation of young people shooting dope and having sex. Triggered by the scene, Layla's body began to cramp up, as if struck by a deep tearing pain! Her body convulsed and she barfed. This initiated a catharsis, and she screamed:

Layla: "They don't feel, they don't feel! Nobody cares anymore! Nobody to stop them! Feel, damned, feel! Feel yourself, feel each other, and feel God!"

Drone observed Layla's catharsis like a freeze frame in slow motion. It almost seemed as if these young couples represented the incarnation of Angels, who were send from heaven to show a society of despair the stairway back to heaven. Drone observed a scenery of intimate interactions in between angelic primates and he associated it with a Safari tour during mating season. Layla began to pick some flowers, which she then hand delivered to one of the many naked couples.

Layla: "The power of love is in a flower!"

The couple smiled and gave her a kiss on the cheeks! Layla looked over to Drone and said:

Layla: "We can change the world with the power of love! Don't you think?"

Drone: "Maybe that's the reason why we came to this planet?"

Intuitively they felt that the answer to that question would reveal itself when they would be ready to welcome it. As they walked back to the hotel, Layla suggested:

Layla: "Drone, would you be receptive to experience a state of Meditation during our sex act?"

Drone: "Are you suggesting that we should bring more consciousness into; the Wild Thing?"

Layla: "Yes, I would love that! When one enhances a prolonged state of sexual awareness, then the mastery of that skill will result in a benediction, a blessing!"

Drone: "So we build up our sexual pleasure until we're about to climax and then we just stop?

Layla: "Sort of like that! We have to learn to hold back our orgasms and allow the sexual energy to dissipate into a super awareness!"

Drone: "What is the 'benediction' aspect of it?"

Layla: "A cultivation of heavenly energies! Your lower sexual drive can thus be transformed into a higher form of heavenly bliss!"

Drone: "I'm open to it!"

That same evening, they experienced their first meditational Tantric exercise. Layla had set the mood by burning candles and incense. The scent of fresh Jasmine enhanced a deep longing inside of Drone to merge with Layla's body. Layla approached him naked and eased her receptive vortex over his extended self. Drone sensed that she was aroused, because her juices were flowing and she welcomed him without resistance. They sat erect with their vortices deeply interlocked and the natural pulse of their heartbeats moved their bodies with a gentle sway. Gently they rocked back and forth until the beat of their hearts became as one. Their breathing patterns were deepening and again they began to breathe in tune with each other. Layla's breath was hot and fresh and it continued to deepen, as if descending into the abyss of new feelings. Drone kissed her on the lips and he began to inhale her hot breath. The sexual act of mutual resuscitation soon triggered a state of hyperventilation and he drifted away into a world of white clouds. The Tantric breath of fire is like a rebirthing experience and it unlocked visions of life times, which felt very familiar to Drone. His eyes were teary, and slowly, but with certainty, he now became able to relax at his inner core essence.

Drone: "It feels as if I'm slipping and sliding in and out of different realities!"

Layla's face was changing and it took on different personalities. The visions kept coming at a very fast rate and as soon as Drone tried to have a closer look at them, they disappeared! Drone discovered that if he remained relaxed and did not zoom into the changing apparitions of Layla's face, then these visions would keep coming at an ever-increasing rate. The trick was to remain relaxed and stay connected with the inner observer. The changing complexion of Layla's face reflected men, women, animals and even some unknown extra-terrestrial appearances. Reality was playing a trick on Drone's Mind and it made him wonder if he was being deceived by the incapacity of his nerve system. A moment came, in which everything became dark within his inner sky and the reflection of Layla's face completely disappeared from the sensors of his retina. Drone felt like he was falling into an abyss of no-thingness. The room around him became empty of his Earthly reflections. For a moment, there was nothing! Then, gradually the space within himself became filled with divine light particles. The fairies were doing their little dance inside a world of fluid perception. Akashic records of fiber optic light were woven into the soul matrix of his being. His old self began to fade out and a renewed self, zoomed into his liquid sense of reality. It was as if a new image was woven, which was soon to make its appearance. A new brighter light began to fade in on the retina of his inner eye. Slowly, but with certainty, this light then began to form itself into the most exquisitely beautiful being he had ever seen. It was neither man nor woman, but its form was recognizable human. Its matrix was made up of myriads of tiny lights shooting through a lattice of optic fiber tubes, moving constantly in ever changing colors. The face was a face of a thousand ancient beings. This apparition radiated all and everything he could ever wish to be 'love, peace, grace, freedom, bliss, wisdom', and other divine qualities, which he could not describe in words.

Drone: "What is your name?"

Being: "I have many names collected from a multitude of incarnations, but my true spirit is only a light frequency, not a name. I am that, which cannot be named! If you seek me by name, then you may refer to me as Altazar, Lord of the Star system called Deneb. I am that, which you have always been. It was your longing for the truth, which has brought me here. These, are the moments of your awakening, treasure them! You are a response system and I interface with you. I have been aligning your circuitry through Layla, which enables you to better receive me. Attune to me for a better calibration. Remember your true home always! When time began, you were a pure lattice of white light. You will always have the characteristics of light with many colors, many nuances, many experiences!"

Drone felt his body being caressed by a soft gentle breeze. The immense love of this being wrapped itself around him and it felt as if this being was absorbing his pain! Drone felt uplifted and waves of sheer joy ran through his body vehicle. He was on fire! His entire being was consuming the flame of love and he experienced an overwhelming feeling of bliss, which he could have never imagined before. From within, an indescribable force of passion began to well up and Drone did not know what to do with this strong feeling. The firmness of Layla's breasts against his hairy chest brought Drone back into the here now. Her heartbeat was pounding against his chest and he said:

Drone: "Thank God you are still here!"

Layla: "Just feel and hold me darling!"

Drone allowed himself to melt into the arms of Layla and it gave him the sensation of a free fall into the eternal abyss of bliss. He looked deeply into Layla's eyes and said:

Drone: "Did you feel that?"

Layla: "Yes, it felt like a melting with the matrix of a silken God!"

Drone: "Yeah, like a nuclear meltdown!"

It was a miraculous evening and they both felt expanded by the intrinsic nature of love. Layla was happy with this new discovery and she expressed her excitement by wanting to teach her experience to those who are willing to learn!

Layla: "You and I should teach Tantric sex to a 'willing to learn' type of audience!"

Drone: "You know you might be on to something!"

Layla: "You think so?"

Drone: "Yes, because the religious limbo of oblivion is that everybody covets to be clothed with a heavenly dwelling as a means to cover up their naked shame and blameful selves!"

Layla: "Do you think we should write this stuff down?"

Drone: "Yeah, I think you should!"

Layla began to write and she cuddled up against Drone's naked body. Drone was the first to wake up the next morning, and he realized that his vacation was almost over. There were three more days left to party, before they had to return to the reality of the red-light district!

Drone: "Your face looks sad Layla! What's going on?"

Layla: "Last night I had this strange lucid dream and it made me feel sad!"

Drone: "Tell me about it!"

Layla: "My Pleiadian brothers and sisters appeared to me in the dream state and they extracted my embryo! They informed me that my child needed to complete its growth inside the divine matrix of the Pleiadian star constellation!"

Drone: "Can you translate that in layman terms for me?"

Layla: "My soul aspects have extracted our baby and it was teletransported to the Pleiadeans, where it will be born with a full brain capacity!"

Drone: "Will we ever see our child again?"

Layla: "Yes, but we will have to be prepared."

Drone: "Prepared for what?"

Layla: "Molecular tele-transportation through the Androgynous Stargate into the outer Galaxies!"

Drone: "What kind of mumbo jumbo is that?"

Layla: "My Pleiadian brothers and sisters have informed me, that you were to follow the directions of Isua Dow, who is the Shaman of the Hummingbird tribe!" Layla was speaking in tongues as if hosting the Holy Spirit.

Drone: "Your meta babble is distracting me from the pain I feel caused by the loss of our baby!"

Layla: "The child didn't belong to you Drone; it belongs to God!"

Drone: "Is that the reason why you are not grieving?"

Layla: "God will return his child whenever we are ready to receive it!"

Drone: "That is a poor excuse!"

Layla: "God does not need excuses and you are in no position to accuse his actions!"

Drone: "God is playing our feelings behind the reflection of his image!"

Layla: "Yes, isn't it fun, when God allows his inner child to come out and play with us?"

Drone: "Any suggestions on how to prepare for our merit in heaven?"

Layla: "I pray that our life will be strong in love and be built on love. Moreover, I pray that you and all of God's holy people will have the power to understand the greatness of Christ's love. I pray that you can understand how wide, how long, how high, and how deep that love is. God's love is greater than any person can ever know. But I pray that you will be able to know that love!"

Drone: "Are you saying; Love is the preparation and the merit?"

Layla: "You're catching on, aren't yah!"

Drone: "You are a beaudaceous cosmic babe, Layla!"

Layla: "For now I need to record all the information, that the Holy Spirit is revealing to me, and I want you to buy me a cassette recorder! Please!"

No time wasted! They took a cab into the city, where Drone bought Layla her own personal cassette recorder. When they returned to the hotel, Layla whispered softly into his ear:

Layla: "Let's get naked and continue our Quest for Fire!"

Layla held his hand as she walked him into the bathroom. She grabbed his razor blade and shaving cream and said: "Shave me darling!"

She ushered Drone down onto his knees and allowed him to disrobe her voluptuous body. Drone foamed up her vulva and he shaved her private area with the precision of a barber. Her sacred vortex was responding to his trembling touch and her lips began to swell up from excitement. Layla grabbed him by the ears and pulled his face straight towards her private lips. Drone slithered his tongue deep inside her crevice and it made her nectar flow as if it was in the midst of a monsoon season. Layla orgasmed in no time and Drone waited until she was ready to receive him.

Layla: "You are the best French kisser I've ever had!"

Drone: "It's the scent of your pheromones that drives my tongue crazy!"

Layla: "Do you know why I asked you to shave me?"

Drone: "Because you like to be clean and fresh!"

Layla: "That too, but the real reason is that I want us to have a perpetual intercourse during our long train ride home!"

Drone: "Perpetual Motion, Hugh?"

Layla: "When we have intercourse, and especially when you give me the cunnilingus treat, it feels like the whole Universe is being channeled through me!"

Drone: "So you want an uninterrupted coitus?"

Layla: "Yes, because I want to record the information that comes through me!"

Drone: "Why do you want to record it?"

Layla: "Intuitively I feel that the recorded information will have a directional purpose for us!"

Her new idea excited Drone and since it was the day before their departure, he decided to pack his suitcases early. Together they took some time to say goodbye to all the wonderful people who hosted them, after which they tucked in early. The next morning, they boarded the train at 7 a.m., and got settled in their private compartment. Layla enjoyed her private space, because it made her feel cozy and safe. Layla was wearing an above the knee sensual skirt and it reminded Drone of a cheerleader outfit. They made themselves comfortable and the rocking motion of the train soon made them fall asleep. It was about an hour later, when Layla suddenly sat up straight and said:

Layla: "The Holy spirit is now ready to speak in tongues through my body vehicle!"

Before Drone realized what Layla was doing, she had unzipped his jeans and revitalized his vortex. She claimed her squatters right and jumped right on top of his lap and Drone immediately felt that she was not wearing any underwear. Her vortex was well lubricated and her labia fully embraced and welcomed his erected self. Layla began to massage the sensitive sensors of his vortex with a circular motion of her cervix. She rubbed her G-spot against his hardened shaft and at the same time, she began to breathe heavily into his ear. From time to time, she alternated her approach by sticking her wet tongue into his ear. The sexual juice of her vortex now began to flow freely around the base of his shaft. Layla kissed him on the lips and pushed her tongue deep into his mouth for a French kiss! His brain responded to the invasion of her tongue with the release of an excessive amount of endorphin. Drone's body felt uplifted by the electrical tickling sensation, which was sparkling in between the tips of their tongues. Suddenly Layla stopped and retracted her intimate self. She reached over and grabbed her cassette recorder. Layla then looked Drone in the eyes and said:

Layla: "Are you ready for our long ride home?"

Drone smiled, kissed her and said: "Yes I am!"

Layla closed her eyes and reconnected with her inner self. It seemed as if she arose herself into a state of trance. Layla now began to speak with the tongue of the Holy Spirit.

Layla: "I am 'She' who is an integrated aspect of God's light lattice. My home is in a Starlight system called Hunab-Ku, and my name is Deneb! God send for me to be Layla's mentor!"

Drone: "What is it that we need to learn?"

Deneb: "Layla's body vehicle will teach you how to love Drone. I am pleased with the progress you have made on the path of love. Do you have any questions?"

Drone: "What is my mission on planet Earth?"

Deneb: "To understand the answer to that question you have to understand the difference between 'Reincarnation and Resurrection'! Do you understand?"

Drone: "Enlighten me!"

Deneb: "Resurrection is the transformation of body and soul into the higher planes of God's creation, whereby your body is glorified in humbleness and becomes spiritually free in the fullness of the Holy Spirit. Any sinful soul can be restored in the Father's image through Christ, into the heavenly perfected Adam & Eve. Resurrection pertains to the courage to stand naked in front of the eyes of God until he finds you worthy to wear the full garment of the Father at the time of the collective resurrection. You are resurrected according to your degree of glory as a temple of the Holy Spirit!"

Drone: "Are you saying that when we humans become able to accept our nakedness in the eyes of each other, that then our flesh will be sanctified as; The temple of the Holy Spirit!"

Deneb: "Exactly! Anything else?"

Drone: "What does 'sin' mean and what is this 'garment' stuff?"

Deneb: "Seriousness is the worst of all sins! When we do not allow the everlasting living light of the Holy Spirit to shine through our body vehicle, then we miss God and everything divine all together! Always be in search for the miraculous outside your comfort zone and you will never miss God in the magic zone. To sin means to miss God! God's garment is the cloth i.e. the presence of the Holy Spirit. As the energy potency of the Holy Spirit becomes increasingly greater, the density of his invoked presence will become greater and it then becomes increasingly powerful in your body vehicle. Light is a high-energy substance, which conducts the innate intelligence of God. God's light is stored in each cell of the human body and it will gradually become the same form of your body cells but with a different molecular rearrangement. Your cells hear your thoughts and feel your feelings, so you have to take response ability to allow only the highest. Your material body will become a superconductor of light ~ wave particles and you will then effortlessly merge with the Unified Force Field i.e. 'The Matrix of God' as an inter-dimensional full consciousness pattern. This is also, what we refer to as the ascension. You will look like an ordinary person from the appearance. The only difference is that you will appear younger than those, which are of your age. Certainly, the bad things in your body will have to be removed, including illnesses. Your skin will become delicate with a healthy peach color. Serenity, Grace, Rhythm, Peace, Freedom and Balance will be the benefits, when you accept the living light of a silken God.

Drone: "Then, what is reincarnation?"

Deneb: "Reincarnation is the birth after birth of the same soul until the lesson of resurrection is learned!"

Drone: "So, what is my mission on this Earth?"

Deneb: "The living light has the intelligence and the power to uplift the veils from your memory banks!"

Drone: "Are we supposed to have some kind of love affair with God?"

Deneb: "Start simple by awakening the passion in those people, who are send by the Divine to bathe in your presence!"

Drone: "Bathing as in Sun tanning?"

Deneb: "Yes, but realize that Sunshine is only a reflection of the real God light!"

Drone: "What is love?"

Deneb: "Every human being is the reflection of God's image, which can only be seen and felt when his living light shines through your body vehicle. Love is the art of knowing oneself as another yourself, but love as a sensation is a gift from God. Once known, you then have to go beyond the small family and find out, what it is that lays beyond yourself. Love is the surrender to the beyond of yourself, each other, until you learn to be intimate with all of God's creations. Love is not safe, because it is free in the expression of itself. Love is ferocious, because it makes you feel your pain and shed your tears. Love is not about hiding or sugar coating your pain, but instead it is the art of feeling it with the intent of discovery. Love is about building a relationship with an orgasmic Universe. Love is about entering and sharing your sacred temple called heart. Love is not the practice of a ritual, but instead, it is a relationship with everything divine. Love is about going to Church, Naked! You Drone are in search of the miraculous and you have found the force of love dormant within the abyss of Layla. Your path of love will be blessed with eternity and it will be challenged by the time warps of separation."

Drone: "What about sex?"

Deneb: "This is a sexed Universe, and the force which you refer to as God-love has violently expelled man and woman from their balanced condition of being tension free within the full flowering of their being. Man and woman are now fully charged and dually unbalanced by their sexual opposite electric pressures of compression and expansion. These two opposite unbalanced conditions violently desire to return to the oneness of balance from which they were divided into two.

Drone: "Sort of like the workings of a rubber band?"

Deneb: Yes, Sex is the compression of your light body into two opposite tensions, which desire release and expansion from their opposition. Your sexual pulsation seeks rest and unification with your opposite vortex partner. Every action of motion in this Universe is a result of sex desire for motion from a state of stillness and rest, or for rest from a state of motion."

Drone: "Help me to understand this in Layman terms. Are you saying that the force of sex is like an elastic band being pulled apart, and that the nature of its inner tension wants to pull itself back together so that it can be in a state of rest?"

Deneb: "Yes, in the near future you and Layla will be challenged by a timeless force called separation. It is important for the both of you to move into the deepest space of love within, before this separation takes place. It is predestined that Layla will leave her body and incarnate almost instantly as Maneesha with her shadow self twin sister Maleeka!"

Drone: "What is a shadow self?"

Deneb: "A shadow self is the unconscious aspect of a twin soul. Its lesson to learn is; Growth towards the light!"

Drone: "What is my part in all of this?"

Deneb: "Drone, you will be guided by a shaman named: Isua Dow! Go totally into the deepest intensity of love that is possible. Let love be an opening in you, an abyss for the divine to enter! As far as I know, except God, everybody is ultimately a woman, because one has to be receptive for the Holy Spirit to appear."

Drone: "I always knew that if I were to be born a woman, I would become a lesbian!"

Deneb: "Drone, you will have to endure an arduous pilgrimage for eighteen years, during which you will come to learn the integration of your grief. From your heart, you will become a mad devotee of love and always in search of your beloved. At the end of the eighteen years, you will be reunited with Layla and enter a new era of being. I will be present during your ceremonial reunion. Until then my friend, may the force of love take care of you."

Layla moved her pelvic region, sighed and shivered as Deneb's spirit was leaving her body vehicle. Her precious vortex was still interlocked with the seal of intimacy and the mechanical cadence of the train kept

Drone mesmerized with the sensations coming from her calibrated G-spot. Layla was breathing heavily as if still in trance. She dug her nails deep into his flesh and bit him in the shoulder. Her body was contracting and from deep within, she then released a frightening primal scream, which reminded Drone of some pre-historic creature that had been abstained from a mating season for over more than a decade. Her nectar was now flowing abundantly around the base of his vortex and her sweet musky pheromone scent induced him into an altered state of trance. It felt as if they were merging into one being. Her body was releasing orgasmic after shock vibrations and their bodies began to slide apart like two dolphins beaching on a mud bank. Layla's hoarse voice brought Drone back to his senses.

Layla: "Water, water, water, I feel dehydrated!"

She gently withdrew her embracing vortex and disengaged herself with a gentle sound of suction. Drone stuck his tongue deep inside her crevice and slithered it up and down a couple of times. Next, he sucked on her swollen lips and released them slowly with a succulent grace. Layla moaned. Drone stood up and handed Layla a glass of water. Layla gulped down the water as if she had just crossed over the Sahara Desert. She sat down and stared at Drone with gleaming bedroom eyes and said:

Layla: "Do you want to drink me? My juices are flowing and I know you love the taste of it!"

Drone kissed her on the lips and with his hands; he then opened her legs spread Eagle. She then opened her labia and granted him a full access to her lubricated crevice. He suctioned her again and made full circle with his slithering tongue. His kisses moved down towards her perineum and he stretched it out as if molding it into a spoon. Now her juices were collecting themselves in the cavity of her spooned perineum. Her nectar tasted warm and sweet and Drone drank it with a feeling of love-joy!

The suctioning motion on her labia kept her glands activated and Layla continued to flood out from her pores.

Drone: "We should bottle this stuff and market it for consumption!"

Layla: "Never! My juice is for your taste buds only!"

Drone: "Why don't we create a love potion that can benefit this whole planet?"

Layla: "Are you serious?"

Drone: "Our commitment to love is to be taken seriously, because in all of the time on Earth, no progress has been made by those who preach about love, but don't practice it. People do not know how to walk the path of love. Of course, we cannot expect a fictitious entity like a church to vibrate love, but the people who are a servant to this fictitious entity should be held accountable for the vibes that they create. Religion is considered opium for the people, because it keeps them subdued into believing that denial is the stairway to heaven. First, they condemn you, and then they control and subdue you with shame and blame issues. Even the Pope originated from some type of copulative experience. My heart and my body are telling me, that there is absolutely nothing wrong with sex. My Mind however still holds on to the emotional grip of condemnation and that turns everything into a plastic reality. Denial is the acceptance of feelings one likes and the rejection of feelings, which one dislikes. Nobody should be allowed to put a guilt trip on another person. Most churches tell us that without the presence of Jesus Christ in your heart, you will be incapacitated to love another human being. The love I feel for you Layla is teaching me how to keep my heart open for the rest of humanity. I now know with a deep sense of certainty, that when I continue my quest for the miraculous, then someday I may become able to totally open myself up to a divine being called God. If God created you Layla, then he must know that I love him through you. Christians say that a person can only love God through his son Jesus Christ, but I know that I can love them both through you Layla! The question arises if that would stigmatize me as being gay! Is God the only man and are we all but in a feminine devotion towards him?"

Layla: "Religion should be brought to actual reality and once it comes to the actual reality it will be the very essence of the love we all seek."

The rhythmic cadence of the train brought Drone back to his senses and he felt Layla's tongue swirl around the sensors of his vortex. She pulled back the foreskin of his vortex and with her tongue; she then followed the swollen profile of his glans. As soon as Drone signaled Layla of his upcoming orgasm, she then smiled and pushed with confidence on his prostate gland. Layla looked up at him and said:

Layla: "It is extremely important that we remain connected together at our deepest core level my darling!"

Drone: "Why is that?"

Layla: "We are downloading our genetic information into the memory banks of our vortices; this will enable us to recognize each other's pheromones in my next incarnation!"

The thought of losing Layla suddenly frightened him and she noticed a concerned look on his face.

Layla: "Everything will be in divine order my beloved!"

Layla gently reconnected their vortices and the cadence of the train calibrated her G-spot to the level at which Layla began to orgasm again. They were not copulating anymore, but instead it seemed as if the entrapped primal forces of the ancestral line were now being released by means of a bone thrilling orgasmic primal scream. With her convulsing body, Layla was now expressing all of the painful holographic images she was seeing inside her Mind. She was breathing heavily and her breasts were sliding over his wet chest. Drone could feel the pulse of her heartbeat pounding inside of her excited body. Their bodies were in harmony with each other and it almost felt like they were cruising on automatic pilot. Layla's invoked catharsis began to unravel the veils of her suppressed shadow side. More and more visions kept coming and her body continued to contract and release the energy of what seemed to be very traumatic events! It was a frightening process because neither of them was controlling the situation anymore. The intelligence of her electrical body was in charge and it felt like she was being pressed through a major purification process. Internal forces greater than her power to resist moved Layla's being into purification. Her body was cleaning up the harm caused by the eternal denial of being an orgasmic being. Drone lost track of time, space and self-identity! It must have been a couple of hours later, when he noticed that the convulsions of her body began to subside into a graceful swaying cadence. A moment came, when everything became serene and reflective like a mirror. In that moment, all of his fears and pains, which had been entrapped inside of his self-I-dentity body, seemed to give way to a blinding beam of light. Softly, but with certainty an intense light arose within his being and the shape of an exquisitely beautiful being with a myriad of tiny light pulsations was now being impressed on his Mind's eye. The being that called himself 'Altazar' was waiting patiently for the right timing to break the code of silence.

Altazar: "Greetings! The reason for my appearance is that you both just had a glimpse of the mirror in which the reflection of human love disappears and the original light of God will make its appearance. Only a chosen few extra ordinary people have been able to love each other to this point. This is the point of no return. The both of you are not ready yet to be just that, which you covet to be! Your love life needs a ripening like the grapes of a good wine."

Like a sponge, Drone was absorbing Altazar's message into the heart of his being. It felt as if his love vibration was expanding out and into the Universe. His energies were shifting as if accelerating to a level, which was too overwhelming to bear.

Drone: "What's happening Altazar?"

Altazar: "I am amplifying your love vibes so you can be calibrated to my level of being!"

Drone: "Why?"

Altazar: "Just feel and adapt yourself to it!"

Drone: "It is unbearable for me so I command you to stop it!"

Altazar: "Forgive me for testing you, but I needed to know if you would be able to expand your love vibes to the level of a Deity!"

Drone: "Hello, have you ever heard of informed consent over there on cloud nine!"

Altazar: "Forgive me for intruding!"

His image faded away as quickly as it appeared and Drone's sensory system began to readjust to its normal condition. Layla was the first to break the magic spell, which their host had created and she said:

Layla: "I'm hungry, let's go out and eat!"

Without the utterance of a word, they were dressed and moved towards the restaurant. When they finally sat down Layla said:

Layla: "I've got two 90 minutes tapes of channeled material and I would like to type it out and edit this new material."

Drone: "We'll need time to process it!"

Layla: "We will darling, we will!"

They both felt exhausted and in overload of the new information they just received. Their body vehicles needed a deep resting sleep and they slept straight on through until their arrival in Amsterdam.

Layla woke Drone up and said: "I'm thankful for the divine intervention, which must have guided the train conductor to refrain himself from interrupting our beauty sleep!"

Drone: "Yeah and I'm happy to be back home!"

Layla: "Home is where the heart is darling!"

Light my Fire: by the Doors

You know that it would be untrue
You know that I would be a liar
If I was to say to you
Girl, we couldn't get much higher

Come on, baby, light my fire
Come on, baby, light my fire
Try to set the night on fire

The time to hesitate is through
No time to wallow in the mire
Try now we can only lose
And our love becomes a funeral pyre

Come on, baby, light my fire
Come on, baby, light my fire
Try to set the night on fire

The time to hesitate is through
No time to wallow in the mire
Try now we can only lose
And our love become a funeral pyre

Come on, baby, light my fire
Come on, baby, light my fire
Try to set the night on fire

You know that it would be Untrue
You know that I would be a liar
If I was to say to you
Girl, we couldn't get much higher

Come on, baby, light my fire
Come on, baby, light my fire
Try to set the night on fire
Try to set the night on fire
Try to set the night on fire
Try to set the night on fire.

Chapter Four ~
When the Music is over

And if people are not raised from death, then God never raised Christ from death. If the dead are not raised, Christ has not been raised either. And if Christ has not been raised, then your faith is for nothing; you are still guilty of your sins.

1 Corinthians 15: 15-17

We had great burdens there that were greater than our own strength. We even gave up hope for life. Truly, in our own hearts we believed that we would die. But this happened so that we would not trust in ourselves. It happened so that we would trust in God, who raises people from death!

2 Corinthians 8 – 9

But if the watchman sees the enemy coming and doesn't sound the alarm to warn the people, he is responsible for their captivity. They will die in their sins, but I will hold the watchman responsible for their deaths.'

Ezekiel 33: 6

The next morning Drone woke Layla up at 10 o'clock a.m. and he suggested starting the day with a red-hot Swedish sauna. The tantalizing heat soon opened up his pores, which then released an excess of bodily toxins. It was a Wednesday morning and this meant, that he had two more days to himself before he had to go back to work. Drone glanced over at Layla and he enjoyed looking at a stream of water drops gliding down smoothly over the accentuated curves of her heavenly body.

Drone: "Babe I love it when you sweat!"

Layla: "Yeah, it feels good!"

Drone: "I bet it tastes good too!"

Layla: "That is only if you like salty oister!"

Drone: "I would love to taste your salty pearls of transpiration!"

Layla: 'Then come on over and have a go at me, here kiss me down under!"

Layla teasingly leaned backwards and arched her spine. Slowly she then opened her legs spread Eagle and exposed her private insecure self. With his tongue, Drone began his journey at her feet and in between her toes. Layla giggled and Drone moved on up, slowly following the wet surface of her inner thighs, until he made a tender contact with her private lips. With his velvet tongue, he then dipped the pearls of perspiration from her delicate skin. She widened her legs even further and with her fingers, she now opened her labia, which then gave his tongue a full access to her private joy chamber of womb awakening. He began to kiss Layla's electric spot until her vortex was about to explode with squirting pleasure. Layla commanded him to: "Stop, stop, stop!"

Drone's tongue was determined to guide Layla into the pleasure zone, and he continued to spark her electric spot until she finally lost control over her surging orgasm. Her heart was filled with joy and the muscle contractions of her sexual area ejaculated a stream of juicylicious sacrament straight against Drone's chest. He became so aroused by the explosion of her pleasure zone, that he wanted to do her right then and there! His hard and erected droning stamen found his way to her love shack and he began to usher in and out of her climaxing vortex. With his velvet skin, he began to excite the sensors of her G-spot, and together they entered a perpetual orgasmic state of being. Layla climaxed her Lovejoy, repeatedly, over and over, and the abyss of intimacy was deepening itself by the second! Finally, he could not hold back his horses any longer and Drone blasted his hot semen deep inside of her womb. At a cellular level, their Souls were absorbing the massive amounts of blissful energies, which were now being released by their orgasmic vortices. His body was contracting and convulsing, as if triggered by a primal release phenomenon. When Layla came back to her senses she said:

Layla: "Why don't you go run some errands in town, while I type out my channeled material?"

Drone: "Do you need anything from the store?"

Layla: "No, I'll be fine! Just enjoy yourself and think about me!"

Drone: "I'll miss you!"

Layla: "Ditto!"

For more than three hours Drone cruised all over town, and when he returned home he expected Layla to be behind her type writer, but instead she was sitting in a reclining chair with her headphones on! As Drone approached Layla, he noticed that she was totally drawn into her own world. She had her eyes closed and she was touching her private self with an expression of joy written all over her face. With her left hand, she was touching her breasts and with her right hand, she was finger diddling her vortex area. In a flash of a second Drone grabbed, his Camcorder and he began to eternalize his ultimate fantasy. Layla had one leg hanging over the armrest of her chair. Her panties were shrugged off and her G-string was pulled over to the side, exposing her vortex. Her pink oister was filled with the excitement of her pulsating blood-flow. She now began to prod her vortex with a little red hummingbird vibrator and it got Drone so excited, that his eyes nearly popped out of their sockets. Layla slid her humming vibrator back and forth through her succulent erotic zone. Her rosebud squeaked as it slid back and forth across the leather chair. Meanwhile, she moaned and gasped for air as if her dream stud was banging her like a jackhammer at full throttle! Suddenly her body contracted and her vortex ejaculated the juice of a massive G-spot tingling orgasm. Layla continued to finger diddle her vortex and she sucked on the little red humming bird. She slumped back in her chair for a breather and slowly opened her eyes and looked around. Somehow, she must have sensed Drone's presence, because she felt a slight invasion of her privacy.

Layla: "Hi Drone how was your day?"

Drone: "Fine! Did you get any work done?"

Layla: "Can't you tell? I was celebrating!"

Drone: "Can I celebrate with you?"

Layla: "Come on over here, you wild man of mine!"

Drone walked over to Layla, and she sensing what he wanted, then reached out and unzipped his protruding pants. Before Drone could ask what she had in mind, he felt a hellacious lip lock around the bobbing sensors of his erected vortex. In no time, her French kissing tongue made him ejaculate his life force deep inside of her velvet throat. To his surprise she did not gag, on the contrary, she welcomed the energy dance of his bodily fluids and swallowed! Layla squeezed and sucked the last drop of proteins from his reservoir and she made a sticky clicking sound 'click a dee clack' with the tip of her tongue. She closed her eyes and Drone could now sense a shift in energy taking place, which was an indication that she was about to speak in tongues again! The channel to the other side was now open again!

Layla: "As you may have sensed, it is the holy spirit, which is being hosted in my body vehicle. The blue print of your semen is now merging with the blueprint matrix of my Soul. It is a necessity for my Soul matrix to be encoded with a full color spectrum of your reproductive DNA. This merging will program my Akashic memory bank and recognize you as my beloved during my future incarnation. It is then that we will earn the garment of immortality. The path of love will teach us how to bloom like a Lotus flower! Our sexual intelligence will unlock our brain potential and the way of our hearts will show us how to tap into a full brain capacity. We will learn how to merge with the Unified Force Field and as such, we shall then obey the Law of One! According to the Law of One, we are all One! When one is harmed, all are harmed. When one is helped, all are helped. When one enters the Great Cosmic Orgasm, all will benefit from its ripples of intense bliss! Therefore, in the name of my being, which is one with all there is and is all-powerful and all loving; I am one with the living light of the Holy Spirit. I ask for that only, which be for the highest Good of everyone involved in this matter. On the physical plane, the greatest health, beauty and love! On the emotional plane, the acceptance of all feelings. On the mental plane, the greatest illumination. On the spiritual plane, Rhythm, Peace, Freedom and Balance! Lord God, I ask for these things in your name! So be it!"

The vibrations of Layla's being were so powerful that it made Drone shiver to the bone.

Drone: "Layla, you're blowing my fuse box!"

It took Drone a little while before he was able to pull himself back into the present time, where he compared notes with his 'normal' self! Any 'normal' person would have stopped this flow of Meta-babble lingo. Indeed, within the boundaries of the world of language, it was a definite confusing and Mind upsetting experience. Drone decided to grant it the benefit of doubt, because at this time he was not able yet to comprehend the total picture of what just had been revealed to him. His body seemed to be able to allow the flow of divine intervention run through the vessels of his being. Who would have known at this time that he was being prepared for a Quantum leap into the silken matrix of an eternal Father? The way Layla and Drone were exploring their sexual spirituality would have upset any faithful Christian into a judgmental call of 'Sinners!' God has nothing to do with the morbidity of our Sins! It is man himself, who brought these into being, and man is the only one, who can erase his problem seeds of thought! When one is one with the law of love, then one will no longer produce sins, but to merely refrain from producing sins does not place you within the benediction of God's grace. It is doing truth, not merely refraining from that which is not truth! Ignorance has a way to trigger the Rothweiler on LSD within Drone's system, which in essence wants nothing but to express the celebration of life itself. Religion needs not to be a grim affair. It does not have to be negative, because there are positive sides to life too! The force of life can be positive, a liberation and a joyful experience. It is a God given task to edify Christian indoctrinated people, and Drone is driven to blow his Rams horn 7X around the walls of their defended selves.

Layla: "Most people are polarized in their spirit and this is how they are avoiding many things, which they don't want to surface and feel. They have, literally, drowned and buried these things in darkness and hoped they would never find their way to the surface again. People are dissociating by jumping over their entrapped gapped rage."

Drone: "Unfortunately, most of the Spirit polarized people will not take you seriously here!" Instead of allowing movement in whatever emotions they have in order to find out for themselves if these teachings are right for them or not, they have been dismissing their gut feelings, because their primal emotions do not fit in with the plastic image of a God they already have conditioned within the memory cells of their brain. Lucifer has been getting away with passing himself off as God because he disdains all sensuality and passion for life, teaching that it is all the trap of the material world. Lucifer is involved in all the passions in a state of denial, which means he is in reversal against them, punishing all who have desires they believe are wrong, trying to force them to give their life up to him. If you are not sure how what I am saying here could possibly be correct, you need to feel the undercurrent of rage these people hold in the reflection of religious righteousness versus poetic justice. This rage is self-hatred in a state of denial that does not include the ability to recognize itself for what it is."

Layla pulled Drone back into this reality and said:

Layla: "You know Drone, this great idea dawned on me and I want to see what you think!" Layla knew she had his attention and she continued:

Layla: "I would like to organize a spiritual sexual awareness course with the girls who work for you. I want them to experience, what we are experiencing as a couple, and maybe some of it will rub off on their clientele. Your girls are wasting their lives, because they are sharing their most intimate body parts, without ever daring to open their hearts nor give up their finest female energies to their lovers. They are missing the God given opportunities to move into the deepest intensities of love that is possible and hence they are missing the blessings from the Divine!"

Drone interrupted Layla by saying: "It is not good for business, when my girls fall in love with their customers!"

Layla: "You don't understand love, because what I meant to say was; If they would allow their sexuality to freely circulate within the feeling center of their being then that acceptance will transform them into higher levels of consciousness! It is a rising, and not a falling!"

Drone: "The scripture says; A man who joins himself with a prostitute becomes one with her in body. But the one who joins himself with the Holy Spirit is one with the Lord in spirit, 1 Corinthians 6: 16-17!"

Layla: "Exactly! If we can teach our girls to open up to the Holy Spirit then that will have an effect on their customers!"

Drone: "How?"

Layla: "According to the Law of One, if one is helped all are helped!"

Drone: "How are you going to convince my girls?"

Layla: "I want them to be free human beings, to have an open heart and learn how to be intimate with everything divine on the face of this Earth!"

Drone: "Do you really think they'll go for that?"

Layla: "It is essential for their survival as a human being!"

Drone: "Why is that?"

Layla: "Orgasm is a nutritional state of being. It is like having a little taste of heaven. When we train ourselves to be in a state of perpetual orgasm, then and only then, will we become able to create a Heaven on Earth!"

Drone: "Let me get this straight, you want me to give up our source of income in exchange for their freedom?"

Layla: "No you silly, I want to start a mail-order business, that supplies sexual toys and I want your girls to have some form of residual income, which will enable them to alter their occupation if they desire to do so!"

Drone: "Have you picked a name yet for your business?"

Layla: "Heavenly taste or Celestialmente gusto!"

Drone: "Why did you pick a Brazilian name?"

Layla: "Because Brazilians are juicy people and my intuition tells me that they know how to allow the Holy Spirit to move through their body vehicles!"

Drone was taking it all in and he concluded that Layla might be on to something big. For the next couple of days Layla began to cruise all over the Red-Light district in search for creative ideas. She made an in-depth inquiry about the existing product line of sexual toys. Every afternoon she would invite one of the working girls to his home, and together they analyzed the existing Sex-catalogue business. Layla then listed the selected products and discussed different ways and means of how to give each product a creative twist. The days flew by and after a month of intensive teamwork, Layla had established the groundwork for her new business. During her meetings, Layla would share in detail with the girls about her new spiritual insights, which she had discovered while having sex with Drone 'the Boss man!' The girls were excited about Layla's newly gained spiritual insight and it motivated them to assist Layla with the organization of a class about Tantra & Spiritual sex. The initial layout of her Tantric program was as follows:

1) The rapture of sexual dis-eases
2) Anatomy of the reproductive organs
3) Virility enhancers
4) Mood setters
5) Intimacy skills
6) Sex tools and how to use them
7) Primal release
8) Extended orgasms
9) From sex to super consciousness
10) Practical guide of the Kama Sutra.

The initial class was a success and the word got out that Layla's program was hot and educational. The mail orders for her Sex-catalogue began to flood in, and Layla was being pressured to expand her business. She rented an office space and committed herself to a full-time business adventure. In the beginning, Drone felt left out, but Layla was reminding him every day, that it was her mission to uplift this planet to the vibration of love!

It was not her words, which made him a believer, but more so, her actions, the efforts she made to be together! It was during these special moments, that Layla began to experience extended states of orgasm. Her primal screams were a nuisance to the neighbors, who from time to time called 911! They filed an official complaint, which stated that somebody had gone orgasmic in their next-door apartment. Layla explained to the police officer that it was too hard for her to control a socially inhibited God given right to pleasure herself, which is a protected right under the first amendment of the Constitution of the United States of America; 'Congress shall make no law respecting an establishment of religion, or prohibiting the free exercise thereof; or abridging the freedom of speech, or of the press; or the right of the people peaceably to assemble, and to petition the Government for a redress of grievances.' The police then cited a city code to her, which she had to adhere to as a law-abiding citizen. Drone wondered if this police officer ever had pledged his allegiance to uphold and protect the Constitution of the United States of America. The city code was a joke, because it was in direct violation with the first amendment, but Drone decided to do something about it anyways! He insulated his bedroom with one of the best soundproof materials available on the market, which then enabled Layla to express her inhibited self; Freely! Layla's daily catharsis helped her create new business ideas and she expanded rapidly with a social media following that demanded her full attention. The word was out and the Tantric gatherings earned the name of 'Garden of Eden!' In their hearts, they knew that this was the calling they stood for. The message was; any sexual person should have an understanding of how the basic laws of Creation are mirrored in human thoughts, bodies, emotions and all existing systems. With this knowledge, one learns how to master the antagonistic, yet complementary nature of sexed opposites in humans, nature, institutions, matter, and all expressing systems in this electric Universe. Until sex is presented as a scientific explanation of the natural processes, which are common to every expression of creation in this electric Universe, the youth of our world will continue to suffer the ill effects of their misconceptions regarding sex. The Holy Spirit, which was hosted in Layla's body, informed Drone that there would come a time in his future life, in which he would make himself available as a servant to God's sacred womb awakening temple body. At this time however, Drone was not prepared to take on this gigantic responsibility. Society had not matured yet to the level of a social, political and religious level of tolerance towards its citizens. Drone's work at Zorba continued, and Layla would always find the time to be close at his side. Their mutual affection had grown stronger and they had grown very much in tune with each other's energy. Everything felt balanced, just as their perfected selves would have intended it to be. They were blessed with a deep feeling of love for each other and it was not until that fateful Friday night, when the Moon was in Scorpio, that Drone felt like they had become immortal lovers. It was about 8 o'clock in the evening, when Layla stopped by to hang out with Drone at Zorba. The doorbell rang and Drone peeped through the looking glass and he immediately recognized the smile of Layla's Angelic face. Just as he was about to open the door, a car drove by and Drone heard three shots, Bang…Bang…Bang! The door opened and Layla fell straight into his arms with her blood gushing out of the back of her neck. As the car drove by Drone captured the shooters profile and he recognized him as one of the bouncers from across town. Everything seemed to happen as if in slow motion, and as Drone turned Layla's body over, he felt her life force slipping away. The expression in her face was one of 'joy' as if returning to a better place! Her gentle Soul was able to look Drone into his eyes one more time as if saying: "Don't worry Drone, we shall be together again, because it is our destiny!" Drone's voice was seeking strength and courage to speak:

Drone: "I will find you my beloved, I will find you!"

Everything became quiet around Drone and it was as if the birds had stopped singing. The immense silence was broken by a soft gentle breeze, which caressed the body of his beloved Layla. In the back of his head, he heard the song: "Peace Frog, by the Doors!"

There's blood in the streets it's up to my ankles
Blood in the streets it's up to my knees
Blood in the streets of the town of Chicago
Blood on the rise it's following me
She came....
Just about the break of day
She came, then she drove away
Sunlight in her hair

Suddenly Drone became aware of the presence of an overwhelming feeling of love and he could clearly see a luminous being wrapped around the Soul body of his beloved. Drone felt lighter, and waves of sheer joy began to run through his body vehicle. From within, the apparition of Lord Altazar made an appearance to him.

Altazar: "We know you are stunned, shocked and in pain. Rest assured, Issua Dow will be the guide to reunite you and Layla in a future incarnation!"

Drone knew in that moment that this being of light would always be with him and he would never be truly alone again. How, at times he had struggled on and on with clenched fists and set teeth, seeing and knowing that the light was there; although there seemed to be but one last flickering ray and, at times, it seemed that that last ray had gone, and a shadow was cast in its place. His uncle Danny Steel shoe was standing next to him crying his eyes out. All he could say was:

Danny: "We'll get those bastards Drone, we'll get them!"

A crowd had begun to gather itself around Drone and a voice spoke from the crowd:

Voice: "Satan will not force his own demons out of people. A Kingdom that fights against itself cannot continue. And if Satan is against himself and fights against his own people, then he cannot continue; Mark 3: 23-26."

Voice: "Death comes to everyone because of what one man did. However, the rising from death also happens because of one man. The scripture says, God put all things under his control; 1 Corinthians 15: 21, 27."

Drone looked around to locate where the voice came from, but he did not see anybody. Danny relieved Drone from his duty for that evening and all he wanted to do was to guard the body of his beloved. He escorted her body to the City Morgue, where he watched over her dead remains like a Rothweiler on lethal LSD. From that moment on, Drone remained at her side until the final moment of her cremation. After the ceremony, Drone was given an urn with Layla's remains, and Danny and Hemp boy drove him to the beach, where he offered her ashes to the ocean. Hemp boy rolled a joint and added some of Layla's ashes. He asked the ocean to take her heart back to Bora Bora and God was asked to welcome her spirit body! Feelings of love despair and rage were all part of his grieving process. Drone did not know whether to forgive or seek revenge and it confused him. His uncle Danny knew what to do and he was determined to go for the kill. He left them by saying: surrender your wrath to God.

Danny: "We've got to take care of business Drone, and I'll pick you up next week!"

Hemp boy and Drone spend the night on the Beach, and smoked pot until they were stoned immaculate!

Drone: "I've got to go back to school and complete my studies!"

Hemp boy: "Sell your IQ "cleverness" and take an EQ walk on the wild side. Give up your vows to headucation and become one with the wind in the trees, the moon and the stars."

Drone: "Yeah, Social conditioning has stunned the force of life in me!"

Hemp boy: "Five to One babe, No One gets out of here alive; Seek the light my brother!"

Drone: "Any attempt to 'get enlightened' is in fact a resistance to it, and an avoidance of that which always is."

Hemp boy: "God is always giving. The Devil is always taking and feeding into your neediness. For as long as people are needy they will attract the Devil and create their own misery."

Drone: "Did God create the Devil? Do you know man?"

Hemp boy: "The God quality arises, when you vacate the time and space of other people, who are a reflection of your needy self. The acceptance of life as 'suchness' creates a pregnant vacancy, a fullness filled with emptiness. You become a host to a loving God energy. When your own pure heart opens up the core of your being, then you will come to know your beloved, the lover of lovers, who is silently waiting there for your coming home!"

Time stood still and Drone was filled with grief! The sound of the waves breaking on the beach took them into other dimensions and together they reminisced throughout the night.

It was a cold and gloomy day when Danny came to pick up Drone. All he said was:

Danny: "It's payback time! Are you ready?"

Drone: "What did you find out?"

Danny: "I'll tell you when we get there!"

Danny drove to the other side of town, and parked his car around the corner of a club called: 'The Stallion!' They both knew that the bouncer who worked there was one of the drive-by shooters at Zorba, and Danny said: "Their shift ends at five!"

Danny handed Drone two bottles of pepper spray, and said nothing. It was about a quarter after five a.m., when three men came walking into their direction. Two of them were instantly recognized as being the bouncers of the joint. The third person appeared to be a friend and Danny anticipated on the possibility that he would probably help out his friends. Drone did not hesitate for a second and he walked up to them and emptied his pepper spray! Their vision was now impaired and Drone delivered his devastating low kicks. One by one, he brought them down to their knees. The guy whom he recognized as the drive by shooter appeared to be a tough cookie, because he refused to go down on his knees. Danny stepped in with a Stanley knife and began to slice the Achilles tendons of his opponent. This brought him down to his knees, which triggered Danny into becoming like a raging bull. He continued to slash his opponent with superficial skin-deep cuts and the scene became a bloody mess. Drone stepped in to stop Danny from finishing off his opponent, before he was no longer able to speak to them.

Drone: "Stop Danny, he still has to give us the information we need!"

Danny stopped and grabbed the guy by the balls.

Danny: "Who was with you? Who paid you to kill his girl?"

Danny squeezed harder and the Choirboy now revealed the name: 'Dado', who is a well-known drug Lord from the Red Lights. They left the guy to bleed and were on their way to find Dado! Dado's office was in a back street alley and heavily guarded by sinister looking dudes. They seemed to be expecting Drone; as news travels fast in the Red-Light district. Danny tried to reason with them and said:

Danny: "Look you guys, we only came to get even with your boss and we have no business with you!"

He did not seem to impress them a bit and a big goon walked up to Danny, who remained dead calm as usual and said:

Goon: "Shorty your mouth is just about at the right height for my Dildo!"

Danny replied: "Well son, do you go to church?"

Goon: "Why?"

Danny: "Because they always have a need for new choir boys!"

Danny grabbed him viciously by his gonads and the big guy extended above and beyond the weight bearing capacity of his toes, as if prepping himself for a ballet lesson. His distress call sounded like one of those extended versions of a whale song! Danny threw the guy against the wall and said:

Danny: "Nephew, put in your teeth protectors and let's turn this place into a church choir!"

They had to finish this fast, because Dado could get away while they were kept busy!

Dado must have felt over confident about his men, because he never tried to escape. When they finally got to him, he was sitting at ease in his recliner and acted surprised!

Dado: "How are you boys doing?"

Danny: "Get up and let's go Dado!"

They escorted him out the back door and Danny jump-started a car parked in the back alley.

Drone: "Where are we taking him?"

Danny: "To the Docks!"

The Docks was a sinister place, where the misfits and rejects from society had created their own tribal laws. Extreme places had been popping up like mushrooms, which thrive on the darkness of lost souls. There was S & M joints, Vampire gatherings, Nazi clubhouses, satanic churches and the leather Boy and Girl's clubs. Danny's choice fell on the leather Boy's clubhouse named: 'Billy Boy!' Drone rang the doorbell and a humongous bouncer nicknamed 'Moby Dick' opened the door. He seemed to recognize them from across town, because he said:

Moby Dick: "You guys are the Zorba dudes, Hugh?"

Danny: "Yes, that's who we are!"

Moby Dick: "Are you here for a lube job?"

Danny: "The works!"

The bouncer let them in and they cruised straight on through to the dark room, where Dado was delivered to a sick looking gang of thirty humongous Gay leather boys. They were doing their fist fucking thing and the room gradually silenced as they began to notice Dado's presence. Danny broke the spell by saying: "This ass is for you! Do not disappoint us and leave some of his ass for us. We'll be waiting at the bar!"

The dudes looked like a hungry pack of hyena's waiting for a bone to pick. Their gestures were obnoxious, but under the given circumstances, Danny did not feel offended.

Danny: "You don't have to use a rubber on this one, because he deserves whatever it is that you've got!"

They removed themselves from the agonizing scene and returned to the bar, where Drone ordered a Calvados to sooth his distressed body. Danny was smiling and by the looks of it, one could never tell just what was going on inside of his head. Therefore, it happened that this huge leather boy noticed Danny's smile and interpreted it as an invitation to intimacy. He walked over to Danny and said:

Leather Boy: "Your mouth is just about at the right height for my Moby Dick!"

Danny without changing the grimace on his face grabbed him by the gonads and locked on like a vise grip.

Danny: 'We are not going to hurt each other, are we?"

Leather Boy: "I thought you were hitting on me man!"

Danny: "When I hit on you, you go down my man! Next time pick one of your own kind!"

Leather Boy: "Whatever man just let me go!"

Danny loosened his grip and the dude walked away. In the background, they could hear Dado scream like a pig on a troubled farm and Drone began to relax. It took the boys a couple of hours to enjoy their gift and they left Dado for wasted. This was only the beginning of Drone's payback time. He felt like he was on a Geronimo warpath, and he was to take this all the way to the gates of Hell. They dragged Dado back to their car and locked him in the trunk. Danny took the wheel and drove to the countryside, where he seemed to know a good place to finish off the job. After an hour or so, they came across an abandoned old windmill. The huge propellers were catching high winds and the sound was pretty impressive. They dragged Dado inside the mill and threw a rope over the support studs. Dado was told to get naked, but he refused and cursed at them with words, which Drone had never heard the likes off! They threw him to the floor, tied the rope around his ankles and hung him upside down. Danny grabbed his Stanley knife and stripped-down Dado's clothing until he was bear naked!

Danny: "Grab the boom box and my bongos Drone, because we are going to throw ourselves a little African party!"

Drone walked out to the car to get the boom box and Danny's bongos. This was a ceremonial thing and it was Danny's way to help him move through the entrapped rage, which he had held suppressed within! Instead of Dado, they could have chosen a punching bag, but at the time, Drone was not that evolved yet. Years later, he would come to realize, that if he had given Dado his compassion, he could not have endured his pain. At this time, however he was not able to picture the whole enchilada of his spiritual quest. According to God everything is in divine order, but Drone could not perceive, that the divine would pan itself out in due time. Danny duck-taped Dado's mouth and smothered his filthy speech. The rhythm of Drone's African drumming tape motivated Danny to play his bongos. Danny first snorted a line of coke on the surface of his drum and then he picked up the beat from the Capoeira tape. Capoeira is the Brazilian art form of African dance, which over time had evolved into a martial art. Many of the moves Drone had picked up at the 'Bahia

Mia' dance club, and the rest he improvised with what he'd learned from the other styles. The beat of the music was hypnotizing and his body was getting into the swing of things. Drone began to loosen up and as soon as he broke a sweat, a jungle spirit took possession over his body vehicle. The energy dance of his body became ferocious and Drone began to fall from grace. Danny sniffed another line of coke to numb out his civilized inhibited self and sank deeper into a state of trance. Flashbacks appeared, which reflected the times when Layla and Drone were doing the Lambada dance and every picture seemed to trigger him deeper into the ferocious revenge of painful feelings. His flying roundhouse kicks were now landing with full impact on Dado's body, but he never confessed anything. When Drone came back to his senses he noticed that blood, sweat and tears were running over the skin of his body. Danny was still drumming and Drone could not tell if he was in a state of trance or high as a kite. From exhaustion, Drone fell down to the floor and waited until the drumming stopped. Danny hugged Drone and they both cried their hearts out! Danny cut the rope of Dado's remains and together they dragged his body outside. To their surprise, Dado was still alive and Danny kicked him in the face. Danny went back inside the building and he turned on the brakes of the windmill. The speed of its wings began to slow down and finally they came to a halt with a squeaking noise. There was a moment of silence, then the sound of a compressor kicked in, and Danny returned to the scene with a nail-gun in his hands. Together they tied Dado's body to the wing of the windmill, and Danny finished the job by nailing his hands and feet.

Danny: "Looks like Jesus Christ, doesn't he?"

Drone: "Are we done now?"

Danny: "Not yet!"

Danny squatted down and began to prepare a heroine fix.

Drone: "Are you taking that shit?"

Danny: "This one is for Dado!"

Danny injected the needle into Dado's neck, and he immediately responded with a primal scream, while trying to fight off the heroin shot. Finally, Dado surrendered to the invasion of bliss, and he opened his eyes to a sky, which was now glowing with a deep pink-purple radiance.

Drone: "Are we done now?"

Danny: "Yes, we're done, just go inside and release the brakes!"

When Drone returned to the scene, Danny was standing there as if in a state of shock. In his right hand, he was holding his Stanley knife and in his left hand, he held the castrated balls of the drug Lord Dado. Danny threw the balls at Dado's body, and together they watched his body going round and around on the wings of the mill. Blood was splattering all over the place! Victory was in their blood and stunned they left the crime scene, as if in a daze. They drove back towards town and did not speak a word. Within himself, Drone began to pray:

Drone: "**Our father who art in heaven, forgive us for our sins. Just as we forgive those, who sinned against us. Do not cause us to be tested, but deliver us from the Evil one. Amen!**"

Drone: "Danny, we need a priest, because I don't want to carry this burden for the rest of my life!"

Danny: "As far as I am concerned, we are even with God!"

Drone: "It's not about getting even Danny! It is about the acknowledgement of having remorse and the opportunity to start with a clean slate!"

Danny: "If it makes you feel any better, I know this old Catholic church right on the beach of Noordwijk aan Zee!"

Drone: "Just take me there!"

It took them about an hour and a half before Danny found his freaking church. They walked straight into the church and found themselves a priest, who seemed to be disturbed by their bloody appearance. He instantly fell down to his knees and began to pray to his God. Drone begged him to stop and informed him that he was in need of his services.

Priest: "What do you want from me?"

Drone: "Well we did something really bad and we want to confess our wrongdoing to you!"

Priest: "I do not have the powers to forgive you, but he does!"

The priest pointed at the crucified man, who was hanging on the cross and said:

Priest: "His name is Jesus Christ, and he died for our sins!"

Danny: "Correct me if I am wrong, but didn't 'We the people' nailed him to the cross, because 'We the people' did not have the courage to stand up and acknowledge him as the Son of God!"

Priest: "Yes, he died for our sins!"

The priest gestured them to get down on their knees and pray. The moment Drone closed his eyes he began to see visions of himself being crucified on the cross. As Drone looked down from the cross, he could see Layla approaching, gracefully as if in slow motion. She climbed up the ladder and wrapped her naked body around his tortured flesh. Everything started to spin around and inside of his head and it felt like the wings of a windmill were moving him. In the eye of his spinning world, a massive column of light made its appearance and Drone passed out. It was a pain in his face, which brought him back to his senses. As Drone opened his eyes, he saw Danny slapping him in the face. Danny helped Drone get back on his feet and together they walked out of the church. Drone felt like going for a long walk on the beach, and it seemed that a fresh sea wind would do the both of them good. Little sandy trails guided them through the dunes towards a humongous building in the middle of nowhere. As they approached the building, Danny read a sign: 'Humaniversity', and he interpreted it as a place for humanitarians. They both looked at each other and said: "You look like shit dude and you need a shower!" The main entrance was open and they walked straight towards a receptionist at the front desk. She giggled when Danny asked her:

Danny: "What would you charge us if we took a shower at your place?"

Receptionist: "It's not a standard procedure to allow outsiders take a shower at our Institute, but for the two of you I will make an exception to the rule!"

Drone: "We appreciate that! By the way, what is this place all about?"

Receptionist: "I'll explain everything as soon as you guys are all cleaned up and fresh!"

Drone: "What's your name?"

Receptionist: "Luna, now let me call somebody to escort you to your showers!"

Within two minutes a young girl showed up, who introduced herself as Inga!

Inga: "My name is Inga and I will escort you to your showers!"

Danny and Drone followed her to the showers, where they were instructed to undress themselves. Inga kept looking at Drone, upon which he asked her:

Drone: "Would it be too much asked, if you gave us some privacy?"

Inga: "My instructions are clear, and I'm not to take my eyes of the both you until you've had your physical exam!"

Danny did not have the slightest idea, what she was talking about, and Drone was just about to pick her brain, when a wild bunch of naked people jumped into the showers and joined them.

Danny: "What is going on Inga?"

Inga: "This is the Tourist program and if you are interested, you can request for an intake interview!"

Danny: "We'll talk about that after our shower!"

When they were finished taking a shower, Inga then escorted them to the coffee shop, where they sat down with Luna and Isabelle. They explained to them, that the Humaniversity is a therapeutic community with a mission. People that come here can experience the unseen role of denial. It is a place where one can move through the deepest fears and discover the 'Who am I!' under the guidance of excellent trained therapists. As the name Humaniversity suggests, it is a human University, which is concerned with enriching and fulfilling each individual's potential as an authentic human being. Then, in the course of working with other people, one can confidently, responsibly and excellently assist others in doing the same. The Humaniversity calls itself a School for Masters, in the sense that it teaches people to become masters of their life - masters in the Art of Being Human. The entry to the Humaniversity is determined by your willingness and commitment to learn about yourself. The Humaniversity is interested in developing, integrating, realizing and accepting the totality of your intelligence as a human being - your mental, physical, emotional and spiritual intelligence; then you can be, truly and fully, who you are and enjoy being that which you are. What you learn will be first - hand, direct knowledge about yourself and others around you. This knowledge will come from personal experience resulting from circumstances specifically set up to create that experience. Your principal frame of reference will not be books, but your own living experiment. The Humaniversity is concerned primarily with the artistic approach - The Art of Being Human. It is concerned with the deepest level of understanding of the human psyche through personal exploration and subjective experience. While it readily embraces all the value and benefits of the scientific approach, the wealth of such knowledge can be fully realized only if the psychologist proceeds from the wisdom of his own personal experience and insight. The Humaniversity is an independent organization, free of any educational or policy influence by state, church or business interests. It has always operated without government or commercial subsidy of any kind, and in that sense, it is able to operate clearly without any Social, Political or Religious conditioning. It also encourages a sense of personal freedom; it welcomes students of all nationalities, cultures, spiritual traditions, academic backgrounds and scholastic ability. The Humaniversity's work is responsive to real human needs and is focused on solutions for the future. The cost of the Program is €1500. US Euros for every two weeks, which includes food and lodging, and which is variable according to the attendance of additional 'guest' programs. Since Drone had plenty of money in the bank and nobody to go back to, he decided to sign up.

Drone: "I'm intrigued and I have nothing left to lose, so I want to sign up!"

Danny: "Are you out of your Mind! This might be one of those cult things!"

Drone: "I've got to do some Soul-searching man!"

Danny: "Well I am not staying; I'm going back to Amsterdam!"

Drone: "Are you sure, and will you be able to manage Zorba in my absence?"

Danny: "I'll take care of it my friend!"

They hugged each other goodbye not knowing when they would see each other again!

When the Music's over: by the Doors

When the music's over
When the music's over here
When the music's over
Turn out the lights
Turn out the lights
Turn out the lights

When the music's over
When the music's over
When the music's over
Turn out the lights
Turn out the lights
Turn out the lights

For the music is your special friend
Dance on fire as it intends
Music is your only friend
Until the end
Until the end
Until the end

Cancel my subscription to the resurrection
Send my credentials to the house of detention
I got some friends inside

The face in the mirror won't stop
The girl in the window won't drop
A feast of friends alive she cried
Waiting for me outside

Before I sink into the big sleep
I want to hear
I want to hear
The scream of the butterfly
Come back, baby
Back into my arms

We're getting tired of hanging' around
Waiting around
With our heads to the ground

I hear a very gentle sound
Very near
Yet very far
Very soft
Yet very clear

Come today
Come today

What have they done to the Earth?
What have they done to our fair sister?

Ravaged and plundered
And ripped her
And bit her

Stuck her with knives
In the side of the dawn
And tied her with fences
And dragged her down

I hear a very gentle sound
With your ear down to the ground
We want the world and we want it,
We want the world and we want it, now
Now? NOW!

Persian night! Babe
See the light! Babe
Save us!
Jesus!
Save us!

So, when the music's over
When the music's over, yeah
When the music's over
Turn out the light
Turn out the light

For the music is your special friend
Dance on fire as it intends
Music is your only friend
Until the end
Until the end
Until the end

So, when the music's over

Chapter Five ~
Roadhouse Blues

God has been waiting for you to change. But you think nothing of his kindness. Perhaps you do not understand that God is kind to you so that you will change your hearts and lives.

Romans 2:4.

Unless you change and become like little children, you will never enter the kingdom of heaven.

Matthew 18:3.

I the Lord do not change.

Malachi 3:6.

Know God and his ways. God's will is for you to be holy, so stay away from all sexual sin. Then each of you will control his own body and live in holiness and honor not in lustful passion.

1-Thessalonian 4: 3-5

*I*sabelle: "The founder and president of the Humaniversity is named 'Veeresh', who was born and raised in New York (1938). He became famous for his work in the European growth movement, and he earned a reputation for strong, searching confrontation. Veeresh has created many techniques and structures, such as Flushing (a combination of Primal, Free Association and Tantra), the Pressure Cooker (an intense form of Encounter that takes the participants through the four basic emotions i.e. pain, anger, fear, sadness), three day Socio Structures (interactive role playing within a community setting), Experimental Seminars (wherein the audience is guided into an experience of the subject discussed), and the Multi- Symptomatic Approach (having people with different symptoms, such as alcoholics, junkies, bulimics, healthy neurotics and spiritual seekers all in the same basic program). He is the founder of the Osho Free-State Network, a worldwide network of people living from the heart. He is a creative and innovative teacher, whose work is beyond therapy. He is a successful painter, a poet, and an Executive Music Producer. Veeresh runs the show with his well-trained and supportive staff. Before one is accepted into the Tourist program, one has to be tested for Aids and other Venereal diseases."

Drone; "Let's do it!"

Drone submitted himself to a thorough physical exam, and he was checked for lice and dis-eases, a procedure, which because of the intrusion of privacy could be considered therapeutic! The A.I.D.S.-test results were all negative and that made Drone feel good about himself. That same day he had to go to a local Bank and withdraw a couple thousand euros, which then would enable him to enroll into the Tourist program! Drone did not know what he was getting himself into, but the people were nice and this place invoked a magical 'Yes feeling!' inside of his Soul. Drone's medical checkup was clean and Inga escorted him to his team leader Maya, who introduced Drone to his tribal family of twelve members. They were all given a nickname and Drone was nicknamed 'Coconut'! The meaning of his name was obvious: 'Hard on the outside with a tropical surprise on the inside!" There was a total of six participating tribes within the Tourist program and from time to time, they would all inter-mingle and function as one group. The groups were to be guided and challenged by their team leaders and the Grand opening statement was: "Who does not do what we ask them to do?"

Naturally, there is always the underdog, who does not understand the simplicity of a challenge! The hook is: 'What 'mumbo jumbo' do you identify with as a person?' As soon as the underdogs raised their arms, and questioned the 'Why', they then were asked to leave the program. Apparently, the participants were not allowed to ask questions, but instead they were expected to do what they were told to do! The therapeutic container was set, and it was not one, in which Drone felt safe! There were quite a few German therapists, who because of their cultural indoctrinated denials had to push other people's **first chakra** buttons. Unexpectedly, they would be right up in your face and scream their guts out, but Drone was a fast learner and he took their intimidations with a grain of salt. The Tourist program began at six a.m. with the Dynamic meditation as developed by the enlightened master: 'Osho'. Dynamic meditation is a contradiction in itself, because it demands much effort, and meditation means silence, no effort, no activity. You can call it a dialectical meditation that consists of five stages. First stage; ten minutes of breathing rapidly in and out through the nose and with a full focus on the exhalation! The breath should move deeply into the lungs, and the chest expands with each inhalation. Be as fast as you can in your breathing, making sure breathing stays deep. Do this as totally as you possibly can, and without tightening up your body, make sure neck and shoulders stay relaxed. Continue on until you literally become the breathing, allowing breath to be chaotic i.e. not in a steady, predictable way. Once your energy is moving, it will begin to move your body. Allow these body movements to be there, use them to help building up even more energy. Moving your arms and body in a natural way will help your energy to rise. Feel your energy building up; do not let go during the first stage and never slow down. Second stage; Follow your body. Give your body freedom to express whatever is there… Explode! Let your body take over. Let go of everything that needs to be thrown out. Go totally mad…Sing, scream, laugh, shout, cry, jump, shake, dance, kick, and throw yourself around. Hold nothing back; keep your whole body moving. A little acting often helps to get you started. Never allow your Mind to interfere with what is happening. Remember to be total with your body! Third stage; Leaving your shoulders and neck relaxed, raise both arms as high as you can without locking the elbows. With raised arms, jump up and down shouting the mantra: Hoo, Hoo, Hoo… as deeply as possible, coming from the bottom of your belly. Each time you land on the flats of your feet and making sure heels touch the ground, let the sound hammer deep into the sex center. Give all you have, exhaust yourself completely! Fourth stage; Stop! Freeze where you are in whatever position you find yourself. Do not arrange the body in any way. A cough, a movement, anything will dissipate the energy flow and the effort will be lost. Be a witness to everything that is happening to you. The fifth stage; Celebrate…with music and dance, express whatsoever is there. Carry your aliveness with you throughout the day. At seven o'clock in the morning, Drone was feeling invigorated and ready to face the day. Being sweaty and all, Drone jumped into the showers, where he was being surprised again by the all-embracing nudity of his fellow Tourists. What a shocker it is to get to know one another bear naked. After the shower, it was time for breakfast, during which every group was being subdivided into smaller groups. The house needed to be cleaned and it was to be experienced as a working meditation. The cleaning session lasted for about an hour, during which everybody was informed to move on to the Ping Pong room. This was a larger room that could contain groups of at least 100 people. Everybody was given a blindfold and instructed to get naked. 'Oops', Drone thought to himself, but he did it anyways. Butt naked he was standing in a large room filled with naked people, who in appearance were total strangers to him! Thank the Lord for the creation of blindfolds! The next command Drone heard was: 'Walk around and meet each other'! Touch each other and allow yourself to be intimate with the divine! Don't hold back!' Drone reached out from within his comfort zone and he could feel breasts, butts, hands, chests, breasts, pubic hair, vortices and etc.… The following command was: ' Hug each other and continue to change partners!' The energy in the room now became increasingly 'juicy' and before Drone knew what was happening, he felt this hellacious lip lock around the sensors of his vortex. He peeped down from under his blindfold and thanked the Lord again for sending a woman, who knew how to give a hellacious fellatio. The free expression of sexual energy was allowed to be experienced and it sounded like everybody was having a good time. After thirty minutes or so, the group was commanded to stop and witness the energy stirred within their bodies. The whole group began to meditate on their inner turmoil and to Drone it felt like this silence would last forever. Finally, the spell of silence was broken with yet another command: "Take off your blindfolds and hug each other!" Drone looked around and he saw strangers reaching out to him as if to pull him into their naked discomfort zone! The team leaders now moved themselves onto the podium, and one of them was trying to get every person's attention by blasting a primal scream into a wide-open microphone.

Team leader: "Your next challenge will be to get here on stage 'Butt… Naked!'

Have the courage to express yourself freely about your deepest pains, fears, rage and sadness. When you take this microphone, you must speak your truth and only the truth will set you free! Do not be tempted to lie, because we will feel it and you will then be asked to step down and pack up your gear and leave!"

On the inside, Drone felt scared shitless, but the urge to express his real authentic self became unbearable, and he stepped forward and grabbed the mike! Drone was sweating, because he was about to unlock doors, which he had never opened before!

Drone: " Ugh…. Hello…! My name is 'Coconut' and I'm scared shitless to stand here in front of you all, and moon shining my private self!"

Crowd: "Hello coconut what's hanging?"

Coconut: "Well, I would like to talk about my beloved Soul mate Layla who recently passed on to the other side!"

Crowd: "Silenced"

Coconut: "She used to make me laugh, but now I can only cry! I do not feel self-pity, but I feel stunned and confused by the reality of her death! She was a junky when I met her, but somehow she pulled herself out of it, and welcomed the light. Layla carried herself like a goddess and she kept telling me that our Souls are immortal! Just before she died, she told me that we would be together again because it was written in our destiny! I want to believe her, because otherwise I think, I would fall apart. I had a lucid vision in which I was told, that it would take me eighteen years to find her again, and I am looking for her. I love her with all of my heart and I feel that, except for this journey, I have lost everything worth living for! My heart is broken, but my hope to find her gives me the strength to make the journey."

Drone paused and noticed that there was a piercing silence in the room. He looked up and around at a large teary-eyed naked crowd, who all seemed to be affected by the sadness of his speech!

Coconut: "Well I guess that's all I have to say about that!"

Team leader: "How do you feel now Coconut?"

Drone scanned his body for an honest answer and said: "Pain!" The Team leader then asked the group: "Do you feel his pain? It is your pain!" Silence!

Team leader: "I want everybody to put on their blindfolds and walk around!"

After a minute or so the therapist instructed again: "Stop and grab a partner!"

Drone's hands were reaching out and carefully explored the space around him. With his fingertips, he touched the soft skin of a woman's breast. The woman giggled and said: "My name is Sarah!"

Team leader: "I want everybody to sit down, embrace each other intimately and rest your heads onto each other's shoulders!"

Sarah was not timid at all and she wrapped her legs around Drone. Their bodies bonded but within his spirit Drone had visions of Layla being wrapped around him and it triggered his libido. The hardness of his erected vortex excited Sarah, and before Drone realized what was happening, she had merged her vortex with his. Sarah slowly began to move her pelvic area back and forth and they both now began to enjoy their intimate union. Her pelvic thrusts grew stronger and her breathing pattern began to deepen. With each exhale she expressed a moan of pleasure, a sound which gradually would change into the purr of a pussycat. This Feline definitely had a wild streak, and she was eager to come out for a taste of her freedom! Her inhibitions were on the loose and it was up to Drone to enjoy the ride! His joy ride was not to last for too long, because the Team leader interrupted them again by saying: "I want you to hug tighter and scream with all of you might the following words: '**I feel your Pain!**'"

Drone's state of sexual arousal was now seriously being disturbed by the distracting noise of one hundred people screaming: "**I feel your**

Pain!" The word pain had the effect of a hook digging deep into the walls of his defended self. His body began to vomit out the emotional toxins of his past traumas. Old girlfriends, friends, parents, feelings of pain, anger, fear, sadness were being projected out of his body. Psychically he could feel Layla's body embrace his pain. She was reaching out to him from the other side of no return. In effect, she was absorbing his pain like a sponge, and his tears were flowing abundantly. Her eyes were filled with happiness, and her heart was overflowing with compassion. Layla's reflection was dancing on the retina screen of Drone's inner eye and all he wanted to do, was to dance with her. Thirty minutes must have passed when a gentle hand touched his shoulder and a soft-spoken voice whispered to him: "stop screaming!" Sarah and Drone's bodies were perspiring profusely. With his lips he sucked the salty taste of sweat from her shoulders and Drone began to cry: "Mamma, mamma, where are you?"

Sarah's body was contracting and convulsing, and she began to cry: "Daddy, daddy, where are you?" Their bodies entered a stage of catharsis, and they surrendered to a primal scream coming from within. Wave after wave of suppressed emotional distress forced them to face their traumatized selves. The Force was too strong and it took control over their emotional bodies. Like a giant tropical storm, it flushed out the emotional charge of not accepting who one really is.

When the catharsis finally subsided, they lifted up each other's blindfold and were captured by the vulnerability in their eyes. Drone began to rock her body as if she was back in the cradle. Sarah continued to cry: "Daddy, daddy, daddy, where are you?" People were getting up and moving towards the showers. Life was returning to his vortex again and Drone reconnected one more time with Sarah, who guided him back to her most intimate zone. Through the speaker phones they were now being informed that this session was to be referred to as 'flushing' and everybody was to participate in it three times a day. Sarah asked Drone: "Do you think we will survive this three times a day?"

Coconut: "I don't know it may be a little too much!"

Gently they disconnected their vortices from a loving embrace and headed for the showers.

In the showers, Sarah and Drone washed, each other's body, and Sarah felt an inner urge to submit Drone to fellatio after treat. How could he resist? Drone looked around, but nobody seemed to pay any attention to what she was doing! Drone closed his eyes and concentrated on his surging orgasm, and he blasted his load all over Sarah's breasts. For a moment or two, he felt dizzy on his feet and he leaned back against the wall. Sarah laughed and said:

Sarah: "Your name suits you well Coconut, hard on the outside and a tropical surprise on the inside!"

In that moment, Drone felt guilty for having sex with another woman. The damage was done and it left him with feelings of guilt, shame and self-criticism. In the back of his head, he heard Layla's voice looping around:

Layla: "It is okay Drone, the sun shines for everybody, I want you to open up your heart to other people and romance your shadow side. Shed light where there is darkness and be happy!"

Just as quickly as the voice came, it disappeared and Drone got out of the shower and followed his tribe to another house cleaning assignment. The cleaning session took him about an hour, after which we had to put on his jogging suit for a workout on the beach. When he returned from the beach Drone thought he was going to get a break, but nothing of that kind. Instead, he was informed to participate in a session of Martial Arts. The structured program continued and he had to scream his guts out. After lunch, his group was being divided into cleaning shifts, which gave him the necessary quiet time to process his intense experiences. His quiet time did not last for long, because again he was being instructed for yet another 'flushing' session.

Team leader: "Get naked and get down to it! Find a partner and put on your blindfolds!"

Drone sat down with his blindfold on and waited for somebody to approach him. A girl jumped on his naked lap and she said: "My name is 'Yuka' and I am yours for the next thirty minutes!"

Drone touched her with his fingertips, and he observed that she was petite with a fine complexion. Yuka took his fingers and encouraged him to touch her all over. Her move was innocent and she taught Drone how to trust the touch of his fingertips. Drone had a driven curiosity, and she welcomed his touch with a welcoming 'yes'! Yuka's body scent was sweet like Jasmine and she instantly noticed the effect she had on his erotic zone.

Yuka: "Can I touch it?"

Coconut: "Yes, but be gentle!"

Yuka gently touched his shaft with her finger tips and asked him gently:

Yuka: "Would you allow me to sit on you?"

Coconut: "Be my guest Yuka!" In addition, to himself he thought: "Here we go again!"

Yuka lubricated his shaft with her saliva and merged her private self with his extended vortex. Her love opening felt tight, but with her body weight, she was able to stretch and welcome his extended self. Yuka rested for a breather and said: "Coconut you fill up my senses!"

They began to breathe in tune with each other and Yuka now was being aroused by the tingling sensations erupting from her G-spot. Her love juice was flowing and the perpetual drive of Drone's piston created a suctional sound. The joy of their ride was being disturbed again by the instructions from their Team leader who said: "Hug tight and scream I hate you!"

Together they began to scream from the top of the lungs for about twenty minutes or so, and all of that time their vortices remained sealed and delivered. After ten minutes or so, Drone felt a hand on his shoulder and a soft-spoken voice instructed him to stop and witness the inner turmoil! His muscles were spasmodic with uncontrollable contractions and all Drone could do was just to allow it to happen. When he came back to his senses he noticed that something strange had occurred, he felt stuck as if glued together like two dogs doing their wild thing! It seemed that the rocking motion of their bodies had created a vacuum inside her pleasure dome. Yuka tried with all of her might to get up and shake him loose, but Nature's law kept them sealed vacuum. It was an embarrassing moment for the both of them and they needed help! Their Team leader walked up to him laughing and she covered them up with a blanket. Drone had to stand up with Yuka wrapped around him, and together they were escorted to the community Van, which then took them to the Hospital emergency room. The doctor on call seemed to have experience, because he immediately acted with confidence, precision and a steadfast hand. He asked their permission to insert a plastic tube alongside the length of Drone's shaft and into Yuka's vortex. They consented to the procedure and when the tube was in the right position, he then blew on his end to equalize the pressure in Yuka's body cavity. Slowly they were able to disengage from each other under a loud applause of the surrounding nurses. The whole situation was so ridiculous, that it triggered the couple to laugh about them. The E.R. doctor had some words of advice for the two of them, and his points were well taken.

Doctor: "The next time you two love birds try this number again, please stick to the recommended 'two inches' of penetrative depth, as a preventative measure for a repeat fiasco!"

Coconut: "Thank you Doc, we'll take your advice into consideration!"

When Drone returned to the Humaniversity, he was welcomed with a celebration party at the Boozeria. He danced until twelve at which again he was instructed to find a partner to sleep with. Drone had enough sexual experience for one day and he decided to ignore the assignment. At three a.m., he woke up with his vortex erected and embraced by a warm juicy feeling of somebody playing with his private parts. It was dark so he did not recognize, who invaded his privacy!

Coconut: "Who's there?"

Voice: "Inga, we are here to make sure that you follow through with your assignment!"

Coconut: "We?"

Inga: "Yes we! Luna is also here to keep you in line!"

Before he could figure out where Luna was, she whispered in his ear!"

Luna: "Would you like to eat me? Can I sit on your face?"

Drone: "Yes, but you can't claim your squatters right?"

Luna had squatted herself above his face and was waiting patiently for his approval to engage.

The sweet scent of a flower lured him towards her private zone. He reached out and placed his hands on her firm buttocks. Gently he ushered her into the right position and he began to breathe on her swollen lips. The love juice from her hotspot was now dripping straight onto his tongue. Drone extended his tongue and began to French kiss her down under hot swollen lips, which covered her electric spot. A shiver went through her spine and she trembled from the overwhelming sense of pleasure. As he was kissing her lips, she then repositioned herself and leaned forwards to French kiss Inga. With his tongue, he followed her crevice until he reached her little rose bud. Luna giggled, but it was soon to be replaced by a deepening of her breathing as he slid his tongue back and forth through the trench of her vortex. The tension of their electrical excitement was rising and it accelerated their drift of passion. Their sexual desires were now burning and exploding like a wildfire. They all climaxed and erupted at the same time! Flashes of Layla made Drone feel guilty again, and he felt ashamed for his betrayal. Slowly he drifted away into the Dreamtime, where he was hoping to find her. Her energy body became more visible to his inner eye and she spoke to him with wisdom.

Layla: "Nature is for freedom, not for any kind of bondage. A Mind that can be jealous cannot be giving; a Heart that loves cannot be deceitful. Your joy, your happiness is my happiness. You enjoy, because I know whenever you come back, enjoying a fresh love will make you fresh also. A fresh love will bring fresh youth to you. I will be waiting as a friend eager to know and share all of your adventures. Only love is, only love is, only love is!"

A constricting sensation around the sensors of his erected shaft brought him back into the here now. Inga and Luna had changed places and Luna had inserted his erected vortex into her well-lubricated rose bud. Her vortex was facing him as she was doing her aerobic exercise. Inga had repositioned her electric spot right above his face and he reached out to suck on her labia. She enjoyed his special treat and leaned forwards to submit Luna to the same cunnilingus teaser! Luna was in a state of ecstasy as she slid her rose bud up and down over his erected muscle. She kept moaning: "Only love is, only love is, only love is!" It almost seemed as if she had become a temporary vessel for Layla's divine words. Inga's erotic tongue had brought Luna into a state of convulsive orgasm and Inga quickly arose her body as to get out of the way of Luna's orgasmic contractions. Luna roared a primal scream and released her sexual self with a massive squirting orgasm. Her love juice exploded with an eruptive force, and she sprayed her potion all over Inga and Drone, whom felt like little kids dancing in a mid-summer rain! There was a level of intimacy in between them, which gave them a sense of safety, and together they fell asleep into each other's arms. The scent of Inga's sweet musky vortex was a nice wakeup call at a quarter to six and Drone enjoyed his view of two sleeping beauties at his side. They took a quick shower together and headed for the Ping Pong room, where they were to participate in the dynamic meditation. His body felt exhausted and the thoughts of becoming a 'dropout' began to grow on Drone. It takes the staff an average of three days to break down a person's resistance to change. In addition, Drone noticed within his body, that they were getting under his skin! What kept him going was that he realized that he was not the only one having a rough time. His body was tired and aching and he observed his inner feelings resisting an opportunity for change. The staff was supportive with their feedback, and the individual groups were allowed to recoup during an extended break. One of their favorite pep-talk quotes was: "The only certainty in life is that everything is in a flux of constant change! Adjust, go with the flow and you'll be fine!" At five p.m. Drone's group was scheduled for a sherry hour with Veeresh and his staff. Everybody was given a shot of sherry and an opportunity to exchange their individual feelings about what was going on emotionally! Veeresh would ask the team-leaders: "How are the groups doing!" His staff would fill him in on the progress and he would then counsel the groups on an individual basis. It was fun and juicy to be in the presence of Veeresh and his loving personality reminded Drone of a 'Cheech and Chong' classic! The staff also informed the groups, that the first three days of the Tourist program were considered the toughest, because of the physical catharsis, and readjustment to constant change. From the fourth day on it would go up hill and the group would begin to feel an energy boost, which would help them to move on. After the sherry hour with Veeresh, the groups were to celebrate at the Boozeria until deep into the night. The next morning it was hard to get up, but the dynamic meditation was necessary for everyone! Following the dynamic meditation, the program continued with 'the flushing exercise', and a morning jog on the beach.

Then after lunch 'the flushing exercise' was repeated, and the group naturally unfolded into the: "Fear of Intimacy Course!"

The whole group was instructed to strip down naked and put on a blindfold. The women grouped themselves on one side of the room and the men were gathered on the other side of the room. The specific instructions were: "Start touching yourself and allow yourself to fantasize about your most perfect turn on. Allow you to be touched by yourself and enjoy it. Make love to yourself and with yourself and know that nobody is watching. Do not climax but instead contain your sexual energy until further notice!"

This exercise was a definite turn on for Drone, and he began to imagine himself having sex with Layla. The sexual tension grew intense, and Drone was about to blow off some steam, when he received the next set of instructions.

Voice: "All the men will now be escorted over to the women's section, where they are to perform cunnilingus until all women are satisfied!" His escort matched him with a woman, who waited patiently in spread eagle for his tender approach! The woman grabbed Drone by his ears and pulled his head in between her legs. Her vortex had a sweet scent to it and with his tongue; he gave her the treat of her life. She was a little hot thing and Drone's tongue made her climax in no time. She wanted Drone to stop but he now began to suck on her labia, which then triggered her electric spot repeatedly. She came two more times and her love juice was flowing lavishly! The next instructions were to take off the blindfolds and observe all the females being in a state of orgasmic bliss. The men were now allowed to masturbate while watching the felines laying spread Eagle. This was the hottest experience he had ever witnessed and Drone came in no time. When a woman is in a state of orgasmic bliss and she looks you straight in the eyes, man I tell you, that is an experience you do not want to miss in this lifetime. Yet, Drone felt he was still terrified of a woman's depth of love and the energy that moves as a woman's sexuality and emotions. And, at the same time, Drone wanted nothing more in this life than to merge completely with a woman's devotional love and wild energy.

> Only as a man outgrows his fear can he handle a woman's tremendous love-energy without running. And only such a man is worthy of your devotional offering in a committed intimacy

The lesson Drone learned was: "**Make your love stronger than the denial of it**!"

When one is in a state of bliss, it becomes hard to move. It feels as if one moves in slow motion, and it almost feels like one hover above the ground. Many of the fast movers and shakers among the commoners are escaping a deep feeling of inner bliss. Their thrills have a short life span, and such a moment of release cannot be compared to the Eternal bliss found heaven. Every orgasm is like having a little taste from heaven, but it is with the extended state of orgasm that the instant thrill seekers are left far behind. Drone's group moved towards the showers and a sense of innocence was being shared amongst the group members. After dinner the group participated in one more flushing session and the rest of the evening was celebrated at the Boozeria. The group partied until twelve o'clock and just as Drone wanted to call it a night, his group was instructed to go to the Ping Pong room and get crazy. Imagine a room filled with people, who just surrendered their last sense of inhibitions, what would you do? His group members were given an opportunity to face and act out their internal fear of going insane. Going into this feeling all the way, stirred up a deep-rooted fear of survival. It was hard to give up everything Drone knew about himself, because his 'self' image was based upon the control of primal feelings. However, it is within the great nothing, where all the magic seems to happen. What he needed to learn was not to separate himself from the bigger picture. A thought, which is captured, is in itself never created by a person. Thoughts belong to the Universe and it is only the form of a thought, which is created. Drone believed that there is but One thinker, one feeler, one being, one body, one heart, one sex pulse in this Universe; that his thinking is God's thinking, and that every person's thinking is an extension, through God and his Unified matrix, of every other person's thinking. Drone therefore thinks, that the greater the exaltation and ecstasy of his thinking a feeling, the greater the standards of all man's thinking will be. Each person is thus empowered to uplift all other persons, as each drop of water uplifts the entire ocean. One must not be the part; one must be the whole. The crazy group brought forth primal forces of which Drone had not encountered the likes yet. People all around him were behaving like primal beings, which could only speak but 'gibberish'! All he could do was to laugh at the whole scenario and that somehow moved his energy. Laughter became painful and he became unable to stop this tremendous release of energy, which he thought would be detrimental to his body. The crazy group lasted until six a.m. and it blended in naturally with the kundalini flow of the break of dawn dynamic meditation. After the dynamic meditation, Drone felt wasted, and he was allowed to take a long hot shower, which helped him to get back into his body. The group was given an hour and a half to digest their breakfast and process the newly gained experiences. The most frightening thing for Drone, and probably for anybody, who visits the Humaniversity, is to always be confronted with the fact that: "I am another yourself!" Moreover, if you react to something, you are really reacting to yourself, and that is the frightening thing of it all! It takes a while to realize that every triggered emotion is all, but your projection of it. After breakfast the group was instructed to participate in their next adventure called: "the Slave Market!" The group was split into two divisions; one division was labeled slaves, and the other half was labeled masters. The masters were instructed to buy the slaves from the auction master and the proceeds would then go to the Humaniversity. The masters were allowed to do anything with their slaves within the save container of: "No beatings, no rape, no drugs, no murder etc." The role-play of being a slave was set up so that one could explore the limitations of one's subjective inner self! The therapeutic goal was to learn to transcend the limitations of 'denial' and to allow it to effortlessly unfold itself as the acceptance of such-ness. The role of being a master was set up to explore and allow fantasy to unfold by itself, without hurting self or the other person in doing so. Informed consent of the participants was needed so that everybody could explore and experience 'the great unknown' within the safe container of trust! Drone was selected into the group of masters and as soon as the bidding began, people were being exited. When Inga and Luna appeared on stage, people kept bidding, but Drone had the final say with a bid of $1000. = For the two of them. The girls felt relieved and delighted, that they now belonged to Drone, but his team-leader created a catch 22 for them. Drone was to be handcuffed to both of his female slaves. With one hand cuffed to Inga and the other cuffed to Luna, he felt trapped! The girls seemed to enjoy this type of bonding, because they felt empowered by the freedom of their opposite arm. It dawned on Drone that he had become the slave instead of the master, and that was not a fair deal! Inga and Luna were laughing, because of the unforeseen reversal of role-play and it angered Drone!

Coconut: "Listen, I am your master and I am in control!"

Luna grabbed him by the gonads and said: "We are not going to hurt each other, are we?"

Coconut: "Luna, I want you to kneel down in front of me!"

Luna: "Doggy style boss?"

Coconut: "Yes, and Inga I want you to lubricate both of our vortices!"

Inga kneeled down and said: "Yes boss-man!"

Inga spit her saliva on their vortices and slid her tongue back and forth until they both were well lubed. She then grabbed his shaft, and guided his erected vortex into the welcoming matrix of Luna's body. With every thrust of his stamen, he electrified the sensors of her G-spot. She then responded rhythmically and began to ride his vortex in reverse slow motion, and with every thrust, she would reposition her G-spot back in the line of fire! Inga felt left out and wanted to be included in their circle of pleasure. Drone instructed her to slide her head in between their legs and French kiss Luna's electric spot. Inga grabbed his scrotum and gently held it positioned in a forward stretch. Whenever Drone withdrew, Inga would then pull him back into Luna's vortex. The stretching pull on his scrotum triggered a sensation of pain and pleasure at the same time. With his jackhammer at full throttle, he continued to pump up Luna in doggy style, while Inga was laying spread Eagle in a 69 opposition. Luna now began to French kiss Inga's electric spot and it did not take long before the three of them convulsed simultaneously with a massive orgasm. The scent of musky pheromones triggered the endorphin levels within his brain. It truly felt great to liberate each other with a spirit of celebration. When the scent is right, a woman's body is like a field of wild flowers and that scent just drives a man crazy. United they dissolved and for a couple of seconds they drifted off into a parallel Universe, where all the forces of 'life' seemed to be in a state of bliss. One by one, they returned back into their bodies and moved towards the showers. Playfully and with tender care they washed each other's private zones, which felt just as good as the initial foreplay. Playfully they held their sponges on high and pretended like they were the three Musketeers, who acted out their favorite One liner: "One for All and All for One!" It began to dawn on Drone, that this would include all of their personal bathroom breaks. In order to relieve himself, his 'slaves' had to cross over and humbly wipe his behind and wiggle his vortex. The humiliation of being exposed while taking care of one's personal hygiene directed his level of intimacy to a completely different level of functioning. What topped it off was that Inga and Luna both had started their menstrual period and that would seriously be a testing ground for Drone's level of tolerance. The female hormone levels were fluctuating and they had to pay special attention to their personal hygiene. The sight of blood made him feel sick to the stomach and he did not want to be stigmatized by what he thought at the time to be an impurity of the flesh. Drone lost his appetite for sex, but his slaves did not take his 'no' for an answer, and they continued to seduce him.

Luna: "What if we clean ourselves up with a tampon and you skewer us from behind?"

Coconut: "Please give me a break, let's just hold hands!"

Luna squatted down on her knees and wiggled her rose bud. When Drone looked down he could see her tampon retraction string hang loose from her crevice and his knees got weak. Inga lubricated his vortex abundantly with warm massage oil. Luna begged Drone to make a move and she said: "Do me Coconut, make me a Pina Collada!"

Drone ushered his hardened stamen forwards and gracefully slid his vortex into her welcoming rose bud. Luna was breathing heavily as she was trying to adapt to the stretching sensation of her anal opening. Inga had positioned herself under Luna in a 69 position and she began to tantalize her electric hotspot. His 'slaves' changed their positions frequently and their rose buds were now getting used to the ever-expanding pulse of his droning vortex. The girls became totally engaged into a mutual cunnilingus treat and in the chaos of their excitement, they had twisted his arms into an awkward position. The girls climaxed simultaneously and the rhythmic contraction of Luna's anal muscle had a numbing effect on the sensors of his vortex. It took him some time before he was ready to blast his load into Luna's cavity. The inner feeling of bliss was so overwhelming that it swept away the boundaries of his master ~ slave relationship.

The lesson Drone learned was: **"I allow myself to move into my denials with the intent of discovery!"** Their level of intimacy had deepened to the point where they felt as if functioning as one body. They completed their assignment, and at the end of that week, it felt strange, when his handcuffs were taken off. The program continued and this time Drone had to do a reversal of role-play and he was to be auctioned off as a slave. Luna and Inga bought him back for a $1000. = And they immediately demanded his full and undivided attention to their yearning desires. Their private parts were delicately sanitized and it tasted great to lick the juicy nectar from their velvet vortices again. This week's 'theme' was pornography and all the team members were instructed to dress up and wear sexy clothes. For inspirational purposes, the group members gathered around this big screen television to watch an X-rated video. After an hour or so each team was handed, a camcorder and the groups were instructed to produce their own skin flick movie. The best producer and the best leading actor/actress would be awarded with a night out on the town. Drone continued his master ~ slave relationship and they were able to make a very enticing X-rated bondage flick. Luna and Inga were so in tune with each other's bodies that they were unanimously awarded with being the best leading actresses. The award for being the best producer was to be received by Drone. He was happy and the lesson he learned was: **"The free expression of my being, nurtures the love of my being to grow little by little, every day, moment by moment!"** The three of them felt like they deserved a break away from the intense program they were engaged in. His two girls were thrilled to death by the idea of going out on the town and they expressed their excitement by squeezing Drone playfully in the buttocks. The girls were dressed to kill and Drone loved the bright colors of their seductive short skirts. The restaurant, which the girls had picked out, was a fancy place and they were seated in a private booth. As soon as they sat down Inga began to rub her feet against the insides of Drone's thighs and it was only seconds later, when Luna disappeared under the table. By the looks of pleasure radiating from Inga's face Drone concluded that Luna was giving her a French cunnilingus treat on the lips. The expression on Inga's face intensified and the razor edge signs of pleasure on her face forewarned Drone of her upcoming state of grace. She grabbed her napkin and bit hard to silence the pleasurable sounds of eternal bliss! Finally, she relaxed and the sensual expression of joy-bliss was now shape shifting her face into a state of erotic grace. The waiter came and Drone ordered two Margharitas, one beer and an oyster appetizer. He felt Luna's hands unzip his pants and her tongue and lips were now giving him a hellacious lip lock around the sensors of his bobbing head. She gently massaged his pounding vortex with her tongue and yet at the same time she maintained a firm grip at the base of his shaft. Her tongue was moving round and around the swollen profile of his pulsing vortex and she alternated her moves with a suctional kiss on the tip of his droning stamen. Her hands began to pleasure him with gentle strokes and with her skilled oral techniques, she was able to maintain the pressure on his load down. Inga smiled and Drone closed his eyes and exhaled. Luna kept sucking and Drone could no longer hold back his horses. With a sigh of relief, he blasted his load deep into the oral cavity of Luna, who is a master in the art of deep throat. Inga interrupted his magical moment by telling Luna: "Save some for me girlfriend!" Luna quickly arose herself from under the table and positioned herself next to Inga. Luna stuck out her tongue, which was covered with his milky 'power of life' and Inga leaned over to suck 'the force' from her tongue!

Coconut: "True love starts with a healthy protein shake!"

Luna: " I love this stuff!"

Inga: "You know if people would allow each other to express their fantasies within the safe container of trust, then that would give birth to the long sought after reality of tolerance and truth!"

They continued their lovely meal and when they were finished, they decided to go for a walk on the beach, where they reminisced about the intense experience at the Humaniversity.

Luna asked Drone: "Coconut, would you be interested in becoming a therapist at the Humaniversity?"

Coconut: "What would it take?"

Luna: "It's a four-year commitment to your inner growth!"

Coconut: "I don't think that even Superman is able to complete a program as vigorous as this one. I don't think I have what it takes to make that kind of a commitment, but thanks for the offer anyways!"

Inga: "Coconut you do have it in you, but you just don't realize it!"

Coconut: "I feel really thankful to the both of you for keeping me on the path of love! However, I'm driven by my passion and commitment to find my beloved Layla!"

Luna: "If her love means more than the love we feel for you, then your Layla must be a special lady!"

Coconut: "That she is, that she is, and I hope that you will have the opportunity to meet her some future day!"

Talking about Layla made the sweet memories of her return onto the screen of his visual Mind and Drone got the message to move on. Drone was convinced that it would be a tremendous important healing experience for him if he were to stay at the Humaniversity. However, for now he had to move on. Time is moving faster than his ability to process a past experience, and yet at the same time, Life as such was passing him by like the beating of his heart! On the other hand, time can slow down and ultimately become non-existent, when one makes an effort to truly enjoy and capture the stillness of each moment. The time for an exit interview with Veeresh had arrived, and Drone informed his two female friends, that it was time for him to move on! They took it to heart, because they felt close to Drone, and it is always painful to say goodbye to those we love.

Veeresh did a reality check on Drone's emotional status and then unexpectedly he mentioned the following: "You know Coconut you should check out the origin of the brotherhood of the seven rays!"

He did not say much more about the subject, but it had stirred up Drone's curiosity. They gave each other a goodbye hug and Drone trembled in the embrace of his arms. Veeresh then grabbed him by the shoulders and said: "Coconut, I sense that you are on a mission and I would like to tell you that what you seek is right here and now! But maybe you need to go places where you will find it right here and now!"

Coconut: "When I find my beloved then that will bring me back into the Here Now!"

Neither of them knew, when they would meet again, but it felt good to know that the species called 'Human Being' was not extinct yet! Thank you Veeresh!

Roadhouse Blues by the Doors

Keep your eyes on the road
Your hands upon the wheel
Keep your eyes on the road
Your hands upon the wheel
Yeah, we're goin' to the roadhouse
Gonna have a real good time

Yeah, in back of the roadhouse
They got some bungalows
Yeah, in back of the roadhouse
They got some bungalows
And that's for the people
Who like to go down slow

Let it roll, baby, roll
Let it roll, baby, roll
Let it roll, baby, roll
Let it roll
All night long

Ashen lady
Ashen lady
Give up your vows
Give up your vows

Save our city
Save our city
Right now

Well, I woke up this mornin'
I got myself a beer
Yeah, I woke up this mornin'
I got myself a beer
The future's uncertain
And the end is always near

Let it roll, baby, roll
Let it roll, baby, roll
Let it roll, baby, roll
Let it roll
All night long

Chapter Six ~
Waiting for the Sun of God

Then the angel showed me the river of the water of life.
The river was shining like crystal. It flows from the
throne of God and of the lamb down the middle of the
street of the city. The tree of life was on each side of
the river. It produces fruit 12 times a year, once each
month. The leaves of the tree are for the healing of all
people. Nothing that God judges guilty will be in that
city.

Revelation 22: 1 – 3

If a person believes in me, rivers of living water will flow
from his heart.

John 7 : 38

He who sees me sees the One who sent me. I have come as light into the world. I came so that whoever believes in me would not stay in darkness.

John 12: 44 – 46

So, believe in the light while you still have it. Then you will become sons of light.

John 12: 36

Luna and Inga escorted Drone to the train station of Egmond aan Zee, where they gave each other a long swaying hug goodbye. Their passion was charged with a painful silence. Drone felt insecure and he allowed his 'inner child' to cry. The girls had their eyes closed, but their bodies were trembling, and Drone enjoyed the reflection of their inner beauty. The girls were emanating strong emotions, and Drone finally gave in to the embrace of sweet surrender. The window of his Soul was now wide open and it felt as if God was blowing a gust of freshness through his windowpanes.

Drone: "God it feels so good to be alive and to be loved by two women, who share their heart lavishly!"

Luna and Inga responded to his freshness by grabbing his hands and guiding his fingers into their lingerie.

Luna: "When a woman opens up her heart to a man, it will make her love juice more alkaline and it has a sweeter taste to it!"

Inga took of her panties and the one from Luna and put them playfully into Drones mouth as if pheromone anointing him with their sacred womb juices.

Their vortices were moist like a peach and they were inviting him to stay, but a force greater than the thought of eating their passion fruit was ushering him forwards into the train. Drone turned around, and sucked the juice off his fingers, while with the other hand he waved his friends goodbye. It took Drone two and a half hours to return to the big city of Amsterdam. He was on his guard because Dado's boys could have tipped off the police and he did not want to do jail time yet! His gut feeling was to check up with his friend Hemp boy, and find out what happened to Danny. Hemp boy informed Drone that Danny had gone into hiding and he recommended that Drone should do the same. His apartment was like a safe haven, because Drone had registered himself under a false name and only a few good friends knew the entrance to his place. Drone waited patiently for the night to set in and he used the darkness of the streets to sneak back into his empty apartment called 'home'. Some of Layla's clothes were still hanging over a chair and the rest of her stuff was neatly folded in her closet. Drone opened up a drawer and brought her lingerie to his face. He sniffed her silky lingerie as if scanning for any leftover traces of her bodily scents. Within his memory bank, he was trying to revitalize her image, and he continued to breathe deeper into the scent of her clothes. The memory of his beloved triggered his tears to flow and he had to use her undies as a hanky. Drone walked around and decided to heat up his sauna, because he wanted to sweat out his sadness. Hot and steamy he then jumped into the ice tub to numb off his emotional state of being, and that made him feel better! He put on his Levis and a Hemp- T-shirt with a slogan, which read:

"I didn't inhale my shit,

I didn't ejaculate my shit,

I am the Hemp man!"

Drone called Hemp boy and asked him if he could run by the library and pick up some books about: "The brotherhood of the seven rays!"

Hemp boy: "Sure Be~Jah, need some Chinese food too!"

Drone: "That'll be great!"

They ate together and Drone exchanged in detail, his traumatic experiences from the last couple of weeks. Hemp boy did not comment on Drone's crime of passion, but instead he shared a deep understanding and a lot of dope. Halfway through the night Hemp boy fell asleep and Drone began to read the books from the library. There were seven different books that dealt with the ancient mysteries of South America. The origin of the Brotherhood of the seven rays can be traced back into the ancient times of Lemuria. Lemuria is the name for the last part of the great Pacific continent of Mu. The actual destruction of Mu and its submergence began before 30,000 B.C. This event continued for many thousands of years until the final portion of old Mu known as Lemuria was also submerged in a series of new disasters that were terminated between 10,000 and 12,000 B.C. This occurred just before the destruction of Poseidon, the last remnant of the Atlantic continent, Atlantis. Lord Altazar was one of the great Lemurian sages and the keeper of the Scrolls encrypted in the memory chips of the great Atlantean crystals during the last days of doomed Mu. It was well known to the Masters of Lemuria that a final catastrophe would cause gigantic tidal waves to take the last of their land down into the sea. Those working on the left-brain path continued diabolic experiments and heeded not 'the handwriting on the wall', just as today, on Earth, millions of inhabitants are continuing to 'eat, drink, and be merry', even though the signs of the times are clearly discerned by the true people of the Infinite Father. The Masters and Saints on the right brain path began to collect the precious records and documents from the libraries of Lemuria. Each Master was chosen by the Council of the Great White Hierarchy to go to a different section of the world, where in safety, he could set up a School of the Ancient and Arcane Wisdom. At first, for many thousands of years, these schools were to remain a mystery to the inhabitants of the world; their teachings and meetings were to be secret. Hence, they are called even today 'the Mystery Schools' or the 'Shan-Gri-Las of Earth!' Altazar, as being one of the enlightened teachers of Lemuria, was delegated by the Hierarchy to take the sacred crystals in his possession along with the enormous Golden Disc of the Sun to the mountainous area of a newly formed lake in what is now South America. Here he would guard and sustain the focus of the illumination flame. The Disc of the Sun was kept in the great Temple of Divine Light in Lemuria and its main function was that of a dimensional doorway into the higher Godlike realities. While the final portions of the former continent were breaking up in the Pacific Ocean, terrible catastrophe was taking place all over the Earth. The Andean Range of mountains was being born at this time, and it disfigured the west coast of South America. The ancient city of Tiahuanaco (Bolivia) was at that time a great seaport and a Lemurian Empire colonial city of magnificence and importance to the Motherland. During the ensuing cataclysms, it was raised from sea level and a mild, tropical climate to a high on a barren, wind-swept plain and created a frigid Arctic-like climate. Before this took place, there had been no Lake Titicaca, which is now the highest navigable lake in the world, over twelve thousand feet above sea level. Moreover, it was here, where the Monastery of the Brotherhood of the Seven Rays came into being, organized and perpetuated by Altazar. This Monastery, which was to be the home of the Brotherhood throughout all ages on Earth, was placed in an immense valley that had been created during the days of the birth of the Andes, and was a strange child of Nature in that its exact disposition and altitude gave it a warm, semi-tropical climate where fruits and nuts could grow to phenomenal size. Here, on top of ruins that had once been at sea level, like the City of Tiahuanaco, Altazar had the Monastery constructed of gigantic blocks of stone cut only by the energy of primary light force. The other Masters of Lemuria, the Lost Continent, journeyed to other parts of the world and also set up Mystery Schools, so that mankind would have throughout all time on Earth the secret knowledge hidden away, not lost, but hidden, until the children of Earth had spiritually progressed to study again and to use the Divine Truths. The valley of the Monastery of the Brotherhood of the Seven Rays is located high in the Andes Mountains on the northern, Peruvian side of Lake Titicaca. Each student of the Monastery came into existence on one of the Seven Great Rays of Life, as we all do, and these Rays were to be blended by each student weaving his, or her Ray, as if it were a colored thread, into the tapestry which symbolized the Spiritual Life of the Monastery. Therefore, it was called the Brotherhood of the Seven Rays, also known as the Brotherhood of Illumination! The information was overwhelming to Drone, who by now was stoned immaculate, and he needed a break to process the information. He woke up Hemp boy and told him to get dressed, because they needed to hang loose at Bahia Mia's. They took the Metro down town, where they crossed a couple of streets to get to the designated club. The bouncer knew who Drone was and he let the boys in without hesitation! Inside the club, Hemp boy and Drone went their separate ways and they mingled with a dancing crowd. The Brazilian chicas at this place really love to dance and Drone had no trouble finding a girl to move and groove with. One of the bartenders at Bahia-Mia was an active member of the Santo Daime church, and Drone knew that he always kept a bottle of 'Daime' behind the counter. He charged Drone $25 per cup, who shared it with his dance partner Maria. Daime is like a liquid light bulb, which slowly illuminates the internal dark corners of despair. When his body reached the critical mass of saturation, it then felt like he became like a moth flying into the flame of no return. Little sparkly lights were like fairies dancing all around him. Drone's body was being moved by the rhythm of the Salsa and it felt like the divine was guiding him. His hands were taken from the dancing wheel and he began to leave his body and merged with a Condor flying over the Andes Mountain range. His eyes were scanning the ground below in search for his secret Shan Gri La. The faces of places made their appearance and an Amazon elder introduced himself as: 'Isua Dow!'

Isua Dow: "Welcome my brother! I am awaiting your arrival in the big iron bird! It is here, where I will guide you to dance your way to God. Come, come, and yet again come!"

The vision disappeared with a blinding flash and Drone felt his spirit returning into his dancing body. When he opened his eyes, he noticed that Maria was as high as a kite. She had the stars twinkling in the abyss of her eyes and Drone was drawn into the infinity of her Soul. Her dancing body had a language of its own and Maria led their dance towards a dark corner. She then unzipped his pants and seduced his vortex to stand proud with full erective force. Maria jumped up and latched on to Drone with her legs wrapped around him. She was dressed in a flirtation mini skirt, which barely covered up her naked loins. Gently she now lowered herself over his hardened shaft and his breath was captured by the pleasure arising from his loins. A warm embrace of her private lips welcomed him deeper into the abyss of this Latino feline. The Daime was working like a charm and it kept him hard and going like one of those Dura cell batteries. Maria and Drone were fishtailing their bodies to the rhythm of the Lambada beat and they lost themselves in a never-ending dance of passion. Maria's voluptuous body vehicle climaxed at least three times and her fluids of love were running down her inner thighs. She came time after time, and her vortex kept convulsing, while she dug her teeth deep into the flesh of his shoulders. Maria relaxed and dozed off while maintaining sealed and delivered on top of his lap. The force was with her and Drone let her bath into the divine beauty of it all. As she finally came back to her senses, she seemed to be in another world, and it took Drone quite some time to get her back on her feet. They straightened out their clothes and walked out of the club to gaze at the stars, which were bright that night. Maria sat down on the sidewalk, and Drone went inside to call for a cab to take them home. He said goodbye to Hemp boy, and headed for Maria's place, where he tucked her in bed with a long kiss goodnight. The vision he was given during his trance state invocation was now pushing him forwards to undertake a life changing adventure. It took him three days to get his shit together and Drone notified his immediate family and friends that he was going on a long trip around the world. The plan was to board a freight ship to Turkey and from there to Peru. Drone was still on the run, and he was not aware that Dado's men never did inform the police about his killer's identity! It appears that the rules of the underworld are the same as the laws of nature. The survival of the fittest is ruled by natural selection, and Drone was not yet aware of his newly gained identity of 'Godfather'! He felt torn between the pull of his shadow side and the push forwards to find his beloved Layla. The force was with him and he hitchhiked to the Docks of Rotterdam, where he lobbied for a free-be cruise going from ship to ship. His efforts seemed hopeless, and he finally sat down on a dock to kill time by throwing pebbles in the water. Suddenly he was being pushed from behind and Drone fell into the water. When he surfaced, again he recognized two familiar faces laughing at him: "Danny and Hemp boy!"

Hemp boy: "What are you doing broh?"

Drone: "I'm running from the law you ass holes!"

Danny: "No need to run brother, we are the Boss now!"

Drone: "They never told on us?"

Danny: "No siree!"

Drone: "I'm still going to Peru!"

Hemp boy: "We know broh and we're going with you!"

Drone: "Why? You guys didn't lose anybody!"

Hemp boy: "We know broh, but I had a vision that Danny and I were to keep you on the right path!

Drone: "So where do we go from here?"

Danny: "Back to Amsterdam, because we have the plane tickets and Visas!"

Drone: "How did you do that?"

Danny: "Connections my friend, connections!"

They drove back to Amsterdam and took the train to Schiphol airport, where Drone's mother was waiting for him with warm open arms. It was hard to say goodbye, because Drone loved his mother dearly. She tried to make it easy for him and said: "We can always meet again in our next incarnation!"

They headed for Terminal C: Gate 33 and the custom service let them through, except for Hemp boy! Danny and Drone were sweating it out, but Hemp boy was giggling like he was on Helium or something. There were Drug dogs sniffing out their luggage and they stopped to sniff on Hemp boy's attire. All of his clothes were made from Hemp, but he was smart enough not to smuggle any of 'the real stuff' on board of this airplane. The Custom service strip-searched him, but they had to let him go due to lack of evidence! The men were now allowed to board the big bird and they bought themselves a couple of beers to celebrate their new adventure.. The flight took about sixteen hours and it was the beers that helped them overcome their jet lag. In Lima-Peru, they boarded a connecting flight, which flew them to La Paz, and at this time, Drone was able to see the scenery below. As he looked down at those isolated mountain ranges below, it filled him with feelings of awe, which seeded a deep respect for some being, which was greater than him. A being larger than life had the power to create all of this beauty! At the La Paz

Airport, it took them about two hours to go through the Custom service and gather their luggage at the other end. With the use of a little Spanish, they were then directed to a bus terminal, where they bought their tickets to Lago Titicaca. They had landed on the top of the world and it gave them a sense of power! Lake Titicaca was situated at an altitude of 12,000 feet and it took the bus another 15 hours to arrive at their final point of destination. It was August 21, 1991 when they arrived at Lake Titicaca, where they made camp. That night Drone experienced a lucid dream during which Isua Dow contacted him again, and this time he gave him a more detailed description about the location of the hidden valley.

Isua Dow: "What you seek is an area of magnificent natural beauty, a place of peace and tranquility, where blood has never been shed: a location with abundant, clean, pure water: a nearby rushing stream or river; a place where vegetables and fruits could be grown in soil not contaminated by chemical fertilizers and sprays, but a soil designed with Sacred Geometry; a land of happy, contented people, who are apart from the Outer World, yet in it!"

Isua Dow paused and Drone awaited his continuance!

Isua Dow: "An Amazon woman dressed in Monks clothes by the name of Deneb will contact you! Follow her instructions and do not allow her beauty to distract you from your path!"

The name Deneb flashed back his memory and Drone remembered her as being the Mentor from Layla's lucid dream states. The recognition triggered his inner flame of excitement. A few days later Deneb appeared and she unfolded herself as envisioned in his dream. Her feet treaded lightly as if barely touching the Earth and Drone felt a definite shifting in his aura as she approached the campsite. Deneb waited until she was spoken to.

Drone: "Where do we go from here Star sister?"

Deneb: "To Zion!"

She turned around and began to head for a distant mountain range. It left the three men in awe for a couple of seconds and then they hurried to get their gear together.

Deneb continued her pace and did not seem to have the time or courtesy to wait for the trio! Hemp boy felt 'gay' and he began to sing with the expression of joy in his heart.

Hemp boy: "Marching, marching, marching to Zion. Oh Beautiful, beautiful Zion!"

As for Danny and Drone, they did not want to lose sight of the mysterious lady and they sped up their pace. Together they journeyed many miles to the east over great Andean passes filled with snow, and attacked by howling, bitter winds, which sweep the barren land. The way to their Shan Gri La was over narrow mountain roads, where avalanches and landslides are common threats. They were definitely walking a path on razor's edge, full of hazards and life-threatening physical demands. Deneb walked with a steadfast stride and she seemed to be the only one who was not impressed by altitude or danger. The men were cold, hungry, thirsty and exhausted, but Deneb just kept going and going. Hemp boy finally fell down and he needed a break to gain back some of his lost strength.

Hemp boy: "Sister is there not another way to your heaven?"

Deneb: "There is only one way to reach this valley and this is it!"

After long hours of travel, they arrived at a small village perched high on a fantastic precipice. Above them towered the majestic snow-capped Andes. At the cold village, there was a long delay, while mules were prepared for the descent into the hidden valley, which lay thousands of feet directly below the tiny sky village. All were wrapped in native Quechua woolen ponchos and caps, and finally they began the descent in a cold, steady rain. Gradually the climate and the scenery changed. It was as though one were watching winter fading into summer. The rain stopped…it became warmer, the woolen clothing was soon discarded and shirtsleeves were in order. The snow and ice that had been so evident just a short time before completely disappeared, and Drone felt like he was actually descending into Heaven. This was, indeed, a Shan Gri La, a hidden valley away from the cares of his chaotic planet. Yet, it was a place where a great work could be accomplished in its peaceful atmosphere, where blood has never been shed, and where Quechua-speaking Indians, descendants of the great Inca Sun Empire, live quietly in a semi-tropical paradise. On all sides of the valley, hundreds of beautiful waterfalls dash down great rock walls to bring clear, pure water from the Andean glaciers into the valley. In addition, there was a great and rushing river, a beautiful thing to behold as it wound its way through the entire length of the valley like a shining silver thread. Drone soon learned that practically anything could be grown in the valley. A place where temperate zone products grow side by side with those of the tropical zone! Corn, beans, squash, yucca, peas, beets, carrots, lettuce, cabbage, papayas, mangos, cherimoya, avocados, tomatoes, bananas, lemons, oranges, peaches, apricots, grapes, etc., grow in abundance, and these are only a few of the fruits and vegetables available. It was until later that Drone would find out that only organically grown, natural foods are consumed and which are free from poisons. The planting season is throughout the year and no chemical fertilizers or sprays are used; everything is grown organically and naturally within amazing crop circle designs. The Sacred Geometry and color spectrums of all those fruits and vegetables truly reminded him of the Garden of Eden as described in the Holy Scripture. He knew he had arrived at the center of his Universe, because the world felt more alive here than he had ever imagined it could be. Colors burn and flicker; sounds vibrate like plucked strings, and each breath he drew made him feel a little giddy and light headed as if he was inhaling a purer element.

Hemp boy: "Man, I'm telling you, I'm tripping with serious altitude! This is awesome and it just makes me want to cry to see all this beauty! I could sing a happy song, but I can't find the words!"

Danny: "Too much Hemp on your brain boy?"

Deneb: "I urge you to move on!"

Therefore, they did, they moved on towards what at first sight appeared to be a lucid dream of some kind! The valley was filled with a series of majestic Domes, which seemed to blend in naturally with its breath taken environment. It was here that Deneb uncovered her Monastic garments and all three men were being struck by the finesse of her beauty. There, before him stood a radiant majestic woman, who weighed about 150 pounds of sensational curvaceous female flesh. Her Lagune blue eyes caressed Drone with an all-knowing embrace, and they looked into each other's eyes, for what seemed to be a very long time, as Drone grew increasingly self-conscious. The sunlight, sifting through her long black hair, formed a shimmering halo. Drone was so startled, and mesmerized by her beautiful clarity that he literally forgot to breathe! Those all-knowing, all accepting eyes seemed filled with dancing lights and her skin had a transparency like a million tiny lenses reflecting and magnifying the colors of her personality's life field or aura. The light reflection radiating from the stars in her eyes had a dazzling effect on his inner perception. Her body's curvature began to shape shift according to the erotic polarity of God's blueprint. She took on the features, complexion and curvature of the memory projection of his 'Layla'. It stunned him for that moment, and his Endorphin and Pheromone levels were being triggered by the reflection of his beloved. Drone felt driven to release the sexual tension that had risen, and again Deneb seemed to be one step ahead of his intend to release the rush. The central control system of her Mind was shape shifting repeatedly her body, but this time she transformed into the reflection of Drone's perfected self. Seeing the reflection of his perfected self-shifted his sexual energies back into neutral zone, and Deneb touched his face, smiled and began to speak.

Deneb: "I am another yourself. What you see in me is what you see in yourself. You are vibrating an unbalanced sexed condition, which violently desires to return to the oneness of balance from which you were divided into two. Our sexual pulsation seeks rest and unification within the intimate realm of our opposite vortex partner. Sex is the compression of light pulsation into two opposite pressures, which desire release and expansion from their opposition. What you refer to as sexual sin is nothing else, but the denial of the return to the oneness of balance from which you were divided into two. You are preventing the living light of the Infinite Mind of God from being creatively recycled through your body vehicle. My body vehicle reflects your subconscious desires and projections of sexual polarity and it is my task to neutralize your polarity. Only a sexual neutralized person is able to receive the light from our Cosmic Babe who resides in the Temple of Life."

The three men were now being struck by a gap of awe in which they experienced their learning curve to rise to unbelievable heights.

Hemp boy: "I'm tripping man and I see the light babe!"

Danny: "I have no idea what the heck she is talking about, but she sure is a gorgeous babe!"

Deneb: "What you see in me is nothing but a reflection of the Cosmic Babe!"

Drone: "How do we neutralize our sexual desires?"

Deneb: "The way for the Monk students to neutralize their sexual tension is by allowing oneself to melt with every hug from the opposite vortex partner!"

Drone: "Are you saying, that even when we get sexually aroused we should not act on it?"

Deneb: "Just allow your hugs to dissipate the polarity and you will be fine. All students of life are now allowed to enter the valley and experience the Monastic Way of Life as directed by the Great White Brotherhood otherwise known as the inner circle of discipleship. The students Monastery is separated from the Brotherhood's Temple of Life for reasons of sensory perception. The so-called rules and regulations are followed at the Abbey so that all Students of Life may partake of a great Spiritual unfolding. The Brotherhood does not believe that the following way of life is necessary for salvation, or even that such a routine would be right for all people. Responsibility lies within and cannot be blamed on an external dark force, nor can it be replaced by the Salvation of some external light force! We are all children of the light and we have to grow up and take responsibility for our every decision we make. Truth is always there and it cannot be masked, hidden or deceived. The routine at the Abbey has been developed to bring about certain Spiritual Illumination for advanced Students on the Path of Cosmic Understanding. The Student of Life applying for entry into the Abbey must, first of all, be seeking and serving Truth, and living a clean and upright life.

There are absolutely no restrictions as to age, sex, marital status, race, religious affiliation, nor is the Brotherhood interested in anyone's past history. The important thing is that the individual Student, at the time of application, desires Truth above all else. There is no religion higher than Truth! The student must come to experience the Cosmic Babe Christ, who came in the flesh to mentor the Earth and who has returned to mentor our cosmic valley."

Danny: "Are we still allowed to sin in this valley?"

Deneb: "Sin is the fuel for your salvation! Sin is the driving force behind your quest for paradise. We can have a forgiving attitude even toward those who caused the most painful hurt if we allow Christ's love to flow freely through us. Anything that prevents the 'Living Light' of the

Infinite Christ from being creatively recycled through the body vehicle is a sin. The believer's forgiveness is to be limitless. Failure to forgive will result in God's withholding His forgiveness for our sins.

Hemp boy: "When can we see the Cosmic Babe?"

Deneb: "Watch yourself dreaming, hear yourself screaming, open your heart, and receive the 'Living Light' to shine through your body vehicle!"

Hemp Boy: "Trippin sister, what are you smoking?"

Deneb smiled at Hemp boy, but she did not reply to his comment, instead, she continued with her informative lecture.

Deneb: "The students rise at dawn for their morning lecture from the Cosmic Babe and the rest of the day is being used for work shifts. At sunset, everybody participates in Satsang and Darshan in the presence of the Cosmic Babe, after which the evening is being used for dance and music.

Danny: "What is Satsang and Darshan?"

Deneb: "It is like a baptism, an anointing!"

Hemp boy: "What does Babbletism and Anointing mean?"

Deneb: "It is when you receive the 'Living Light' from the Cosmic Babe to shine through your body vehicle! In addition, to continue my story, at eleven o'clock p.m. everybody returns to his or her quarters for a good night sleep. The entire experience of a Student of Life at the Abbey, the Primary Outer Retreat of the Cosmic Babe, is one of initiation into physical, mental, emotional and spiritual illumination. This initiation consists of; dedication, purification, discipline, instruction, service and work. No one will be saved because they join the Abbey or because they follow the monastic way of life of the Brotherhood. However, the rewards to the individual student in the form of universal lessons learned are great."

Hemp boy: "What do you mean by: No one will be saved?"

Deneb: "Exactly that! Help does not come from the outside; salvation occurs when one receives the 'Living Light' of the Cosmic Babe within the matrix of one's Soul! Even when you surrender to the Christ, that is not a security that you will be saved. It is Yahweh, who chooses who will be saved according to the Predestination teachings. *You will then receive a white stone with your name written on it!*"

Then, without speaking, Deneb touched his hands and gestured the men to their work quarters. They were shown their working robes and a Monk guided them to the fields of fruit and plenty. A group of Monks greeted them silently and one of the Monks instructed the trio what they were to do. It seemed important that they did not create any tension, remained flexible, trusted and allowed their doing to become prayer, without attachment to the outcome. Then they were explained the effects of stress on growth and taste of the crop, which then would affect the person consuming it. The silence in which the Monks work, was at first unbearable, but in due time it began to grow on Drone. He became intensely alive in the work he was doing and Drone did whatever was humanly possible. Repeatedly a Monk would tap him on the shoulder to redirect his raw bursting energy.

Monk: "Don't try to prove your worth and reduce yourself to a commodity. Remember, the greatest experience of life comes not through what you do, but through love, meditation and prayer. Just being ordinary is a miracle. Not thirsting to be somebody is a miracle. Let nature take its course. Allow it. Be like this tree. If you are useful, you will be cut and you will become furniture in somebody's house. If you are beautiful you will be sold in the market, you will become a commodity. Be like this tree, absolutely useless, and then you will grow big and vast, and thousands of people will find shade under you. Move in the world as if you are not. Do not be competitive, do not try to prove your worth, there is no need! Remain useless and enjoy!"

Drone thanked him for the correction and from that moment on, he began to touch the Earth and its vegetation with the joy of love.

Hemp boy: "See, that's why I smoke pot, be a nobody, hug trees and tripping in the wind!"

Drone: "As usual you are right, but you are definitely not ordinary Hemp boy!"

At six p.m., they were to go to the natural hot springs, which sprung from the surrounding mountain slopes. It was to be the daily naked rejuvenation and water baptism. The three men followed a procession of pilgrims approaching the Wells in silence. Their sandaled feet made no noise. One by one, they stooped and drank the water in cupped hands. When each arose, they appeared to glow with an inner radiance, as if refreshed by the water of life itself! Drone cupped his hands, stooped, drank and waited for the blissful effect he witnessed upon the pilgrims faces. His body tingled and it felt like he just drank a cup of liquid light, which was filling him up like the popping rush of a shot of Daime. Hemp boy and Danny appeared to be blissed out and Drone entered a condition of cosmic lucidness. The three of them lay down and allowed the breast of mother Earth to bring them back to their normal selves. A Monk guided the men back to a Dome, where they were to change their clothes into a white robe for the Satsang or meeting with the 'Cosmic Babe' and the White Brotherhood. There was a long line waiting in the direction towards the Temple of Life and Drone joined in anxiously and filled with explosive expectancy.

Female Monk: "This temple is a place where the remembrance of God is kindled, at least for a short while.

Hemp boy: "I am tripping lady!"

Female Monk: "We should try to keep our minds on God throughout the day, having a fixed time for mantra voice resonance meditation."

Drone: "Should we offer something?"

Female Monk: "Do not go empty handed to a temple. Offer something as a symbol of your surrender, even if it is just a flower."

Hemp boy: "What about a rolled-up Santa Maria Joint?"

Female Monk: "God accepts anything that you offer to Him with love."

Drone: "How do we prepare?"

Female Monk: "You should stand there quietly and patiently for some time and try to visualize your Beloved Deity within your heart."

Drone: "Can I give him back my Mind?"

Female Monk: "You can only offer that to which your mind is attached, but it is the offering of your heart that God appreciates the most."

Hemp boy: "Yes, the heart is His creation and he can assume any form of His choice."

Female Monk: "You should be able to behold your Beloved Deity in everything."

Drone: "I simply cannot accept the heroin drug addicts in my world, so what's up with that?"

Female Monk: "Whenever you feel any aversion towards anyone, your mind becomes impure. To love everyone equally – this is Yahweh's Way."

Drone: "So what about the Temple's way of worship?"

Female Monk: "The temple atmosphere should be vibrant with the chanting of the divine names. When we enter the temple courtyard we should put an end to all useless talk."

Hemp boy: "So, then what do we focus on?"

Female Monk: "The focus should be placed on the regular conduct of worship according to tradition, spiritual discourses, devotional singing, etc.. It is the faith and devotion of the people, not rituals or ceremonies that fill the temple atmosphere with spiritual energy."

The contours of the Temple of Life were shaped like a massive Dome, with a radius of at least 300 feet. A person standing next to Drone informed him that the Dome was made from organic material and that it contained pure consciousness! With a sense of curiosity, he asked her how that could be possible!

Female Monk: "During our Satsangs everybody projects their consciousness with coherency and synchronicity onto the organic life form, which structures the Dome. With mental projection we can redirect and sculpt the organic life form into any Sacred Geometrical shape or form!"

Drone: "Now that is interesting, and who makes this organic life?"

Female Monk: "The Cosmic Babe manifests the substance from a combination of Stardust, Photons and Manna! It is a recycling process of substance from within the Unified Force Field and it is the Holy Spirit, which compresses life into it."

When the men finally made it to the Gate, Drone noticed two gorgeous Student Female Monks sniffing out people from head to toe. When it was finally his turn to be sniffed, he asked them what the occasion was.

Female Monks: "If you want to be close to the Brotherhood and the Cosmic Babe, then you will have to leave your chemical perfumes, colognes and carnivore habits at home!"

Suddenly Drone became afraid of not being allowed to enter! He was still a meat eater, and hence they could probably scent the distress of proteins being digested in his system. They allowed Drone to enter, but he had to wait for his friends to be sniffed out. When the girls' sniffed Hemp boy they giggled and said: "You uplift us brother, we love your scent. It tickles our bellies with laughter!"

Hemp boy: "You can smoke it too, and by the way, when can I sniff out your snuff-box sister?"

The girls giggled and signaled to a Student Monk to usher them forwards into the Temple, where they were seated in a back row. The Temple was filled with a human ocean of white robes and the floors and pillars were all made out of blue marble. The Sacred Geometry of the interior designs was phenomenal and Drone felt mesmerized by its beauty. At seven o'clock sharp a life music band began to play a melodic trance beat and a group of 33 women all dressed in maroon red started to dance freely at the center stage, while everybody was singing hymns in devotion to the Cosmic Babe.

Can you believe in the miracle coming
Can you believe it will take you away?
There will be living where once there was death
There will be living in Jesus.

The music kept going and going until everybody was juiced up to the max. Then there was a sudden silence and a group of twelve androgynous beings entered the center space. They were surrounding a column of the brightest Light he had ever seen. Everyone became quiet and the silence became unbearable. Suddenly the spell was broken by a voice coming from the Light column. As the voice spoke it almost seemed as if the Light column was calibrating the sound spectrum frequencies of the mesmerizing voice. The voice spoke as follows.

Voice: "The habit of seeing only that which our senses permit, renders us totally blind to what otherwise we could see. To cultivate the skill of seeing the invisible, we should often deliberately disconnect our Minds from the evidence of the senses and focus our attention on an invisible world within and without our inner sky. Your senses are Light reflection motion detectors, but they cannot register the essence of light as stillness. When your senses become able to record the whole of each life experience cycle both ways, they would record stillness, not motion, for every action would be voided by its opposite flowing reaction. A Human Being is a creation of God, which is limited by his senses and thus perceives differences only in a strange Morse code language of action and rest. Man is the only unit in Creation, who can bring conscious awareness into the Spirit within him, and have the electromagnetic awareness of Gods dually conditioned light acting upon his senses. These two pulsing light wave extensions of the One still light within your inner sky, is for the purpose of recording and transcending experience patterns in your body of matter. The sound of language, when it is abused becomes a diffused power equal to noise. When our thoughts hold the highest perfection of ourselves and each other, then they will be filled with God light, and language then becomes the spore print of God. Gracefully dawning conscious awareness is but a gradual recollection 'memory' of the All-knowing light spore print seeding, which has always been within man. A divine spore printed word filled with God light, makes the meaning of the word disappear, just like snow melts into the Sun. The God light takes over the meaning of our words, and within that awe, our silence is born. Man and Woman themselves are the sound light spectrum of the Word of God, but only when they abide in and by that Word. The silence of language, when it is rightly used becomes a deep feeling of the words that we may wish to speak. The sound of silence when it is drawn within your feeling center becomes a divine spiritual retreat, where one can be with God to reflect his presence. God is always present within the deepest parts of your silence and within the deepest spaces of your darkness. Just know that the real Stairway to Heaven is through a personal awareness of the limitations of the senses. This is the Way, the Truth and the Life to live. The only way to the father is through me. When you master and transcend your senses, then you will really come to know my father and me! The Light you see speak here today is nothing but a reflection from the Light within the essence of your being. Seek the Light in your most intimate dark corners and you will come to know that your sins are the fuel for your salvation. The truth will set you free!"

Drone: "I can't see him; I can't see him!"

A female Monk standing next to him began to sing a song to him:

Open the eyes of my heart Lord
Open the eyes of my heart
I want to see you
I want to see you

To see you high and lifted up
Shining in the light of your glory
Pour out your power and love
As we sing holy, holy, holy.

Holy, holy, holy
Holy, holy, holy
Holy, holy, holy
I want to see you

Within his inner eye, Drone could now clearly see a matrix of light reshape itself to what he knows today to be the reflection of Jesus Christ. He felt the blissful sensation of his living light conduct through his energy body vehicle. Instantly he knew, that in the near future he would come to lose the meaning of words as he knows them, and that the meaning of his words might grow upon him. As for now, his brain felt fried by the excessive amount of light and feelings of inner joy. His whole being was being stunned with bliss and a female Monk escorted him out of the Temple again.

Drone: "What did just happen?"

Female-Monk: "By meditation on the distinction between the name associated with an object, the object itself implied by that name and the conceptual existence of the object, the meaning of the sounds made by all beings become available. "

Drone: "What did I just see?"

Female Monk: "In the light of the divine understanding of Truth, you do not need a Politician, a Priest or a Magistrate. Expand your perception of the everlasting living light, and be the light that God wants you to be!"

Drone: "Was it Jesus?"

Female Monk: "You seem to appeal to Jesus as a mediator between you and your God, who seems to be a stern and, at times an angry God sitting off somewhere in the place called heaven, located where I do not know, except it be in man's consciousness."

Drone: "Yeah, he is idolized by our Christian society!"

Female Monk: "Instead of the idol, Jesus should be the ideal; instead of being made into a graven image, he should be real and living to you. He intended for us to know that we are all children of a greater God!"

Drone: "Why don't we ever see the man upstairs?"

Female Monk: "God is ever willing and ready to reveal Himself to all men as he has revealed Himself to Jesus and others! Fill the seemingly blank spaces about you with the thought of God only. Then remember; the word God is a seed. It must grow!"

For the next three days, Drone committed himself to working in silence. It was within this solitude that he lost track of time, space and identity. His being was being merged with the divine matrix of a silken God. It felt like finding a home and for the moment, he felt content. However, as he continued his Soul searching, Drone discovered that his subconscious desire for Layla was still there! Just the thought of her would trigger his brain into a frantic search party for proof of life. Drone felt trapped, held hostage in a world of sexual polarity, and he had a violent desire to return to the oneness of balance from which he felt divided into two. His sexual drive was still seeking rest and unification within the intimacy of his opposite vortex partner Layla! The thought of Layla alone was distracting his energies from being centered and at ease within the divine matrix of a silken being called God. Drone was romancing his shadow side and he needed a guide to help him find the way out of a self-created Mind trap.

Danny: "Layla is gone, but your sexual memory of her will always haunt you!"

Drone: "It's driving me insane!"

Danny: "Get laid my friend, release yourself and it will set you free!"

Hemp boy: "Love is like the Sun of God Drone; it shines for everyone!"

Drone: "Are you promoting promiscuity?"

Hemp boy: "The holy spirit can be loved in one way only!"

Drone: "What is the way?"

Hemp boy: "Through his son Jesus Christ!"

Drone: "So what's your point?"

Hemp boy: "The Holy Spirit manifests itself in many different body vehicles!"

Drone: "Are we allowed to love everybody for as long as we allow the living light to shine through our body vehicle?"

Hemp boy: "Isn't that the revelation we've all been waiting for?"

Danny: "Why did God send his son Jesus?"

Hemp boy: "Don't you guys get it? Christ was sent to restore the image and similitude of the actual garment of light that man is to put on, that is, if he is to attain the level of the original Adam."

Drone: "Do we have to get naked in the eyes of God?"

Hemp boy: "Absolutely naked! Jesus constantly held himself in conscious communication with God within. Jesus talked with Him as though He were personally present. He knew that God was abiding in the deepest part of his inner silence! Our bodily cells hear us dreaming, they hear our every thought and they feel our every feeling. God is always watching!"

Drone: "I've got to move! I feel restless in this place and I need a change of scenery."

Hemp boy: "Just go my friend, because your beloved is awaiting your arrival."

Drone: "You guys are staying?"

Danny: "Home is where the heart is and this is where our hearts belong!"

They hugged each other with deep intensity and Drone was on his way to say goodbye to Lady Deneb and Lord Altazar. They were expecting him, and their luminescence responded to him in a mirror like fashion. The matrix of their being reflected his desire to unite with his Layla. It made Drone giggle to see Layla and his perfected self-reflected in the mirror of a living light. Deneb waited for the right moment to break the mesmerizing spell, which Drone was being entertained by.

Deneb: "We can feel your pain, and it is your sexual tension which prevents the 'Living Light' of the infinite Mind of God, from being creatively recycled through your body vehicle!"

Altazar: "You are in grave danger, because now you know where God lives! At any moment you may be loving, laughing, intensely alive and realize that your journey has ended right here in the house where God lives! Once you leave this valley, you will not find it again until you find the divine within your inner no self. The only way back into this valley is by tele transportation of the Androgynous Stargate, also called the Cazimi Climax Portals. The Stargate will neutralize your sexual tensions into Zero-point energy, and you too will become One with the Unified Force Field of all that is. It is important for the survival of this Universe that you bring light into the dark corners of your denial before you project radical judgment unto others. We know, that you and Layla will succeed in the return to the Oneness of balance from which you were divided into two! So be it, and it is done!"

Deneb and Altazar escorted Drone to a friendly Quechua Indian, who would be his guide back to Lake Titicaca. Deneb informed Drone, that if he were to find Layla, he needed to contact the Santo Daime trance dancers at the 'Gate of Heaven' in the Amazon basin. Drone was familiar with the Santo Daime ritual and he felt relieved by this new information. He had a purpose again, and suddenly he felt no longer lost in this vast no-man's land. It was hard for Drone to leave the hidden valley, for it had captured his friends, and the atmosphere of peace that hangs over the place is powerful and unforgettable. Picture, if you can, the narrow, winding foot and mule paths that have never known the brutal wheels of modern vehicles, the Lama trains, the silent, friendly Coca leave chewing Peruvian Indian, who awaits the appearance of his reincarnated Inca ancestors, when they will again be led in a new Inca Sun Empire of a Golden Dawn on Earth. These people, although isolated in this hidden valley, know what is going on in the world today, and patiently await the return of Viracocha, the Great White Brother. "The Great White Brother has returned and people don't even know it, because of the limitation of their sensory perception", Drone thought to myself. Life is processing emotion, and it takes a lifetime to clear all traumas, be clean, clear and able to receive a higher perfected being like the 'Cosmic Babe!' Most of the time, we do not even see each other, let alone see ourselves!

Waiting for the Sun; by the Doors

At first flash of Eden, we raced down to the sea
Standing there on freedom's shore

Waiting for the sun
Waiting for the sun
Waiting for the sun

Can't you feel it, now that spring has come
That it's time to live in the scattered sun

Waiting for the sun
Waiting for the sun
Waiting for the sun
Waiting for the sun
Waiting...

Waiting for you to come along
Waiting for you to hear my song
Waiting for you to come along
Waiting for you to tell me what went wrong

This is the strangest life I've ever known
Can't you feel it, now that spring has come
That it's time to live in the scattered sun

Waiting for the sun
Waiting for the sun
Waiting for the sun
Waiting for the sun

Chapter Seven ~
Wild Child

I was praying in the Temple, and I had a vision. I saw the Lord saying to me:

Acts 22: 17

Speak to each other with psalms, hymns, and spiritual songs. Sing and make music in your hearts to the Lord.

Ephesians 5: 19

The Spirit speaks to God with deep feelings that words cannot explain.

Romans 8: 26

When you are weak, then my power is made perfect in you. And I am happy, because when I am weak, then I am truly strong.

2 Corinthians 12: 9-10

If my people, who are called by my name, will humble themselves and pray and seek my face and turn from their wicked ways, then will I hear from heaven and will forgive their sin and will heal their land.

2 Chronicles 8: 14

I am the vine; you are the branches. If a man remains in me and I in him, he will bear much fruit.

John 15: 5

When Drone returned to Lake Titicaca, he said goodbye to his Indian friend and hitch hiked to La Paz, where he boarded a smaller plane to Rio Branco. Endless jungles down below, mesmerized him with their emerald green beauty. The Amazon jungle is truly one of the last frontiers left on Earth, and the Amazon basin measures nearly the same size as the Continental United States. Imagine, that everything west of Washington D.C. was a huge, virtually impenetrable jungle filled with anacondas, jaguars, crocodiles, savage Indians and lost cities. The Amazon jungle is situated primarily within the borders of Brazil, but significant parts are located in Bolivia, Peru, Equator, Columbia, Venezuela, and the Guianas. It is generally these border areas that are the least known or explored. Within this dark world, rarely penetrated by civilized men, the Trance Dance of the Santo Daime Church takes place.

A gentle breeze invigorated his soul from deep within and thoughts of eternal paradise were lingering on inside of his Mind! After his arrival at Rio Branco, it then took Drone another two hours delay; before he could board his connecting flight to Boca do Acre. It was in Boca do Acre, where he strolled around the hood, driven to find a jungle guide, who would be able and willing to take him up the Purus River. As he was cruising the back street taverns, Drone stumbled upon a Santo Daime member by the name of Joao, who for a small fee was willing to take him up stream to 'Ceu de Mapia' or otherwise referred to as; 'the Gate of Heaven'! Joao informed Drone in a broken form of English, that 'Ceu de Mapia' is the headquarters of the Santo Daime church, and that any sincere spiritual seeker is welcomed by its community. He continued to explain the history of the Santo Daime religion with a sense of deep nostalgic passion and servitude. Thus, spoke Fardado 'Joao' the following:

Fardado Joao: "The Santo Daime religion emerged from the Brazilian rain forest to the Amazonian town of Rio de Branco in the 1930's, and reached the cities in the eighties. The founder was Raimundo Irineu Serra, a remarkable tall black man, whose occupation as a rubber tapper in the twenties brought him into contact with indigenous people and their use of Ayahuasca, a 'magic potion', valued as a medicine and to make contact with plant and animal spirit entities seen in visions. Irineu was brought up a Catholic, but his visions were of the Queen of the Forest, a white woman clad in blue and indistinguishable from the Virgin Mary, who told him, that his task was to found a new religion making use of Ayahuasca. She appeared to him many times, instructed him how to use the tea as a sacrament, and guided him through the political hurdles establishing the church in the Amazon town Rio Branco. In addition to visions, Irineu 'channeled' hymns containing teachings, which formed the doctrine of the new religion. The word 'Daime' (Portuguese for 'give me') occurs in so many of the hymns, that the religion became known as the Santo Daime! Members also use the word 'Daime' as a reference to their sacramental form of Ayahuasca. The doctrine of the church, as revealed in the hymns, is all-inclusive. The predominant theme is that the spirit of the Ayahuasca vine is a teacher, but hymns also consist of prayers to the Queen of the Forest i.e. the Holy Virgin Mary and the Christian God. Some hymns refer to resurrection and salvation, but the religion is mostly concerned with enlightenment in the here and now. The church spread, particularly amongst poorer Brazilians attempting to settle in the rain forest. However, the authorities harassed it to the extent that in 1981 Irineu's successor Sebastiao, decided to leave Rio Branco. Like Moses, he led them on an arduous journey to a site deep in the jungle, where they could practice their religion as part of a community lifestyle. Their Ashram like village is called 'Ceu de Mapia' and now has about 700 inhabitants, who live a simple, ecological sensitive life without money, electricity or running water."

The journey would take the men two days by canoe, because Ceu de Mapia's location was situated far up the Purus River.

Drone: "Pretty impressive, when can we go?"
Fardado Joao: "At the break of dawn, meet me at the river!"
Drone: "Do you want to go out for a drink? I am buying!"
Fardado Joao: "Sure!"

Joao guided him to a local tavern, which was located in a dark alley. As they entered the joint, Drone immediately became aware of the overwhelming scent of Santa Maria Marihuana. They sat down at a table to drink a beer and have a smoke. Joao said that the Santa Maria was still considered illegal, but all the locals were smoking it, and hence the police was more tolerant to its consumption. Within no time, the stuff had Drone flying as high as a kite, and little did he know that the place was soon about to be raided! It was a rude awakening, when the bartender screamed: "Policia, Policia!" Before Drone knew what was happening, he witnessed all these little plastic bags with white powder flying through midair, and most of them magically landed on his table. People were running in chaos, and everybody was trying to get out of the place in a hurry! Stoned immaculate Drone opened one of the bags, and stuck his tongue in to taste the contents. His timing was right, because the Policia just walked in and witnessed his act of sampling the coke harvest. They forced him to the ground, handcuffed him, and dragged him outside to their S.W.A.T. van. At the police station, they roughened him up, but Drone was still too stoned to resist. With his face down to the ground, they then dragged him into a van, and drove off! After a twenty-minute drive or so, they pulled him and another guy out of the van, and forced them to walk towards a deserted fishing pier. There were three police officers present, and one of them had a machete, which he began to sharpen on a leather belt. They forced the other prisoner down on his knees, and made a cut in the back of his legs. He was bleeding like an ox and screaming like a pig. His hands were tied around a wooden pole, and his lower torso was then lowered into the dark muddy river. The river became alive, and the expression on his face became one of terror and despair.

Drone: "What the hell is going on my friends?"
Police Officer: "Piranha's my friend! Piranha's!"

This time Drone knew that he was in serious trouble, and he was determined to put up a fight as soon as they would free up his hands. After three minutes or so, they reeled in the brother, whose legs had been stripped to the bone. Drone was the next runner up, and he knew they had to release his handcuffs in order to hold him down on the pier. Drone had seriously been sobered up, and they had yet to experience his crushing low kicks. As soon as his cuffs were being released, he then executed his devastating low kicks, and took possession of the machete. With his long knife, he then sliced and diced his opponents. One by one, he kicked them into the deep muddy Purus River, where their razor-edged friends welcomed them. The other prisoner had bled to death, and out of compassion, Drone dug him a small grave. The keys of the van were still in the ignition and he drove back to town to find himself a place to stay.

The rest of the night was spent at an old shaggy Motel, and the owner woke Drone up just before the break of dawn. At the river, he reunited with Joao, who had his boat ready to go. With a Winchester rifle, two revolvers, machetes, food, hammocks, jungle clothes, medicine, mosquito nets and other equipment, they ascended the Purus River to a secret jungle trail, which lay two days upstream. It was here that they abandoned their boat and began the final journey to 'Ceu de Mapia' on foot. As they drew nearer to their final destination, his guide then prepared himself for the reunion with his people, and he straightened out his clothes. It impressed Drone, that his guide had been able to keep himself clean in an all-embracing muddy jungle. A minister named Fardado James welcomed the men, and he assigned Drone to a Madrinha named 'Maria', who was to be his personal ceremonial mentor. Maria guided him to his quarters, which Drone was to share with four other Fardado's (initiates). Maria requested that Drone left his belongings in the cabin, and he was to follow her to the kitchen, where his service was needed. In the kitchen, there were about twenty men and women working with jungle vines and leaves.

Maria: "The male Padrinos pray over the male part of the Santo Daime sacrament and the female Madrinhas pray over the feminine part of the sacrament. The alchemy of the Daime is being orchestrated by a Shaman-minister, who will mix the male and female plants together in the large pots on these open fires."

Drone was taking it all in, and as soon as Maria noticed that he was receptive again to digest more information; she then continued her lovely teachings.

Maria: "While each Shaman has his own secret formula for the Daime mixture, it has been established that true Daime or Ayahuasca, always contains both beta-carboline and tryptamine alkaloids, the former (harmine and harmaline) usually obtained from the male Banisteriopsis caapi vine, and the latter (N, N-dimethyltryptamine, or DMT) from the female leaves of the Psychotria viridis bush. It is significant to note that neither one of these plant substances by itself is normally psycho active in oral doses. The minister always stresses the necessity of a diet-, which includes also sexual segregation- to learn from the teacher plants. The body has to be purified to communicate with the spirit realm. The Daime must never be combined with any amphetamine-type drug or any food with aged protein, because of the potential trigger into *paradoxical hypertension*! A prohibited food list includes, but is not restricted to; cheese, beer, wine, pickled herrings, snails, chicken liver, yeast products, figs, raisins, pickles, sauerkraut, coffee, chocolate, soy sauces, cream and yogurt. Only in the way of diet and purification, will the Trance dancers acquire their spiritual helpers and learn the Hymns or Icaros power songs. The apprentice here drinks Daime every week for months until he/she is able to hear his or her own melody. The tune one seeks and finds must be remembered, for it will be the healing chant for one's spiritual awakening. The search for one's own melody initiates the apprentice into a personal relationship with everything divine. The nature of one's Soul is musical; therefore, it is the Souls most adequate form of expression. Hearing one's own melody may be simply an expression of the experience of establishing contact with one's deeper self-imbedded within the divine matrix of life. Daime, Yage or Ayahuasca is a special gift from God, that teaches us about Good and Evil!"

Drone: "So you think, that Drug usage is not a satanic temptation, which is out to destroy the moral characters of all the 'good' citizens?"

Maria: "There are no advantages for those who, in the name of any morality or goodness, avoid confronting the experiences that bring knowing. Now is the time to unite and to have the certainty that Satan is not our enemy, because God is also in control of his fallen angel. We need to work always with the good, for the sake of good, so as not to feed that which we do not want. We try to 'stop' feeding into the negative! When seeing, only seeing the thorns in others, never in oneself? Look inside of you, don't you know where it is?"

Drone: "I can't look inside of myself, because I'm in search of my beloved, who lives outside of myself!"

Maria: "Suppose we all refuse to use 'negative words', would that create peace on Earth?"

Drone: "I don't know, but it sounds great!"

Maria: "By using right words, right thoughts, right actions, every word impinges upon that great vibratory influence called love. Your heart accepts and stores everything that is thought or spoken; hence, it is important that our words are pure and charged with the ideal state of being! We imprint 'negative words' upon our body cells by our own thoughts, feelings and speech. Whenever we use a 'negative vibration' for whatever reason, we betray the Christ within ourselves!"

Drone: "Inside it feels like I can't live without my beloved!"

Maria: "When we use the word 'I can't' we deny the power of the Divine within! When you accept the 'I can't' attitude, you have accepted a separation from God! Each individual should become aware of his oneness with God and the Christ."

Drone: "What about 'Osho, Buddha, Mohammed, Krishna'?

Maria: "Search ever deeper within yourself, see your deepest habitual impressions and notice how they have clouded the self-identity and obscured self-realization. Look into that which you feel, then surf it and ride the waves of light coming from within your heart. Magnify yourself with the presence of God coming from within, and burst forth his waves of light!"

Drone: "It is quite conceited to think that 'Christ' is the one and only savior."

Maria: "Jesus taught in simple terms that the object of this life is not death, but a greater expression of life! The entire Bible is a complete bringing forth of that, condition in which everybody will radiate the Everlasting living light from a living God. Prepare yourself to bring forth his love from within your heart, and then pour it out to the entire Universe!"

Drone: "I knew love once, but then God took it away!"

Maria: "Everybody is in essence another yourself, but you did not come here to know me, because I already know myself. You came here to know yourself!!"

Drone: "I still feel like I can't live without my beloved!"

Maria: "In the context of self-pity we feel our difficulties and suffering are unique and under this pretext we then want to exclude ourselves from a greater surrender and transformation. Under the false pretense of material happiness, we then further regress in the density of our attachments and inflict injury to those who seek a communion with the light! Did you come here to inflict injury upon us?"

Drone: "I came here to find my beloved!"

Maria: "First know the love that lies dormant inside of you, and cultivate an awareness of God's constant presence. Live the Christ life and get your attention away from your limitations. Abandon yourself recklessly, and give yourself unto the Lord for he will set you free!"

Drone: "What is Love?"

Maria: "Love is the Art of knowing oneself as divine such-ness! In the heart's fire, we are asked to grow in love and skill in search of the greatest perfection possible in everything. In the Christian flame, the one inside us wants very much the merging of him and us! The fear of God is great, because if you knock on his door and he opens the door, then what? Then everything is finished, your journeys, your pilgrimages, your great adventures, your philosophies, your search for thrills, all the longing of your heart, all is finished! It will be suicide! Like moths attracted to light, these lost Souls then ricochet back into society and inflict damage in the name of being politically correct."

Drone: "How can we live in communion with God, and yet at the same time function in a society, which is bar-coded with the undercover Mark of the Beast?"

Maria: "When the infinite fits into the mundane, and each day partakes of infinity, a spiritual potential is brought into fulfillment, attaining Christ's spiritual Utopia. Each vessel should feel, that the life that dwells in him- or her is the same as in others. Each man that is perfect in Heaven should be also perfect on Earth. We cannot remain in denial. We are made of the same essential light matrix, and we are all emanations of the same spirit called Christ. This understanding is necessary so we can live together as a community!"

Drone: "I am in a mental overload here, and I'm about to blow my fuse box!"

Maria: "Know that your Mind can only comprehend what the seed can endure!"

Drone: "What is that supposed to mean?"

Maria: "There are great differences in the ways individuals handle their experiences; some persons can welcome all experiences without feeling threatened, while others cannot. Thus Daime, by confronting us with the apparitions of our inner demons, who control the layers of our denials, perhaps can help us bring light into the shadow aspects of our Souls. In symbolic form the participant of a Daime ritual comes to see the goodness of what was considered evil and the ultimately divine nature of that which was rejected within one's nature. We believe this shift from self-rejection to self-acceptance is the essence of the Santo Daime ritual. The Santo Daime Trance invocation is an exhausting procedure, and the drinkers may not engage in another session for weeks, even months, at a time, though on rare occasions we repeat the sacred ceremony two, three, even four nights in a row. The men and women live separately, but dance and harvest Gods sacred plants together from deep within the jungle. We dance every night, and practitioners are being monitored for their individual electrolyte imbalance and dehydration symptoms. The participation in the weekly sweat lodge ritual as a means for detox is highly recommended, as is the appropriate white and blue church dress code! Furthermore, we request from you that you make a commitment to Jesus Christ, who is our Lord and Savior! We recommend not engaging in any sexual activity one week before the Daime ceremony, but this rule does not apply after completion of the ceremony. The Daime ceremony starts at seven o'clock p.m. promptly, and it continues until the break of dawn! Our community supports itself through individual service and donations. Any questions Drone?"

Drone: "How can I commit myself to somebody, who I can't see, and whose life is based on hearsay?"

Maria: "Complete devotion to an ideal is the secret of its attainment! Persistently work, love and celebrate your God-self towards the goal of perfection. When you can live in the light, as you now live in your sense of body, you will be immortal for the light never dies. Only the individual, who taps into and draws from the presence of God, can know exactly what that light is like. This is the power of direct knowing and manifestation."

Drone: "I am a free spirit and I have a hard time with commitment!"

Maria: "Well, you are committed to find your beloved Layla, aren't you?"

Drone: "My beloved is tangible and there is nothing greater than her love vibes!"

Maria: "Love comes and goes with your every heartbeat, and I pray that your life will be strong in love and be built on love. Moreover, I pray that you and all God's holy people will have the power to understand the greatness of Christ's love. I pray that you can understand how wide, how long, how high, and how deep that love is. Christ's love is greater than any person can ever know. But I pray that you will be able to know that love."

Drone: "If his love is greater than any person can ever know, then what is the sense of ever knowing it."

Maria: "It is beyond the limitation of your senses and it can be found only in a state of No Mind! Rise up out of your circuitry and allow the law of nature to work through you, let it breathe!"

The Daime steam coming from the boiling pots started to have a yellow mellow effect on Drone, and he excused himself to join the male section of the kitchen crew, who were preparing the vine. The energy of brotherhood and camaraderie in between the men was noticeable, and Drone came to learn, that this time was being used to rehearse the Hymns and Icaros of the sacred ceremony. The lyrics were all in Portuguese, but with easy to catch on verses like:

Hino do Paulo Roberto

I am the shine of the sun
I am the shine of the moon
I give shine to the stars
Because they all follow me
I am the shine of the sea
I live in the wind
I shine in the forest
Because it belongs to me

It felt good to resonate the sound of Drone's voice within the cavities of his body. The realization dawned on him, that his voice was in search for a personal melody, while his hands were working with the sacred plants from mother Earth. The intoxicating effect of the Daime fumes had a disorienting effect on his senses, and Drone felt scared, sort of like being 'in the gap' just before a quantum leap into hyperspace. Nothing to hold on to, no sense for direction, not even a hint of what choices might lie ahead! It was a state of pure potential, and all he could do was to feel the pulse of his heartbeat, hear the mesmerizing droning sounds of the jungle and seeing the popping light effects of the Daime. His heartbeat was guiding him into the experience of an inner emptiness, a pregnant state of no~thingness. The absolute potential for all inner possibilities within this Universe was mapped out in a sacred place inside. Drone's perception was moving as if in slow motion, and he began to see sparkly auras around all other life forms. His presence was being welcomed by a world of liquid light, and it dissolved the illusionary boundaries of his Mind. In the distance, he could hear the singing voice of Maria, and it was she, who brought him back into the here now. Maria instructed him to get ready for his first jungle Santo Daime Trance dance. She had organized his clothes, and waited patiently for him to get ready. With her hands, she escorted Drone to the sacred dance grounds, where he was to meet a congregation of well over 100 people, most of them were in between thirty and fifty, and two-thirds of them were women. The attire of the men reminded Drone of the Wild West, when Sheriffs wore their black trousers, white shirts and a brass star embossed with a flying eagle, while the women wore calf length heavily pleated dark blue skirts, white shirts and bow ties. Chairs were neatly laid out to face a central altar, a table displaying an incongruous collection of religious icons, including a double barred crucifix, a statue of Mary and a star of David besides a twisted piece of vine, which Drone learned was the sacred Ayahuasca. The men and women sat on opposite sides of each other, with senior members at the front around the altar. The Santo Daime dance is as simple as line dancing, but its spiritual catharsis is a little bit more intense than the loss of your mamma or your papa. The meeting and merging with your creator through the expression of dance is an ultimate orgasmic experience, which is driven by a force that reminisces the good old days in Paradise.

Maria: "Allow the Rain of Blessings to flow through your body vehicle freely, without crossing arms or legs when seated, as that may block the flow of the living light to be recycled through your body vehicle. The urge to barf is to be welcomed as an expression of 'catharsis' or purification, and should not be resisted. Our assistants will provide buckets for barfing when needed!"

During the breaks in between the dances, there were healing rituals and silent meditation. Prayers were followed by hymns, which were orchestrated by an accordion and other instruments brought along by the congregation. The simple repetitive tunes were sung with great gusto in Portuguese, more like sea shanty lullabies. The group had hardly settled into the singing, when it was time for them to receive the sacrament. The dancers lined up, and just like going up to the altar for the Holy Communion, they followed a precise route to a side table behind which a Brazilian elder stood in uniform. He held a jug of dark brown liquid, which was as thick as a milk shake, and as people approached, he would look them in the eyes as if measuring a quantum boost of rocket fuel to fly into hyperspace. When it was Drone's turn to lock in with his eyes, he then gave him a glass of Daime, which Drone accepted with a smile of pleasure.

Drone said to himself: "Why Walk when you can fly?"

There was no scent to it, but the taste of Daime was bitter and full of a scintillating awe! Back in his seat, Drone leaned back and began to see flowing geometric patterns as if all matter was being born within a twinkle of a star. This time around, the effect was stronger than before, and he had to hold onto the back of his chair. The nausea was excruciating and he had to stand up and move around. With the strength of his Mind Drone was able to hold back his urge to gag, but his body wanted to push the sacred jungle juice all out. He felt as sick as a cat, which eats grass to regurgitate hairballs. One of the assistant fardado walked over and put his hand on Drone's back to check if he was O.K! He gave Drone the insight, that his inability to vomit was a metaphor for being unable to let go emotionally. Drone's body felt blocked and he was holding together the walls of his defended self, terrified of the fear, which lay dormant beneath. The regurgitating reflex responses accelerated, but Drone's body kept resisting the constrictive contractions. The strength in his legs grew weaker and a force greater than his self, brought him down on his knees. His sociably inhibited self, wanted to express itself by means of movement and sound. To Drone's surprise this was not allowed and a gentle hand helped him back on his feet. At first, he felt angered for being restrained in the free expression of his personal catharsis, which is a God given right! It was on reflection much later, that he came to understand how this 'formal' safe container was a way to direct the flow of energy, while observing the light bursting forth from within the Daime. The discipline provided a secure setting, in which one was to allow the congregation to go deeply into their own religious experience, while discouraging individuals from spacing out into other realms. The jungle juice has a strict discipline to it, and it seems as if it is even more difficult to inhibit oneself in the higher subtle realms. The Kingdom of the Gods is truly for those, who are able to crawl through the eye of a needle. As Drone opened his eyes, he was facing the dancing Madrinahs, and he noticed that many of them were glowing with a divine inner joy. Some were apparently miles away, perhaps having deep spiritual experiences. A few made the appearance as if facing their inner demons of denial, and the helpers, who cared for them with the obvious expression of love and devotion, were attending them all to. The whole scene made the impression of a divine matrix, woven by a silken God. Drone's inner self was trying to refocus on Maria, who radiated a luminous energy, which was not from this world. It was clear to Drone, that the Holy Spirit was having a free ride through her body vehicle. She almost looked translucent, as if her aura was being filled with a million sparkly lights. The group danced until the break of dawn, and Drone felt like he was walking on cloud nine. Maria walked up to him, and hand guided him to her private cabin, where she began to make love to his body. Her love seduction came unexpected, and Drone felt distant and aloof as if he no longer needed an individualized experience. She was passionate, and it was a strong experience for Drone to see her ride his Stallion. Maria gave him a little taste of heaven, but yet at the same time Drone was unable to reconnect to his real inner feelings. For the moment, all he could do was to lie back, and witness the ride. Her heavenly naked body was being moved by divine intervention, which caused her to experience a vulva tickling orgasm. As Maria was enjoying the heights of her climax, Drone witnessed bursts of eruptive liquid light shoot out from her aura. With his fingertips, he reached out to touch the light, and the light responded to his touch with a sense of curiosity! As the light grew dim, Drone then drifted away into a deep hypnotic sleep. It must have been early in the afternoon, when he gradually came back to his senses, and noticed that he was laying in a hammock overlooking the Purus River. In the distance, he saw Maria washing her clothes in the river, and she was dressed in a white robe. The sun was hot, and Drone convinced himself to get up and socialize. As he approached her, he noticed that she was transpiring, which gave her robe the wet T-shirt look. His eyes met Her's, and he hugged her for a very long time. Hand in hand, they then walked upstream, where she showed him her secret place. There were two huge boulders in the middle of the river, but Drone could not distinguish a path leading up to them. Maybe it was the sunlight reflecting the perception of illusion on this magical spot, but Drone could not see a path! Maria jumped into the water, and it appeared to him as if she was walking on water.

Maria: "When you are in deep trust, that quality of trust transforms your life no matter what the circumstances are!"

She signaled him to follow the ripples of her footsteps, and it was scary to make a jump into the unknown water, based on trust alone. Instinctively he jumped, and he felt his feet being supported by the hard surface of a submerged solid rock. Maria guided him from rock to rock until they reached the huge boulders in the midst of the river. The boulders felt warm, and Maria guided him to the spot, where the rock had been eroded and sculpted into curved shapes, which would fit a human body. Maria gently eased down her curvaceous body, and merged herself with the streamlined molding of the rock. The heat of the rock, and the sound of running water soon caused them to fall asleep. The trees became alive and Drone had another vision of Isua~Dow, who said that the Hummingbird people would be awaiting his arrival.

Drone: "How much longer Isua?"
Isua~Dow: "You will know it when you allow yourself to be transmuted by the Santo Daime invocation! The Daime will teach you!"

His apparition disappeared, and was soon to be replaced by the Angelic form of his Layla, who smiled and then kissed him on the lips.

Layla: "Hi darling, I am here in the spirit form to let you know, that we are getting close to embrace each other again. Drone, do whatsoever is in you might to open your heart and allow yourself to totally surrender your emotional crud to the Santo Daime Trance Dance. Let the music change your sadness into celebration, and all of your fears will be transcended into a luminous resurrection. Dance with the passion of a moth, which is driven to seek the light. Dance and make wild passionate love, for I want you to be at your best, when we meet again!"

The tickling sensation of pearls of sweat sliding over his skin, snapped him out of the dreamtime. Maria was sitting across from him in a Lotus meditation position. She appeared to be in a deep state of trance, and everything was peaceful within the vicinity of her aura. The sun was shining through her hair, and the reflection of sunlight on her skin painted against the emerald green background, made her look like the Queen of the Forest. She noticed Drone's observational touch intruding her sense of privacy, and she challenged the control panel of his lustful self by gracefully stripping her wet clothes from her yearning skin. She laid herself down in the eroded body molded rock bedding of her boulder, and then opened her legs spread Eagle. The sun kept burning hot, and the warmth of its rays made Maria purr like a pussycat. Her skin was absorbing the heat, which radiated from the stony surface, and the heat opened up the pores of her skin. Maria was a definite sun worshipper, and the transpiration pearls, which were bursting now from her pores, began to run down the path of least resistance. They ultimately found their way to her erotic crevice. Her vortex was dripping silvery pearls of perspiration, which furthered their way down over the heated rock bedding towards him. The whole enchilada became irresistible and Drone leaned forwards to touch the pearls with the tip of his tongue. Maria allowed his tongue to touch her lips, and he tasted her sweet peach. The scent of her nectar was now droning inside of his brain, and he begged her to welcome his cunnilingus treat. She welcomed his tongue touching her electric spot, and he slid his slithering lingua up and down her hot crevice. Who wants to go to heaven, when you can have a little taste of it right here on Earth?

Maria now arched her spine, and grabbed Drone by the ears, as if wanting to pull him deeper into her magical forest. The primal sounds, which were being released from Maria's body, were now overriding the mesmerizing droning sounds of the jungle. They were so in tune with the divine forces of nature, that it almost seemed as if their nerve systems were calibrating themselves to the droning cicada sounds of the jungle. Butterflies were landing on their rock, and Drone could definitely hear them scream for a mate! Maria's body responded to his tongue and began arching her spine again as if wanting to shoot an arrow.

Drone: "Come, come, yet come my Lady. Let it rise and pop your butterfly!"

The cumulation of a slow and steady rush ushered her forwards to let-go and from deep within she then released a Mind-blowing orgasm, which caused her vortex to squirt out her blessed nectar of the Gods. Her love juice landed straight on his chest, and for a moment, it left him stunned with awe! It was a warm kind of sensation, and instinctively he felt driven to suck the love potion from her velvet vortex. Her muscles continued to contract for at least a couple more minutes, and when she finally opened her eyes, it felt as if she invited him into the bliss of her abyss. The nipples of her voluptuous protruding breasts were hard, and yearning to be kissed upon. Maria felt what Drone needed, and she leaned over to put a hellacious lip lock on his pulsating vortex. The rotating rhythm of her tongue worked him up to a volcanic eruption. She could sense that his bobbing head was just about to ejaculate its residual fluids, and she then released her vice grip to give way to his blast. There was a pregnant gap in between the two of them, and Maria awaited the arrival of his potent juice. Drone fired with full force ahead, and it felt like he had found his pleasure Dome from Heaven!

Maria: "You know I really like the sensation of God's life force sticking to my tongue!"

She put her lips again around his bobbing vortex, and slowly milked the last drops of God's juice from his reservoir. What can a person say, when the feelings of bliss, serenity, and a higher form of love are actually here to be experienced?

Maria: "Do you want to go for a swim with my river friends?"

Drone: "Thank you very much, but I feel reluctant to swim in a river filled with anaconda's, crocodiles, piranha's and tropical diseases!"

Maria: "My river friends will protect you!"

She grabbed some drift wood sticks, and banged them together under water, while at the same time pursing her lips to make a clicking sound with her tongue. A dolphin pod surfaced, and they swam straight towards Maria. Maria grabbed his hand, and pulled Drone into the water, where he was welcomed by her river friends. Dolphins are very aggressive sexual beings, and they are well known for their continuous sexual interaction as a form of communication. They must have sensed their state of sexual arousal, because some of them were rubbing up against Maria, as if to scan her body and communicating: "Isn't it the neatest feeling to have intimacy with all that is divine and alive!"

Their river friends stayed for an hour or so, after which Drone pulled himself out of the water for a rest on the boulders. Maria was laughing, and the sound of her laughter filled him with the sensation of joy. The river friends said goodbye, and Maria and Drone held hands as they swam away. Slowly they strolled back to the village, where the daily ritual of the church diverted their attention away from each other. The Santo Daime Trance Dance is a Quest for God, and a personal love affair in between a man and a woman should not come in between the Quest and the seeker! Maria and Drone went back to work and prepared the Daime for the dancers of that evening. Standing over the boiling Daime pots, Drone's reality became translucent again, and he traveled in and out of parallel dimensions. The vapors of the jungle juice made him loose track of 'time and space coordinates', and he learned to trust the rhythm of the divine to carry him through his emotional catharsis. All Drone remembered was his daily routine of working with the Daime, and the painful quest of moving through the layers of his denials. As human beings we evolve through the inhibitions of our neural synapses, but at the same time it may also create a conditioned nonresponse to life. Hence, it had become his deepest desire to reprogram his self, and to become absolutely clean from any social, political or religious conditioning. His heart wants to embrace life, but within his Mind, he was still afraid of death. Daime was teaching Drone to love himself as being a divine part of God's creation, and God was inviting Drone to love him as another yourself. Maria had become the extended part of Drone, and he loved that part of him as being a part of God. His heart was opening up like a Lotus flower in bloom, and he felt inspired by the divine light effects of his blessed jungle juice. Time had slipped him by, because he could not even remember what day of the week it was, let alone, what year he was in. The Daime dancers do not seem to care about the loss of their 'time space coordinates', and the only thing that did matter was their Quest for God. The droning sounds of the jungle, the sun, the Daime, and Maria's loving vortex were keeping his heart open and his being afloat. There was a sense of peace, and yet, the seeker inside of Drone was not at ease! God was watching, and he knew that within his self he was still seeking for the thrill, that would return his inner dis-ease to the oneness of balance from which he felt divided into two. Every day his heartbeat, the Daime and the sun were charging Drone into a sexed condition! His sexual desire sought rest and unification within the intimate domain of his opposite vortex partner. Sex had become the obsessed compression of a yearning friction, which desired release and expansion from its opposition. Every action of motion in this Universe is a result of his sex desire for motion from a state of stillness and rest, or for rest from a state of motion. Sex can drive a person crazy; when his or her creative force is not being redirected towards a higher purpose and presence of being. Drone's Mind wanted a woman wrapped around him twenty-four hours a day, and his longing had become an obsession. Maria was well in tune with him, and she felt compelled to release the valve of his blue balls. She offered him a cup of Daime, and kneeled down to blow the breath of life into his well responding vine. The suctional force of Maria's tongue made Drone feel dizzy and he walked over to his hammock for a breather. Maria lifted up her white skirt, sat on top of him and merged her pulsating vortex with his. Their bodies were rocking slowly to the beat of the Daime hymns. The feelings of release, expansion and unification were welcomed within the heart centers of their divine body vehicles. Pearls of perspiration were bursting out from her pores with joy, and the surface area of their skins was sliding with ease and grace over a thin layer of coconut oil mixed with their bodily fluids. It was a lubrication dance of joy! Inside his Mind Drone felt as high as a kite, and as light as a feather. It almost felt as if his pranic currents were flowing in a particular way, hence neutralizing the gravitational pull of mother Earth. A voice from the beyond made him get up and walk with Maria's body still wrapped around his naked loins. Filled with sheer strength and joy, he began to walk towards a jungle, which was silvery lit by a full moon night. His footsteps were rhythmic as if in a trance, and Maria was giggling all the way. In the midst of his dreamy walk about, Drone became aware, that a stalker was watching him! His Eagle eyes were scanning the jungle, and he locked in with a multitude of moonlight reflective eyes. The trees had become alive and Drone asked Maria if she knew who their visitors were?

Maria: "Mmm…those are our friends from the Hummingbird tribe!"
Drone: "Are they dangerous?"

Maria: "They used to be head hunters, but ever since their first contact with the white Missionaries, they have become more selective with their diet."

Drone: "Selective! As in who to eat?"

Maria: "The vision of the Medicine man decides what the intend of the tribe will be!"

Drone: "I hope that we are not mistaken for Missionaries!"

Maria: "By the looks of our sexual position, I don't think that they will confuse our identity dear!"

One of the Indians approached them, and Maria called him 'Isua Dow'!

He was five foot one, his eyes were intense and piercing like an Eagle. Around his waist, he wore little shrunken heads of little people, and it caused a shiver in his spine. He put one hand on Maria's heart, and the other one was placed on Drone's. Maria now retracted her vortex from the delicate position of: "Coitus Interruptus."

Isua Dow: "Thank you sister for being so compassionate to our brother here, but he has to move on in order to evolve into his perfected self!"

Maria: "I understand!"

Isua Dow: "Brother it is time that you come with us to the Androgynous Stargate, and complete your mission!"

Maria: "Go with God Drone, because there are a lot of juicy girls in heaven!"

The tribe began to move, Drone had but one choice, and that was to follow the group butt naked into a magical emerald green jungle. In the back of his head, he could feel Maria's eyes touching the contours of his tight buttocks, and he felt blessed to be loved by her.

Wild Child; by the Doors

Wild child
Full of grace
Savior of the human race
Your cool face

Natural child
Terrible child
Not your mother's or your
Father's child
You're our child
Screaming wild

An ancient lunatic reigns in the trees
of the night

With hunger at her heels
And freedom in her eyes
She dances on her knees
Pirate prince at her side
Staring
Into
The hollow idol's eye

Wild child
Full of grace
Savior of the human race
Your cool face
Your cool face
Your cool face

You remember when we were in Africa?

Chapter Eight ~
Break on through

They will pick up snakes without being hurt.

Mark 16: 18

You will walk on lions and cobras. You will step on strong lions and snakes.

Psalm 91: 13

So now we serve God in a new way, not in the old way with written rules. Now we serve God in the new way, with the spirit.

Romans 7: 6

Their hearts are like a hot oven. All night long its fire is low. When morning comes, it is fanned into a flame.

Hosea 7: 6

But if they cannot control their bodies, then they should marry. It is better to marry than to burn with sexual desire.

1 Corinthians 7: 9

There is no law that says these things are wrong. Those who belong to Christ Jesus have crucified their own sinful selves.

Galatians 5: 23

Grace teaches us to live on Earth now in a wise and right way, a way that shows that we serve God.

Titus 2: 12

As Drone felt, his body move through, what seemed like an impenetrable jungle, his reasoning Mind began to drift away into the spirit world. Drone was afraid of the darkness, and here he was butt naked, following a headhunter, who held him hostage with his tribe.

Drone: "Isua, can I ask you a question?"

Isua: "Speak my brother!"

Drone: "Do you believe in the existence of a God?"

Isua: "There is but one God, and I know him!"

Drone: "Then why do you hurt and kill people?"

Isua: "It is 'I' that maintains the Lord's wrath against his enemies!"

Drone: "So you kill sinners and non-believers?"

Isua: "Remember to trust that with a master any situation at any moment can be used to wake you up. Do not protect yourself. Be insecure, be vulnerable, surrender, and place your trust in your master."

Drone: "Do you consider yourself a sinner?"

Isua Dow: "The everlasting living light of God can no longer sin, when it is welcomed by a host!"

Drone: "Is it true, that a God loving person can be liberated from all conditionings and inhibitions, and hence becomes pure and absolutely clean?"

Isua Dow: "Sounds boring Hugh?"

Drone: "No, no, but I think that a sin in essence means: ' a moment of disconnection, in which one does not feel and celebrate the eternal presence of a living God!"

Isua Dow: "You mean the Son of God!"

Drone: "I mean the Everlasting Living and Dancing Light of God, which is personified as his Son for the purpose of our understanding. Every moment lost, in which a person could have shared his/her love, laughter and friendship, might have been that person's very last chance to enjoy the incarnate breath of life!"

Isua Dow: "Do you want to be reconnected?"

Drone: "Connected to what?"

Isua Dow: "To the entire creation of God our creator!"

Drone: "Am I not connected then?"

Isua Dow: "Isn't it amazing, how little man comprehends his moment-to-moment closeness to God. Man's individual destiny is of as much a moment-to-moment concern of the Creator, as the touch of your most intimate lover is a concern to you!"

Drone: "Christians urge me to confess that I am a sinner, because only then will I be saved!"

Isua Dow: "By what authority do they judge you?"

Drone: "Jesus Christ, the Son of God!"

Isua Dow: "He indeed is the only authority, that taught us not to judge! Did he not?"

Drone: "Then what is it that I'm doing wrong?"

Isua Dow: "You are not allowing the passion of drawing in God light through your feeling center, which because it cannot be compressed, will attract unpleasant experiences in order to release itself! When we attract unpleasant experiences to ourselves, then the other person will label you as being a bad person. The encapsulated energy of denial does not want to be held outside of the nourishment of Gods light. The Christian Sin is a judgment call, in which people that represent themselves (not God!), enslave the freedom of other people to function within their own limits. The exercise of Free will within your self means that you no longer have the Freedom to enslave yourself. In saying 'Yes', to ongoing change from the heart, will have the end result of your judgments dissolving into the joy of Gods dancing light. By taking the time to feel the reflections of Gods pulsating presence in everything alive, one will become able to raise the vibrations of one's own body vehicle to match the lattice of the Omni presence of Gods light! The key is to see the divine restoration and perfection for all. Feeling the picture of perfection and expressing a blessing of thankfulness with every step you make, is what the creation in the image of God is all about!"

Drone: "So I need to open myself to receive the reflection of light, and allow it to flow through my body vehicle until it becomes saturated with the essence of God's light!"

Isua Dow: "Yes, start by loving yourself first and only then you may refer to your body vehicle as being a garment of the Gods. We are to restore the image and similitude of the original man and woman that was lost, and to open the threshold gates to the actual garment of light, that man is to put on if he is to attain the level of the original divine man. When you become one with the law of one, you will no longer sin."

Drone: "So my individual consciousness has to unify with the universal, which is the ultimate cause and therefore, can be truly objective.?"

Isua Dow: "Yes, the universal consciousness objectifies the universe. We can change our vibration and thus produce any condition we desire to manifest in our bodies. Choose your movie, make your feelings about it stronger and then the evidence of your senses appears to support those beliefs. Thus, it becomes your reality and you can have peace with it.

A perpetual divine thought overrides nothing, and yet at the same time, it brings all conditioning into one, provided it is for the highest good of everyone involved. Isua Dow's presence caused Drone to listen to his words with great intensity, and the dazzling meaning of his words caused a sensation of light to move through him like a cosmic fairy dance. They continued to march on, for what in retrospective view must have been a month. The thing that kept Drone going was the chewing on coca leaves and his inert conversations with his mentor 'Isua Dow'. On the thirtieth day, the group came to a sudden halt, and made camp at the base of what seemed to be a massive stone wall built in the middle of a never ending emerald green forest. The stone wall looked ancient, and it was covered with lush vines, which kept most of the inert rock structure in place and together.

Isua Dow: "Behind this wall lies a city called Anjuna. The whole city is surrounded by this wall, which has only two access gates. These gates are so narrow, that they give access only to one person at a time. The plain in the West is additionally guarded by stone watchtowers, which are guarded by female Amazon warriors, who are always on the lookout for their enemies. Anjuna is laid out in the sacred geometry of circles and triangles. Two intersecting main streets divide the city into four parts corresponding to the four universal points of the Gods. The great Temple of the Sun, and a stone gate cut from a single blue marble rock sits on a wide circle in the center. The temple faces due east, toward the rising sun, and is decorated with symbolic images of our former Masters. The most impressive building in Anjuna is the Great Temple of the Sun. Its outer walls are unadorned and made from artfully hewn stones. The roof of the Temple is open aired, so that the rays of the rising sun can reach a golden mirror, which dates from the times of the former Masters, and which is mounted at the front. Majestic stone carved figures, symbolizing 'Tantric lovers', flank both sides of the entrance to the Temple. The interior walls are made out of blue and red marble, which is the color spectrum that rebalances male/female impurities. Next to the Great Temple of the Sun are the buildings for the Masters and their servants. The other adjacent Dome buildings are for the Tantric initiates, and their protective Amazon warriors. Besides the fortress on the surface, there exist a series of chain linked underground dwellings. We have twelve cities, deeply hidden inside the mountains that are called the Andes. Inside the Temple of the Sun, there are twelve entrances to the tunnels that link 'lower Anjuna' with other underground cities. The tunnels are large enough for three men to walk upright, and they are so extensive, that many days are needed to reach one of the other cities. All of the underground cities are artificially lit, by high vertical shafts, which reach to the surface, while an enormous silver mirror disperses sunlight over the whole city. The former Masters, who ruled over Anjuna as if in the hands of God, built these tunnels and subterranean cities. They ruled over men and the Earth by means of their Supernormal powers. These Masters had ships faster than a bird's flight, ships that reached their goal instantly by matter of thought. They had magic crystals to look into the distance so that they could see cities, rivers, mountains, stars and other galaxies. Whatever happened on Earth or in the sky was reflected in these stones. Nevertheless, the underground dwellings were the most wonderful of all. In addition, the Masters gave them to their chosen stewards as their last gift. For the former Masters are of the same blood and have the same father!"

Drone: "Will you be my guide on the inside?"

Isua Dow: "No my friend. This is where we depart! Once you make it to the other side of this wall, the Amazon warriors, who will guide you to the test site of your last temptation, will then escort you! Go with God!"

Drone: "What if I want to come back!"

Isua Dow: "Then my people will have to kill you, because once you've seen God, then there is no way back to your old self!"

They hugged each other and Isua guided Drone to the entrance of Anjuna city, which was covered by jungle bush. The entrance was small and Drone had to squirm his naked body sideways for a better fit. It took him thirty-three steps to make it to the other side of what seemed to be a massive rock wall. Drone moved slowly through the narrow opening, resting from time to time against the giant Rockwall, until he had the strength to move on. Before Drone stepped out into the open, he carefully observed his surroundings for any sign of human presence. It was safe to move forwards, and he pushed his way through the tough jungle, gritting his teeth each time the thorns of its tough underbrush cut into his naked hands. Sweating, he leaned against a giant red wood to catch his breath. After a mile or so Drone became aware that he was being stalked by the piercing eyes of a predator gazing at him from within the trees. Without notice, he suddenly felt a big bang on his head, and he blacked out! A pounding headache brought him back to his senses and he tried to open his eyes, but he could not see a thing. A blindfold blinded his eyes, and his arms and legs were restrained in a cross like position. Drone felt like his body was positioned supine, and slanted to a certain degree. It felt uncomfortable. In the background, he heard a female giggling.

Drone: "Who are you?"

Female: "How do you feel?"

Drone: "My head is pounding!"

Female: "Maybe this will take your headache away!"

Drone felt her kisses descending a happy trail down to his private area. A Mind-bending fellatio worked like a charm on his now subsiding headache. Her French kissing tongue gave him the works, and as his vortex expanded, so did her passionate lovemaking. Suddenly she changed her body position, and wrapped her constricting legs around his naked loins. The crevice of her warm and wet vortex merged with his pulsing shaft. She moved her pelvic region up and down the length of his erected vortex. Her erotic lips now began to milk him, as if wanting to squeeze the juice of life out from his blue balls. She stopped again, and repositioned her wet vulva straight into his blindfolded face. The pheromone scent released by her musky glands began to trigger an endorphin rush inside his brain, and unexpectedly the vision of Layla appeared onto his internal memory screen. Drone whispered her name: 'Layla, Layla, Layla', and the female voice responded in a sensual, but teasing fashion.

Layla: "Drone, my heart soars with gladness that you are recognizing my scent! My Soul is painted with a new name, and it is now: 'Maneesha!'

Her scent lifted up the veils, which had covered up his memory bank of what seemed to be eons ago. Tasting and scenting are but one sensation of feeling light wave particles reacting upon mouth and nostrils. The scent of her juicy vortex created an amazing rush like feeling inside of his brain, and it felt like he was given a little taste from heaven. Drone felt yet another energy source makes its presence, and Maneesha introduced him to her shadow sister Maleeka. His blindfold was now being removed and he glanced at his two female companions. Their complexion was identical, and it was hard to tell them apart. Layla's appearance was fading in and out of what seemed to be a reflection of an identical twin. The experience thrilled, stunned, confused and aroused Drone all at the same time. It felt like he was having a holographic hallucination, and the vibes were so intense that it stunned his breathing.

Drone: "Wow, what a trip girl! Wake me up Lord, because I must be dreaming!"

Maneesha: "There's absolutely nothing wrong with your eyes Drone, it's just that we are now vibrating at a higher frequency, and you are a little bit out of phase with us. Given time, you will soon come to know the gap, which you will learn to bridge!"

Maleeka: "For now let's get dressed, because tonight we shall meet the high priestess Deneb, who will marry us before we burn up with sexual desire!"

Drone's circuitry was in overload, and he felt stunned and driven to catch up on the 'gap' of lost time, with his beloved Layla. Finally, after all these years of searching for his beloved, he now was given the opportunity to relax, and feel just how tired he really was. His female companions anticipated the point of his collapse, and they simultaneously grabbed his arms to support his buckling knees. When Drone woke up from his catnap, it was time to meet Deneb. Hand in hand, they walked in the direction of a small Dome, which seemed to be the designated area for their ceremonial reunion. When they entered, he became aware of the exhilarating radiant angelic form, which forewarned him of the manifestation of Deneb's presence. She had kept her promise, and Drone became a believer of the Dreamtime.

Deneb: "And the two people will become one body. So, the people are not two, but one. God has joined the two people together. So, no one should separate them." Mark 10: 8-9.

Jointly: "And so be it!"

The three of them were as happy as a bunch of kids, having their first birthday party. They thanked Deneb with enthusiasm, and she in return was able to receive their human gratitude! The three of them left the ceremonial Dome in search for a place to celebrate. The Amazon garments, which his two ladies were wearing, had a very enticing effect on the endorphin levels inside of his brain receptors. The sound and scent of a woman moving around in a natural leather outfit somehow triggered Drone into a lustful fantasy, in which a Black Stallion is pumping his long reproductive organ in and out the succulent vortex of his female counterpart. Picture this for a moment and absorb its sensuality like a sponge does water. Then picture two women walking next to you in tight leather outfits, which are rubbing against their succulent vortices. The aroma of musk, sweat, and wet leather combined, really worked like a charm aphrodisiac on his never resisting libido. His two ladies noticed his sexual droning, and they stopped their sensual motion for a second or two. This gap of silence was supposed to give Drone a breather, but instead it drew him deeper into the longing for it! They each grabbed a hand of his, and prodded his fingers into their leathery lingerie, where he then finger diddled their well-lubricated crevices. Maneesha was the first to break the silence of their magical sensual vibrations.

Maneesha: "The reason we were reunited Drone, is for the three of us to become one in the spirit and in the flesh. Only with the Force of One will we be able to transmigrate ourselves through the Androgynous Stargate into the house of God! We are a trinity with the mission to balance our inner male and female counterparts into the unity of his being!"

Drone: "I seem to be missing the point. What's your drift?"

Maneesha: "In the beginning when God created Adam and Eve, they were given a choice, which they acted upon, and that has separated man and woman into two opposite unbalanced conditions of electric pressures; compression and expansion! Our sex drive is a violent desire, which wants to return to the Oneness of balance from which we were divided into two. Our sexual desire seeks the stillness, in which it can receive the magnetic light directly from God."

Maleeka: "Here in Anjuna we are blessed with the tools and teachings of the Androgynous Tantric Masters, and we would like to introduce to you, a process called: 'Acoustic Levitational Transcendence!' But first we will have to go through a piercing initiation, which will ultimately maximize our sensual impressions."

Joined together by their arms they walked over to a small round temple, which was referred to as: 'The Tantric Body Shop!' The needles were being run and stung by two gorgeous Amazon sisters, who greeted them with a warm hug. The two sisters Mitzee and Mayak explained to Drone the procedure of body piercing, which according to their expertise was sweet and not painful.

Mitzee: "It is sort of like a love commitment with God!"
Drone: "So, you girls are going to harpoon my whale?"
Maya: "Yeah, we are going to pierce the septum of your foreskin!"
Mitzee: "Who wants to go first?"
Milika: "Drone?"

As Drone looked over to Maleeka and Maneesha, they had already undressed themselves. With eagerness and in a spread-Eagle position they were awaiting their ceremonial piercing. They were given a calming drink of Daime, and as Drone drank the liquid light, he could feel his body relax. Maya helped him get undressed, and Drone hung his private part out in unknown territory. Strange hands finger diddled his extended body part, and the pulsing Daime woke up his Moby Dick.

Mayak: "Wow, it is so big!"

Mitzee responded with a professional finger click of her index finger against Drone's pulsing shaft.

The penetrating lash of her finger had an immediate numbing effect on his libido. His vortex relaxed, and Mitzee took advantage of his momentary absence of Mind. Swift, and with precision she suddenly harpooned his whale, and Drone shrieked 'Héh!'

Mitzee: "Next I will insert a small stainless steel interconnecting shaft, which will connect two metal pearls and form into one bipolar G-spot stimulator."

Maya: "You will have to abstain for one week from any sexual intercourse and your wound will heal! Take these herbs to stop the bleeding, calm your nerves, and ease your pain!"

Drone: "How will this all work sexually?"

Maya: "When you take your woman from behind, it will stimulate her G-spot!"

The girls were up next to be pierced by Mitzee, and again it was a swift and painless procedure. Following, she inserted a golden ring in each Labium, and attached them individually to a golden chain, which was connected to a pair of golden plated Garter belts. Once the chains were in position, Milika and Maneesha tested them out by spreading and closing their legs. The spread-Eagle motion definitely exposed their sacred vortex opening to Drone's liking! God is good, and God was getting better, because he had sent him his two Angels to teach the lesson of Acoustical Levitational Transcendence! For their own edification, his two ladies also purchased themselves a set of jade love eggs on a string for the sole purpose of exercising their inert vortex muscles. In layman terms, it meant the practice of a tight squeeze, and in addition, his girls were given a pair of oval shaped glass probes with different diameters, which would assist them in the training of their Lotus. Maya gave Drone a bottle of libido stimulating herbs with the following contents: "Avenue

Sativa, Saw Palmetto, Sarsaparilla, Velvet deer antler, Yohimbe Bark, Fo-Ti He-Shou-Wu, Siberian Ginseng, Ashwagandha, Muria Puama, Damiana, Diosores Composita, Orchic powder." Now they were packed, loaded, and in good shape to resolutely deal with the problem. For the next couple of days they were at leisure, enjoying a daily total body massage, soaking in hot mineral water, and detoxing their bodies in hot and steamy natural springs. There was no sexual interaction between the three of them during this time of healing and purification. It was a nurturing communion of reunion, meditation and prayer. The garden around the Lotus Pond was pregnant with scents of Roses, Jasmine, Lilac and Lotus, and their fragrance was subtle, which gratified his compulsive longing for a passionate thrill. The healing of the small puncture wounds was swift, and Milika informed Drone that it was time to prepare their sacred love shag. She forgot to mention that they had to remain in the sacred Dome until the three of them were being transformed into a higher level of consciousness. They walked through the herbal gardens to a larger interconnected Dome structure, which when seen through a bird's eye view resembled the geometrical pattern of the Flower of Life! The subdivided smaller Domes were Tantric training sites for initiates, who wanted to graduate to the level of Master Alchemists of 'Love potion 69,' which were ultimately the initiation towards the ascension level of androgynous beings! The ceiling of the Dome had the appearance of a dark sky filled with a million of sparkly lights. In the center space of the Dome there was a round King size bed, and above it was a large mirror suspended in midair to enhance the special effects of the visual cortex. On a table next to the bed was a variety of culinary sexual tools displayed and disposable accessories! On one side of the Dome was a small round kitchen, where they were to eat their daily juices and meals. The rest of the Dome was filled with empty white space, captured by a large window overlooking the Lotus Pond. The three of them sat down in a Lotus position, and they connected with each other by holding hands. Maleeka was the first to break the silence, and she spoke as if in a state of trance.

Maleeka: "Welcome my beloved and sister. Sex is the driving force, the thrill that brought you here to be reunited with me! Let your sexuality be the first step to heaven, but not the last! When two lovers are in a state of deep sexual orgasm, they melt into each other, then the woman is no more the woman, the man is no more the man. They become just like the circle of yin and yang, reaching into each other, meeting into each other, melting, forgetting their own identities. That is why love is so beautiful. This state is called 'Mudra', and the final state of orgasm with the whole is called 'Mahamudra', or the Great Cosmic Orgasm! Orgasm is a state, where your body is no longer felt as matter, it vibrates like energy, electricity. It vibrates so deeply from the very foundation, that you completely forget that it is a material thing. It becomes an electric phenomenon, and it is an electric phenomenon. Moreover, when you feel love, and you surrender to each other, then you surrender to this moment of being energy, and fear loses its grip. When the body loses its boundary, when the body becomes like a vaporous thing, when the body evaporates substantially, and only energy is left, a very subtle rhythm, **you find that it is, as if you are not**. Only in deep love can one move into it. Love is like death, you die as far as you think you are a body, you die as far as your material image is concerned, you die as a body, and you evolve as energy, vital energy of Godlove. In addition, when the partners start vibrating in a rhythm, the beats of their hearts and bodies come together, it becomes a harmony then they are two no more! Now the circle is complete, and they vibrate together, they pulsate together. Their hearts are no longer separate, their beats are no longer separate, and they have become a melody, a harmony. It is the greatest music possible, all other forms of music are just faint things compared to it, like shadow things! When the same thing happens not with another person, but with the whole existence, then it is 'Mahamudra!' Then it is the great cosmic orgasm! My name is Shunyata, and I am your Tantric guide!"

Maleeka opened her eyes, and Drone looked deep into the abyss of her Laguna blue eyes. In silence, but with tender care they undressed each other, and playfully Drone touched his bare-naked lady. Maneesha initiated a French kiss on his lips, while Maleeka teased his pounding vortex with a hellacious fellatio. Maleeka's tongue played around with his pierced ornaments, and Drone enjoyed the exploration of her tongue. His muscles contracted from sheer bliss, and his tongue reached out for Maneesha's breasts, which responded softly with the hardening of her nipples. Driven by his oral reflex, he sucked on them gently, as if drinking from her milk. The sweet musky scent of her Labia now drew him straight down towards her juicy vortex, and with his tongue, he made sweet passionate love to the lips of her vortex. Her she-bob was dripping joyously, and he began to drink from her fountain of love. The suctional power of his mouth was teasing her with a push pull, stretch and relax motion. Maleeka was lying comfortable on her side, while her tongue continued to give Drone's vortex a work over. Maneesha leaned over towards her, and gestured Maleeka to open up her private parts. Her legs winged spread Eagle, and Maneesha buried her tongue deep in between Maleeka's delicate self. The Sacred Geometrical pattern of their sexual position made them rise and fall to unbelievable heights. Maleeka felt that Drone was about to come, and she pushed her thumb deep into his prostate gland. This was the distraction he needed to immediately reverse the flow of his upcoming orgasm, and Maleeka commented teasingly: "We have come together to practice the extended valley orgasms, and we should not allow our vortices to lead us into the ultimate pleasure zone!"

Drone's 'Moby Dick' was as solid as a rock, and he sat up for a breather, during which Maneesha merged her vortex with his. With her cervix, she began to ride and massage his vortex, and Drone loved it. Drone now rhythmically began to massage Maneesha's G-spot, and her labia were being pulled apart by her Garter belt contraption. She was purring like a pussycat, and Drone intuitively felt that she could not hold back the rush of pleasure any longer! Suddenly her whole body contracted, and with her muscles, she locked a deadly vice grip on his pleasure zone. Her spine was arched, and with her tongue pressed upwards against the roof of her mouth, she now began to pant like a dog in heat. They sat like this for five minutes or so, and then a moment came in which Drone could feel her body relax again. The velvet feeling returned, and Maneesha opened her eyes to make contact with Drone. For a moment in time, they felt deeply connected within the abyss of their Souls, and there were these tiny sparkles of light everywhere. Yet, another feeling made her close her eyes again, and it appeared as if she was sliding into yet another state of trance! Her voice spoke out aloud, and then paused again, as if she was searching for the right words to be channeled.

Maneesha: "When the electric sensors of my G-spot are being activated by your vortex, it also heats up my ovaries, which is a buildup of energy that needs direction and expansion! As my erotic tension builds up for a total orgasmic release, I then make a conscious effort to postpone the saturation level of pleasure with a squeeze hold and control of my bladder and vortex openings. My level of control then moves towards a squeeze hold and control of my Rosebud. This way I contain and preserve my sexual energies for the next cycle of passion. The heat rising from my ovaries, then needs to be redirected down into my sex chakra, and from there to the sacred hiatus or bottom opening of my sacrum. Next, I place my tongue against my palate, and I suck my sexual energy upwards, using my spine as a straw. The blissful feeling of liquid light is then pulled upward, and redirected straight into the cortex of my brain. This is what we call the rising sexual energy, which moves like a snake, and hence is called Kundalini! The blissful feeling continues to move on forwards through my third eye, and into the tip of my tongue. From there it descends into my throat chakra, and further on down into my heart chakra, which then becomes saturated with the flow of liquid light. Once my heart is dancing and singing on the wings of love, I then redirect my sexual energy to cascade on down into my Solaris Plexus, and again further on down into my Hara! From my Hara, or otherwise called 'center of Life and Death', I then recycle all of the Divine energy back into my ovaries. Since my ovaries were given a break and cooled off their heat, they are now ready again to be recharged with the liquid light of life! This is what in Tantra sex is referred to as 'Running the inner orbit', and this process is quite the same for men! The difference with a man is that he draws the heat from his testicles into his prostate gland, and straight into the bottom of his tailbone or 'Sacral Hiatus!' During multiple extended states of 'Valley Orgasms', one becomes able to also revitalize, rejuvenate and immortalize each organ and its cellular tissue, by supercharging them with blankets of liquid light. The tightening of the sexual exit holes i.e. 'Urethra, Vagina, Anus', during this process is of extreme importance as it contains the sacred energy within the inner orbit. Thus, we remain healthy, because Health in essence is the accumulative effect of body cells being saturated with sexual electric conscious energy. When a man or a woman allows their sexual energies to be ejaculated during a state of orgasm, then 50% of their basic life energy, which is fed by the basic mineral supplies of 'Magnesium and Selenium', will be lost and wasted! The repetitive loss of basic life nutrients and electrolytes in its turn will affect the life expectancy of your heart muscle, and in due time may results in heart attacks, strokes etc…! Senile decay, which is the common experience of man, is but an expression that covers his ignorance of cause, certain disease conditions of mind and body! In order for us to mature towards becoming healthy immortal beings like the Cosmic Babe, we will have to master our 'Coitus Interruptus', and learn to redirect our sexual energies into the inner orbit of our sacred body vehicle!"

Drone: "Wow, I wish somebody taught me that in High School had! What is Kundalini again?"

Maneesha: "It is the rising of your sexual energy in the spine, which moves like the snakes of Aesculapius and Caduceus!"

Drone: "Aren't those the Western symbols of Medicine!"

Maneesha: "Yes, the old Tantric Schools taught us, that when the Kundalini or snake energy rises in the spine, it sets into motion the running of the inner orbit, which in essence is the doorway to immortality, which is now being held open by our Master Jesus Christ."

Drone: "Why do Doctors use the symbol of Caduceus?"

Maneesha: "Satan has led them astray from the Path of self-healing, because that would aid people to remember a conceptual God!"

Drone: "Is it bad to feel this sexual snake energy?"

Maneesha: "Our religious leaders have condemned our intrinsic nature of sexuality, and that caused us to fear ourselves, each other, and God! Now they control your fears by calling you a sinner, and yet with the same breath they preach to you, that sin is the fuel for your salvation!"

Drone: "Is it sinful to Sex?"

Maneesha: "It is a sin **not to allow** 'the living light of God' to move through the inner orbit of your body vehicle! And again, Satan seduces you to direct your sexuality outwardly instead of inwardly, and that will distract you away from abiding within the stillness of God's presence!"

Drone: "Are you in fact saying, that the flow of sexual energy is the living light of God, trying to direct our ways back to the source, where he can be found?"

Maneesha: "Yes, we are all fallen Angels from an infallible silken God, and we are on a journey to reunite with our beloved!"

Maleeka and Maneesha were now alternating their Tantric positions with each other, and Drone went with the flow! For the first time he began to listen to his body, and he noticed that his sexual sensations were made off pure energy, which now was being recharged with a desire to express itself freely! The way they were touching each other and themselves, felt like the way hummingbirds' lands on a flower bud to drink its nectar. Drone was engaged in a cosmic dance, and he experienced a transformational process, that would never take him back to be the same person he was before he entered the Sacred Temple! The sound of water running through the walls of the Dome had a soothing effect on his libido, and there were these moments in which he would just float and drift, while being drunk with the Divine. The experience of time was expanding, and he lost his sense of reality. He never slept, but instead rested his body consciously. It almost appeared as if his sexual energy had become a form of liquid light, which now had found the doorway to the waking centers of his brain. The girls took a break during his training sessions, and together they spend it in the flower gardens. The penetrating scent of Jasmin and Magnolia saturated his being to the ultimate level of inner bliss, and it left him bathing in a sense of mystification with the Divine. Tropical birds sang their harmony songs to the receptor membranes deep within his inner ears. The practice of sacred sex was to be practiced daily, which at its height was a drifting away into the valley experience of inner bliss! The running of the inner orbit began to have a life of its own, and Drone's energy kept turning like wheels within wheels. After three weeks of Tantric practice, both Maleeka and Maneesha were being reminded of their monthly returning menses cycle.

Maleeka: "The gravitational changes in the field of the Earth caused by the Moon, easily penetrates all of our physical bodies, and it also has a rhythm-entrained effect on the opening, and closing of our female reproductive organs. The electromagnetic fields surrounding our body vehicles, are relatively strong, and they serve us by holding our atoms and molecules together. Certain tissues will interact more with one kind of vibratory energy than others, but our reproductive organs are the most sensitive to change. The gravitational or magnetic effects will affect the body as a whole. No matter how small the lunar rhythmic effects are on our bodies, our psyches will always respond strongly to it. Female mood swings during their Moon cycle are caused by the unwillingness to dance to the rhythmic changes in her body caused by the Moon pulse. Great Cosmic forces are being released, when a woman tunes in and dances to the rhythm of her menses pulse. This is a woman's most powerful time for prayer and meditation; hence we are to interrupt our Tantric sessions with the preparation of our sacred ceremony in Grandfather Redwood."

An Amazon woman came to guide the girls away to yet another sacred site inside the city of Anjuna. It took them an hour to walk through what appeared to be a magical jungle garden, until they arrived at a 33-foot cross-surrounded by majestic Giant Red Wood trees. Maleeka and Maneesha were instructed to put on their climbing gear, and the guide informed them, that the women were to remain up in the tree tops until their menstrual period had subsided. She then continued with some more personal instructions, and this was definitely not meant for his male ears at the time. Each was handed a small catheter with a transparent looking probe, and the girls were signaled to say goodbye to Drone. They gave each other an intense, but tender hug goodbye. The girls secured and attached their climbing gear to the cords, and an unknown force pulled them straight up into the crown of the trees, where one can only imagine that the sky is the limit. Drone's eyes followed them high up into the trees, until he lost sight of them, and rays of sunlight replaced their silhouette with a cosmic dance of delight on the retina of his eyes. The female guide took him by the hand, and guided him to a secluded magical spot in the jungle, where he was to soak in natural mineral water gushing out from the rocks of a mountainside.

The magical hot springs were imbedded in a lavish lush bed of moss, and at a short distance away from the springs, there was a little love shack built for the comfort of recreation. Sparkles of light were dancing all around him, and there was this sense of presence, a knowing that the forest spirits were observing him. The mineral water was hot, and at about 108F one could definitely describe it as a lobster pot. His body vehicle was to enjoy itself here, until his girls had completed their menstrual tree ceremony. The presence of a nurturing scent of red wood was tickle pleasing the core of his being, and the ancientness of their gigantic sacred geometrical foliage drew Drone closer into their magic spell! This was definitely a magical place in which one could truly feel, that God is watching! As he was soaking in the bubbly spring water, Drone could feel part of his spirit soar over the Emerald green jungle, and their colors made him slip and slide into other dimensions. It was a time of processing and integrating his 'religious' experiences. The Holy Spirit began to speak to him in tongues and the emptiness within him was now being filled with a spore print impression from the other side.

Holy Spirit: "Discovery is all about making an internal connection with the external reflections, and it is driven by a curiosity to reveal the veils of the Divine. Soma is another word for your body vehicle, which is being controlled by the Cybernetics of your Brain. The Human Brain uses a Biological Morse code language of action and rest nerve impulses, which in their turn control your body vehicle muscle contractions.

Your nerves are your senses in motion; therefore, your nerves sense only that, which they themselves are. I AM this Universe experiencing itself. Sensation is but an electrical awareness of wave motion caused by other waves within your liquid body of water. Sensation is the strain of resistance to the separation, which exists between all separated bodies of substance. In order to tap into the knowing of other dimensions, one must bring awareness into the smallest particles of soma matter. It is in between the fine line of Matter and Non-Matter, where one may find a glimpse of God. Close your eyes for an extended period of time, and for a moment, you will be exposed to immediate subjective world of the ultimate beyond! It is within your inner sky, where your external world begins. Being unraveled is what it is all about, until one breaks on through to the other side of no return. The smallest particle of your body is the atom, which consists of a nucleus or center within a **void** filled by vibrating fields of light-pulse wave particles. The movement or activity of the light particles is fluctuating in between two states of rest. The information, which a human being feels coming through its nerve system, provides for them the perception of differences within. Your perception functions as a tool to survive the challenges of the external world, yet at the same time it is the key to the Kingdom of Heaven! We are thinking of how dolphins 'porpoises' emit ultrasonic waves, which when reflected back, are interpreted to determine the environment. The neuro-receptor transmitters of your inner reality can perceive something only when the external world reflects the movement of two different input signals. One needs two information signals 'sensory input' in order to have the ability to respond 'movement' to a certain situation. With your senses, you can receive the awareness of seeing, hearing, tasting, smelling and feeling. All of these five senses are but 'the One Sense of Feeling!' Seeing is a sensation of feeling light wave particles landing on the retina of your eyes. Hearing is sensations of feeling light wave particles stir your inner ears.

Tasting and smelling are sensations of feeling light wave particles reacting upon mouth and nostrils. You are frozen light, and yet this sensed light of this sensed Universe of God's creation, is not you. Your senses are Light reflection motion detectors, but they cannot register the essence of Light as stillness. All variations in the sense of experiential feeling are due to a difference of electromagnetic conditioning in pulsing wave matter within your liquid body of water. Conditioning is a limiting neurological pattern based on the juice of negative interpreted emotions like: 'Fear, Pain, Anger, Sadness!' All of your pains are caused by **the original sin**, which in essence is your **resistance** against the flow of the Living Light to freely move through your body vehicle. Your neuro-receptors encode your experiences of chemistry within your Limbic system, which is that part of the brain that stores memories of Primal Feelings of Survival: 'Fright, Flight, Fight.' These primitive survival issues encode the chemistry within your brain, and your emotional juice has been entrapped within your Limbic system. You have been seduced to accept the subliminal Social, Religious and Political conditionings, and your emotional juice feels entrapped in a World that defines Culture as the Art of Inhibition! You must take the time to know the Light of God for yourself, and you must live it, feel it, breathe it, and vibrate it!"

Drone's inner ear drums were sensing the footstep frequencies of two human beings. His heart began to pound with joy, as he sensed the graceful beauty of Maneesha and Maleeka merging with the radiance of his Aura. They joined him in the Hot Spring, and held his hands with a pregnant silence, and tears were rolling over their cheeks from happiness. Maleeka was the first to break the spell of silence.

Maleeka: "The wind in the trees took me away to God. My heart surrendered to the will of the wind, and it melted my resistance to life. The wind, the trees, the stars, and God have opened my heart for love!

I am One with All that is, and I am learning to melt away the limitation that stands between me and my God."

Maleeka's sharing captured Drone off guard, and it spun him straight into a state of receptivity. The poetry of her words and the pulsation of her heartbeat had a definite alternating effect on the essence of his being. His body began to release deep layers of Primal Pain, which had been stored away by the social forces of condemnation and denial! On the screen of his inner Mind, he began to have flashbacks of situations in which he learned to inhibit his true self. Whenever he suppressed his true self, and compromised to the demands of social ethics, he, in effect, was truly traumatizing his inner self. Is it my nostalgic addiction to drama, or am I just scared to unravel the veil of my liberated self? A Primal feeling inside of him desired to include every part of him into all the aspects of his life. The only way of overcoming deep instinctual primal behavior is by going into it! Sex is the essence! Sex is the limitation that separates him from his God, and sex is the ultimate doorway, behind which God lives!

The pulsation of their triangulated heartbeats was now pulsing in sink, and its rhythm activated the blood-flow to their erectile tissues. Maleeka stood up, and placed her vortex straight on Drone's lips, and he sucked on her Labia, which caused her to arch her spine with a deep moan. The windows of their Souls locked in with each other, and the air in between was being filled with a radiant bliss. It was a very intimate moment, in which Drone could feel her whole being vibrate through the light sensations of his lips. God was filling him up with the presence of his Living Light. His happiness was ecstatic, and tears kept flowing from his eyes. It was hard to maintain eye contact, but through the mist of their tears, they kept feeling each other. Peace dawned with the acceptance of just another yourself. The sensation of bliss was being captured by the transgression of his first and final sin, and Drone felt in harmony with the infinite. He was to allow his inner child to receive, and feel the Living Light of God flowing through his body vehicle! When Maleeka finally climaxed, Drone could clearly sense the light flowing through him, and his pores were bursting with joy! Her juices were overflowing and with her blessing, he drank the nectar from the Gods. Maleeka eased her Divine body down, and merged her vortex with his. Maneesha wrapped herself around him from behind, and together they just sat there bathing within the surrender of their bliss.

Maneesha: "I believe Drone is ready for the Temple of the Great Mahamudra or Great Cosmic Orgasm!"

The sun was setting, and hand in hand, they crossed over the river dam. Their clothes soaked up the water, which caused them to slow down their motion, and Drone could feel his body move with the incredible lightness of being. The golden, purple, and pink rays of sunlight reflected over the Dome shaped city of Anjuna, left a magical radiance on the retina of his eyes. The scenery was divine and could only be compared to a Taj Mahal in Machu Pichu. The 'Cosmic Babe' was definite present here, and Drone began to realize that he had found his doorway to God.

Break on through; by the Doors

You know the day destroys the night
Night divides the day
Tried to run
Tried to hide

Break on through to the other side
Break on through to the other side
Break on through to the other side

We chased our pleasures here
Dug our treasures there
Can you still recall
The time we cried?

Break on through to the other side
Break on through to the other side
Break on through to the other side

Ev'rybody loves my baby
Ev'rybody loves my baby

She gets, she gets
She gets, she gets

I found an island in your arms
A country in your eyes
Arms that chained us
Eyes that lied

Break on through to the other side
Break on through to the other side
Break on through to the other side

Made the scene from week to week
Day to day, hour to hour
The gate is straight
Deep and wide

Break on through to the other side
Break on through to the other side
Break on through to the other side

Break on through, break on through
Break on through, break on through

Yeah, yeah, yeah,
Yeah, yeah, yeah…

Chapter Nine

The Spy in the house of love

Greet each other with a holy kiss.

Romans 16: 16

It is not what a person puts into his mouth that makes him unclean.

Matthew 15: 11

God has made these things clean. Don't call them 'unholy!'

Acts 10:15

The first man came from the dust of the Earth. The second man came from heaven. But those people who belong to heaven are like the man of heaven. We will also be made like the man of heaven. We will not all die, but we will all be changed!

1 Corinthians 15: 47-51

You have begun to live the new life. In your new life you are being made new. You are becoming like the One who made you. This new life brings you true knowledge of God.

Colossians 3: 10

God is in the light. We should live in the light, too. If we live in the light, we share fellowship with each other. And when we live in the light, the blood of the death of Jesus, God's Son, is making us clean from every sin.

1 John 1: 7

Drone made an unusual observation. He discovered that the women of Anjuna use their sexual energy to assist their male partners to surpass the sex symbol fixation and gaze upon enlightenment as the ultimate benediction. Here men are being taught to idealize for themselves that, which they wish to bring forth from the within, instead of graving for an idol in the lost world of hollow glamour. Man seeks instant release and gratification, and thus needs a lot of sexual interaction before he learns to let go and relax at his feminine sexual center. The women's objective was to reveal to him that at his core center man consists of pure light. At his core center, man needs to learn to hold his body indwelling with everything divine, and merging that body into the perfect God body just as God sees him or her. In doing so, man can ascend to a plane of consciousness, where the perception of the mortal senses transcends beyond the illusion of limitation.

The complexion of Maleeka and Maneesha is almost bio-mimetric-identical, and whenever Drone was zooming in on them, it felt like he was sliding in and out of the one reality of Layla. This reality shift was sometimes confusing for his subconscious emotional Mind, and it made him long for a miracle. He needed something to transform his feelings, a transgression of the divine law of reincarnation, the ultimate transmutation. The question arose: "How does a human being tap into the Ultimate beyond, and make it his simple cozy home?" The most important relation in creation is to really slowly connect to our inner child and acknowledge for the very first time his-her presence inside of oneself. The time had come to be initiated into the Cazimi Climax Portal at the Great Mahamudra Dome, and the little boy inside of Drone was excited about the adventure of experiencing the everlasting living light . Treading on a new path made him feel more alive, more mystified, and closer to his feminine polarity. The Sky is the limit, and the horizon always kept his dire need for thrills to experience outside the comfort zone. One might question: "If you know where God lives, then why are you on the run?" Drone's defensive answer to such a question would be: "So, tell me more about yourself, so that I can learn more about myself!" Anyway, it seems like Drone had been on a rampage of self-justification, and he was angry with himself for not having the courage to cross the bridge, which was suspended between him and God! Today he realized that God began where the senses of his perception ended and this was outside his comfort zone. God can only be met, when one enters the suppressed territory of awe and mystification. God began where his self-ended, and in that sense, he has to become a nobody, nothing, no where and everywhere at the same time! People are a reflection of each other, and in that sense everybody else is thus but another part of yourself. This means, that what Drone sees in another person, is what he sees in himself, because the chemistry of his world is all happening inside the perception of his brain. All of his senses are but the 'one sense of feeling' the motion of light reflections from God's essence! The experience of interacting with other people was teaching Drone to feel His divine presence within his inner space. The Quest for God requires a process of feeling those feelings, which are locked away deep within the Limbic system of his brain. Feelings of Primal Pain, Fear, Sadness and Anger needed to be engaged and witnessed, as they do come and go! The residue that remains after the primal encounter with these feelings is the essence of God. The reactions of other people trigger daily the denial of these Primal feelings. Denial is nothing but the lack of courage to cross the gap suspended in between man and God. Maleeka and Maneesha were about to teach him that nothing should stand in between him and his creator.

Maleeka: " Remember Drone, you choose your beliefs and then the evidence of your senses appears to support those beliefs. Thus, it becomes your reality."

Drone; "The Dominators on mother Earth have polluted our innocence with make believe convictions as to delude me in thinking that I am not okay unless I breathe like they are thinking.

Maleeka: "It's only true if we submit to it. Our validation and obeisance affirm their intentions. Without that it would immediately crumble into dust.

Lies have no power unless believed. That's the power of the awakening.

See Through It for What It Is. We need to see it for what it is. It only comes into being when humanity buys into it!"

Maneesha: "Feel yourself as a holographic light being. There is no struggle, no limitation and no judgment; only allowing-ness, acceptance and the honoring of the sacredness of self and all else."

There was but one desire remaining, which was to become one with the Beloved and all that is divine. The two girls were warming Drone's hands as they approached the House of Love. At the entrance their body vehicles were again sniffed from head to toe, and the melody of their scents were allowed to enter! What Drone witnessed as he walked into this Miraculous place, will be hard to describe to anybody who is limited by the five senses, but he will give it a try for people's sake. Begin to imagine a three-hundred-foot Monolithic Dome with a majestic thirty-three-foot crystal cross in its center, which is surrounded by sacred geometrical figures in the shape of a thousand Lotus petals blossoming. Picture the unusual observation of a giant Lotus made from transparent porcelain. Each Lotus was filled with a pair of lovers seated upright in a Tantric love making position. The transparent flower was resting on a glass stem, which was connected to the transparent core within the crystal cross. The light reflections coming from the ceiling of the Dome seemed to have the brilliance of a million Star-clusters made from little fiber optic lights. The acoustics of the Dome was droning like a Queens beehive, and it appeared as if the Lights on the ceiling were responding to the hum with the flow of a full Light spectrum. Drone was stunned by the miraculous, and Maleeka grasped his moment of frozen awe with her female ability to communicate!

Maleeka: "Here in Anjuna we are perfecting the body spiritually until one becomes so conscious of the deep spiritual meaning of life, that one comes to see life as God sees it!"

Drone: "Who controls all of this?"

Maleeka: "No part of God's substance can be misplaced or placed where it is not wanted."

Drone: "Are all of these people from another planet?"

Maleeka: "These are the Tantric healing masters from planet Earth! Each elected couple has mastered the Art of sexual transcendence, and hence obtained an enlightened 'full' Heart brain capacity. The Humming sounds you hear echoing inside the Dome are the acoustic vibration of orgasm, which keep the crystal cross activated. The devices you see on top of each person's head are called S.Q.U.I.D.S., or Spectrum Quantum Units Integration Device Systems. They record a full sound and color spectrum from the recipient's cortex, which then is transmitted to a central computer, which analyzes and complements the missing octaves. A serial linked converter then activates the sound and color spectrums with harmonic feedback to compensate for the missing energetic Solfeggio gaps! When a couple is out of sync with the Harmonic overtone, then the central computer maintains a perpetual feedback loop of Light and Sound reflections to the Tantric recipients. The reason why it is so important to be in tune with the Harmonic overtone is, that the couples are producing a substance called 'Baji Baji' which in essence is a superconductor of Light. The orgasmic state of being creates so much light, that it manifests itself in the liquid form of their sexual secretions. Each couple is positioned above the Lotus bud, which has a reservoir to collect the 'Baji Baji!' The 'Baji Baji' then runs through the Lotus stems into a larger reservoir surrounding the crystal cross. Inside this reservoir, the 'Baji Baji' is filtered away from the human secretions and bacteria. The 'Baji Baji' is then potentiated with an orgasmic sound and color spectrum, which was received and transmitted by the S.Q.U.I.D. systems. The potentiated 'Baji Baji' then is pumped into the central reservoir of the crystal cross, where it has to age and mature before harvesting. Every seventh day of the week, the apparition of the Sun of God appears, and he grants us his Pillar Peace of "I"! His presence is so intense that it creates a pillar of Light, which in essence is the force, which transforms our nectar into its final stage. We refer to our Tantric end product as: 'Love potion 69', and it is then bottled for a worldwide export to our connected churches of Light. The Tantric discipline is strict and arduous, and the responsibility to create 'Love Potion 69' and 'Poçao do Sangre di Cristo 33' is demanding, for each potion unlocks the Gateway to our Heavenly father.

Drone: "What happens if a person is in love with another person?"

Maleeka: "Personal love is a feeling, which is limited by the five senses. Godly indwelling love is a state of being beyond the sensation of the five senses. We see only the Christ or God quality in all at all times, and in that way, we surrender our problem seeds of thought. God expresses through us the perfect way of the Divine."

Drone: "How different you are!"

Maleeka: "We are in no way different from you, we have only developed our God-given powers to express directly from God!"

Drone: "What is 'Poçao do Sangre di Cristo-33?'

Maleeka: "It is the blood of the Cosmic Babe, which is potentiated into higher Geometrical Light patterns! His blood is evolving our current single pair DNA molecules into the reassembly of six double stranded DNA molecules via bliss-induced braiding. Christ's DNA has a superconductivity that creates a pathway for the imbedding of an inter-dimensional full consciousness pattern. His blood is the symbol of the atonement 'at~one~ment', and he who consumes his blessed blood will be given universal resurrection and the eternal life. We have been made right with God by the blood of Christ's death, because it was Christ who said: **'You will not change me into yourself as you would food of your flesh; but you will be changed into me!'** The Mahamudra or Great Cosmic Orgasm creates a 6th to 12th overtone of successful recursive bliss induced braiding, evident in the spectral emissions, which cause the crystal cross to charge and transform our blood into a pure Christalization. Do you remember, when Maneesha and myself were doing time in the Redwood Crowns?"

Drone: "Yeah, you girls had your menstrual periods!"

Maleeka: "Exactly, and while we were up there swaying in the wind, we tapped our blood into a container, which then was handed to our caregivers! The substance is then potentiated and enriched by Starlight impressions captured by a Schmidt-Cassegrain telescope with gold and silver-coated mirrors, which then further directs the Light into a quartz bottle filled with extremely pure water suspended directly in front of the eyepiece! Once our blood molecules become saturated with Starlight, it then merges into a higher receptive matrix of Lightwave particles, sort of like a 5th dimensional Light body. The potion is then placed in a separate reservoir, which is suspended inside the crystal cross. There are three Domes with a 33-foot crystal cross in each of them, and the potions rotate in between of them. Every Tropical and Sideral mooncyclus, the apparition of our Cosmic Babe appears holographic, after which the men drink this purification potion only. This is your ever upward blessingway. The women can only drink Love potion 69, while the men can drink either Love potion 69 or Sangre di Cristo 33. Each woman is assigned to her specific Lotus, and it is the men who rotate their positions quarterly. The Sangre di Cristo potion is unique for every woman, and should not be mixed with the essence of other women. This potion opens a man's heart and brings him in tune with the essence of his female counter part. The blessings of the Cosmic Babe, then elevates and merges the couples Low-self frequencies with the over-soul matrix of the Lightbody of Christ. The men, who drank from the blood of the lam, are now completely fused with the highest form of Love possible on the face of this Earth! This potion will bring down the walls of the male's defended selves, because it was tapped from a woman's essence in E-motion, and moved by the wind, the Moon and the Stars! A woman on her Moon cycle has to listen to the voice of her body, and the wind is telling her to become One with all that is. The wind is rocking her into an internal sense of Peace, and she then allows the wind to move through her towards the womb of the creator. This atonement is so unique, that some men are able to scent the fragrance of Redwoods, while they drink this sacred potion. It is only when men are not in tune with a woman's need for inner listening, that she can be triggered to act out the unheard message of her raging hormones. A woman needs the nurturing sensation of a listening wind blowing through Redwoods, which calms down her nerve system, and this will make her receptive to receive the Light. These powerful Moon cycle patterns have caused us to readjust our religious practice, into a more flexible and enjoyable flow."

Drone: "Isn't sexual looseness an act against the word of God?"

Maleeka: "It is better to marry, than to burn with sexual desire! However, do not refuse to surrender yourself, because All have to become One in the body of Christ! The real Freedom comes from the obedience to the Word of God. And Mind you, the original dominators have left out and falsified many scriptures as to remove our ability of conceptual Godlike feeling. All positive words or words of accord add energy to our bodies every instant that we are giving them out, and we create an influence that returns and surrounds us with emanating energy. Each word carries its vibration to the very soul of all who speak, hear, or see the word God, and as the soul responds to that vibration, the body from which the radiations come forth is lifted and exalted correspondingly as the soul is exalted by these vibrations. Every word is abstract, a reflection withdrawn from the perfect mirror of God's law! A mirror doesn't do anything, it simply reflects, and in doing so, aids the recipient to transgress the meaning of the word, and feel the 'gap' of the beyond. We have to learn to transcend the limitations of our senses and prepare for the Kingdom of the Beyond!"

Drone: "So we have to obey God's word, and yet at the same time prepare for the transcendence of the beyond?"

Maleeka: "When you make the two One, and when you make the inside like the outside and the outside like the inside, and the above like the below, and when you make the male and the female One and the same… then you will enter the Kingdom of God!"

Drone: "So, we can remain together without mingling with the others?"

Maleeka: "God loves everybody, and his Sun shines for everybody! We can choose to open our hearts, or remain closed like an oyster captured by the limitations of its senses! The majority of women here are able to have their Moon cycle in synchronicity with one another, but there are those that have a different cyclic melody. The first week post menses, a woman makes herself available for the creation of the Love potion 69. The second week post menses, she has to go to the Trance dance Dome, and she then connects herself to the remote S.Q.U.I.D. circuitry. Her bliss induced Trance invocation will then braid and potentiate her menstrual blood suspended inside the Christal cross. During the Trance invocation, the participants are allowed to drink the Daime juice, but this is not a requirement. Daime as you know is a form of liquid light, that enables the dark side of the Soul to be illuminated."

Drone: "Trance dance and romancing your shadow-side!"

Maleeka: "A full spectrum color & sound biofeedback system will assist the participants to express and release deep Primal catharsis at their individual DNA levels. The first 24 hours the dancers release their Primal sexual inhibitions, and this catharsis will bring them to the point of exhaustion. Once the expression of catharsis has been discharged from their body vehicles, a turning point of ecstatic joy kicks in, off which the likes have not been seen on this Earth! A turning point takes place in which the dancers become super charged with the Holy Spirit itself. This is the moment in which everybody spontaneously disrobes, and continues to dance their way to God. A true divination takes place, and the dancers touch each other, while maintaining eye contact with the essence of Soul. In a way, it is a Dreamtime-Sundance, which invokes the participants to surrender their pain into the hands of the Cosmic Babe. The S.Q.U.I.D. systems record and harmonize all frequencies, which then Christalizes the female menses blood suspended inside the crystal cross's reservoir, with a 6th to a 12th overtone of successful recursive bliss induced braiding. In the third week post menses, the women make themselves available again for the production of Love Potion 69. In the fourth week post menses, the women return again to their Trance Dance invocation, and it is during this cycle that their hormones are triggering a phase of ovarian heat. In male terminology, you might say that they become aroused and ready to mate. The conditions are now optimum to experience the Great Mahamudra or otherwise called; 'the Great Cosmic Orgasm!' During this cycle, their juices will flow abundantly and surge at an all-time high. Their nectar now brings forth the best aroma to produce the Love Potion 69, and their male counterparts intensely enjoy the succulence of their vortices. On the last day of the feminine ovarian heat wave, the women naturally perform fellatio on their male counterparts, because their semen now has become so potent, that it becomes a necessity for the women to energize themselves with the force of life before the discharge of their Menses. As soon as the Menses cycle begins, the women retreat, themselves into the crowns of the Redwoods, and the men gather at the hot springs. It takes about four years of intense training to master the Great Mahamudra, and only a few succeed to transmute into an Androgynous being. Only the Androgynous Tantric Masters are eligible for time travel by means of our Golden Christal Disc. Our Masters work for the Cosmic Babe and his Heavenly Father. They travel to the so-called Shadow Star Systems, where the presence of their being illuminates the Dark side of Gods Universe. Hell, and Heaven are both created by our Heavenly Father, and both are under the auspices of his power. Hell in essence is, when a person is not able to receive God's Light directly into the feeling center, because one is being misled by the limitations set upon the reception of one's senses, which by their intrinsic nature are only able to detect the motion of God's reflection of Light. Your senses are Light reflection motion detectors, but they cannot register the essence of God's Light as stillness! A Quantum Leap of Faith is needed in order to learn how to merge with the presence of God's stillness. "Be still, and know that I am God" is a verse from Psalm 46:10 in the Bible, emphasizing the importance of quietness and trust in God's sovereignty and power. It encourages individuals to find peace in recognizing God's presence and authority in their lives. This is a path, where you will have to move beyond the daily distractions of your Earthly life as you know it, and it demands a commitment to authenticity. It is the thirst to know the original behind the reflection that makes you worthy of the 'Ultimate Accident/Quantum Leap' into the stillness of God's presence. So always be prepared for the Ultimate Accident, the unknown, ready, waiting, and receptive. God is the balanced stillness of Omnipresent White Magnetic Light at eternal rest within itself, waiting to be received by a host. Without the invitation the Guest 'Holy Spirit', will never come."

Maleeka gave Drone a pregnant pause of silence to digest her spirited lecture, and as soon as their breathing cycles were in accord with each other again, she continued.

Maleeka: "Drone, in order for you to participate in the Great Mahamudra, you will have to pass the Holography regression test. This is a tool that will enable us to sense if you are able to tap into the Power of Zero-point energy."

Maneesha guided Drone out of the Love Dome, and the three of them walked over to a private Tantric chapel, where they undressed each other. They sat down naked, and triangulated a Lotus position. It was time to meditate upon the temptation of the flesh, and it was a challenge for Drone to resist their surging pheromone levels. Maneesha stood up and placed one foot on his shoulder, and her Garter belt, which was chained to her pierced labia, opened her private self, spread Eagle! Her vortex invited

Drone to give her the cunnilingus treat, and with his lips he juiced her right up to the point, where she was wet enough to slide right on top of him. Drone loved the sweet taste of this woman! Maneesha looked him straight in the eyes as he kissed her vortex, and Maleeka still seated in her Lotus position began to channel the Holy Spirit!

Maleeka: "It is important at this time, that the both of you run your inner orbit of liquid light. This energy will open up your Full Heart-Brain Capacity, which is needed to fully comprehend the Holographic principle of remote viewing. The Ancient Mother knows that the flesh must be illumined by the light of the flame, which is first kindled from within, then allowed to shine forth to the world without!"

Maneesha was charging up her vortex by riding her G-spot over Drone's extended self, and the scent of her pheromones now really began to arouse his inner world of imagination. Within no time they were both humming like a pair of humming birds in mating season, and Maneesha dug her nails deep into his back as an expression of her joy. Her hum now changed into the purr of a pussycat, and they rocked each other's cradle to the rhythm of their heartbeats. The voice of Maleeka interrupted their passionate love making, and the vibes of her voice felt like a shockwave disturbing his lily pond.

Maleeka: "Can you not see that man's true vibratory sphere is the whole vibratory sphere of God if he lives in that sphere? To make God alive and vital to you, you must think and know that you are God!"

Drone: "Stop talking!"

Maneesha: "Surrender and listen!"

Maleeka: "You will find that the vibrations of your body will change from the human to the God vibration. As you think, feel, live, move, and become one with this vibration, you become it!"

Drone: "Stop talking!"

Maneesha: "Surrender and listen!"

Maleeka: "God loves you when you stand steadfast with your eyes always fixed upon the light of His being. Meditate only upon the true desire of your heart, and you will come to know that you are the God light!"

Drone: "Be Quiet!"

Maneesha: "Hush, surrender and listen!"

Maleeka: "We lift these bodies up until their shining radiance becomes a blaze of pure, white light and together we have returned to the father from whence all have come forth. The silken matrix of God's substance is the Unified Force Field, this is the source in which all things exist and, because of that existence, the vibrations are so high that none can perceive them. The God habit is to see this perfect presence within you with every breath that you take!"

Drone: "Can you please be quiet?"

Maneesha: "Surrender and listen!"

Maleeka: "Soon the Everlasting living light will shine forth from your Celestial Third Eye, as it has to all enlightened masters. Recall and know that every time you think God, you are part of God's Divine plan."

Drone: "Oh shut up! How can I surrender to a God I can't see?"

Maneesha: "Command your inner self to live true to the teachings of Christ. The instant you lift your thought to the Christ, your body responds to the Christ vibration; thus, you do conceive and bring forth the Christ, who is completely amalgamated with a silken God. Know yourself as one in harmony with the Infinite and transcend this principle to manifest the perfection of the God Love!"

Maleeka: "The Cosmic Babe is where the redemptive energies of the Body of Light are manifested. When they are acknowledged and manifested within you, you become part of his lineage, and his collective Oversoul! When you **drink his blood**, he will be evolving your current single pair DNA molecules into the reassembly of six double stranded DNA molecules via bliss-induced braiding. Your DNA will then Christalize and become One with his eternal body of the Living Light. Christ's DNA has a superconductivity, that creates a pathway for the imbedding of an inter-dimensional full consciousness pattern, which enables you to see in Universe beyond Universe. One must recognize All Universes 'his Domain' in order to see God. We will only be able to relate to the world around us, when we understand the world within us, because we experience everything within ourselves as a Morse code perception of the World around us."

Drone: "How can your menstrual blood transform into the unique DNA pattern of an ascended Christ?"

Maleeka: "The S.Q.U.I.D.-systems record and harmonize all frequencies, which then Christalizes the single pair DNA of the menses blood suspended inside the crystal cross's reservoir, with a 6th to a 12th overtone of successful recursive bliss induced braiding into six double stranded fully Christalized DNA molecules. This is the evolved blood of Christ!"

Drone: "How do I transgress beyond my inert social conditioning?"

Maneesha: "The voice inside knows that every man/woman must transcend the mortal, the fleshly desires, the doubts and fears, until he/she comes to the perfect knowing of the indwelling everlasting living light of an awesome God. It is His omni-presence in which we all live. We live it with every heartbeat and with every breath we take. Everything is breathing Him"

Maleeka: "The most attractive model of our nervous system is the holographic imagery, which gives the basic principles upon which memory is established. These principles of holographic imagery appear to spread throughout the body, relating with input (the sensory system), the central nervous system (Cybernetics), and output (functions of the body).

Drone: "Can you explain it in a more down to Earth language?"

Maleeka: "Imagine God to be pure light that splits of in a reference beam of light that shines through a Lense of his creations called human beings. God wants us to create and to find him in this creation. We humans can witness our bodies, our emotions, our thoughts, our soul, but only when we witness the witness within can we find him as the One who is really seeing.

Drone: "I get it!"

Maleeka: "Holography is the study of pictures produced by using laser light to illuminate subject matter (your internal world), or a three-dimensional picture created by energy interference patterns. Two beams from the same source interacting produce a hologram. It is a unique principle in nature, which shows that every piece can contain the essence of the whole. Many individuals will reach out to touch a quality hologram, only to find a handful of empty space."

Maleeka's metaphysical meta-babble lingo made Drone lose his erection, and she immediately shifted her gear to a level, where he could relate to her information in a more enchanting manner.

Maleeka: "Every Human Being is a sexed creation of God, and all are limited by their senses, and thus perceive differences only in a strange Morse code language of action and rest. **Man is the only unit in Creation, who can bring conscious awareness into the Spirit within him, and have the awareness of Gods dually, conditioned reflection of light acting upon his senses. These two pulsing Lightwave extensions of the One still light, within your inner sky, is for the purpose of recording experience patterns in your body of matter.** Experience is recorded electro-magnetically in your body of matter with the impression of two pulsing, interchanging lights. Man and woman alone can be freed from their body vehicles when they see themselves as the centering light of Creation. This divine vision may shock many of you, but it has to be understood by the analogy with the Hologram. The Laser **reference** beam of God's light is pure and virgin within the essence of origin, and as such can be compared to the absolute Witness within us. This is the light that cannot be experienced by our nervous system. The absolute Witness within us is in **essence** the eye of God looking into our subjective world. The Laser **object** or **working** beam, is a light beam that splits of from the absolute reference beam as a semitransparent light. This is **the reflection** of light, which comes from God's essence, but is not his essence, because we are able to perceive this type of light with our sensory nervous system. The Laser **working** beam can be compared to the Seeker, the Searcher, your Questioning Mind, which can encounter objectives like: 'your physical body, and the chemistry of sensation that takes place inside of it!' Your nervous system can sense anything that is within motion like: 'movement, muscle contractions, heartbeats, breathing, E~motions, thoughts, dreams, Soul!' The veils, which cover up the semitransparency of your memory bank, can be unraveled with the experience of Orgasm and Primal Scream! Our Mind's eye '**working beam**' is a seeker on a journey of experiencing the duality of life, seeking to merge with the Beloved or the Absolute Witness 'God's **reference beam**' within! When this ultimate merging takes place, then all of your experiences as you know it within this dimension will cease to exist. For, if your body substance is recording the electromagnetic waves of experience, then electromagnetism, which records experience, and the experience itself, are non-existent! Within our moments of inner peace, we expand as consciousness, and we accelerate the life vibrations of our body vehicles with the blissful infusion of God's light encompassing our atomic matrix. Our blood and flesh are illuminated by the light of the flame that is first kindled from within, and then allowed to infuse with the all-encompassing axiatonal lattice of God's Universe within

Universes! We are frozen Starlight waiting for our beloved to defrost our essence, and to fill us with his Living Light. We are the manifestation of 'living' Stardust that came traveling upon the waves of Starlight; hence, we who are God's atomic matrix became able to receive the reflections of his light. It is the Living light that gave us life, and it is through intentional prayer that we can request from God, that which is already in existence! We are the Hosts that can invite our beloved Guest to shine through our body vehicle, and to fill us up with the Living Light of his divine presence. By nurturing Gods essence within our lucid vehicle, we can celebrate existence and bathe in the presence of his Light, with brilliancy far greater than the biggest Starlight eruption ever! God created us in his image, but we deny ourselves the courage and luxury to see ourselves as a reflection of him, the One, who is one with all that is! Our courage is being hooked and subdued by the boring emotions of Social, Political, and religious conditioning, which in their turn are addicted to the primal Adrenaline chemistry of 'Fight, Fright and Flight' reactions! These emotions are draining the Living Daylights out from your body vehicle, and *they intentionally distract you away from your authentic thirst to know God's stillness!* That is why it is said in **James 4: 4. 'To be the World's lover means becoming the enemy of God!'** A courageous person will move into the Son-light provided by his Heavenly Father, who reins within our inner skies, and she will allow the flame of awareness burn away that which belongs to the World. We shall fly into his divine flame of no return. How long shall it take before you can look God straight into the eyes and say out loud: 'forgive me Lord for not recognizing you, forgive me for neglecting you in everything that I experience! From this day forth, what I see in you is what I see in me, so I must be you!' Once we become able to look God straight in the eyes, then we will be able to accept and merge with the image of his Universe within Universes. If we are to participate in the ongoing divine evolution of continuity and change within the creative continuum of the higher evolution, we must allow the Son of God to redeem ourselves in order to quicken the collective ascension of each and every one of us! Consciousness seeks and gravitates towards consciousness, and the Seeker within each of us can cover long distances in space and observe many aspects of itself within a very short period of time. As our ability to capture an expanded state of consciousness increases, our inner time increases, so we can start remembering some information we may have received while traveling and exploring our inner skies. The Seeker within our inner sky is searching for other aspects of itself in order to feel complete again. Every search for thrills is in essence the search for the stillness of God's presence within a world of sensory deception. All of us are in search of the Eternal Witness within or otherwise referred to as our Eternal Redeemer, which is the absolute reference beam and pillar of pure God-light."

Maleeka paused, and Maneesha moved her pelvic region in circular motions in order to reactivate the blood-flow back into Drone's relaxing vortex. The movement within her pelvic region helped him to be calibrated again with the pursuit of his physical endeavors. The gratifying feeling of bliss in his loins distracted Drone from remaining centered in spirit, but then again, that might have been the challenge of his training!

Maleeka: "The Witness or Absolute observer within our inner sky is the last 'missing link' within our world of experiential perceptual awareness. It is not that it is not there, but we continue to keep on missing it. This Witness within our inner sky exists in all of our life experiences. When we learn to witness the Witness within as a continuum under all circumstances, then we create the soil upon which our Heavenly father can tread. We are pure content-less consciousness, and that is God's presence, which has been guiding us through a long and eventful trip back to itself! Allow yourself to move into this area, where you may not have been touched before, exhale and welcome this inner bliss! Calibrate yourself to your Heavenly father, and welcome the pouring out of his blessings with an open heart. When in doubt like your Grandfather Thomas once was, then breathe into this fear, and allow the Primal Pains take over the expressions of your catharsis."

As Maneesha exhaled, Drone inhaled. Her breath was fresh and sweet. Drone intuitively felt that he was being filled with something divine. His sexual Ener~'chi' was now clearly running through the energy channels of his inner orbit. The sensation of Maneesha's hands on his back was sensational, and he became aware that she was breathing energy through the palm of her branding hands. It made him aware of his breathing pattern, and how the energy, which was being created inside of him, was now moving through his hands into Maneesha's body. It felt as if they were melting effortlessly into a space, where only the sky is the limit. They French kissed and captured a gust of Prana, in and out, on and on! Drone felt like he was about to hyperventilate, and his body became charged with tingling sensations. A spell of dizziness kicked in, and he simply lost it! Spacing out! Within his Mind's eye, he could clearly see Light particles 'photons' dancing all around him, and they were touching his skin as gently as the landing of a shower of snowflakes. There were these fluffy white clouds in the sky, and Drone felt himself being a guest, drifting in the house of the heavenly Father. As his Soul slowly returned to his body, he noticed that his body was in a state of wordless bliss! The voice of Maleeka requested him to open his eyes and pause. His right hand was to be placed onto the back of Maneesha's head, thus activating the Gate of Jade. The palm of his left hand was to be placed on Maneesha's heart, and they were to breathe through their palms, while at the same time maintain eye contact and run their inner orbit!

Maleeka: "Bring all the sufferings of yourself, each other, and the World into your heart, and pour out all of your blessings. When you breathe in, feel that you are breathing in all the miseries of all the people in the world. All the darkness, the shadow sides, all negativity, all the Hell that exists anywhere, all Problem Seeds of Thought, you are breathing it all in. Moreover, let it be absorbed in your heart. Allow God, his son the Cosmic Babe, and the Holy Spirit to release, cleanse, and transmute these energies into the Light of mutual Love! In addition, when you breathe out, breathe out all the joy that you have, all the bliss and benediction that you feel! Breathe out, pour yourself into existence."

Drone's body would shiver as Maneesha moved her pelvic region, and it made his abdominal muscles contract spontaneously, as if responding to the release of Primal feelings entrapped within his body vehicle. In the depth of his being, Drone felt fear for the unknown, but at the surface, the shivering felt good. For a man it is hard to have intimacy at the core level of his being, and waves of energy in motion 'E~motion' were rushing through Drone's body vehicle. Doubt clouded his Mind, and it kept firing the stigma of non-sense! His body was contracting and relaxing, pulsing in accord with Maneesha, and within his heart, he could sense her sensations of pain and bliss. Together they were surfing their innate primal feelings of pain and joy. Maneesha's essential juices were now flowing abundantly, and the sweet scent of surrender made his abdomen contract increasingly. Maleeka observed and explained the physical phenomena they were going through.

Maleeka: " There is so much survival stress stored within our bodies at a cellular level, that for most of us human beings, it takes a life time to *discharge and transmute* our primal pains. The key is to move your sexual energies through the E~motional forces of inhibition, and then to allow your catharsis to naturally unfold itself. The memory of your unity with God creates your sexual desire to return back to the ultimate immediate Beloved! Sexual interaction stirs up the psychic flashbacks and the physical pains, which were suppressed in order to serve the guilt of shame and blame hallucinations. The discovery and embracing of your pains naturally unfold themselves into catharsis of your primal self. Catharsis sometimes appears to last forever, but given time, it will naturally loop back into an extended state of orgasm. The deeper one moves into it, the more profound the final feeling of bliss will be. Catharsis is an essential part of orgasm, because pain and pleasure are energies in motion, and in search for the presence of God's stillness. The joy of sex lies dormant within the private domain of your Limbic system, which is the memory bank for your primal suppressed feelings. The free expression of primal feelings will deepen the level of intimacy shared between two partners, to a depth, which is not of this world. The gentle intrusive force of sex will assist you to move your E~motions out from their cultural conditioned gridlock patterns. Sex will unlock the cave man and woman, and their mutual catharsis will open up all possibilities for an unlimited access to becoming orgasmic. We can feel your pain, we know your longing to be One and whole again, hence the more E~motional crud you become able to express and release, the closer you will come to be to that which you seek! God is waiting for you to prepare yourself well, so that you become worthy to be in the Presence of that beautiful area of 'Silent Solitude' infused with the reverence no man knows."

Slowly Drone opened his eyelids, and as he looked into Maneesha's eyes, there were these Stars within stars reflected upon the retina of her eyes. She drew him in, and the flickering and flaming of candlelight's all around them had the effect of moving him deeper into the indwelling of his being. A gentle force moved Drone through his cellular membranes, and into the braiding factory of his single pair DNA strings. There were strands of Heli(xes), colorful, shady, rotating irregular due to the heavy attachments of unresolved E~motional crud. Bliss induced braiding of these DNA-strands can only occur, when you become able of E~motional catharsis and elevation of consciousness. The rhythm of his breathing pattern was pulling his attention in and out of his body, and Drone, the way he knew himself was melting, pausing, surrendering, and merging with God's Universe reflected onto the retina of Maleesha's eyes. The gravitational forces of his cellular awareness pulled him back into a blissful braiding of his Heli, and there was light 'photons' being created and directed into the crud attached to his DNA! The experiences of the ancient mystics were coming through, and they flashed him by at a high firing rate, which induced a fear that astounded him. For a couple of seconds Drone was stunned by awe, and he gasped for air. Maneesha sensed his despair, and she tightened up her succulent grip around his loins. She grounded him, and Drone became able to bring his awareness back into his emotional crud, which upon the presence of his attention, now was being transmuted into an energy force that observes itself. His body was trembling with tiny shockwaves, a feeling that he remembered from the times when he felt more alive. Tiny muscle ripples, which when traced back to their source of origin were caused by the emotional energy shifts at a cellular level. Deep within the electron orbits of the atomic matrix he found himself in a process of emotional detox, a catharsis, and a blissful braiding, which was increasing his vibratory levels of perception. With his awareness he was dissolving and transmuting his emotional crud into an Axiatonal light lattice, which was rebuilding the essence of his Soul. The flickering of candle lights made Maneesha's complexion shape shift as if she was time traveling through her projection of her past life memories. At a cellular level, she seemed to be in a process of catharsis. Her body had stored old feelings of pain, which was trapped within the energy levels of her DNA. Her complexion shape shifted into the appearance of a man, a woman, a deity, an animal, a child, a baby, an embryo, a tree, an ocean, psychedelic colors, aliens, Universe within

Universes. Drone's body felt compressed, and yet he was expanding at an accelerated rate, moving in and out of his own cellular memory! There were these waves of feelings, which kept coming and coming. Feelings like awe, thrills, shock, bliss, pain, ecstasy, fear, love, contractions, and flashes of orgasm! Her complexion kept moving in and out of a recognizable imagery, and Drone felt himself moving deeper and deeper into the world of the atom. Within his Mind's eye he could clearly see atoms and electrons spinning around within their orbits, and God's light was being created within the matrix of their empty space. At a subatomic level, God was commanding Drone to defrost his Starseed potential and rekindle the eternal flame of awareness. God was assisting Drone to let go of his emotional crud. His divine being invited him to merge with a higher light receptive matrix, which at its best could be described as a 4th or 5th dimensional Lightbody. His surrender to the exquisite axiatonal lattice of this Divine being caused the excitement of raw bliss! Thank you Lord for your precious gift of the living Light. Within his Mind's eye, Drone now became aware of an increased intensity of light. It almost felt as if somebody was turning on a light bulb of a 100,000-Watts! This light was alive and it made him feel as if his body no longer limiting him! Within these movements of time, space and energy, his field of dreams was being opened, and he could clearly see high frequency bodies ascend and descend within space. His heart felt connected to everything alive and kicking within this Universe, and it felt awesome! His being was being calibrated in coherent resonance with the Holy Spirit, and he felt himself expanding into God's domain.

Maneesha was rotating the lips of her uterus around the sensors of his glans, and this feeling thrust him right back into his sexual orbit. Deep within the magical jungle of their loins, they just had to feel each other again. The rhythm of his breathing pattern made him slip and slide in and out of her Amazon basin. From time to time, there were these spastic convulsive contractions, which pulled Drone deep into her vortex area. Maneesha's inner and outer succulent labia were swollen with excitement, and her breasts were being enlarged by the pumping blood-flow coming from her strong heart. With his Mind's eye, 'remote viewing' Drone was capturing pictures from Maneesha's past life events, and yet at the same time he was witnessing a Christalization, which took place at his cellular level. Her reflections were moving in and out of his being, and suddenly, as if struck by lightning, all of the reflections disappeared, and Drone was facing an empty space! To himself he thought; 'Somebody must have zapped her out of my reality, or I'm being misled by my senses!' With all of his might, Drone made an effort to focus, and she reappeared. Maleeka must have noticed his energy shift, because she started to speak again.

Maleeka: "Drone, I noticed within my Mind's eye that you were embracing the emptiness of your orbital electron matrix, and I salute you for your courage. You will come to learn how to nurture this place of stillness. Allow your 'self' to relax, and then move forwards to melt with it. It will be scary at first, because we are built and conditioned to detect things in morse-code motion only. The bliss induced braiding of the Axiatonal lattice of your body vehicle will increase your vibratory rate to the level of Galactic Harmonic Resonance. One needs to be calibrated and in accord with the Heavenly Father, because once you are granted the ability to tap into this Zero-point energy or Unified Force Field, then your feet may tread upon his divine domain. His Unified Force Field contains within itself the baseline power source of all energy manifestations. The Harmonic Resonance Rate of your light body vehicle enables you to travel through a resonant matrix of Axiatonal gridlines, within which information transmission is virtually 'instantaneous!' Knowing the capacity of how to feel and merge with his Unified Force Field by means of sexual unification will teach you how to access God's supernormal power resources. These powers will teach you how to remain ordinary within an extra ordinary world of creation. The energy created by your conscious acts of being intimate sexually is the force that will transform your body into becoming a superconductor of light. Ultimately you will grow and become one with the love of Christ, and it is by the powers of his character that you will overcome the duality of your male female polarity."

Maleeka touched Maneesha and Drone lightly on the shoulders, and it was time to return to the senses of being active in the here now! Maneesha disconnected her succulent labia from his pulsing vortex, and they replenished themselves with a drink of electrolytes. Her smiling face and the touch of her grace kept them feeling connected. They were to contain their level of intimacy, because they were most vulnerable. There was an open bathroom, where they each took turns of relieving themselves from excessive waste fluids. The sharing of a private affair deepened their level of intimacy. It excited Drone to see his two women squat down spread Eagle in order to relieve themselves from their excessive bodily waste products. Only God knew that he loved these two women more than anything, and yet, at the same time Drone realized that he had to meet his maker!

The Spy - by the Doors

I'm a spy in the house of love
I know the dreams that you're dreamin' of
I know the words that you long to hear
I know your deepest secret fear.

I'm a spy in the house of love
I know the dreams that you're dreamin' of
I know the words that you long to hear
I know your deepest secret fear

I know ev'rything
Ev'rything you do
Ev'rywhere you go
Ev'ryone you know

I'm a spy in the house of love
I know the dreams that you're dreamin' of
I know the words that you long to hear
I know your deepest secret fear

I know your deepest secret fear
I know your deepest secret fear
I'm a spy
I can see you
What you do
And I know

Chapter Ten ~
You make me real

Everything that God made is waiting with excitement for the time when God will show the world who his children are.

Romans 8: 19

We know that everything God made has been waiting until now in pain, like a woman ready to give birth.

Romans 8: 22

So, we are waiting for God to finish making us his own children. I mean we are waiting for our bodies to be made free.

Romans 8: 23

But the light makes all things easy to see. And everything that is made easy to see can become light. This is why it is said: 'Wake up, sleeper! Rise from death, and Christ will shine on you.'

Ephesians 5: 13 – 14.

I leave you peace. My peace I give you. I do not give it to you as the world does. So, do not let your hearts be troubled.

John 14: 27.

Peace to all of you who are in Christ.

1 Peter 5: 14.

But the Spirit gives love, joy, peace, patience, kindness, goodness, faithfulness, gentleness, and self-control. There is no law that says these things are wrong.

Galatians 5: 22 – 23.

For a person is a slave of anything that controls him. They were made free from the evil in the world by knowing our Lord and Savior Jesus Christ.

2 Peter 2: 19 – 20.

God invites people to feel the ultimate experience of immediacy.

Drone: "What is the ultimate way to God?"

Maneesha: "Ultimate? God is immediate; hence, there is no way!

Drone: "Why does God use his Son Jesus Christ as a mediator?"

Maneesha: "God's love is so intense, that we need his mediators to gracefully adjust to his level of being, sort of like the electricity of a sudden clash of thunder."

Drone: "People make the impression to be drawn to Jesus as being a mediator between them and their God! To me the birth of Jesus, the Christ symbolizes the birth of Light within every human cell of consciousness. Jesus came to show us that God not only dwells in the Universes around us, but His presence can also be found in the Universes within us. God never intended for us to be separated from him or any of his creations. God is all-inclusive, and this means that his light is also to be illuminated within our inner and outer worlds of darkness. We have to romance our shadow side, and God will then enlighten our darkness with the brilliance of his light. This is the hardest nut to crack for all those stubborn believers, who have put their trust into their fluctuating emotional stock market. When somebody truly radiates the sunlight of God, then his or her mission should be to shed Light into the Dark corners of shame, guilt and fear. Man is not allowing the living light of God to shine through his body vehicle, because of his inborn fear of rejection. However, fear can only depart within the allowance of love in man's fragile heart!"

Maleeka: "WOW ! the visible invisible of inner true being, back on rise to inner space where emptiness become wholeness. When the Holy Spirit comes upon you, the God power will manifest in the flesh! Jesus said: 'you shall be perfect even as your Father in heaven is perfect. He who walks and lives as I have lived, shall not walk in darkness, but shall have Eternal life, and shall be free from all limitations.' Man and woman are struggling to be free from the limitation of sensory perception, and yet their search for thrills leads them on towards the insane polarity of extremes! Is there not more life to be found in the arms of a woman, who can immerse you with the virgin light of her essence being with her womb awakening?"

Drone: "I need my testosteron thrills in order to feel alive!"

Maleeka: "Your thirst for thrills has led you away from your inner Quest for a feminine nurturing God. The average human being has become emotionally cocooned & mummified, and their true feelings have been replaced by a plastic braided identity. It is only to the degree that we are not in tune with **God's** rhythm of breathing as it is in fact, that there is a discord in your own nature. The human body becomes perfected in the flesh, when man lives true to the God vibration. Your sex-drive is in search for the immediate experience of a silken touch, which when released may cause to dawn a true reverence for the sublime purity of God. The great 'condemnation of sin' can be forgiven, when we allow His everlasting living light to shine and dance through our body vehicles. A great many have taken false comfort in the belief that man is a 'born sinner' and that man can never be as perfect as his infallible God in heaven. The power of sin is rooted as the result of wrongful thinking. Erase the false belief and sickness vanishes. Always fix your Celestial eye steadfastly on the living God and His divine perfection. His everlasting living light will transform your shadow pain!"

Drone: "How can I communicate with a God, who is immaculate?"

Milika: "By constantly connecting, communicating, praising, praying, blessing and giving thanks and glory to His divine love and by singing and glorifying His divine name, you increase His light, and as you do this, it becomes more potent and readily accessible to you. You will come to know that as you keep your body in the divine vibration, you never grow old and will never die, because the gift of God to the God-man is eternal life. It takes courage, because every fear of mortal thought and limitation must be erased, you must come to know without fear or manmade belief, that you are a child of God, who has the power to master the principle of His silken matrix; 'the Unified Force Field'!"

Drone: "Will this change my body?"

Maleeka: "We reassemble ourselves within a new garment of pure white light. This sacred light shines steadily on, and its purity shines through the receptive souls and hearts of those who cultivated their inner beings. When you live freely in this light vibration, then all who are near to it will be drawn to man's true abiding place."

Maneesha: "Tantric sex is a way to build a safe container, in which fear will be dissipated and transformed into a higher form of love. All men and women are created equal into the image of God as One body. With our brain we can receive God's divine messages, which when heard, are to create our divine reality. God impresses gracefully his divine will on the courses of our life, and when we surrender and redeem ourselves to his will, then that relationship will return our Heaven on this Earth! When the living light is being welcomed to shine through our body vehicles, then he will free us from the consequences of sin. In order to live we must surrender ourselves with the right use of will to the still light of knowing how to live in communion with him. The mighty works of Jesus can and will be done by All of those who live in immediacy with the stillness of His presence. Once understood, one will come to realize, that there is nothing mysterious about these works. The mystery is only in man's mortal concept of them. All of your previous perceived limitations will end the moment you enter the domain of his divine centering source of stillness. The Eternal divination of the beloved awaits you at the other end of your projected self, within space, where it will ultimately await to void you, and resurrect you with the presence of his seeing light. Resurrection provides no provision for the division between the world within and without. The in goes on flowing into the out, and the out goes flowing into the in; it is a non-dual presence of breathing. Prayer does not tire, because it is relaxation itself within everything that is the source of heart. One has simply merged with the overall indwelling of a living God, and that being is the same as the being of all. The invocation of the Holy Spirit is the immediacy of a purer element, which is not in search for thrills. Instead, the Host is in a state of silent pregnancy for the Eternal Guest to come. All power is born out of the polarity of friction creating electricity. The power that originates from peace, non-friction, non-fight, non-manipulation, is the power of a rose flower, a wild child, a man crying, the dewdrops of a mountain. It is immense, but not heavy; it is infinite, but not violent. Prayer is the knowing of the beyond as another greater yourself. You cannot bring it in, but you can learn to be open to it. It lifts you up beyond you, and you have to disappear into it, in order for you to be born into His image and similitude."

Maneesha sighed, and the warmth of her breath brought Drone back into the here now.

Maleeka: "Are you ready for your next session?"
Drone: "That I am!"

With his legs crossed in a Lotus posture, Drone awaited Maneesha to merge her intimate self with his private self. His vortex was relaxed at first, but as Maneesha approached him with her naked self, his heart became excited. Her succulent vortex embraced him like a suction cup, and he could feel that she had mastered the coordination of her innate private parts!

Maleeka: "In order for this session to be successful, Maneesha will have to create a vacuum in between your interlocking vortices, as to prevent the higher creation of energies from draining away! Maneesha will pump out the excess of air from her procreation cavity by using the constriction valves of her vortex muscles. This vacuum seal is needed, because either one of you may lose consciousness during this exercise, due to the excessive amounts of bliss that you will come to experience. It is important that the flow of your sexual orbits is not to be broken, because such an interruption would damage and alter the Christalization of your DNA patterns. This process of blissful braiding and the reorganization of your Christalized DNA into the reassembly of six double stranded DNA molecules will need your total commitment until the cycle is complete.

This exercise will take you all the way into the level of Tantric mastery of electric circuitry."

The thought of being sucked into a vacuum seal triggered Drone into a past experience, which at the time was a very embarrassing experience with Yuka.

Drone: "Are you able to deflate us afterwards?"
Maleeka: "Most certainly!"

Maneesha activated her succulent constrictive muscles, and it felt as if his vortex was swelling, and stretching at maximum capacity. Waves of pain and pleasure were surging in the primal zone of his brain, and Drone allowed himself to expand into a space of total freedom.

Maleeka: "Are you comfortable and calibrated my beloved?"
Drone: "Yeah, let's get it on!"

Maleeka's hypnotic voice soon brought Drone into a space of trance induced imagination, and he could feel that Maneesha's belly button began to breathe in accord with him.

Maleeka: "Emptiness is there only, when it is full of content-less presence. It is there, when all of your obstructions have been dropped. It is there, when you do not have anything inside, when nobody is there to be an observer to it. This emptiness is not even an experience, because if you experience it, it means that you were there to fill the empty space. The emptiness in essence is you, who can no longer experience itself as a self. Experience implies duality, the observer and the observed, the knower and the known, the subject and the object, the seer and the seen.

Full emptiness is filled with a no-thingness, and it is this gap, which will invite you into the stillness of His presence. Sex is not about having tingling sensations in between the polarity of sexual organs. **Sex is about our longing to return to the oneness of balance from which we were divided into two.** God gives us a little taste of heaven with every orgasm that we may experience, and it is this taste that will guide us back to his Garden of Eden. God puts us to the test, and in order for us to receive the Great Mahamudra or Cosmic orgasm, we will have to master the shadow side within ourselves, and become worthy of his approval to enter his garden! Maneesha will guide us through it!"

Maneesha did seem absent up to this point, but the revival of her presence made Drone realize, that he was the one, who was too much occupied with his inner world.

Maneesha: "Close your eyes and begin to breathe in accord with me. Sex is the snake, which took us out from Paradise, but sex is also the snake, which will take us back to His Paradise. We must conquer this snake with Godly guided right use of will. *We shall ride the snake to the lake!* Imagine yourself in a supine position facing the stars. Know and feel deep within yourself, that you are a child of God, who came traveling as stardust from the galaxies of the omni-galactic source. Tune into the stars with all of your senses, and allow yourself the time to feel and merge with their unique pulsations of light. Become One with the pulse of Starlight. Allow yourself to feel this light pulsing inside the matrix of your body vehicle, then bring your awareness into your heartbeat and feel God's living light pulsing through your body vehicle. Feel and merge with the light. Listen to the echo of your heartbeat pulsation, and feel the moment in which your heartbeat begins to beat in accord with this starlight pulsation. You may notice a sense of expansion, and without warning you may observe, that you are actually leaving the body in and out. Within the safe container of your consciousness, you can now surf the waves of starlight back to their original source. Ride these waves of light, and it may actually feel as if you are sliding in and out of different emotional realities. Ride these waves of emotional joy! Surf the light, and the light will serve you! Let it rip and slide…! Allow yourself to pause and melt. Ride the wave in harmony with the infinite! Your visual eyes are now on the verge of becoming centered into your third eye, and as you are becoming centered, and comfortable, you begin to notice, that you have closed your visual eyes without any effort on your part. As you have closed your eyes, it seems as if the Stars are still there, but now they are being reflected on the screen of your Mind's eye. Gradually, but with certainty, we become aware of a magnetic pull within ourselves, and as this pull becomes stronger, we then surrender to this cosmic energy dance! God's silken matrix appears to be a Void, and your senses are not getting a reading on it. The Void pulls in your inborn curiosity to explore, but your inborn survival mechanism wants to usher you into the opposite direction. This is a very painful and frightening experience, and it feels like one is drifting in eternal darkness. There is no way out, no exit door, and this experience has to be taken all the way to the end of your existence as you know or remember it. Embrace and welcome this fear for non-existence. Amnesia kicks in, and it seems as if the ever-increasing pressure makes you forget the things you know about yourself, and yet at the same time, this pressure is opening up unrevealed divine Galactic doorways. As you are sliding through the pores of your memory cell membranes, you become enchanted to break on through to the other side of the veil, which kept these cells together. This magnetic pull comes from a black hole, which overrides all forces known to man. The resistance felt in your body finally gives in and surrenders. This all-encompassing pull into the Great Nothing, makes you feel drunk with existence, and all matter that falls into a rotating black hole loses its point of reference! You feel lost, but you persist on scanning the movie screen of your Mind's eye, and increasingly you become senseless and disoriented. Your physical body now becomes so dense, that the gravitational pull on your body compresses all of your light-body particles into a compacted glow of mass. This is what we refer to as the compression of light into the liquid mold of matter. It becomes obvious now, that your body vehicle is a collection of Stardust particles being held together by an Axiatonal lattice. Stardust Atoms are being held together by the electro-magnetism of electrons engaging with their anti-matter counter matrix. The denser they become, the larger the crushing forces on it: and the larger the crushing forces, the denser your physical body becomes. It feels almost like your physical body is compressing itself out of existence. This phase is what we refer to as the Dark Night of the soul, because whatsoever you knew about yourself is dying out, and the new has not been born yet. The compression continues and you drift deeper and deeper into the Great No~thingness towards the passage of no return. You enter the domain of Zero-point energy, which is a state of being, wherein all aspects of your consciousness are being integrated and merged with the Unified Force Field. All of your bodily sensations are now being united into a singular point of massive stillness, sort of like a pregnant phase of expectancy and despair. Man needs to have the expectancy of God to break through whatever circumstances you are in, and we need to be the vehicles for His mighty works. This state of emergency shall pass, and this too you are not! As you move yourself through this point of no return, and without looking back to the old Universe, you may now perceive your survival mechanism kicking in. You feel like you want to escape the inner buildup of confining pressure, and you are about to explode. You feel like self-destruction, and you begin your final countdown towards ignition and combustion of your physical body into a new perception of reality. Allow yourself to melt and adapt to this final countdown, and begin to count: 'ten, nine, eight, seven, six, five, four, three, two, one, and take off.' Your compressed physical body now explodes into trillions of Starlight particles, which expand rapidly into hyperspace. These photons or light particles are now afloat and drifting in deep space, waiting for a ride from another light wave to come. All of these light particles have the appearance of fireflies in the sky, which are being gravitated by some unknown force, and effortlessly migrates them back to their original Star systems. Because of the sudden combustion of your compressed physical reality, you were unable to release all of your entrapped particles of light. Now is the time to let it all out, and you can observe hidden parts of yourself ignite themselves like the explosion of fireworks and fairy dust. Give yourself time to move into the deep feeling of this, and witness the fallout of your blissful release. What are you holding back? What do you want to release? What do you want to activate? Let it go! The freedom of your inhibited light-body is now being driven to recollect and unite itself with the virgin rays of His Starlight domain. It almost feels like the Star people are assisting your Soul to build an eternal awakened 'You!' As your Soul collects all of God's floating light particles, your newly awakened 'born again' light-body has now become a gravitational field for your garment of the Living Light! When all of your Light particles are fully integrated and activated on all levels of your being, it is then that you are able to remotely reflect on the world, which inhibited you from becoming one with all that is divine! This is the devouring fire against the fallen lords of light who have kept the root races of the planets in karmic bondage, oblivious to the infinite love of the father. Allow yourself to pause, reflect, melt and view your own personal history of worldly conditioning. Imagine yourself being the president of your life, one who reviews the creation of his world with a sense of awe, and discerning the essence of self from the imposed plastic self. The essence of self lives in the domain of God, and it is the stillness of His light, which you have been searching for eons of lifetimes. Allow yourself to melt and merge with the stillness of His presence. Know that your eyes have now become the mirror that reflects the peace of His presence. Your voice now resonates with a full spectrum of sound against the background of the stillness of His being. Your Aura or energy body has now absorbed a full spectrum of colors, reflected by the Light of His being. Your energy field has a transparency to it, which enables us to see through the blissful orbital dance of the Great Cosmic Orgasm. You are now totally and blissfully saturated with the majestic stillness of His presence. You are it! Every person that will now come to bathe into the communion with your energy field will have a first glimpse of what it feels like to be divine dancing on the waves of light. Receive this gift of being ordinary, humble and gracefully. A person touched by the Divine may even faint, because of the overwhelming presence of His eternal bliss! This will harm no one. The function of his Light is to romance the shadow side of His creation, and in doing so, reorganize the DNA patterns of his subjects into a higher light receptive matrix. Light upon light will create a white holographic Torus hole, which emits the Infinity of God's presence eternally. The pure essence of your being is now able to receive and reflect the Starlight of His Universe within Universes. It is through the windows of your Soul, that we now become able to touch the brilliance of His domain. It is the light upon light, wave upon wave, which uplifts your energies to dance with all of God's creations. Continue to dance your way to the realm of his domain, and he will glorify you upon your arrival. Be a womb to this divine Guest, and welcome the vortex of His light in Harmony with the Infinite. Do not shy away from His light, but let him magnify you with the oceanic waves of peace and bliss. Scan yourself for any trace elements of pain, and know that the comfort of suffering here will be a poor excuse for the one glance of his eyes. Observe your shame and blame issues, and make yourself worthy to be in the presence of that beautiful area of 'Silent Solitude' infused with the reverence of the beyond. Enjoy your healing bubble, and as you feel completed, then allow yourself to return to this reality with ease and grace. You will feel refreshed and rejuvenated. Know and remember God only! On the count of zero you will be fully awake and present: '10 ~ 9 ~ 8 ~ 7 ~ 6 ~ 5 ~ 4 ~ 3 ~ 2 ~ 1 ~ 0.' A blinding light flashed straight through Drone's being, and it reconnected him to his senses. His vortex was still locked in a vacuum seal with the succulence of his opposing beloved! The come back from his inner journey made him realize, that God once again had divided them into two opposite energy forces. At the same time, it made him realize, that the male and female polarity in essence does not exist! In comparison, it is sort of like an elastic band stretched apart into two opposite unbalanced conditions, which has the intrinsic desire to return to the oneness of balance, from which it was divided into two. If life is like an elastic band, then man and woman are in essence made from the same rubber, and their intrinsic nature should not be separated into the imposed manmade plastic image. 'God, the One knower, becomes three by his imagining. The still light of the knower and the moving lights of his thinking, are the Trinity, which God is in all things in this Universe. God, the one ancient father and mother, divided his sexlessness to extend the ancient mother and father bodies from his oneness of being. The One desire of these separated male and female particles or masses, is to unite and to void their separateness. Upon this formula God's electric Universe of motion is founded!

Maleeka leaned over and touched the both of them as if saying: "You guys are doing great!" She also touched the area of their vortices (sexual organs) as if to check if they were still connected to each other and God! The gentle exploration of her fingertips caused a ripple of excitement to surge through the vessels of his heart.

Maleeka: "Sorry to intrude, but I had to check! You guys are not done yet, because I still detect some remaining emotional crud! In order for you to be a participant in the production of love potion 69, it is necessary that you purify yourselves from the conditionings of cellular pollution by means of catharsis!"

Drone: "WOW ! the visible invisible of inner true being, back on rise to inner space where emptiness become wholeness .?"

Maleeka: "Your DNA Heli will not be able to reorganize itself into a higher geometrical matrix, if you do not release and transform your emotional crud completely!"

Drone: "How do I release and transform!"

Maneesha: "Surrender your resistance to change, express yourself the way you truly feel, observe yourself with the eyes of discovery and awe. Empty yourself completely, and allow the Living Light to take over your domain of hope and despair. Surrender your belief and know your God from a state of absolute innocence, then he will induce a blissful braiding of your DNA, and Christalize you in harmony with the infinite!"

Drone: "How can I return to a state of innocence, when the voice of judgment criticizes me?"

Maneesha: "Simply drop it like an object! The necessity to purify is rooted in the fact that our SQUID devices are capable to transmit your holographic light images, and this includes any remaining emotional crud. It is crucial that only the purest light images are being impressed into the virgin matrix of Love potion 69! Human emotional crud creates an out of phase lower cellular frequency, which absorbs the problem seeds of thought from your shadow self. This caused us to separate ourselves from our divine garments of light, hence it is crucial that you increase your light bearing capacity, and continue to ingather the Christalization of the Living Light."

Drone: "You don't want me to induce stress upon myself, do you?"

Maneesha: "No, but allow me to explain this purification process to you! Your large intestine represents a place in your body, which indicates your overall poisoning at a cellular level. Through deep listening we have come to learn how to use this organ as an indicator for the cellular poisoning with E~motional crud!"

Drone: "Define E~motional crud?"

Maneesha: "Human Beings attract toxins into their being, simply because they are unwilling to face and resolve their E~motional issues!"

Drone: "What is the resolution?"

Maneesha: "A deep feeling from the heart, and a deep listening with the heart! Those in power of the shadow side of Society manipulate us by means of the subliminal occupation of our Minds with abstract life draining concepts. It is the shadow side that clouds our clear vision with the distractions and decoys of the world."

Drone: "Is it always going to be them and us?"

Maneesha: "One cannot serve two Masters! Jesus true mission here on Earth was to show us that we as God's children can create as perfectly well as God does. Jesus was sent by the Father to show us that the Father intended us to create exactly as he creates!"

Drone: "How do we pollute ourselves?"

Maneesha: "Christianity is not about inter-denominational bickering, but instead it's about an inward Journey towards His dancing light, a transcendence of sin! We have become unable to breathe deeply at a cellular level, simply because our life force cannot penetrate through the clogged pores of our suffocated cellular membranes! Unresolved traumata and conditioned E~motional crud have a gravitational effect on the addictive intake of, and or exposure to external toxins like: 'Sugar, Alcohol, Drugs, Medication, Fluor, Chlorine, Salt, Radiation & Radioactive Fallout, Hormones, Industrial toxins, Insecticides, Heavy Metals, Quartz watches etc....' As one masters these feelings of E~motion with the Art of discovery i.e. looking into it, and the catharsis of it, one then becomes able to detoxify oneself. The Large Intestine produces a harmonic sound, when it is in a healthy state of functioning. This harmonic sound may fall out of spectrum, change, or disappear altogether due to the out of phase overload of E~motional toxins. In most cases the Intestines will cramp up into a spasm or cause ulcers, and in due time this will harden the lining of your tract, which then will stagnate the blood flow of your metabolism!"

Drone: "WOW ! the visible invisible of inner true being, back on rise to inner space where emptiness become wholeness. I would have never thought this sensation could be possible!"

Maneesha: "Every E~motional attached Seed of Thought has an alternating effect on your metabolism. Your brain functions best, when it produces the so-called Alpha waves at the rate of 5 – 7 Hz per/sec. Alpha waves are very beneficial for the rhythmic functioning of your Intestinal tract."

Drone: "How do I get to work my brain at that frequency?"

Maleeka: "When we think, our brain produces rhythmic electric currents. With their magnetic components, these currents 'thoughts' spread out into space at the velocity of light, as do the electric waves or sounds produced by our hearts. These waves all mingle to form enormous interference patterns, spreading out and away from the planet. Thoughts of selfishness and self-interest separate us, isolate us from the rest of humanity, *and this sense of separateness makes people immune to their needs for 'true feelings', thus throwing the social structure out of balance.* Those who allow their mental and emotional natures to recoil, refusing to let their senses to reach out into the undiscovered domain of God, destroy their own capabilities. This choice will always keep them entrapped in the limitation of their senses! It should be observed that this prison is only the recoil or reflex of his or her own nature. Genius is that which goes on through challenging conditions and circumstances, while witnessing an expansion of consciousness and engaging in the celebration of the heart.

The more Godlike the thought, the realization, and the consciousness, the greater the power involved in the process. The moving force of God is the gift of receiving his everlasting living light to shine through your body vehicle."

Drone: "Is it not blasphemy that we uplift ourselves to the level of God?"

Maleeka: "Blasphemy is the act of expressing lack of reverence for God! It's not so much an uplift; it's more like veils are being lifted from a divided space of infinity. When we declare ourselves enlightened before un-illuminated people, those steeped in ignorance regarding the true state of all creation, they then accuse us of blasphemy today just as they did Christ two thousand years ago! When we empty ourselves through Meditation, through the Art of discovery i.e. 'witnessing', then we become a 'Host' for the sacred 'Guest' the Beloved. We learn to empty ourselves and become a vehicle for his ever-lasting living light. Look for yourself immediately into His light, and know that thou are that. Then there is nobody left to act out the act of blasphemy, only an empty space filled with His everlasting living light remains!"

Drone: "You blow my Mind!"

Maleeka: "We must shake our electro-magnetic or gravitational thought field to its roots. We must resurrect ourselves into a new art of being. Jesus, when he was crucified, gave His flesh and blood, to prove that there is really a deeper spiritual body, which is the light-body that he manifested, when he resurrected Himself from the tomb."

Drone: "So the raising of Christ body on the cross symbolizes but the elevation of our Minds above sense delusions. We are tasting the luminous gap of infinity?"

Maleeka: "As your Mind dissolves you become one with the Unified Force Field, which is the matrix of our silken God! All consciousness is a trance induced state of limitation and essence wants to break free and catch the wind under its wings to fly. We need to bridge this gap in consciousness wherein dwells all sense of human limitation. To free the consciousness is to free the ancient mother Eve, who was birthed into existence by the fallible man Adam. As you become one with the Law of One you will no longer sin, as the everlasting living light of God is now flowing freely through your body vehicle. Finding your calm in this eternal unity of all things is a position of power, where all contrary illusion is dissolved into the peace and tranquility of illumination. What better attitude could there be than viewing the world through the eyes of a Goddess?"

Drone: "What about the Ten Commandments i.e. God's laws?"

Maleeka: "The Law of God is written in your inward parts, and to outwardly obey what is moving within is to bring the inner capacity into outer manifestations. God brings out the bliss in man and that is the true emotional state of man, born from his inner release of joy into the truth of his being. Feelings of separation and anxiety begin with the loss of Joy. It is only when we get out of that condition of Joy and harmony that we begin to feel separated from the Highest."

Maneesha: "It is because our next therapy session is based upon this principle, and I want you to be a conscious participant!"

Drone: "I am all ears!"

Maneesha: "We are spiritual beings having a human experience. This shift in perception causes a tremendous difference in the way we perceive ourselves in our personal time-space continuum."

Drone: "What do you mean?"

Maneesha: "In our physical body of volume everything is energy and matter and it is not as solid as we perceive it to be. When we allow it, we then can feel at our deepest level that we are not separate, as a body, as a spirit, as a soul — we are just energy-beings. This is the level of consciousness being opened to us from which a new experience is emerging for the purpose of healing all separation. Everything is Divine and Sacred, thus So are we!"

Drone: "How can I understand 'divine and sacred'"?

Maneesha: "When we upgrade our consciousness, we can then see that everything is everything else, there are no boundaries. There is no "this" or "that;" no you or me. It is a pure field of awareness – consciousness. We are not meant to ignore our physiology, but recognize the body as energy, vibrating at a very dense frequency."

Drone: "I just love your good vibes!"

Maneesha: "When we allow Sound to resonate inside the core of our being, we can then experience a knowing deep inside that the emptiness of nothing will create the everything in our beautiful womb of creation. I AM experiencing a re-birth with the Sound of my Soul's voice."

♫ Crystal Bowls Singing ♫

Drone: "Why was I never inspired before like this?"

Maneesha: "Because the Master Key to God Power was kept sacred by the Church rulers."

Drone: "Yes, but they never kept away their Psalms from us?"

Maneesha: "Yes, I know, but there is a catch 22 which nobody noticed!"

Drone: "What is it?"

Maneesha: ""Pope Johannes later became a saint - Saint Johannes - and then the scale was changed. The seventh note "Si" was added from his name. "Si" later became "Ti." These changes significantly altered the frequencies sung by the masses. The alterations also weakened the spiritual impact of the Church's hymns. Because the music held mathematic resonance, frequencies capable of spiritually inspiring mankind to be more "Godlike," the changes affected alterations in conceptual thought as well, further distancing humanity from God."

In other words, whenever you sing a Psalm, it is music to the ears. But it was originally intended to be music for the soul as well or the "secret ear." Thus, by changing the notes, high matrices of thought and to a great extent wellbeing, was squelched. Now it is time to recover these missing notes."

Drone: "So, how do we recover to original cause?"

Maneesha: "The origin of **Unisonic Ascension** and what now is called the missing Solfeggio Frequencies can be found in the singing of Mediaeval Gregorian chants. Thus, by singing, chanting, humming these frequency notes, high matrices of thought and to a great extent wellbeing, shall be recovered when we resonate these missing notes." This is Acoustical Soul Levitation. So now, let us begin to relax and enjoy. ♫ Crystal Bowls Singing ♫

174-Hz – reduce pain

285-Hz – influence energy fields

396-Hz - turn grief into joy

417-Hz – facilitate change

528-Hz – transformation & miracles

639-Hz – reconnecting, relationships

741-Hz – expressions/solutions

852-Hz - return to spiritual order

963-Hz – awaken perfect state

Maleeka: "Allow me to clip some Alpha wave producing electrodes onto your ear lobes. These waves will bring you into a very relaxed state of being. It does not hurt, and it feels like little prickly feelings, which will synchronize your brainwaves into an Alpha state level of 5 – 7 Hz per/sec. Every organ within your body vehicle has a bioelectric trigger point or 'dermatome area', which projects itself onto your skin. It appears as if your organ projects its sound outwardly, and this sound can be detected with the use of a highly sensitive microphone strategic placed on the dermatome area. The combination of sound and silence now becomes a feedback loop to the therapist."

Drone: "So, how can these Alpha waves be of use as a therapeutic tool?"

Maleeka: "My Soul essence will communicate with your Large Intestine by means of a bio-dynamic touch. With my hands I will make gestures, which to you will have the appearance of fluffing air, but in essence I'm realigning the Axiatonal lattice of your Auric body."

Drone: "Axia what?"

Maneesha: "Axiatonal means the emission of sound and light through my fingertips!"

Drone: "Are you a hummer?'

Maneesha smiled affirmatively, and continued with the flow of her speech.

Maneesha: "Listening to the sound spectrum of your Large Intestine, and by means of intuitive feeling, the Holy Spirit guides me to the places where your E~motional crud is anchored down. The treatment will feel pleasant at first, but as soon as the crud dislodges and moves, you may be experiencing pain. Detoxing is a cramp induced feeling at a cellular level, which results in the catharsis of a self-inhibited E~motional built up!"

Drone: "Am I allowed to express myself freely?"

Milika: "Yes, you may want to scream, cry, rage, moan, but you are not allowed to break your energetic cycle with Maneesha."

Drone: "Let's get it on!"

Maleeka taped a mini microphone to his Large Intestine trigger point area and she clipped two ear electrodes to his ears, which produced 5 – 7 Hz per/sec Alpha~stim waves.

Maneesha: "Increase your flexibility, the Powers you possess. Hear yourself dreaming, and watch yourself screaming. Give me your heart, make it real or else forget about it!"

A gurgling sound came from within his belly, and it had a relaxing effect on Drone's being. Maleeka stood about three feet away, and indeed, it appeared as if she was fluffing the air around him. Her hands were remotely touching his insides, and it gave him an unusual but likeable sensation.

Maneesha: "What do you feel?"

Drone: "It feels like I am on a butterfly farm!"

Inside his being, things started to move around and Drone became restless. Pain arose, and he felt his body contracting into a spasm. The movements were uncontrollable and from a distance, it must have made the appearance as if he was on a roller coaster ride. Maneesha was going along for the ride, and her presence functioned like a mirror to the distractions and decoys of his inner pain. A mirror does not do anything, because its function is to reflect. It is the person, who looks into the mirror that does the doing. Drone's body was being warped into a marathon catharsis of seven days and nights. Maneesha was riding the waves of his E~motional ripples, and the contracting motions of his catharsis had kept her succulent vacuum pump activated. From time to time, they would change their Tantric positions, and in doing so, they gave their exhausted bodies a well-deserved break! Maleeka would sponge them off daily, and they felt blessed by the gift of refreshment. On the seventh day, Maneesha induced deep belly laughter, and it was so affective, that it caught on to them.

Drone: "Free, free, free, Lord, set me free!"

His laughter kept going, and Drone could not stop the painful contractions inside of his belly. The deeper he moved into his laughter, the more he felt the pain of his rejected, inhibited and defended self! His body had a language of its own, and it took over his laughter as if being moved by a deeper primordial force. Maleeka's laughter was contagious, and she triggered the mirror like qualities of laughter and tears. This catharsis became a marathon of seven days and nights. As their laughter eased off, they began to notice that their bodies were extremely exhausted, and it took a couple of hours to return to their normal selves. There was this overwhelming feeling of bliss and peace, and the world of Drone's inner silence could not be expressed into a single word. Maneesha now twisted her safety valve, sighed and relieved Drone as she unplugged her succulent vortex. Gently he leaned forwards, and she allowed him to kiss her swollen lips.

Maneesha: "Laughter is such a transforming force, that nothing else is needed to liberate the iron grip from the emotional mind! If you can change your sadness to celebration, then you will also be able to change your death into resurrection! Moreover, remember that seriousness is the worst of all sins, because existence in itself is playful. Hand in hand, they left the Tantric Dome, and walked into the direction of the sacred hot springs. At the springs, they took their time to bathe one another with a silent nurturing care. They hugged each other extensively and repeatedly, which left them in a state of divine bliss. It is not the 'suffering' that gives access to Him, but it is a 'deep feeling' of His intrinsic presence deep beneath the layers of pain, which had blinded Drone's traumatized self.

You make me real: by the Doors

I really want you
Really do
Really need you, baby
God knows I do
'Cause I'm not real enough
without you
Oh, what can I do?

You make me real
You make me feel
Like lovers feel

You make me throw away
Mistake and misery
Make me free, love
Make me free

I really want you
Really do
Really need you, baby
Really do
I'm not real enough without you
Oh, what can I do?

You make me real
Only you, baby
Have that appeal

So let me slide in your tender
Sunken sea
Make me free, love
Make me free

Roll now, baby, roll
Well, roll now, baby, roll
You gotta roll now, baby, roll
Roll now, honey, roll
You gotta roll now, baby, roll

Make me free
You make me real
You make me feel
Like lovers feel
You make me throw away
Mistake and misery
Make me free, love
Make me free

Make me free
You make me free

Chapter Eleven ~
Ride the snake to the lake

When you make the two one, and when you make the inside like the outside and the outside like the inside, and the above like the below, and when you make the male and the female one and the same…….then you will enter the Kingdom of God.

Gospel of Thomas.

But those people who belong to Heaven are like the man of Heaven. We were made like the man of Earth. So, we will also be made like the man of Heaven. We will not all die, but we will all be changed. And this body that dies will clothe itself with that which never dies.

1 Corinthians 15: 48 – 54.

God is in the light. We should live in the light, too. If we live in the light, we share fellowship with each other. And when we live in the light, the blood of the death of Jesus, God's son is making us clean from every sin.

1 John 1: 7.

And once Man has gone beyond his physiological limitations of Self and desires only to serve his fellow creation and the Father – he has purified himself from his carnal predilections and manifested Love sufficient to receive the outer garment of Light.

Keys of Enoch: key 104 : 45.

Seven days had passed during which Drone had entertained himself with the warm and bubbly hot springs. With his eyes closed, he could sense the approaching presence of Maleeka and Maneesha, and he could feel his heart pounding with excitement. As he opened his eyes to check on the accuracy of his intuition, their eyes locked in with his and it made him smile. His girls emanated a scintillating angelic glow on starry grounds. Sparkly light reflections were twinkling in their eyes as if a new Star constellation just had been born inside of them. It was these twinkles from within their eyes, which now captured Drone's undivided attention. It was as if a transformation into something on a grander plane had taken place and yet it felt as close as a deer dancing in the flower world of a mountain meadow.

Drone: "Amuro Angiocina di Sorrento Napoli-What's happening?"

Maneesha: "The Cosmic Babe helped us align and rebalance our inner selves with everything that is divine within His Universe. The divine force of love has cleansed us from the abstract trance induced conditioning of our causal rooted chauvinist Minds, and our inner child was liberated like playful fawns in the enchanted flower world, that's all!"

Drone: "As if that's not enough?"

It was noticeable, that their old self had now transformed into a new sort of energy, which best could be described as: 'Deity!' Maneesha and Maleeka were in a rebalanced state of being as if hosting the Infinity of His Living dancing Light. With his Mind's eye Drone began to scan their luminous transparent bodies, in search for any leftover animal magnetism, any surging hormone level that would display their human heritage. None whatsoever, there was no scent to be detected, and their fragrance had a different vibe to it, a higher vibratory energy level. The conditioned response and release of musk and pheromone fragrances were now being replaced by the emissions of dancing 'photons or light particles. The scent of a flower can ascend into something not from this planet, and Drone's sense of nostalgia was being replaced by the sound and color spectra from the beyond. A soft beam of coherent Starlight radiated straight from their third eye and it entered him through his Nadis or acupuncture portals. This light felt nurturing, and it impressed itself deep within the matrix of his Soul. This felt like magic, and Drone's body was being filled up with a new emission of light. Thousands of butterflies were touching him with the tips of their wings, and he tingled on the inside. Drone allowed his body to slowly submerge into the bubbly hot springs, and he felt stunned by the stunning beauty of his lady friends. Maneesha and Maleeka quickly acted upon his vanishing, and with their hands, they pulled him back to the surface. Maleeka asked Drone to breathe deeply, as if touching himself on the inside with a breath of air. His body felt like it was being warped into hyperventilation mode, and this created more oxygen into his bloodstream, which then unlocked the cellular memory of his ancestral experiences. From a distance, he was remotely viewing the emotional flashbacks of his ancestors. The E~motional crud attached to his DNA appeared to be embedded within a spider web of Angelic hair called: 'Akashic records'. Akashic records are the memory banks of this Universe, and they are being created by the E~motional touch of each life containing vehicle. It is a network of invisible fiber optic threads that attach themselves to any object, which it is being touched by or thought of. The Aboriginals from Australia refer to these threads as: 'the Songlines from the Dreamtime'. From the beginning of time and creation, people have inflicted E~motional pain on each other and other life forms, which was being stored within the cellular matrix of the Akashic records without being realized by the recipient! Karma or the production of psychosomatic E~motional crud, has a boomerang effect in reference to the original cause of sin. **Anything i.e. 'E~motional crud' that prevents the 'Living Light' of the Cosmic Babe from being creatively recycled through the body vehicle, is a Sin.** Throughout our lives we project our negative E~motions onto other people, which causes pain, and which blocks the Living Light from dancing the free flow of life! This projection of pain results in the creation of Karma or indebtedness to the creation of God. The pain we feel today triggers a chain of events, linked back to the original cause of sin, which in the beginning was nothing but an act of innocent curiosity. The original Adam and Eve responded to a voice, which was a temptation created by their creator. God created a fallible fallen angel, who tempted a fallible man and woman, who disobeyed an infallible God! God tested the infallibility of his creation, and he discovered that it was fallible, hence he created two attributes: 'REMEDY and RECOURSE'. Remedy is a way to get out from under the law, Recourse is the way of dealing with any damages you may have sustained under the law: the way you go about recovering your loss. God's REMEDY for his Ten Commandments is: **'Your Sin is the fuel for your Salvation; hence Seriousness is the Worst of All Sins'.** God's RECOURSE for his Ten Commandments is: **'Admit that you are a Sinner, and give all of your Sins to my Son Jesus Christ, and he will save you from Eternal condemnation!'** Serious blame and shame issues which, when taken seriously will create the E~motional crud that prevents the Living Light of the Cosmic Babe from being creatively recycled through your body vehicle. Now it dawned on Drone how many times he had been missing opportunities, in which he could have received the Living Light to flow through his body vehicle. Blame and shame issues had caused him to deny his own feelings, and in doing so, he had been projecting his unhappiness onto the misery of other divine people. A desperate need was urging him to forgive others and himself, for that which had caused pain in his circle of life. The more he forgave, the more the Living Light began to flow and dance through his body vehicle. Drone felt alive, and the realization dawned on him that his senses are light reflection motion detectors.

Drone: "Maleeka, how does one get close to God, when my senses are not able to register the essence of his light as the illuminated stillness? How can I find internal Peace within a world of oscillating atoms and electrons."

Maleeka: "One must accept both, action and rest. From that acceptance, one moves into the observer self. Observing the observer within, is the last link in the chain of 'distractions' we may observe. Within the melting and merging of the observer with the observer, one will find stillness and peace!"

Maleeka and Maneesha were gently rocking Drone in the water like a little baby, and it made him curl up into a fetal position. Their motherly breasts were encompassing him, and he felt safe to enjoy his healing bubble.

Maneesha: "Drone, you have prepared yourself well, and you deserve to be in the presence of that beautiful area of 'Silent Solitude' infused with the reverence no man knows!"

The gentleness of her message silenced the ripples of his inner questioning, and in a flash of a second, he was able to see the reflections of his original face. It was time for his inner child to come out and play the way God had intended him to be a reflection of his similitude.

Milika: "You are now ready to participate in the cocreation of Love potion 69".

A ripple of excitement surged through his being and it activated him to sit in an upright position.

Drone: "Yeah, let us claim a well-deserved position in the 'Great Mahamudra Dome'."

They helped each other get up and out of the water. Hand in hand, they walked towards the Tantric Love Dome, naked! At the entrance, they were sniffed, scanned and touched from head to toe. The Stargate girls sniffed them in, and they were directed to the Hair Salon, where their heads were to be shaven bold.

Salon girl: "In order to obtain a better Holographic light imagery conduction through the SQUID electrodes, we'll have to shave you completely bold and beautiful"

When the three of them were done, they looked at each other and laughed.

Maleeka: "Love can be a true Paradigm shift, isn't it?"

The girls ushered Drone forwards into the Center for Dis-ease control, where they were scanned with some high-tech laser scan of which he hadn't seen the like. The machine gave the green light, and they moved forward to step into the calibration room, which was being monitored by the Androgenous beings.

The presence of a highly evolved luminous being made itself visible to the perception of their senses, and Drone could not identify 'it' as being a man or woman. The Similitude of his image resembled the memory Drone had of the Eternal Babaji, and like him, 'it' reflected a balanced beauty of Divine love and peace. The being introduced itself as: 'Punya', and it handed to the three of them a SQUID device. Punya then linked them up to the outlet of his SQUID system, and he scanned their bodies for any leftover E~motional crud. The three of them were standing there butt naked in the presence of this Godly luminous being. Drone observed his features shape shift into a million-fold of different realities, which upon a closer look appeared to be a remote reflection of all of his past life incarnations. A thought from Milika captured his attention as she said: "All Androgenous beings have a full brain capacity, and remote viewing is one of those gifted qualities!" Punya gestured his hands into the direction of the Love Dome as if saying: "God bless you my children, you may now enter!" He blessed each of them individually with a kiss on the third eye, which to Drone felt like a blinding flash of light rushing straight through the essence of his being. The encounter with Punya left him stunned with awe, and yet at the same time he felt like was able to walk on fluffy clouds. Together they entered the 333-foot Mahamudra Dome, which because of his extensive personal growth, now appeared to be larger than life itself. The fragrance of Lotus flowers was permeating the air, and it appeared as if many of the Tantric couples were not disturbed by the invasion of their privacy. Their eyes were filled with sparkly lights as if painted by the fairies. They took position in the Lotus, and Drone began to meditate on the tune of his new environment.

A voice started a prayer for the consecration of the sacred space; "Inside the infinite circle of the Divine Presence which completely surrounds me, I affirm:

There is only Presence here, it is Harmony with the Infinite, which makes all hearts vibrate with Joy and Happiness. Those who choose to enter here will feel the vibration of the Divine Harmony.

There is only one Presence here, it is Love. God is love, which embraces all beings in one feeling of unity. This place is filled with the presence of Love. In Love I live, I move, I exist. Those who Choose to enter here will feel the pure and holy presence of Love.

There is only one Presence here, it is Truth. All that exists here, all that is spoken here, all that is thought here is the expression of Truth. Those who choose to enter here will feel the presence of Truth.

There is only one Presence here, it is God, the Beneficent. No evil can enter here. There is no evil in God. God, the Beneficent lives here. Those who choose to enter here will feel the Divine Presence of the Beneficent.

There is only one Presence here, it is God, the Life. God is the essential life of all beings, the health of body and mind. Those who choose to enter here will feel the presence of Life and Health.

Through the esoteric symbol of the Divine Wings, I'm in harmonious vibration with the universal currents of Wisdom, Power and Joy. The presence of Divine Wisdom is manifested here. The presence of Divine Joy is deeply felt by those who choose to enter here.

In the most perfect communion between my lower self and higher self, which is God in me, I consecrate this place to the perfect expression of all the Divine qualities that are in me and in all beings.

The vibrations of my thoughts are the forces of God in me, which are stored here and radiate to all beings, thus making this place into a center for emission and reception of all that is Good, Joyful, and Prosperous. God is Prosperity because he makes everything grow and prosper.

I thank you, oh! God, because this place is filled with your Presence.

I thank you, because I live and move for you.

I thank you, because all those who enter here will feel your Presence.

I thank you, because I am in Harmony, Love, Truth and Justice with all beings."

Maleeka was the first to express the force of the Kundalini; Maneesha and Drone soon followed her example by being honest with themselves. Playfully they began to please themselves first before engaging with one another sexually. How strange it is to love oneself first, but it felt right for that moment and Drone was not ashamed. The playfulness they shared with each other helped them to be more intimate, and in doing so, it relaxed them into being juicier. The flow of a woman's juice is a good barometer for her preparedness to mate and be intimate. Their nectar was now flowing abundantly! Maleeka was the first to claim and take her succulent spread Eagle position on Drone's extended vortex. She rotated her cervix around the sensors of his divine flesh, and it kicked in a Kundalini rush, which now began to rise slowly inside the center of his spine. Once his sexual energy found its sense for direction, he shifted gears and tagged it with the purpose of running his inner orbit. Slowly, but with certainty the walls of his defended self, began to give way, and Drone transcended towards the Zero-point energy. A moment presented itself to him, in which he felt the presence of his being everywhere and nowhere at the same time. This moment was hard to grasp, and the more he tried, the less it was there. Maleeka noticed an energy shift inside of his being, and she kissed him on his third eye and gazed deeply into the beyond of his being.

Drone: "How can one merge with the Unified Force Field when it seems impossible to attain?"

Maneesha: "Man has not learned to do the greater works of God, because he has not realized the greatness of God's power and has not known that God's power is for man's use. Jesus recognized that the one in Christ consciousness knows no limitation. Christ looked to God as the source and creator of all and he gave thanks for the power and substance right at hand to fill every want. All supplies exist in Universal substance of God's silken matrix. When we become one with the 'I am' presence of God, we then can tap into this substance and bring it forth as our very own. We use a Sutra created by the Indian Master Patanjali! A Sutra is a very, very special thing to be understood. It is a spell, a magic formula. It implies the phenomenon that whatsoever you have is not really there, and whatsoever you think you have not got, is there! A magic formula is needed. Your Sabeeja problem seed of thought is not real! – That is why a magic formula is needed. It makes sense to use it in order to get there, but once you are there it makes no-sense to use it at all. One cannot grasp a nonsense state of Being with a state of Mind that makes sense! The sound of the Mind will bring you to the domain of stillness, but in order to enter you must request the Divine to erase your problem seeds of thought, then it will allow you to merge with all that is!"

Maleeka began to chant her Sutra and she gave Drone it's meaning.

Maleeka: "Ajym~Nama~Samjama~Udana~Jayajala~Panka~ Kantaka~Disvasanga~Utkrantisca~Pranayama, uplift your energies to the highest reflection of God!"

The Sutra echoed in his inner ears, and Drone began to rehearse the Sutra within his inner self. The sound rippled harmonious throughout the matrix of his liquid body. Maleeka had her legs wrapped around his loins and this kept their vortices locked, sealed and delivered. A weird sensation now began to surge through his body, and it made him open his eyes to discern the within from the without. To his surprise everything seemed normal, and he shut his eyes again to repeat the Sutra: "Ajym~Nama~Samjama~Udana~Jayajjala~Panka~Kantaka~ Disvasanga~Utkrantisca~Pranayama~Kaivalya."

Maleeka: "Who are you really at your essence core level? Does it still need your protection or can you now rest eternally in God?"

The Sutra's sound echoing against the walls of his defended self, drew him deeper into the gap of silence, and Drone entered a state of being, where there were no Seeds of Thought, Mind, or Unawareness left. This Domain of No Mind, in which one's being naturally merges with the Unified Force Field, had welcomed him to have a taste of heavenly bliss. Suddenly, and unexpectedly came this blinding ecstatic beam of light surging throughout his body. The inner feelings of bliss were seriously testing his tolerance for happiness, and Drone made tremendous efforts to adapt to it. The intensity of his inner bliss, which in retrospect was nothing but the approach of His –I AM- presence, made him open his eyes, and Drone noticed that his body was in a levitated position two feet above ground level. The doubt within his Mind distracted him again from his inner source of light, and his body began to descend. Maleeka had sensed Drone's confusion, and she commented:

Maleeka: "It is important to stay connected to the inner source of light! However, if you do feel the need to open your eyes, then you must lock yourself into the light-source reflected within my eyes. As a unit we will reinforce and unlock the powers, which God grants us? The Love potion 69 can only be produced with the uplifting force of Love.

Drone: "How can I remain in tune with this overwhelming feeling of inner bliss?"

Maleeka: "Get out of your own way, and surrender to the Love of the Heavenly father! However, you are doing fine, and a little more trust and courage is needed. It is now time to position our SQUID devices."

They rubbed a highly potent superconductor of light imagery onto each other's naked skulls, and Maleeka placed the suction cup electrodes on the designated transmission points. Maneesha looked strange with her SQUID suction cups planted on her naked skull. Again, she noticed his distraction, and by squeezing her inner vortex muscles, she grabbed Drone's attention and pulled him straight back into a meditative focus.

Drone: "God has a strange way of punishing those people, who are distracted by worldly things!"

Maneesha intensified her python grip on the extension of his private self, and it made Drone realize that God is watching over the most intimate areas of his life. The sound of the Sutra echoed again, as if being triggered by an automatic redial button.

"Ajym~Nama~Samjama~Udana~Jayajala~Panka~Kantaka~ Disvasanga~Utkrantisca~Pranayama."

This time around Drone was able to remain centered within the blinding pillar beam of light, and the uplifting force of love made them rise closer to the domain of God. They were hovering like a hovercraft, and when he opened his eyes for another reality check, he noticed that he was able to maintain his status quo in mid-air! Within the abyss of Maneesha's eyes, he could see Galaxies filled with stars being born, and he felt expansive and all-inclusive. It was a deep feeling of being intimate with everything that is Godly and Divine within this Universe, and yet it was strange to think, that people refer to this experience as having sex! Instead, it felt more like he was given the opportunity to observe God's sexless Universe. This expansive feeling of going beyond the limitations of his sexual organ left him in a state of awe, magic and bliss. When the Holy Trinity: 'Father, Son, Holy Spirit', completes and seals itself into a sexless force of non~polarity and nonduality, the God seeker now becomes able to love him-herself. The divided male female polarity is now being united into the essence of being One body vehicle for the Eternal Father.

"God the creator, divides His one white Light by extending its Oneness into electrical tensions of vibrating red 'male' and 'blue' female pairs. The tensions of His electrical divisions are equaled by a desire for unity, which is attained at the point of White incandescence in matter. Unity thus attained is repeated forever by the same dividing uniting process of electrical action reaction pulsations. Reproduction cannot take place until the red and the blue lights of sex-divided motion are voided in the still White light of the Creator. Man alone, of all Creation, ever knows of his Omniscience!" Walter Russell: Atomic Suicide.

Maneesha and Drone were hovering two feet above ground zero, and they were immersed deeply in a state of heavenly bliss.

Maleeka: "Our DNA is now in a process of the blissful braiding of Christalization, and our bodies are now being molded into becoming a superconductor of His light. Any superconductor no longer has the flaw of friction; hence, there is infinite durability to the high-energy usage, while being in his presence!

Drone: "So we are becoming like the Duracell rabbit, which can't stop doing the wild thing!"

Maleeka smiled, and Drone noticed that his Mind chatter had disconnected him again from the force. They were descending, and this seemed to be a good moment to take a break, and overcome his jetlag. Maneesha disconnected herself, and Maleeka reconnected herself.

Drone: "But, I need a break!"

Maleeka: "No butts for you buddy, but you may enter my vortex and attain eternal life!"

Maleeka calibrated her G-spot, and they began to chant their Sutra again: "Ajym~Nama~Samjama~Udana~Jayajala~Panka~Kantaka~

Disvasanga~Utkrantisca~Pranayama", and the force of love lifted them up into His domain. For six 'eight hours' days they remained suspended hovering in mid-air, and continued to live in the unusual presence of His domain. At the end of their eight-hour shift, they returned to ground zero and rested in the flower gardens.

Drone: "What is the secret behind this super-normal capacity of levitation?"

Maneesha: "The self you see, that is able to perform with super-normal capacity is a truer, deeper self. It is what you know as God, who is the all-encompassing matrix of the Unified Force Field. First we tune in and become one with the Unified Force Field and then we allow God to work through us. It is He as another 'I AM' that does these things. Every good desire man has is God's desire, therefore there is an unlimited supply in the Universal God substance all around us to fill every divine desire." JUST FEEL IT!

Maleeka: "A fully awakened human being will no longer need sleep, because he/she knows how to live without wasting energy nor separating him or herself from God's silken matrix. Withdrawing your consciousness away from the creative source of His eternal light causes failure. To draw from the Universal life that flows freely throughout infinite space is the privilege of anyone, who is in search of the miraculous. No one can truly become alive, until he/she knows that life is moving in and through him/her, and that **God is eternally seeking a fuller, freer, richer expression of Himself always!**"

On the seventh day, they were invited to partake in a Heart driven Trance Dance invocation, which was a time for celebration. In the daytime, they participated in Sufi, Nataraj, Lambada and Salsa dance, which enabled them to socialize with other God seekers. At eight o'clock sharp, the Goa Trance Beat would kick in. They were asked to put on their SQUID devices, and surrender their hearts to the Heavenly

Father. The sound of Goa Trance is rooted in a full spectrum brain wave circuitry, and their rhythmic response to this music created more life into their Heavenly bodies. It felt like swimming in a body of lucid liquid light! The sound of music assisted their bodily tissue to be nurtured by the rhythm of life, and it helped Drone to adapt to the irrevocable change of transmutation. Rhythm = Life = Laughter = Light = Love = God! Trance dance is the last surrender of the heart to the eternal nothingness, the presence of His stillness: 'the Light of His domain!' Drone heard the voice of silence and thus the Holy Spirit spoke to him in a personal way.

Holy Spirit: "Be silent and allow the God-mind in all of its splendor to illuminate the caged consciousness of man and woman. Infuse yourself with the everlasting living light of a living God. We have to build but one temple – the temple of the living God within our very selves. Silence is a pregnant power, for when we reach that place of silent solitude, we have reached the place where all is one, where all is God and Divine. Be still and know that 'I AM that I AM' is God!" Drone danced from Dusk to Dawn, and the braiding of his inner bliss was now being conducted through the SQUID device into the Crystal cross, where divine intervention would Christalize the female sacraments into the Sangre de Cristo.

At the break of dawn, they sat together and watched the sun rise. The early rays of sunlight were a completion to his total recall for God light. His pursuit for happiness was enshrined within his driven Quest for enlightenment, and not ultimately, but immediately it had led him into the domain of God. Drone's behavior had been legislated by strong Christian fundamentalism, people who desire to control and inhibit his authentic search for truth. The Fundamental Christian Legislators are ostracizing, exorcising, exteriorizing his inalienable rights to find the authentic God within his inner world of beyond language, and yet it is there, where he treaded with baby steps upon His domain. Little do they know that the entire Bible is a complete bringing forth of that condition in which everybody will radiate His everlasting living light from the world within. Is it the accuser Satan, who enforces a guilty plea, or should the defender 'God' be persistent in his defense of religious conviction: 'I did not accuse?' Legislature is a decoy 'Con' game, with only one purpose in mind: 'Lead the sheep away from finding their shepherd!' God's domain is beyond the paradigm shift of his written word, and a religious experience cannot be compressed into the impotent abstract meaning of the written word. Why do you think the Bible needed so many words to express the existential experience of: 'Love~Peace~Truth~Light~Life~Heaven~God~Jesus~Innocense~in~no~sense', etc.! The day Drone met his creator; he became saturated with the presence of His stillness. The eleventh stone tabled was fractured in a Million pieces, because it read: 'There shall be no law written to restrain my people from finding me in the corner stones of my Universe!'

After they finished their sun worshipping meditation, they bathed at the Hot springs and rested! For seven nights in a row, they were Trance Heart dancing their way to God, and He streamlined their hearts with a sense of inner complexion of light dancing. The pores of their skins were wide open, and they were now sensing the flow of life around them. With gratitude, Drone observed the heavenly bodies of Maleeka and Maneesha rocking their spots, and they responded to his visual touch with a vibe of love ripples coming straight from the heart. On a Soul level, they grew as close as one could possibly yearn to be. A state of Bliss had become an essential part of the sensation within his nerve system, and to Drone it felt like he could not get closer to God. Light felt all-invasive, but it did not allow him to get a grip on it.

Maleeka: " Drone, why do you tremble?"

Drone: " It is the way you are touching me. It is the way in which you may have become part of me."

Maleeka: " This light you see, it moves with me, it moves with each of my steps. This light walks with me, this light knows me."

Drone: " I shake because I AM alive and your touch is like medicine water flowing through the veins of my body."

Maleeka: "Yes, I AM the sweet medicine of your heart and I AM here to teach you how to rest in His perfect beauty."

Again, it was the pulse of the Moon, that activated the menses cycle of his two women, and Maleeka and Maleesha prepared themselves for another Redwood retreat. This time around, Drone was being prepared for a brand-new experience. His Amazon caretakers escorted him onto a platform suspended high up in the sacred crowns of Grandmother Redwood.

Caretakers: "The trust in God has to be earned, and cannot be taken for granted. Every male initiate of the Great Mahamudra has to go through a test of trial and tribulation during their partners menses cycle!"

They did not wait for Drone to ask what this test was all about, but instead he instantly knew as they tied the Bunji vines around his ankles. With his eyes closed, he jumped and performed a swan dive. The free fall seemed endless, and to himself he thought: "My quality of trust will transform my life no matter what the circumstances!" A massive sensation of instant traction pulled him straight out of his Mind, and back into his body. His popping spine was talking to him with strange sensations: 'C1-C7 Pop~pop, T1-T12 pop~pop, L1-L5 pop~pop!' Blood was rushing into his brain, and as he opened his eyes, he noticed that he was hanging six feet away from a deadly impact with mother Earth. This rush towards death felt like the best healing sensation he had ever experienced. What can a person do when death smiles him in the face? Exactly, one embraces it, and smiles back! His caretakers released him, and Drone allowed himself to fall onto the soft-breasted moss of Mother Earth.

Caretakers: "Good, you passed your first test!"
Drone: "What's next?"

Again, they did not reply, but instead escorted him to the Kundalini Dome.

Caretakers: "Inside this Dome you will encounter God's symbol of Temptation, and you must master the force of seduction!"
Drone broke out in a sweat and asked about the size of the snake!
Drone: "How big is the snake?"
Caretakers: "The last man that survived the snake said it was twenty-five feet!"

They escorted Drone to an indoor jungle pool, where he found himself to be all-alone. The door behind him closed, a burst of sunlight broke through from the other side of the pond, and it beckoned him to swim across. Drone entered the muddy water and began to swim. Half way across the pond, he suddenly felt a massive bite into his calves, and an invisible force pulled him under the lilies. With his hands, he reached down to grab whatever it was that bit him, and with his thumbs, Drone tried to crush its skull. The pool was not deep and he quickly erected himself to gasp for air and face his attacker. The coils of a giant anaconda continued to wrap itself around Drone's body, and it was trying to squeeze the life out of him. Drone kept walking to the other side, and with his hands, he intensified his chokehold. The snake pulled him back down under, and it felt like his lungs were about to collapse. Drone gasped for air, and his adrenaline was pumping at an all-time high. The snake suddenly let go of Drone's calf, and it reached straight for his neck. With the swiftness of his hands, Drone counter attacked the snake, and set his teeth into its neck and bit her head off. With the snake's coils still wrapped around him, Drone stumbled out of the pool. Exhausted he fell down in the mud, and his caretakers came to his aid and unwrapped his ferocious attacker. They hugged him, and began to massage his bruised body. Special attention was given to the snakebite marks in his bleeding calves, and an herbal cream was massaged into the bite wounds. Drone's time for healing and recovery did not last for long, because the rest of the day he was being instructed and prepared to participate in a four day 'Dreamtime Sundance'! The Sundance is about the sacrifice of the 'Living Flesh' to the 'Living Light' of the Heavenly father. A Kingdom of Light is to be built within the reality structure of this world, ultimately knowing that this body of flesh will give way to a garment of Light. Drone's caretakers escorted him to a secluded open area surrounded by giant Redwoods. In the center of the dance arena was a 33-foot crystal cross standing majestically in the midst of two Redwood trees, and their size provoked a sensation of awe. Ropes were hanging down from the Redwoods, and to himself Drone thought: "Hanging is better than crucifixion!" The arbor had an open gate to the East, and from the East the Holy Spirit was invited 'in' to listen to the prayers from the dancers. They walked around the arena to the West side, where low circular grass huts were positioned around a hot burning fire. The fire contained lava rocks, which were being heated for the sweat lodge ceremony. One by one, the men were ushered into the sweat lodge, and the medicine man began to sing his hymns. They all sang aloud, and Drone did not have a clue what they were singing about, but somehow it felt to him as if the words had an ancient meaning. The rocks came in, and Drone counted thirty of them, which began to burn like a heat wave on his delicate skin. The heat became unbearable, and Drone had to sing louder to counter act the burning of pain on his scorching flesh.

Drone: "Grandfather have mercy on me, pity me and forgive me for I am a sinner!"

The pain now became unbearable, and Drone jumped out from the lobster pot. The cool black soil of Mother Earth absorbed his painful distress symptoms, and the light of a trillion stars were captured by the retinas of his eyes. The medicine man gave him a cup of Daime, and the Dreamtime kicked up some more stardust of his archaic revival. For the next couple of hours, the world became surreal, and it must have been the divine intervention of Mother Nature, which kept Drone afloat. The next morning his caretakers returned with a red paint, and the Sun-dancers were all initiated with an Aztec body-paint design. The drums were beating, and the Amazon natives were chanting their bone chilling nostalgic songs. Soft Earthy hands guided Drone to lie down on a Jaguar's skin, and its velvet touch felt soothing to his fingertips. Without warning an Amazon warrior woman slid two small cuts into the flesh of his chest, and she inserted two Eagle claws through the loophole of his skin. An excruciating pain ripped straight through his body, and for a moment, Drone's spirit left his tormented body. His astral body was hovering aloof, and Drone witnessed his caretakers' drag his body to the cross. The hanging ropes were attached and sealed to the pegs. A line of Amazon women grabbed the other end of the rope, and with a united force, they pulled his body up into the arms of the cross. Drone's body and spirit were now spiraling upwards into an ever-expanding sky. His skin was being stretched to the limit, and finally it snapped like an elastic band. Drone landed softly and fell back onto the mossy breasts of Mother Earth, where his caretakers were attending his wounds. With his Mind's eye he performed an internal body check, and noticed that the pain, which he felt was not coming from the infliction of his wounds, but instead it felt like a primal pain originating from the beginning of time. It was the time during which the original Adam and Eve separated themselves from their creator God. The pain, which Drone felt was a deep nostalgic longing for the reunion with his creator God. The beat of the drums inspired him to get back on his feet, and Drone continued to dance his way to God, who now filled his body vehicle with His Living Light. God was weaving his axiatonal light lattice into the electron orbit of Drone's being. The Spirit of the jungle was droning on the background of Drone's perception, and a feeling of wellbeing immersed within the chambers of his heart. The sun was setting, and the sky fairies painted it pink and purple like the similitude of His sanguine image. With the setting of the sun, Drone was allowed to rest and enter the Dreamtime. At the break of dawn, the dance continued under an all-consuming burning sun, and Drone's skin was blistered by the excessive exposure to His Light. When his spirit returned to his body, he felt weakened. The Amazon women carried him to a shelter, where they rubbed him down with healing ointments and cool refreshing spring water. They attended to his wounds, and to his surprise, Drone witnessed the closure of his wounds in response to their healing touch. To have peace with God is like a silver thread of life that weaves itself through all types of challenging circumstances. The Pillar of His Light had finally dissolved the walls of his defended self, and the surrender of his imperfection gave him strength to hold the picture of perfection for all beings. In order to regain his strength, he drank some of the Sangre de Cristo potion, and it boomeranged him straight back into the memory pulse of his two female companions. Drone tapped into the organic memory bank of His divine living being, and Maleeka and Maneesha returned into his reality. They kissed, hugged and cuddled. Feelings of the Heart were exchanged with the touch of their fingertips, and a sense of overwhelming inner bliss opened up the doorway to a state of No Mind! The next day they prepared themselves for another uplifting marathon inside the safe container of the Love Dome.

Maneesha: "Jesus's vision was fixed upon unchangeable; eternal, omni-present life and that life transcends all the emotional crud and all the problem seeds of thought of the here now. With our vision held steadfastly toward the ever-present reality of a living God, we can behold His finished work. Was it not Jesus' true mission here on Earth to show that we as children of God can create as perfectly well as God does? Jesus was sent by the Father to show us that the Father intended us to create exactly as He creates."

Maleeka: "We are to do the perfect works of God, to raise our consciousness to the Christ consciousness. God is holding the ideal perfect world in Mind in every detail and it is bound to come forth as a heaven or perfect home, where all His children may dwell in peace and harmony."

Drone: "This I do know, that we must all ascend to the very highest in consciousness to receive our illumination. Then from the heart, the love center we must let love flow forth to uplift our brothers and sisters. 'I AM' embracing the Christ within!"

As they walked their way over to the Love Dome, they ran into Punya, who signaled them to follow him. He led them into another 333-foot Dome, in which a large crystal cross was connected to a geometrical configuration in the shape of the flower of life. The structure was hovering on top, and it seemed to be able to move up and down over the circumference of the cross. As Drone looked into the structure, he could see pyramids within pyramids, mansion within mansion. The entire structure made the appearance of fiber optic tubing through which liquid light was flowing, and it stunned him with a sense of awe. The tubes were interfaced with 33 large hummer crystals, which were strategically placed inside the structure. Within the bud of the flower of life, there were two terminals i.e. SQUID devices interfaced as a continuum with the light tubing system.

Punya: "The 33 hummer crystals are series linked with the crystal crosses inside the Tantric – and Trance Domes, which energies loads our Stargate for Startravel! The recipient's brainwaves will interface with the interference patterns of the Father, His Son, and the collective Holy Spirit of the Tantric Trance Dancers! When God thinks through our brain, He produces rhythmic electric currents. These electric currents have magnetic components, which spread out into space at the velocity of light, as do the electric waves or sounds produced by our hearts. They all mingle to form enormous interference patterns, spreading out and away from the planet towards the stars. Our planet itself is producing shock waves in the plasma that fills the solar system. These shock waves interact with those caused by other planets and produce resonance between the planets and the stars. Your micro-reality is made up of a vast empty space filled with oscillating fields. It is an interlocked web of fields, each pulsating at their own rate, but in harmony with the others, their pulsations spreading out farther throughout the cosmos. When a strong harmonizing rhythm of bliss is applied to this matrix of interlocking fields, its harmonic influence may entrain parts of the system that may have been vibrating off key. It will restore the orderliness in a world of constant movement and chaos! The faster something moves, the closer it exhibits a 'space-like' behavior. In a meditative- or altered state of consciousness, we have time that is more subjective on hand. This time we can use to explore our inner Minds and expand rapidly into the space of God's domain. In the year 2012, a Galactic synchronization with the beyond will take place. All the Galactic pathways will be lined up in coherent resonance between planet Earth and the Omni Galactic source or the house where God lives. The Christalization of your DNA is necessary for a merger with a mega dose of God-light coming to this planet. We have been using 'Stargate traveling' to evolve towards the center of our Galaxy and reign with the 'Sons of Light'! **You should ingather His living light with every breath you take, because in every breath you are fulfilling the God function of this Universe.** You should realize that with every action you take it creates a vibration, which can be traced back to the first Adamic evolution set in place upon this planet. Within the true House of Prayer, each molecule is encoded with a blissful braiding of faith towards the Father, so that each molecule becomes a Temple filled with His Living Light! Only when you have broken through to the other side of the beyond limitation of your senses, captured the Word of God with the Body of Light, and pulled it within you can your inner consciousness be coded into His Living Light. The structure you see here in front of you is a Stargate into His Living Domain! Only a fully integrated and evolved Adam or Eve can access the Androgenous Stargate."

Drone: "When will we be ready to travel into His Domain?"

Punya: "You must serve the Living God of all mansions, and complete a four-year commitment to the production of Love Potion 69, only then will you become eligible to travel into His Domain."

Drone: "God should be accessible to everyone!"

Punya: "His Love is accessible to all who seek it, but very few want to make a commitment to the Domain in which he resides! People are thrill seekers, and they are in love with the journey of differences. If you were to suggest to people that the time of seeking is over and that the chore is now to face the answer, that's more of a challenge! It takes courage to take Daime, and Trance Dance your way to God! It takes courage to take psychedelic mushrooms, and love your way into His Domain! Everybody is searching for God, because they are in love with the journey. They know where he lives, but all people do is to avoid that place of Eternal Serenity, and they go on searching for Him everywhere else. God's domain, the house of many mansions haunts them, and people avoid that which they fear. If by chance a person accidentally entered the House of God, then all is finished, because you may accidentally find God!"

The silence of his pause made Drone melt and he yearned for the melody of his next phrase.

Punya: "In four years your body will have transmuted into what I am today: 'an Androgenous being'! The reason why your presence is needed here today is, because we expect two visitors from the Pleiades."

Drone: "How does the Stargate work, and who is it that we may welcome?"

Punya: "Our Stargate is activated by the energy created in the Tantric and Trance Dance Domes. It is all about the right timing, and the calibration of two parallel dimensions. As the Hummer crystals are being charged up to their saturation level, an Androgenous being may step into the device and think itself to a desired destination. As for now, I would like for you to direct your Love into the Flower of Life, and welcome our guests!"

Punya paused and turned around towards the Stargate.

Within seconds, Drone was able to see two young adults manifesting themselves out of thin air. Their physical appearance glowed with a blue radiance, and with his eyes, he zoomed in on what was clearly a blending of Layla and him. It was an intense moment of shape shifting realities, and Drone was in awe, stunned by the reflection of his own complexion.

Maleeka: "Maneesha and myself are the embodiment of Layla's oversoul, and these are our children. Remember Amsterdam?"

Drone: "Is this the fulfillment of Layla's promise to me?"

Maneesha: "That it is!"

A blinding light flashed onto the retina of his Mind's eye, and their two names: 'Rishi & Ashen' were impressed telepathically. Holographic impressions from their world of existence were now being seen in his visual cortex. They were downloading their experiences of growing up in another world into Drone's memory bank. Not a single word was being exchanged, and their silence was being gapped by the magnificence of their telepathic impressions. The interference waves of the telepathic connection were Galactic in nature, and Drone's DNA structure was being coded with the Living Light from the beyond. Their message was: "Come visit us, when you are ready to meet your Creator. We will be waiting for you!"

Drone's heart soared with joy, and his Soul was content in knowing that his children were Gods children.

Five to one: by the Doors

Five to one, baby
One in five
No one here gets out alive
Now
You get yours, baby
I'll get mine
Gonna make it, baby
If we try

The old get old and the young get stronger
May take a week and it may take longer
They got the guns but we got the numbers
Gonna win
Yeah, we're takin' over
Come on

Your ballroom days are over, baby
Night is drawing near
Shadows of the evening crawl across the years
You walk across the floor with a flower in your hand
Trying to tell me no one understands
Trade in your hours for a handful of dimes
Gonna make it, baby
In our prime
Get together one more time

Get together one more time
Get together one more time
Get together one more time
Get together one more time

Well, c'mon, honey
Get along home and wait for me
Baby, I'll be home and wait for me
Baby, I'll be home in just a little while
Y'see, I gotta go out in this car with these people
And get fucked up

Get together one more time
Get together one more time
Get together, gotto get together
Gotta get together, got to
Take you up in the mountains
Ha, ha, ha
Love my girl
She's looking' good
Looking' real good
C'mon love ya
Feel, hey
Come on

Chapter Twelve ~
Tell all the people

So, live like children who belong to the light. Light brings every kind of goodness, right living, and truth. Try to learn what pleases the Lord. But the light makes all things easy to see. And everything that is made easy to see can become light. This is why it is said:

"Wake up, sleeper!

Rise from death;

And Christ will shine on you".

Ephesians 5 : 3 – 14.

Your eye is a light for the body. If your eyes are good, then your whole body will be full of light. But if your eyes are evil, then your whole body will be full of darkness. So be careful! Don't let the light in you become darkness. If your body is full of light, and none of it is dark, then you will shine bright, as when a lamp shines on you.

Luke 11 : 34 – 36.

Now we see as if we are looking into a dark mirror. But at that time, in the future, we shall see clearly. Now I know only a part, but at that time I will know fully, as God has known me.

1 Corinthians 13 : 12.

My brother, God called you to be free. But do not use your freedom as an excuse to do the things that please your sinful self. Serve each other with love.

Galatians 5 : 13.

Love the Lord your God with all your heart, soul and mind. This is the first and most important command.

Matthew 22 : 37.

Jim Morrison - The White Blind Light

Your home is still here. Violet, uncertain. Thank you, oh lord, for the white blind light. Jumped humped, born to suffer... Made to undress in the wilderness. All of us have found a safe niche where we can store up our riches and talk to our fellows ...in the same premises of disaster. Thank you, oh lord, for the white blind light. Let me tell you about heartache in the loss of God ...wandering, wandering in hopeless nights. Moonshine night, mountain village insane in the wood and the deep trees.

Your home is still here. Violet, uncertain. Oh, I want to be there, I want us to be there, oh, I want to be there...beside the lake, beneath the moon....Woolen, swollen drinking its

hot liquor... I want to be there. Thank you, oh lord, for the white blind light. A city rises from the sea. Let me tell you about heartache in the loss of God. Wandering, wandering in hopeless nights. Let me show you the maiden whit rot iron soul. Out here in perimeter there are no stars. Out there we are stoned... Immaculate...

After a four-year training of intense levitational sex, Drone's body felt changed, as if he had shifted into a world of no-perceptual reality. The very act of observing his internal atomic world had made him a participant and co-creator of a world, which lies 'alive and kicking' beyond the perception of his nerve endings.

Maneesha: "What's going on Drone?"

Drone: "It feels as if my senses are still functioning as motion detectors, and yet I feel aloof and centered within the encumbrance of my inner stillness!"

Maneesha: "Stillness is the Great Mystery. The holy silence is His voice and silence sings. The fruit of silence is self-love. Silence is the cornerstone of character."

Milika: "I understand the blue print of your being, but is your search for thrills now at ease with the stillness of His Domain?"

Drone: "Mmmm... I have been running for thousands of lifetimes in search for my beloved. Now I know where she lives, and my search for thrills has finally accepted the inner bliss of knowing. Now I know myself to be a steward of God's land and His children. I have become a host to the eternal light of His awesome being."

Milika: "May we conclude that your inner boredom with life has motivated you to become a thrill seeker of the Divine?"

Drone: "Yeah, I'm loving the stillness, which God has shown me within His Domain of a non-perceptual reality!"

Milika: "Then tell me why this stillness feels like the burden of boredom?"

Drone: "I am still afraid for the Quantum Leap, the rapid God realization in which I, as I know myself, will cease to be. That scares me!"

Maneesha: "Who is your real essence self and does it still need your protection? If your answer is 'No', then can you rest in God?"

Drone: "What does it feel like then?"

Milika: "When you feed into your fear you've lost touch with your own vibration, your own frequency, and you get invaded by other vibrations. Your waveform gets discordant, wacky! When you are not in accord, you will miss His Eternal presence in the here now!"

Maneesha: "Stay pure and stick to the Unisonic Solfeggio frequencies of 528 Hz (DNA repair) "MI-ra gestorum" in Latin meaning "miracle."

The clearer you get about your intentions, the more light He can pour into your vehicle; the more light He can pour into you, the sooner you can return home. Having clean emotional waveforms is to have a happy galactic circuitry!"

Maneesha: "All individuals are joined together with the whole. The Whole is the Unified Force Field of His Domain! We are being molded by the silken matrix of His being!"

Drone: "Millions of Souls are on the same path, struggling, in misery, in anguish, striving to reach this Gate of Heaven! Where do we go from here?"

Maneesha: "All we need to know is that God dwells within and around us, and that we are completely embedded in His divine being; that we are consciously within the presence of God. This knowing must be a true resurrection in our consciousness – an uplifting of our deadened senses into a higher vibration of life. This resurrection is transcendence through the layers of pain of our traumatized being. It is an awakening to the full realization of eternal life in the here-now!"

Drone: "I'm seeing my own essence; it is the source of mother nature surrounding me. Is that the path that Jesus tried to show to us?"

Maneesha: "Jesus, when he was crucified, gave His flesh and blood, to prove that there is really a deeper spiritual body; and it is His light-body, which He manifested when He resurrected Himself from the tomb to join His eternal father."

Drone: "Can the flesh be transmuted into this light-body called Merkabah?"

Maneesha: "Even the flesh may be immortalized so that the reflection of youth never changes! When all the life force is conserved "Semen retention of Christ Oil", the body can be so charged with life that you can virtually speak life into all forms. Surrender your belief and know your God from a state of absolute immense in-no-cence, then He will induce a blissful braiding of your DNA, and Christallize you in harmony with the infinite. We are living on a planet evolving around a Star in the middle of the infinity of an unknown space. You, as you know yourself simply disappear into the immensity of His existence. You disperse yourself in the wholeness of the cosmos and become the Grand Dreamer."

Milika: "Your nature has to be changed, why? Because if a man is able to surrender himself whole heartedly to his woman, he can pass into the true essence of his being immediately. Just allow the vibration of your body to be changed into the true love of your Soul."

Maneesha: "If you really want to know love, you must go and feel it yourself, and even when you have felt the love vibe, you are unable to relate to others what it really is. The sensation of love is always immediate and hence there is no way to talk about it."

Milika: "This true love is from the Creator; we are only stewards hosting the love of our Creator. Let your heart become a roaring fire for this true love. Let the yearning of your heart run deep to find the Beloved within."

Maneesha: "After all the stages of love have been lived and passed, then the light of the eternal consciousness can clearly be seen as it really is."

Drone: "What about my garment of light?"

Maneesha: "The consciousness, the golden flame of your being, is eternal. It goes on moving into new forms and ultimately it moves into the formless. Soon pure rays of white light will appear within your body; they become aglow with this light; and this soft, yet brilliant living light invades the clear space within you like a white- golden flame. This light increases steadily until it covers and permeates everything about you. Thus, His light is awakening us to the Christ within, and we shall weep because of the problem seeds of thought of those, who watch the awakening of our inner child. However, it is the finite that suffers. The infinite lies stretched in smiling repose. Ride the snake to the lake and reclaim the original Adam."

Drone: "Yeah, From sex to super-consciousness?"

Maneesha: "If God rules all and is all inclusive, then Hell or the Archangel Satan has no abiding place except in man's mortal thought. I have searched every place and I cannot find him a home; so, I must assume that he is right where man is and has all the power that man gives him. You will need to cultivate your inner self and focus on His divine light within your inner realm. His everlasting living light is there where you lost it! The house of God is to be found within the Celestial realms of your God-given consciousness. Your Celestial eye should remain focused on His everlasting living light, and you need to cultivate this light to flow freely through your body vehicle!"

Drone: "Romancing the shadow side?"

Maneesha: "The black substance, which is the devil's abiding place will thus be illuminated and his existence will ascend away from man's morbid thoughts and transform into God's all-embracing light. Your senses crave that which your heart desires, but your Soul has to move on and transcend towards the virtue that comes from the within, the house of many mansions, where God lives."

Milika: "When the Christ within has been lifted from the chain of the material world, then the ever-expanding urge of the Soul leads him to higher vibratory dimensions. There we live in a world of causes where before we moved in a world of effects. The benediction of this exhilaration will be permanent. The immediate benediction of life lies within God expressed through the Christ in the individual. You have now the choice to go through the Androgenous Stargate, and to be beamed to some external paradise, or you move yourself back into the market place, and garden your children of the Light."

Drone: "How can I die, while others have not reached yet? How can I enter Heaven, when my brothers and sisters have not yet entered?"

Milika: "When do you want to be finished with being mortal?"

Drone listened to the Holy Spirit speak to him: "Move yourself totally into the deepest intensity of love that is possible, and be a light to the world!"

Maneesha: "We shall lift each other up, higher and higher, until the luminous love light of the one is opening us up in sweet surrender. *Except for God, everybody is a woman, because when we surrender our hearts, he then penetrates us with the presence of His Divine Being.*"

Drone: "I've always known, that if I were to be born a woman, I would become a lesbian!"

Maneesha: "You are much more than that, Drone! The love potion 69 has increased the vibratory rate of your cellular tissue to that of a Lord of Light, one who is worthy to breathe in the presence of His divine being."

Milika: "Your physical body has become a super conductor of light, and you are now the master of a holographic mirror-like quality, and capable of reflecting those who are looking into the similitude of your abyss! You have matured in becoming an Androgenous being, who is able to shape shift his complexion and sexual gender with a right use of divine will!"

Drone: "I don't believe it!"

Maneesha: "Believe what you want, but first See for yourself and try it out with a mirror!"

Drone walked over to a mirror and looked into it, but he saw nothing but the complexion of his well-known old self.

Drone: "I see nothing but myself!"

Milika: "Imagine you are it! Feel it deeply, and allow yourself to melt and merge!"

Drone looked again into the mirror, and he imagined himself having the complexion of a gorgeous woman. His eyelids shut softly and Drone began to deeply feel like a woman. He touched himself and imagined feeling her female body parts, and she began to enjoy this fantasy. Her eyes opened to have a reality check, and to her surprise, she saw the reflection of Layla looking straight at him as if it was she! Waves of bliss made him close her eyes again, and he began to make love to his Layla. Her erotic zones were being triggered into a state of heavenly bliss, and she climaxed in no time. Her legs gave out and her body dropped to the floor from pure exhaustion. Maneesha brought Drone back to his senses.

Maneesha: "You forgot to run your inner orbit darling! It is the nature of an Androgenous being to neutralize any sexual energy into the void of Zero-point energy, and 'it' does not yearn nor need the thrill of a sexual "Christ Oil" release!"

Drone: "Why?"

Maneesha: "Supernatural powers will only be given to those who obey the Law of one!"

Drone: "Express yourself?"

Maneesha: "Enlightenment is only the beginning; it is only a door. And then there is an unending existence, evolution, expansion!"

Drone: "Are you saying, that once Enlightenment is there, a new kind of pilgrimage will start?"

Milika: "Until the entrance of God's Domain you are an entity; beyond that door you will be pure contentless consciousness!"

Drone: "Mmmm… that makes me think of the fragrance of a flower, which is being spread all over existence!"

Maneesha: "Yes, this fragrance is luminous and full of awareness. The conditioned attraction of our pheromones is now being replaced by a luminous fragrance, which is the very essence of our Soul!"

Drone: "Sort of like we are the Salt of the Earth!"

Milika: "Yes, honey!"

Drone: "Mmm… what an insight! Is it okay then for me to say, that I now know myself and everything without and within, as being a part from God?"

Milika: "Feel and know God, but not as a separate entity. It feels more or less like a merger with a collective luminous being. It is the atonement of many into one organic being of living light. We are the host and God is our guest for eternity!"

Drone: "If that is so, then how do we teach this to those who are desperately hoping for a better tomorrow?"

Milika: "It is our Earthly mission to romance the shadow side inside all of us, and allow God to work His living light through our body vehicles!"

Maneesha: "In the eyes of God we have to humble ourselves and become feminine, receptive to receive the silent invasion of his light!"

Milika: "Everybody is in search for Freedom, but nobody is willing to give up the very wall that imprisons them! We live in a world of wounded traumatized defended selves. It is the essence of Divine love that will lift us up from our veils of pain! The love from God is so great, that you will need other people to un-burden you from the abundance of his grace!"

Maneesha: "This power of love is such a purifying force, that it will trigger spontaneous catharsis in those people, who are clouded by their shadow side!"

Drone: "Do we have to worry about those who empower themselves with the sin of judgment?"

Milika: "When one points one finger, three will be pointed back! Instead, show the people with your actions, that there exists a Path of Love."

Drone: "Sort of like: 'Walk your Talk?"

Milika: "Yes, we like it like that! Remember interruption of intercourse means getting out of sync with your core essence, which is the Beloved within."

This was the magic moment in which the three of them decided to leave Anjuna and return to the Market place of the World. It took them a solid week to get their belongings together and prepare for the return to the civilized world of loneliness and plastic image. A ritual of hugging friends and trees took the most of their time, and it left them in a state of eternal bliss with the Divine. The intimacy of a hug provides an opportunity for any unbalanced condition to effortlessly return to the oneness of balance from which it was divided into two. The sexual fragrance of our planet mother Earth is complementary to God's sexless Universe. Drone had surpassed his E~motional self, and he now felt deeply anchored into his elevated emotional IQ of the domain of his beloved Grand Dreamer Self. The intelligent faith in his Over self-Mind had been transformed by the luminous grace of His presence into a state of blind faith, which could only be experienced with a state of No~Mind! Milika, Maneesha and Drone left 'Anjuna' with a jungle guide, who escorted them back to the city of Rio Branco. From there, they took a plane straight to Portugal for the gathering of their tribe. People felt naturally drawn to the presence of the Essence of Light radiating through their body vehicles. A Monolithic Dome home was being created in the Estrella region for their gatherings, and they called it: **'Silêncio canta!'** On the 11th March of 2011 a grand Tsunami destroyed the Nuclear Powerplant of Fukushima and no scientist would be able to stop a nuclear meltdown, which had devastating radiation sickness consequences for humanity at large. The half-life of Plutonium is 500,000 years and that's how long it needs to be isolated from our environment. All disease (Radiation sickness) is a lowering of frequency and in Time this frequency will become a dissonance an incoherent entropy and everything begins to move out of rhythm, out of balance, out of order.

Opportunity created the right innovative space-timing to engage the Global public by means of Social Entrepreneurship of One Heart, to create a Unified Neo Quantum Tachyon Field of (+) elevated emotions (=Love-Joy-Celebration) that shall override the collective fear of Fukushima's Global Atomic Geno suicide. What would it FEEL like then? When we have to become Breatharians, because we cannot handle the Radioactive memory-information that is attached to our foods & water.

Drone: "What can we do to help all our relations?"

Maneesha: " We need to create a Global Impact of Tachyon Stargate Ingredients: Meditation-Love-Infinity."

Drone: "People always need something tangible!"

Milika: "Yes, so we kiss and sort!"

Drone: "Meaning what?"

Milika: "K.I.S.S. Keep it Simple S.O.R.T. Start-Orchestrate-Release-Train with Tachyon tools."

Drone: "How will the product/service be used?"

Milika: "The Stargate Trainers Market, Network, Attract & Assemble groups of Social Entrepreneurs that feel passion for our cause to transmute the effects of a Global Atomic Geno suicide and we then teach "How to meditate & visualize with elevated neo-emotions and linger into the Neo-One Heart-One Mind Space-Time Continuum.""

Maneesha: "Yes, and the Participants commitment is to buy 4 Stargates by choice and tune in collectively and coherently, once per day on a Global set Time zone. (11:11 GMT ??) (Reason is that if one sleeps between 11 and 2 – it is like one hour of sleep but LIKE 3 hours…. Ie fast charge up)"

Drone: "So, our commitment then is providing an Immediate STARGATE INTENSIVE training in Portugal, Netherlands, UK whereby the Key ingredient is to create a massive T-chain-reaction of collective Elevated (+) Neo-emotions that overrides the polarized fear of Fukushima's Atomic Geno-Suicide."

Maneesha: "Your emotional IQ is soaring high!"

Drone: "How is it a solution to the customer's problem?"

Milika: "What Tachyon does is give our organism, our body, our subtle bodies the chance to produce whatever effects they need. And since our bodies are incredibly intelligent, they always produce the effects that are good for them."

Maneesha: "Tachyon energy is not limited to a certain frequency. Tachyon cannot be influenced in any way whatsoever by any other form of energy. So potentially, all problems we have- mental, emotional, spiritual, or physical- can be positively affected by Tachyon energy!"

Drone: "What might customers be enticed to 'pay 'for value delivered?"

Milika: "To Capture the Value of Health is based on individuals' willingness to pay and on feeling the connection to a cause that the world can get passionate about, can create an army of world-changers motivated to conquer what appear to be unsolvable problems."

Drone: "Why-How-What would this feel like then?"

Maneesha: "The key to this strategy lies in its ability to appropriately compensate both the career-minded social entrepreneur as well as the millions of individuals in the world who would just like to make a difference in the lives of vulnerable children."

Every morning, they meditated on the beach, after which the girls swam with their Syrian dolphin friends. In the afternoon, they would practice their uni-sonic soul voice synthesis, and in the evening from 7 – 10 PM, a lecture was given on the art of levitational intercourse. The evening always evolved into the free expression of live dance music, and the dancing light was celebrated to its fullest potential.

Drone; "How can we reach a greater audience?"

Maneesha: "If you would have 4 great Buffalo drummers come along, and those drummers would have an exquisite rhythm & beat. (=Of such beauty or delicacy as to arouse intense delight)

In No Time, these drummers would begin to entrain everybody that was drumming and they would produce a rhythm, an order, a coherence. This is the way it is; a natural phenomenon of clocks and menstruation bio-rhythms, because there is an order & rhythm to the Universe of One Song sung whole heartedly. The dot particle becomes then the Oceanic wave of dot-particle Membership sites, Webinars, Platform of Services!"

Drone: "How big do we want to grow?"

Milika: "You mean: How large is the target segment? I personally feel we need a minimum of 144,000 Primary Chosen Participants to get the Cumulative Absolute Velocity Index (CAVI) of elevated + emotions going to work for us as a Space-Time Continuum to counter act the FUKUSHIMAS Atomic Suicide. The Secondary audience is someone other than the intended receiver who will also benefit from the tachyon rhythm entrainment. Longterm goal of 1 -3 years we want 10,000,000 Primary Stargate Participants!"

News travels fast, when you are having fun, and people began to flock around the trio in a type of communal living. The demand grew for more space, structure, staff, and they learned to delegate the necessary assignments, which then accelerated the communal growth spurt. People donated useful things, which benefited the needs of their growing community. Computers were installed, and a dedicated group of people created a website, which would then expand the invitation to the world. People from all walks of life flocked in to become a member and active participant of their Global Humanitarian Cause: "WE CHANGE NOW!' The website received ten thousand hits per day and people from all over the world flew in to help and to learn how to Love:

Cosmic Babies

Hear yourself dreaming

Watch yourself screaming

Trance dance your way to God

Have a little taste of Heaven

Cosmic Babies

We like it

Tantric Trance Dance

Dreamtime Sundance

Come to our Church, Naked!

The church was set up on a member ship basis, and the proceeds would help them built an Anjuna Dome complex in the shape of the flower of life. The fast-growing Social Entrepreneurs project, was to build three triangulated 333 feet Domes, which would be designed adjacent to eight 108 feet surrounding Domes. All Domes would be interconnected with each other, and the three center Domes were to be designated as Sacred Grounds for Trance Dance and Cosmic Tantra. The Stargate was to be built in the center of the three triangulated Domes. The Domes, which were built as the outer shell, were to lodge the growing community of members and guests. Private schooling and day-care were to be provided for, which would enable both parent and child to be calibrated to their individual and collective evolution! A special team was assigned to do the P.R. within the local community, which welcomed them with a loving Hawaiian spirit. The promotional mission statement was: "Give to Creator what belongs to the Grand dreamer, and give to Earth what belongs to the Divine Mother. The choice is yours!" From Brazil they imported tons of 'Hummer Crystals', which were utilized to build a 33-foot crystal cross, which was programmed to help remind us to allow the Living Light to flow through our body vehicle. A courier network was set up between Anjuna and the 'Silêncio canta' center. They were able to import the necessary remote SQUID devices, which enabled them to produce the magic potions: 'Sangre di Cristo and Love Potion 69'. Different team leaders were assigned to organize and bring to completion all of the necessary tasks such as: 'administration, building oversight, advertising, marketing, editing and publishing of recorded information, shopping, cooking, cleaning, security, medical, counseling, intake & exit interviews, public relations, gardening etc."

A program was developed for new members, which was outlined and set up as such, that it would be easy to learn the new ways of elevated emotional IQ, which then blessed would create a new and purified Mother Earth.

An introduction period was developed for those who were not familiar with the works, and it gave the team an opportunity to unify everybody into the experience of One Heart, One Mind. Their program contained an innovative flexibility towards the female members, who needed a nurturing window for their monthly Moon cycle. They built a special Tropical Sideral Moon cycle lodge for this occasion, and for the men a sensory deprivation Dome was built, which was part of their training towards the Masterhood of a no-perceptual reality. Nothing relieves deep stress and tension like floating in the 'weightless' dark silence of super-buoyant temperature regulated water floatation tank. 'Floaters' often speak reverentially of how their experiences in the tank have profoundly increased their overall sense of well-being. The awareness center known as the brain, in addition to all its other functions, is also a very complicated reduction/inhibition mechanism. Throughout its evolutionary path, it has permitted only a certain limited frequencies to penetrate to the awareness, which were needed for the survival issues of the human race. By judicious reduction of even these narrow sensory nutrients, such as light, sound, touch, temperature, gravity, etc.... we then begin to activate those areas of our brain involved with the higher faculties: those related to the evolution of higher 'God' consciousness. It stands to reason that when survival is no longer a primary concern and an energy drain, our real reasons for being on the planet make themselves known. These reasons are as unique as the individuals themselves and are explored, slowly and carefully at first, after the first number of floats, which deal with ordinary survival issues. Like a giant and powerful dynamo whose source of energy is little by little leaking, the logical, analytical, scientific, mechanistic and calculating parts of the brain slows its activity down to a mere trace element frequency – making room for, and encouraging the 'higher reasons and functions of life such as creativity, meditation, holism, peace, bliss, love and the perfection of Divinity. We are in a desperate need to master this 'higher' capacity, because it teaches us how to cope with the addictions to different modes of survival to which we are all subject.

The new society blueprint, completed at the equinox on 20 March 2013, represents a self-governing system for holographic co-creation that can be modelled conceptually as the Flower of Life; one of the most recognisable symbols in modern light working. There is no competition only collaboration to care about each other to succeed.

Our Purpose for Existing = P.F.E., was to capture value with fulfilled-people focus. It is our responsibility to increase the global awareness of emotional IQ, changing the way hundreds of thousands of people view and experience life. To give this to a corporate structure doesn't work for my heart, however effectiveness equals profits by combining talented people who are on a journey towards their own P.F.E. with an organization that has a similar P.F.E.

Everything was on a roller coaster, but Drone's Native Blood was calling him to fulfil a Vision he had from when he was very young. It had to be fulfilled; it had to be Done!

Whenever he attributed the source of his power to something greater than himself, he knew that Grandfather the Grand Dreamer would help him to pull the force of many Buffaloes into one.

Drone wanted for All the Native American Tribe to join forces and reunite for a Sundance at the Sundance Rock in Wyoming. Sundance Mountain is a mountain summit in Crook County in the state of Wyoming (WY). Sundance Mountain climbs to 5,810 feet (1,770.89 meters) above sea level. Sundance Mountain is located at latitude - longitude coordinates (also called latitude - long coordinates or GPS coordinates) of N 44.388597 and W -104.376615. This is the Sacred Place where the ancestors danced to give flesh to their Creator. Your own flesh & blood is the best gift we can give to Creator.

Drone was thinking: "If I would have 4 great Buffalo drummers come along, and those drummers would have an exquisite rhythm & beat. (=Of such beauty or delicacy as to arouse intense delight)

In No Time, these drummers would begin to entrain everybody that was drumming and they would produce a rhythm, an order, a coherence. This is the way it is; a natural phenomenon of clocks and menstruation bio-rhythms, because there is an order & rhythm to the Universe of One Song sung whole heartedly."

Drone paused and thought again: "I need to write a letter to all the Chiefs and see if they are once again willing to give flesh to Wakan Tanka, or the Grand Dreamer of our Great Mystery!"

So, the ink moved across the paper and his first letter had begun.

To Sundance Chief Leonard Crow Dog

Crow Dog's Paradise

Rosebud Indian Reservation

South Dakota 57570

U.S.A. Turtle Island

Dear Chief/Uncle I AM petitioning you to organize the Seven Council Fires of the Great Sioux Nation for the Sundance reactivation at Mateo Tipila in Wyoming

Hoka Hey, Pila maya my dear Chief,

In 1996 the Hopi's returned for the first time in 500 years or so to the East Coast of Turtle Island to rekindle their Sacred roots and renew kinships. Spirit invited me on top of Chimney Rock in NC to witness a Hopi Rain Dance. Only 50 people were allowed on this Sacred Rock and Spirit invited me in to participate as a Witness. This experience was so powerful that it simply overwhelmed me with flashbacks to the Sacred Way it was and still is.

You may remember me from the first Austin-Texas Sundance with chief Mike Hull in 1998. The little girl/maiden did not want to touch the Tree of Life because she did not want the tree to die. So, there was a lot of commotion, remember? I was there with my family to support

Yellow Horse. I carried water from the Lake and helped hose down the dancers after the dance was over. After the Sundance we went South to Mary Thunders Ranch and we sweat and ate together. I was sitting outside Mary Thunder's house and you walked by and shook my hand. The Texas Sundance inspired me to Sundance for myself and I petitioned Chief Steve McCullough with my Chanupa at the Salt creek Sundance. Before my first Vision Quest I had a 4-day sweat with John Fire Lame Deer in which I experienced strong Visions. One of my 4-Visions was to be standing pierced in between 4 poles and that 4 women of the four races would pull my ropes and break my skin in the 4-Winddirections. This symbolised for me the return of the Feminine principle on the Mother Earth. This Vision became reality in my fourth year of dancing and just after my break free the Chanupa was offered by the Four races to the Tree of Life. I lived in America from 1990 – 2001 and now I am back in Holland. Sundance Chief Huston Steward is a dear friend of mine and I contacted him also to help realize my dream & vision for this life. So, I want to petition for your help & support in the gathering of the biggest Alliance Intertribal Gathering for the Reactivation of the Redman's Sundance Rock; Mateo Tipila in Wyoming (In the Close Encounter of the 3'd kind movie they referred to it as Devil's Tower, but that's the white man's way!) It's my Vision that Grandfather wants to remove the Devil's presence from the place that is sacred for the Redman.

This may be a healing crusade for All of our Relations. It's not my intention to create a second FBI-standoff like you & others had in 1975, but when all the tribes are moving towards the Tree of Life, then what can they "White devil Forces" do? The Trail of Tears shall become the Trail of the Redman's Celebration. The United Redman needs YOU Chief Leonard Crow Dog and Chief Mike Hull (Lawyer), Chief Huston Steward and as many other Chiefs to get involved and make it into a Redman's Vision come True. Enclosed I wrote a letter for all the other

Tribal Councils as listed that want to give flesh to our grandfather. Turtle Island needs Chief Leonard Crow Dog to ingather the Canku Oyate for a Sundance Rock Council Fire. This may also be the Crown on all your hard work to save the Red Road and to honour All of our Ancestors; the Buffalo Nations.

As you well know; The Lakota Star constellations are a 2000 – 3000-year-old artefact. No doubt, the constellations had been known previously for a long time between 1000 – 100 B.C.

The Lakota people began using the Sun and the constellations as a ritual artifact of atonement, aligning/synchronising their ceremonies and movements on the plains to the motion of the sun through the Stars. Lakota constellations are associated with specific land forms here on the prairie. Quoting Red Cloud's words; "We told them that the Buffalo must have their country and the Lakota must have the Buffalo!" Red Cloud was referring to a religious duty and it will help to clarify the complex nature of this duty if we continue the account of the annual spring ceremony related to the Black Hills.

During this period of time, the names of three hills changed. Grandfather Sundance rock became Pte He Gi "Grey Buffalo Horn" (White man calls it Devil's Tower). Inyan Kaga became Pte He Sapa "Black Buffalo Horn", and Bear Butte became Pte Pute Ya "Buffalo's Nose". The triangle formed by the three mountains was called "The Buffalo's Head".

During the month or so when ceremonies (preceding, during and after Sundance) were going on, this Buffalo head became spiritually alive. After completing ceremonies at the Pe Sla, the People collected stones at Inyan Kaga (hill in WY Black Hills) and carried them; Stone People, to the Sundance Rock to be used in the purification lodge during the time of the Sundance.

The Sundance Tree of Life creates the 4 directions of the world and holds it together. This light will shine on the world when the Tree of Life is once again resurrected. To him who overcomes fear Grandfather will give the right to eat from the Tree of Life. And the leaves of the Tree of Life are for the healing of the nations. No longer will there be any curse. There will be no more night. The Creator will give them Light and they will reign for ever and ever. Rev: 22. The Lakota Tribe and the Kiowa Tribe have a similar mythical story of the Seven Sisters; Blue Star Woman=Wicahpi to Winyan, Red Star Woman=Wicahpi Luta Winyan, White Star Woman=Wicahpi San Winyan, Turtle Woman=Keya Winyan, Corn Woman=Wagmiyeza Winyan, Divine Mother=Ina Wakan, White Buffalo Calf Woman=Pte San Cigana Waste Winyan. According to legend, there were seven young maidens who went out to play. Several giant bears saw them and began to give chase. To escape from the bears and certain death, the maidens climbed on top of a rock and prayed to the spirit of the rock for safety. Hearing the pleas of the maidens, the rock began to rise from the ground towards the Heavens, so that the bears could not reach them. After reaching the sky, the seven maidens became a cluster of stars called the Pleiades. The bears, trying to climb the rock kept sliding back down the steep sides, leaving deep claw marks in the rock called Mateo Tipi. White Buffalo Calf Woman returned with the Chanupa to bring Peace on the Mother Earth. Sitting Bull's wife gave birth to a son at Mateo Tipi and he sadly was buried there. Chief White Bull wintered there in 1864 and hence Mateo Tipi is a very sacred and holy place. So powerful in fact, that it simply overwhelms any sensitive person.

We the people need the Gospel of the Redman to gather the Canku Oyate for the Sundance Rock Council Fire (Close Encounter of the fourth kind). The historical Sioux referred to the Great Sioux Nation as the Ochethi Sakowin, meaning "Seven Council Fires". Each fire was symbolic of an oyate (people or nation). The seven nations that comprise the Sioux are Mdewakanton, Wahpeton, Wahpekute, Sisseton, Yankton, Yanktonai, Lakota. The Seven Council Fires should assemble to hold council with all Native Tribes who want to rekindle their sacred roots connection to the Sundance Rock, renew kinships, and participate in this Resurrection Sundance, because we are now the Ancestors of those not yet born. The seven divisions should select four leaders known as Wichasa Yatapika from among the leaders of each division and they will represent the four wind directions. The last meeting of the Seven Council Fires was in 1850 and it is time to renew kinships and shed light on the white man's shadow side.

As many tribes as the leaves on the Sundance Tree of Life need to participate in the Seven Winter Council Fires;(2011-2012)

1) Rosebud Sioux Tribal Council, Rosebud Indian Reservation, South Dakota 57570.

2) Oglala Sioux Tribal Council, P.O. Box 2070, Pine Ridge, South Dakota 57770.

3) Northern Cheyenne Tribe, P.O. Box 128, Lame Deer, Montana 59043.

4) Cheyenne River Sioux Tribe, P.O. Box 590, 2001 Main Str, Eagle Butte, SD 57625.

5) Mandan, Hidatsa, Arikara nation, 404 Frontage rd., New Town, ND 58763.

6) Shoshone Bannock Tribe, P.O. Box 306, Fort Hall, Idaho 83203.

7) Southern Ute Indian Tribe, P.O. Box 737, Ignacio CO 81137.

8) Ute Mountain Ute Tribe, 125 W Mike Wash Road, P.O. Box 248, Towaoc, CO 81334.

9) Nez Perce Tribal Executive Committee, P.O. Box 305, Lapwai, ID 83540.

10) Eastern Shoshone Tribe, P.O. Box 538, 15 North Fork Road, Fort Washakie, WY 82514.

11) Northern Arapaho Tribe, P.O. Box 396, Fort Washakie, WY 82514

12) Assiniboin, Ojibwa/Chippewa, Salish, Gros Ventre, Crow?

13) Crow Tribe (still enemies?), Baacheeitche Av, P.O. Box 159, Crow Agency Montana 59022

Do not change yourselves to be like the people of this world. But be changed within by a new way of thinking. You must see yourself as you really are. Rom 12: 2- 3

My Peace of –I- I give to you, my Peace of –I- I leave with you, not the world's Peace,

But only my Peace, The Peace of –I-.

…… …… …… …… …… …… …… …… ……

Drone Hummingbirdman,

Sundance or Sungazing is a deep sacred reverence, deep respect tinged with awe, in a Ceremony in which one learns to love the Divine, to delight in the Creator and as a result it teaches you to love yourself first so that all your relations can love your back. By giving our flesh to creator, we do not destroy our body of light, but instead it is a delight, a celebration with our grandfather the Grand Dreamer. Drone was a Buffalo man; he learned to sing native songs while holding the horns of a big Buffalo skull. It was actually an alignment with the ancestors, so that they could sing their songs through the vessel embodiment of Drone. He felt driven like a herd of Buffalos to reunite all tribes into One Heart – One Mind and dance at the Mateo Tipila-Sundance Rock. There are many Christians on Turtle Island that did not and still do not understand the Sundance and so to help them understand the Gospel of the Red Man I would like to quote 2 Corinthians 5: "We know that our body – the tent we live in here on earth – will be destroyed.

Drone: "We know that our body – the tent we live in here on earth – will be destroyed. But when that happens, God will have a house for us to live in. It will not be a house made by men. It will be a home in heaven that will last forever. But now we are tired of this body. We want God to give us our heavenly home. It will clothe us, and we will not be naked. While we live in this body, we have burdens, and we complain. *We do not want to be naked. We want to be clothed with our heavenly home. Then this body that dies will be fully covered with life.* This is what God made us for. And he has given us the Spirit to be a guarantee for this new life. So, we always have courage. We know that while we live in this body, we are away from the Lord. We live by what we believe, not by what we can see. So, I say that we have courage. And we really want to be away from this body and be at home with the Lord. Our only goal is to delight in God. We want to delight in him whether we live here or there. For we must all stand before Christ to be judged. Each one will receive what he should get – good or bad – for the things he did when he lived in the earthly body." 2 Corinthians 5 – Geneva Bible 1599.

Maneesha: "Because the body is the soul made visible, we are in this life constructing the soul and the body that will be ours in the next."

Drone had a story to tell and so he decided that in his next book: "Waiting for the Son of God", he would give a journalistic account of the intertribal gatherings at the Sundance Rock in Wyoming. For now, they had to work as a team to prepare the people to be clothed with a new body of Light, because the people want to transcend their naked shame in the eyes of a pure God. The Ascension teachings for new comers is a simple: "Breaking the habit of being yourself and lose your mind and create a new one. There is a lot of knowledge about Ascension, however for centuries we have been misguided away from true knowing.

Pope Johannes later became a saint - Saint Iohannes - and he changed the chants which were based on the ancient original scale of six musical notes called the Solfeggio. The seventh note "Si" was added from his name. "Si" later became "Ti." These changes significantly altered the frequencies sung by the masses. The alterations also weakened the spiritual impact of the Church's hymns. Because the music held mathematic resonance, frequencies capable of spiritually inspiring mankind to be more "Godlike," the changes affected alterations in conceptual thought as well, further distancing humanity from God." In other words, whenever you sing a Psalm, it is music to the ears. But it was originally intended to be music for the soul as well or the "secret ear." Thus, by changing the notes, high matrices of thought and to a great extent wellbeing, was squelched. Now it is time to recover these missing notes to inspire us to behold conceptual thought and be more like the Grand Dreamer created us in his image."

Learning the language of light is a step-by-step process of learning how to love the Divine, delight in Creation, purify & make amends with the Ego self and loving the divine essence self.

Thus, when Christ was born to a woman who had been impregnated with the semen of the Father in Heaven, he was born a Son of God and therefore had knowledge far beyond what would be expected. During Christ's life, he and only he could perform the miracles of the Melchizedek priesthood, until the time of his crucifixion. After that time, James, Peter and John, the three inner disciples, could also perform the same miracles. According to the Nag Hammadi Library, in the 'Apocryphon of James', Christ gave sacred knowledge to the inner disciples. The term 'Melchizedek', means 'the righteous king', therefore the quote from Revelation 1: 6 means that we are not only to become priests but also kings, especially kings in the order of 'Melchizedek'. Christ himself said that greater things than he had done, we would do also. If we are to be a nation of kings, then we have no subjects and our physical appearance will have changed. We will be able to heal the sick and to resurrect the dead. We will understand and know all things, including what is right and wrong. We will know the hearts and minds of other people. We will know 'Judas' when he is in the room with what his intentions are and us. Will the change come while we are waiting? Will we burn in heaven like we do down here? Is it too late to celebrate our ability to have a little taste of God? Orgasm is like having a little taste of God of what it is going to be like in heaven. How much more can we be judged, other than for God to know our hearts and mind? Will not this judgment occur when we put on our proper garments as the righteous kings? Is the judgment not inherent in our becoming the true and literal latter-day saints? Daniel 7: 22 says, 'the Ancient of Days came, and judgment was given to the saints of the highest; and the time came that the saints possessed the kingdom!' I now know that the original Adam Kadmon, which existed before the 'Fall', is, in fact, what we will be like when we become filled with the spirit and literally walk our talk with God. **Revelation 2: 17 says, 'To him that overcometh will I give to eat of the hidden manna, and will give him a white stone, and in the stone a new name written, which no man knoweth saving he that receiveth it!'**

Milika: "Sex is the God potency to ascend and return to the level of His Domain!"

Drone: "Sex is like a Mustard seed that has to blossom into a Lotus flowering!"

Maneesha: "Sex is the healing force that can liberate the inhibited self from past traumatic events!"

Milika: "The love and blessings from God can only descend into your being when you have fully integrated your divided sexual being into the unity of one orgasm!"

Drone: "I'm Gods seed returning to the source!"

Milika: "Every woman who allows her feminine energies to blossom becomes a doorway to God!"

Maneesha: "Every man, who allows his feminine energies to blossom becomes an equal passage to God"

Drone: "Every spiritual person is a woman in essence. God is the man of all essence!"

Milika: "Orgasm is like having a little taste of God, and that feeling is telling us what it is going to be like in heaven."

Drone: "Let's tell all the people that our next Flower of Life will be built in Crestone, Colorado at the base of the Sangre the Cristo (Blood of Christ)-mountain range in the Valley of the Golden Disc!"

Maneesha: "Build it and they will come!"

Drone: "Why do we praise Him?"

Milika: "Because he gave His everything!"

Maneesha: "Halle- Hallelujah, that's why we praise him, that's why we bow down and worship this King, and that's why we offer him our everything!"

Drone: "Only GOD is, everything else is peripheral!"

Milika: "I hope that one day roses will bloom in the midst of the ashes of Ego. It is my greatest wish that you can walk through the thorny path of love without hurting your feet."

Maneesha: "It is not God's will to be without you, you could no more will to be without him then he could will to be without you. You are the Will of God, because that is how you were created. Because your Creator creates only like himself. You are like Him, you are part of Him, who is all power and glory and are therefore as unlimited as he is."

Drone: "So, when I'm not at peace it can only be because I do not believe, that I AM in Him?"

Milika: "When a brother/sister is sick it is only because he is not asking for peace. Sickness therefore is idolatry, because it is the belief that power can be taken from you!"

Maneesha: "I AM nothing without the father, because by denying the father you deny yourself."

Milika: "The recognition of God is the recognition of yourself, there is no separation between your will and mine. His will to you is his will for you. He would not withhold creation from you, because his joy is in it."

Maneesha: "Creation is the will of God. His will created you to create. Christ is in me, and where he is God must be. Accept nothing that you would not offer to God as wholly fitting for him. You do not want anything else."

Milika: "Only at the altar of God will you find peace. And this altar is in you, because God put it there. His voice still calls you to return and he will be heard when you place no other Gods before him.

Maneesha: "Drone, why do you tremble?"

Drone: "It is the way you are touching me. It is the way in which He may have become part of me! I love Jesus Christ and I AM resting in Him."

Generations come and generations go, but the earth remains forever.

What has been will be again, what has been done will be done again, there is nothing new under the sun. I know that everything God does will endure forever; nothing can be added to it and nothing taken from it, God does it so that men will revere him. When you make a vow to God do not delay in fulfilling it. Much dreaming and many words are meaningless. Therefore, stand in awe of God. So, I commend the enjoyment of life, because nothing is better for a man under the sun than to eat and drink and be glad. Then joy will accompany him in his work all the days of the life God has given him under the sun. No one can comprehend what goes on under the sun. Despite all his efforts to search it out, man cannot discover its meaning. Even if a wise man claims he knows, he cannot really comprehend it. Come to me as children and feel the joy of reverence for an awesome God. Enjoy life with your wife, whom you love, because naked a man comes from his mother's womb. As you do not know the path of the wind, or how the body is formed in a mother's womb, so you cannot understand the work of God, the maker of all things. Follow the ways of your heart and whatever your eyes see, but know that for all these things God will bring you to judgment. So then, banish anxiety from your heart, and cast off the troubles of your body, for youth and vigor are meaningless. Remember your Creator in the days of your youth. Love God and keep his commandments for this is the whole duty of man. For God will bring every deed into judgment, including every hidden thing, whether it is good or evil. (Ecclesiastes 1 – 12). All is well in Wallowa Valley, but my joy is in Zion!

Endless are His praises, endless are those who speak them. Endless are His actions, endless are His gifts. Endless is His vision, endless is His hearing. His limits cannot be perceived. What is the Mystery of His mind. The limits of the created Universe cannot be perceived.

Its limits here and beyond cannot be perceived. Highest of the High, above all is His name. Only one as great and as high as God can know His lofty and exalted state of being.

Only he himself is that Great. He himself knows himself. The Great giver does not hold back anything. Liberation from bondage comes only by Your Will. No One else has any say in this. Priceless is love for Him. Priceless is absorption into Him. Speak of Him continually and remain absorbed in His Love, because he is the Beloved for All your Eternity.

Drone; "By prayer and fasting and high service, we can so raise the quality of our being that we enter the next life with completeness of vision, hearing the Voices, and with knowing of the Great Mystery."

Maneesha: "When you rise in the morning, give thanks and pray for the morning light, your life, your strength, your food, the joy of living, to wholly void my heart of fear, that fear may never enter into my heart to be the guide of my feet."

Milika: "And if by chance you see no reason for giving thanks, rest assured the missing link is in yourself."

2 Corinthians 5: 17: If anyone belongs to Christ, then he is made new. The old things have gone; everything is made new! All this is from God. Amen.

Tell All the People: by the Doors

Tell all the people that you see
Follow me
Follow me down

Tell all the people that you see
Set them free
Follow me down

You tell them they don't have to run
We're gonna pick up everyone
Come on, take me by the hand
Gonna bury all our troubles in the sand
Oh yeah

Can't you see the wonder at your feet
Your life's complete
Follow me down
Can't you see me growing, get your guns
The time has come
To follow me down

Follow me across the sea
Where milky babies seem to be molded
Flowing revelry
With the one that set them free

Tell all the people that you see
It's just me
Follow me down

Tell all the people that you see
Follow me
Follow me down

Tell all the people that you see
We'll be free
Follow me down

Tell all the people that you see
It's just me
Follow me down

Tell all the people that you see
Follow me
Follow me down

Follow me down
You got to follow me down
Follow me down

Tell all the people that you see
We'll be free
Follow me down

Cosmic Babies

The Cosmic Egg and Seed are nourished and nurtured,
Guarded by the Star people,
Guided with loyalty by our Ancestors.
We are now the Ancestors of those,
Not yet born,
And dead again.
Given to the builders,
A blueprint of the force,
Of Mother Christal Earth,
And offered to the Sun,
And father Sky.
To be sown as Star seeds again,
Watched by the Skywalkers,
Mastered by the Surfers of E~motion,
Concealed in death,
Revitalized by the sword,
Of awareness and encompassion.
Ripened by the Storm,
Giving it worth,
Which enters the Human Being,
Through the house of starlight.
And as long as the night is there,
I am truthful open to myself with heart.
Illuminated by the Cosmic force of our Heavenly father,
To return as spirit pure and virgin,
Through the Cosmic Gate,
To in~gather whole 'Mind over Matter',
Just being another aspect of itself.

And seal it with Starseed Harmony,

Creating unity in universal movement,

Complex stability of Polarity.

Rhythm of resonant coherency,

Helps me to go beyond the limitations of my senses,

Helps us to go beyond the comparison of differences.

To experience the manifestations,

In cyclic periodical synchronicity of centers,

Where Harmonic Resonance brings the organic balance,

Of mystical powers of a rose,

With the feminine touch of a butterfly,

And the innocence of a child,

Playing in the realm,

Of being the light of mutual love.

In Harmony with the Infinite,

Where subjective time overlaps the objective space.

God has touched the places,

Where I have not been touched before.

God mirrors my seriousness,

And He stirs up my essence,

Of being sincere playfulness.

I am masked by a Scarface,

Hiding a trail of tears and joy,

A shy sense of innocence,

Not being in search of thrills,

But a silent waiting,

Utterly relaxed.

A state where there are no seeds of Mind,

Thought or unawareness left,

Conscious only of being conscious,

Observing the distractions and decoys,
Of primal pains and fears.
Triggered by the fast lane of living,
Returning to the simple man that I am,
With the child in my eyes,
I will never be able,
To step into the same river twice,
Not even once.
But that's the beauty of it all,
The end and the beginning,
Of a new circle of life.
From the essence of who I am,
For I am another yourself!
I AM Mohanpal Singh
I AM the Snow leopard King
I can do anything
I AM that I AM
God in Everything!